BOOKS BY HARRY TURTLEDOVE

The Guns of the South

THE WORLDWAR SAGA
Worldwar: In the Balance
Worldwar: Tilting the Balance
Worldwar: Upsetting the Balance
Worldwar: Striking the Balance

Homeward Bound

THE VIDESSOS CYCLE
The Misplaced Legion
An Emperor for the Legion
The Legion of Videssos
Swords of the Legion

THE TALE OF KRISPOS
Krispos Rising
Krispos of Videssos
Krispos the Emperor

THE TIME OF TROUBLES SERIES
The Stolen Throne
Hammer and Anvil
The Thousand Cities
Videssos Besieged
A World of Difference
Departures
How Few Remain

THE GREAT WAR
The Great War: American Front
The Great War: Walk in Hell
The Great War: Breakthroughs

AMERICAN EMPIRE
American Empire: Blood and Iron
*American Empire: The Center
 Cannot Hold*
*American Empire: The Victorious
 Opposition*

SETTLING ACCOUNTS
*Settling Accounts: Return
 Engagement*
Settling Accounts: Drive to the East
Settling Accounts: The Grapple
Settling Accounts: In at the Death

Every Inch a King

The Man with the Iron Heart

THE WAR THAT CAME EARLY
Hitler's War
West and East

West and East

THE WAR THAT CAME EARLY

West and East

HARRY TURTLEDOVE

BALLANTINE BOOKS | NEW YORK

Copyright © 2010 by Harry Turtledove

Published in the United States by Del Rey, an imprint of The Random House Publishing Group, a division of Random House, Inc., New York.

DEL REY is a registered trademark and the Del Rey colophon is a trademark of Random House, Inc.

Library of Congress Cataloging-in-Publication Data
Turtledove, Harry.
West and east : the war that came early / Harry Turtledove.
p. cm.
ISBN 978-0-345-49184-8 (acid-free paper)
eBook ISBN 978-0-345-52184-2
1. World War, 1939–1945—Fiction. I. Title.
PS3570.U76W47 2010
813'.54—dc22   2010012947

Printed in the United States of America on acid-free paper

www.delreybooks.com

9 8 7 6 5 4 3 2 1

First Edition

To the memory of Paul Fleischauer, 1942–2009—one of the good ones.
Too soon gone, dammit; too soon gone.

West and East

Chapter 1

Theo Hossbach lay on a cot in a military hospital in Cambrai. All of him was fine except for the last two joints on the ring finger of his left hand. He wouldn't see those again until and unless what the Resurrection of the Flesh preachers liked to talk about turned out to be the straight goods. Theo doubted it—Theo doubted almost everything people in authority said—but you never could tell.

One thing Theo didn't doubt was that he was lucky to be there, or anywhere. Along with the commander and driver, he'd bailed out of a burning Panzer II. They'd all run for some bushes a couple of hundred meters away. He'd made it. Ludwig and Fritz hadn't. It was about that simple.

The bullet that amputated those last two joints came later. He didn't know whether it was aimed at him in particular or just one of the random bullets always flying around a battlefield. The one by Beauvais seemed to have had more of them than most. Theo might have been prejudiced; he'd never had to bail out of a panzer before.

Or he might not have been. The French and English had stopped the *Wehrmacht*'s drive at Beauvais, and it hadn't got started again. This made two wars in a row where the Schlieffen Plan didn't quite work. Hitler's generals came closer to pulling it off than the Kaiser's had, but what was that worth?

A nurse came by. She took his temperature. "Normal. Very good," she said as she wrote it down. "Do you need another pain pill?"

"Yes, please," he answered. Those two missing joints seemed to hurt worse than the stub he had left. *Phantom pain,* the doctor who cleaned up the wound called it. He could afford to dismiss it like that; it wasn't his hand.

"Here." The nurse gave Theo the pill, watched while he swallowed it, and wrote that down, too. He figured it was codeine; it made him a little woozy, and it constipated him. It also left him less interested in the nurse, who wasn't bad looking, than he would have been if he weren't taking them every four to six hours. But it pushed away the pain, both real and phantom.

Most of the soldiers in the ward with him had nastier wounds. Most, but not all: the fellow two beds down wore a cast on his ankle because he'd tripped over his own feet and broken it. "I wasn't even drunk," he complained to anyone who'd listen. "Just fucking clumsy."

Woozy turned to drowsy. Theo was dozing when hearing his own name brought him back to himself. The nurse was leading a captain over to his cot. The pink *Waffenfarbe* on the man's *Totenkopf* collar patches and edging his shoulder straps said he was a panzer man, too. "You are, uh, Theodor Hossbach?" he said.

"Theodosios Hossbach, sir," Theo said resignedly. How was he supposed to explain that his father had been slogging through a translation of Gibbon's *The Decline and Fall of the Roman Empire* at just the wrong time?

He got the panzer captain's attention, anyhow. "Theodosios? Well, well. No wonder you go by Theo."

"No wonder at all, sir," Theo agreed.

"You are a radio operator. You are familiar with the operation of the Fu5 radio set?"

"Yes, sir." Theo knew he still sounded resigned. Every panzer in the *Wehrmacht* used the Fu5 except commanders' vehicles, which carried the longer-range Fu10. If he was a panzer radioman, he'd damn well better know how to use the standard set. A pfennig's worth of thought . . . was evidently too much to hope for.

Then the captain got to the point: "Can you return to duty? A radio operator in a Panzer II is not required to do much with his left hand."

That was true, and then again it wasn't. A radioman didn't need to do much with his left hand to operate the radio. When it came to things like engine repairs or remounting a thrown track, though . . . Theo knew he could have said no. His hand was swathed in enough bandages to wrap a Christmas present, or maybe a mummy. He hesitated no more than a heartbeat. "As long as they give me a jar of those little white pills, sir, I'm good to go."

"They will," the captain said, with a glance toward the nurse that warned someone's head would roll if they didn't. "You'll have it by the time I come back for you, in half an hour or so. A couple of other fellows here I want to scoop up if I can."

A doctor gave Theo the codeine and a reproachful look. "You should stay longer. You're nowhere near healed."

"I'll manage," Theo said. "I'm sick of laying around."

"Lying," the doctor said automatically.

"No, sir. I'm telling the truth."

"Right." The doctor looked more reproachful yet. Theo hadn't thought he could. "Maybe we're lucky to get rid of you."

"Maybe you are. Most of me doesn't need the bed—only my hand."

When the panzer captain came back for Theo, he had one other fellow (who walked with a limp) in tow and a discontented expression on his face. "The last guy I want is shirking," he growled. "I'd bet my last mark on it even if I can't prove it. Well, I just have to make do with you two. Let's go."

They'd laundered Theo's black coveralls. Putting them on again did feel good. The other panzer crewman, whose name was Paul, seemed to feel the same way. Once he had the black on, he stood taller and straighter and seemed to move more fluidly.

The captain bundled them both into a Citroën he'd got somewhere or other and headed west. They drove past and through the wreckage of a nearly successful campaign. Dead panzers—German, French, and British—littered the landscape, along with burnt-out trucks and shot-up autos. Here and there, German technicians salvaged what they could from the metal carcasses.

Just outside of Mondidier, the captain stopped. "You boys get out here," he said. "We're regrouping for a fresh go at the pigdogs. They'll fit you into new crews."

"What'll you do, sir?" Theo asked.

"Head for another hospital and see how many men I can pry loose there," the officer answered. "The more, the better. We can use experienced people, God knows."

Theo felt shy about joining a new crew. He'd spent his whole military career—he'd spent the whole war—with Ludwig and Fritz. They'd understood him as well as anybody did. They'd put up with him. If another driver and commander had lost their radioman . . . He made a sour face. He'd feel like a woman marrying a widower and trying to live up to the standard his first wife had set.

To his relief, he didn't have to do that. The personnel sergeant assigned him to what would be a brand-new crew. The commander was a sergeant called Heinz Naumann. He had bandages on his neck and his left hand—and maybe in between, too. "Burns. Getting better," he said laconically. On his coveralls he wore the Iron Cross First Class and a wound badge. Sooner or later, Theo knew, a wound badge would also catch up with him.

By contrast, the driver was just out of training. His coveralls weren't faded and shapeless; you could cut yourself on their creases. He was a big fellow with dark hair who moved like an athlete. His name was Adalbert Stoss.

Theo was from Breslau, way off in the east. Naumann came from Vienna. Stoss hailed from Greven, a small town outside of Münster. "It's a wonder we can understand each other," he said with a grin.

Grin or not, he wasn't kidding. As far as Theo was concerned, Stoss and Naumann had different strange accents. They probably thought he talked funny, too. "We'll manage," Heinz said.

"Oh, sure." Adalbert went on grinning. He seemed happy as could be to have escaped basic and come out to join the grown-ups at—or at least near—the front. Theo had seen that reaction before. Most of the time, it wore off as soon as the rookie saw his first body with the head blown off. Training was hard work, to say nothing of dull, but you hardly ever got killed there. In real war, on the other hand . . .

"I was hoping they'd give me a Panzer III," Naumann said. "But no— it's another II." He eyed Theo's bandaged finger. "You aren't complaining, though, are you?"

"Not right now," Theo allowed. In a Panzer III, the radioman sat up front, next to the driver. He also served a hull-mounted machine gun. That wouldn't be much fun with a bad hand. Then again . . . "A Panzer III, now, that's a real fighting machine."

"I know, I know. That's why I wanted one," the sergeant said. Along with two machine guns, a Panzer III mounted a 37mm cannon. Unlike the Panzer II's 20mm gun, which fired only armor-piercing ammo, the bigger weapon had high-explosive shells, too. That made it a lot more useful against infantry out in the open.

A Panzer III also carried thicker armor, and boasted a more powerful engine. A Panzer III was a real panzer. A Panzer II was a training vehicle. Oh, you could fight with it. The *Wehrmacht* had been fighting with it, and with the even smaller, lighter Panzer I, ever since the *Führer* gave the order to march into Czechoslovakia, more than six months ago now. But it would be nice to have a fighting vehicle that matched the ones the enemy used.

Would have been nice. Panzer IIIs were still scarce, while there were lots of IIs and, even these days, quite a few little obsolete Is. (There were also Panzer IVs, which carried a short-barreled 75mm gun and were de-signed to support infantry, not to attack enemy armor. There were sup-posed to be Panzer IVs, anyhow. Theo didn't think he'd ever seen one.)

"I know what I'm doing in a II," Stoss said. "They never let us drive a III in training. Most of the practice we got was in those turretless Panzer I chassis—you guys know the ones I mean."

Theo nodded. So did Heinz Naumann. What you used in training was as cheap as the *Wehrmacht* could get away with and still do the job. Theo doubted whether any Panzer IIIs were within a hundred kilometers of a training base. You didn't practice with those babies—you got them into the fight.

Eager as a puppy, Adalbert asked, "You know where they're going to throw us in, Sergeant?"

"Nope," Naumann answered. "Far as the generals are concerned, we're just a bullet. Point us at the enemy, and we knock him over."

Or he knocks us over. Theo remembered the antitank round slamming into his old Panzer II's engine compartment. He remembered opening his escape hatch and seeing nothing but flames. He'd followed his panzer commander out the turret hatch instead. Ludwig hadn't made it much farther. Theo had—which didn't stop that bullet from finding him a little later on.

The new Panzer II looked like the one that had burned. Theo's station was behind the turret, just in front of the bulkhead that separated the fighting compartment from the one housing the engine. He couldn't see out. The smells were familiar: oil, gasoline, cordite, leather, metal, sweat. He didn't smell much lingering fear, which argued that this panzer hadn't seen a lot of action.

He started fiddling with the radio. No matter what the manufacturer claimed, every set was different. Heinz Naumann said something. Theo ignored it. Indeed, he hardly heard it: like the radio, he was good at tuning out anything that didn't directly concern him.

Sometimes, he tuned out things that *did* concern him. Naumann spoke again: "I *said*, is it up to snuff?"

"Uh, it seems to be." Theo came back to the world.

"Good. Pay some attention next time, all right?"

"Whatever you say, Sergeant," Theo answered. Ludwig had tried to keep him connected, too. Sometimes it worked, sometimes it didn't. When Theo got interested in a radio, or in whatever was going on inside his own head, everything else could go hang.

They motored west, toward the front, the next morning. Naumann rode along standing up with his head and shoulders out of the turret. That was how a panzer commander was supposed to do things when not in combat. A lot of commanders looked out even when their machine was in action. The vision ports in the turret just didn't let you see enough.

There was talk of building a Panzer II with a proper cupola for the commander. The Panzer III had one. So did a lot of foreign panzers. Not the II, not yet.

Theo had another reason for liking the way Heinz did things. With the hatch open, some of the mild spring air got down to him. Then a bullet cracked past Naumann. The commander dove back inside the turret faster than you could fart. "Panzer halt!" he shouted.

"Halting," Adalbert Stoss said, and hit the brakes. Instead of using the traversing gear, Heinz manhandled the turret into position with the two handgrips on the inside. The machine gun snarled several short bursts at . . . something, at . . . somebody. Theo couldn't see out, so except for the gunshot he had no idea what was going on. Not counting his earphones, the radioman on a Panzer II was always the last to know.

"Maybe I got him. Maybe not," Sergeant Naumann muttered. Then he spoke into the tube that carried his voice to Adalbert's seat: "Forward!"

"Forward, *ja*," Stoss agreed. As the panzer got moving again, the driver asked, "A soldier behind our lines, or a *franc-tireur*?"

"Don't know. I never saw enough of him to tell whether he had a uniform," Heinz said. After a pause for thought, he added, "Sounded like a military rifle, though—not a little varmint gun."

"Are the Frenchies trying to infiltrate us? That wouldn't be so good," Adalbert said.

"No. It wouldn't." Heinz thought some more. Then he said, "Hossbach! Report this back to regimental HQ. If it's not just one guy with a gun, the higher-ups need to know about it. We're in map square K-4, just west of Avrigny. Got that?"

"K-4. West of Avrigny," Theo repeated. He sighed as he made the connection and delivered the message. Ludwig had always been on him because he was happier with his own thoughts that with the rest of the world. Now Naumann had figured out the same thing in about a minute and a half.

Theo would have liked to do something about that. But doing something about it would have involved changing, and he didn't care to change. His panzer commanders would just have to cope with it . . . and so would he.

* * *

FROM GREASY TO MESSY. Staff Sergeant Alistair Walsh nodded in weary approval. The Anglo-French counterattack, pushing east from the outskirts of Paris, was still making progress. Greasy was actually the hamlet of Gressy, a few miles west of where Walsh was now. Where Walsh was now was in Messy, which looked exactly the way its name made you think it would.

Messy had good reason for looking that way. Only a few weeks earlier, the Germans had bombed and shelled the place to chase the Allied defenders back toward Paris. And then, after the German attack ran out of steam both here and up near Beauvais, English and French guns pounded Messy to push back the *Boches*. A few buildings were still standing and didn't seem too badly damaged, but that wasn't from lack of effort on either side.

Hardly anyone lived in the ruins. People who could get out had done so before the Germans arrived. They hadn't come back to reclaim whatever might be left of their homes and property. A lingering sick-sweet stench said not everybody'd got away. Or Walsh might have been getting a whiff of dead Germans. After three days, everybody—and every body—smelled the same.

As much to blunt the reek as for any other reason, Walsh lit a Navy Cut. Beside him, Second Lieutenant Herman Cavendish looked around and said, "So this is victory."

Walsh hadn't liked the subaltern ever since Cavendish brought the first order to counterattack. The Anglo-French strike had worked, which didn't make the veteran noncom like the very young officer any better. "Sir, when you set this against 1918, it looks like a rest cure," Walsh said.

Maybe Cavendish had been born in 1918, maybe not. If he had, he was still making messes in his nappies. He hadn't seen—or, for that matter, smelled—the Western Front. He hadn't got shot there, either. Walsh had done all of those things, however much he wished he hadn't.

For a wonder, Cavendish heard the reproach in his voice. The youngster blushed like a schoolgirl. "I know you've been through a good deal,

Sergeant," he said stiffly, "but I do believe I am gaining on you when it comes to experience."

That he could come out with such claptrap straight-faced only proved how much experience he didn't have yet. Telling him so would have been pointless precisely because he lacked the experience that would have let him understand what an idiot he was being.

Walsh didn't even try. "Whatever you say, sir," he answered. One of the things staff sergeants did was ride herd on subalterns till their nominal superiors were fit to go around a battlefield by themselves without getting too many of the soldiers under their command killed for no reason.

Cavendish might have been doing his best to prove he hadn't reached that point yet. Pointing east, he said, "Well, we've given the *Boches* a proper what-for this time, eh?"

His posh accent only made that sound even stupider than it would have otherwise. Walsh wouldn't have thought such a thing possible, but Cavendish proved him wrong. "Sir, the Germans came from their own border all the way to Paris. We've come from Paris all the way to Messy," Walsh said. "If you want to call that a proper what-for, well, go ahead."

"There are times when I doubt you have the proper attitude, Sergeant," Cavendish said. "Would you sooner be fighting behind Paris?"

"No, sir. Not a bit of it." Walsh's own accent was buzzing Welsh, and lower-class Welsh at that. What else to expect from a miner's son? He went on, "I'd sooner be fighting in bloody Germany, is what I'd sooner be doing. But that doesn't look like it's in the cards, does it?"

"In—Germany?" By the way the subaltern said it, the possibility had never crossed his mind. "Don't you think that's asking a bit much?"

"Evidently, sir." Walsh left it right there. If the French generals—to say nothing of the British generals (which was about what they deserved to have said of them)—were worth the paper they were printed on, the German High Command wouldn't have been able to impose its will on them with such effortless ease. That had happened the last time around, too. The *Boches* ran out of men and matériel then, while the Yanks gave the Allies all they needed.

No Yanks in the picture now, worse luck. Just the German generals against their British and French counterparts. *Christ help us,* Walsh thought.

As if to remind people who'd forgotten (Second Lieutenant Herman Cavendish, for instance) that they hadn't gone away, German gunners began lobbing shells into Messy. When they started landing too close for comfort, Walsh jumped into the nearest hole in the ground. It wasn't as if he didn't have plenty of choices.

He thought Cavendish would stay upright and make a brave little speech about command responsibility—till a flying fragment did something dreadful to him. But no: the subaltern dove for cover, too. He'd learned *something,* anyhow. Walsh wouldn't have bet more than tuppence ha'penny on it.

After ten minutes or so, the bombardment eased off. Walsh cradled the Schmeisser he'd taken off a dead *Boche*—for throwing a lot of lead around at close quarters, nothing beat a submachine gun. If the Germans decided they wanted Messy back, he was ready to argue with them.

But no hunched-over figures wearing field-gray and coal-scuttle helmets loped forward. This was just harassing fire: hate, they would have called it in the last war. Somebody off in the distance was yelling for a medic, so the bastards serving a 105 had earned their salary this morning.

Lieutenant Cavendish went off to inflict his leadership on someone else. Walsh lit a fresh Navy Cut. He climbed out of the hole to see what the shelling had done to the hamlet.

A skinny little stubble-cheeked French sergeant puffing on a pipe emerged from cover about the same time he did. The Frenchman waved. "*Ça va,* Tommy?" he called.

"*Va bien. Et tu?*" Walsh ran through a good part of his clean French with that. He waved toward the east, then spat.

The French noncom nodded. "Fucking *Boche,*" he said. His English was probably as filthy as most of Walsh's *Français.* A couple of his men came out. He started yelling at them. He was a sergeant, all right.

Walsh checked on the soldiers in his own section. The fellow who'd bought part of a plot came from a different company. That was something, anyhow. After nodding rather smugly, Walsh wondered why it should be. The British army was no better off because the wounded man wasn't from his outfit. And that other company was weakened instead of his. In the larger scheme of things, so what?

But it was a bloke Walsh didn't know, not one he did. You didn't want one of *your* mates to stop one. Maybe that was a reminder you were too bloody liable to stop one yourself. Of course, you had to be an idiot not to know as much already. Still, there was a difference—whether there should have been or not—between knowing something and getting your nose rubbed in it.

"Are we supposed to move up again, Sergeant?" asked a soldier named Nigel. Like Lieutenant Cavendish, he spoke like an educated man. He didn't sound toffee-nosed doing it, though.

"Nobody's told me if we are," Walsh answered. "You can bet your last quid the lieutenant would have, too."

He wasn't supposed to speak ill of officers. He was supposed to let the men in his charge form their unflattering opinions all by themselves. By the way Nigel and Bill and the others chuckled, they needed no help from him.

"He's a bit gormless, ain't he?" Bill said. *He* came from the Yorkshire dales, and sounded like it. The word wasn't one Staff Sergeant Walsh would have chosen. It wasn't one he'd heard before he took the King's shilling more than half a lifetime ago. Well, he'd heard—and used—a lot of words he'd never imagined back in his civilian days. *Gormless* was one you could actually repeat in polite company.

"Oh, maybe a bit," Walsh said, and they chuckled again. He added, "Say what you want about him, though—he is brave."

"Well, yes, but so are the Germans," Nigel said. "Even some of the Frenchmen . . . I suppose."

"They are. We'd be a lot worse off if they weren't," Walsh said.

"Half of them are Bolshies, though. Can you imagine what would happen if the Nazis and Reds were on the same side?" Nigel plainly could. By the way he rolled his eyes, he didn't fancy the notion. "Some Communist official would say, 'The Germans are the workers' friends,' and all the fellow travelers would decide they didn't feel like fighting any more."

"It's not going to happen, chum," Walsh declared, not without relief. "They're slanging away at each other on the far edge of Poland. You ask me, anyone who wants Poland enough to fight over it has to be daft."

"Anyone who's not a Pole, you mean," Nigel said.

"Them, too," Walsh said with more than a little heat. "Look at that bloody Bosnian maniac Princip in 1914. He got millions and millions killed because he couldn't stand the damned Austrian Archduke. Suppose that was worth it, do you? Just as bloody fucking stupid to go to war over Poland."

"There you go." Bill grinned at him from under the dented brim of his tin hat. "Now you've solved all the world's problems, you have. Go tell the *Boches* to quit shooting at us—'twas all a misunderstanding, like. Then get on your airplane and fly off to wherever the hell you go to pick up your Nobel Prize."

Walsh told him where the hell he could go, and where he could stuff the Nobel Prize. They all laughed. They smoked another cigarette or two. And then they were ready to get on with the war again.

SERGEANT HIDEKI FUJITA HAD SPENT more time than he cared to remember in Manchukuo. He'd got used to all kinds of noises he never would have heard in Japan. Wolves could howl. Foxes could yip. If he was wrapped in a blanket out where the steppe gave way to the desert, he'd fall asleep regardless. And he'd stay asleep no matter what kind of racket the animals made. Out there, he lived like an animal himself.

He also lived like an animal here in the pine woods on the Russian side of the Ussuri, the river that formed the northeastern border between Manchukuo and the Soviet Union. He dug himself a hole, he jumped down into it, and he slept. Howling wolves? Yipping foxes? Hooting owls? They didn't bother him a bit.

Tigers? Tigers were a different story. When a tiger roared or screamed, even gunfire seemed to hesitate for a moment. Those noises always woke him up, too, though he'd sleep through gunshots or through artillery that didn't come too close. You had to learn to fear gunshots. Not tigers. If you heard that roar, you *were* afraid, and on the double.

Fujita quickly found out he wasn't the only one who felt the same way. One of the superior privates in his squad, a student called Shinjiro Hayashi, said, "Something deep down inside your head knows that whatever makes that noise wants to eat people."

"*Hai!*" Fujita exclaimed. "That's just it!" He came off a farm himself. He often had the feeling that Hayashi looked down his nose at him, though a Japanese private who let his sergeant know for sure that he looked down his nose at him was asking for all the trouble in the world and a little more besides. Hayashi wasn't dumb enough to do that. And there were times when having a guy who knew things came in handy: Hayashi spoke some Chinese, for instance.

"When we came here from the Mongolian border, they said there'd be tigers here," said Shigeru Nakayama, another private. "I thought it was more of the same old crap they always give new people, but they meant it."

A major in the regiment had had his men drag in an enormous tiger carcass. He hadn't killed it; Russian artillery had. But he took possession of the hide—and of the innards. A tiger's gall bladder was worth plenty to the people who cooked up Chinese and Japanese medicines. You could probably get something for the rest of the organs, too.

But Hayashi spoke another truth when he said, "The tiger will make noise to let you know it's there. You never hear the damn Russian who puts a bullet in your back."

As if on cue, Russian mortar bombs started landing on the Japanese position. Like any soldier with even a little experience in the field, Fujita hated mortars. You couldn't hear them coming till they were almost there. Then they sliced you up like a sashimi chef taking a knife to a fine chunk of *toro*. Unlike the tuna belly, you weren't dead before they started. You sure could be by the time they got done, though.

Fujita jumped into a hole. He had more uses for them than sleep alone. Fragments snarled by overhead. A couple of hundred meters away, a Japanese soldier started screaming as if a tiger had clamped its jaws on his leg. Several rifle shots rang out a few seconds later. Another soldier shrieked.

"*Zakennayo!*" Fujita muttered under his breath. The Russians sent elaborately camouflaged snipers high up into pines that overlooked Japanese positions. Soldiers must have come out to pick up the man the mortars wounded—whereupon the snipers did more damage.

In the Russo-Japanese War, the Japanese had accepted surrenders and treated enemy prisoners as well as any of the soft Western powers did, even if yielding was a disgrace in Japanese eyes. Things hadn't worked like that on the Mongolian border. If you gave up there, you took your chances. And the Mongolians and Soviets weren't what anybody would call gentle, either.

The game was rough here, too. For that matter, Fujita didn't think any army in the world casually accepted surrenders from snipers, any more than most soldiers were willing to let machine gunners give up.

Japanese guns began to move. The Russians had the edge in artillery here, as they did on the edge of the Gobi. The Soviets might not believe in God, but they believed in firepower. And some of the dugouts they built would take a direct hit without collapsing. What they didn't know about field fortifications wasn't worth knowing. They got to show that off in this forest fighting, too.

Somewhere up ahead lay the Trans-Siberian Railroad and victory. Cut the railroad line, and Vladivostok would start to wither away. That would leave the USSR without its great Pacific port, which was exactly what Japan had in mind.

Unfortunately, the Russians could read maps, too. They were going to defend the railway line with everything they had. And if they didn't have more than the generals in the Kwantung Army thought before they started this war, Fujita would have been amazed.

Somewhere up ahead lay Hill 391, the latest strong point the Japanese needed to subdue before they pushed on toward the two parallel lengths of iron track that were the main reason for the attack. Main reason? Sergeant Fujita shook his head. Absent the railroad, this was terrain only tiger hunters would ever want to visit.

The Russians had more of their seemingly limitless cannon up at the top of Hill 391. Down toward the bottom, they had machine-gun nests, barbed wire to guide troops into the machine guns' lines of fire, and minefields to maim any soldiers the machine guns happened to miss. Fujita had already stormed one of the Red Army's fortified hills. He didn't want to do it again. Of course, his superiors cared not a sen's worth about what he or any other enlisted man wanted. Enlisted men were tools, to be used—or used up—as officers saw fit.

Airplane engines droned overhead. Fujita could see only bits of sky through the tall pines and firs and spruces and other trees he had trouble naming. He couldn't make out what was going on up there. Japanese planes had an engine note different from that of their Russian foes: a little higher, a little thinner. Everybody said so. Fujita believed it, but he had trouble hearing it himself.

When bombs started bursting on top of Hill 391 and on the west-facing slope, he felt like cheering. That would give the Russians something to think about! Airplanes full of bombs could counteract their superiority in cannon.

His excitement didn't last long. Once the planes got done pounding the Russian position, what would happen next? Infantry would go forward and try to clean it out—that was what. And then all the Red Army men the bombs hadn't killed would grab their rifles and wait at their machine guns and slaughter as many Japanese as they could.

Sure enough, Lieutenant Hanafusa's whistle squealed. "Come on!" the platoon leader shouted. "Time to dig them out! We can do it! May the Emperor live ten thousand years!" He trotted forward.

"*Banzai!*" Fujita echoed as he scrambled out of his hole. He didn't care about living 10,000 years himself, though he certainly hoped the Emperor would. He did hope he would last another thirty or forty. Going up against another one of these hills made that a lot less likely.

But he couldn't hang back. It wasn't just that his own superiors would do worse to him than anything the Russians could dream up. They would, yes, but that wasn't what got him moving. You couldn't seem a slacker in front of your men. You were brave because they watched you being brave. And they were brave because you had your eye on them— and because they didn't want to let their buddies down.

Ahead, machine guns started hammering. Fujita shook his head as he dodged around trees. No, the bombers hadn't cleared out everybody on the ground. They never did. By the nature of things, they couldn't. That was up to the infantry.

Red Army khaki was a little darker, a little browner, than the color the Japanese used. Neither was very well suited to the deep greens and browns of these pine woods. Fujita scrambled behind a tree. He raised his rifle, made sure that the helmet had an unfamiliar outline, and pulled the trigger.

Down went the Russian. *One less round-eyed barbarian to worry about,* Fujita thought. Somebody ran past him, toward the higher ground ahead. A moment later, the Japanese soldier wailed in despair. He was hung up on barbed wire cleverly concealed among the ferns and bushes that grew under the trees. The way he jerked and struggled reminded Fujita of a bug trapped on flypaper.

A trapped bug might struggle for quite a while. One of the Russian machine guns soon found the Japanese soldier. He didn't jerk any more after that, but hung limply, like a dead fly.

Fujita shivered. That could have been him, as easily as not. If that private hadn't rushed forward, he might have done it himself. Rushing forward was what the Japanese Army taught its soldiers. Aggressiveness won battles. If it also got people killed, that was just part of the cost of doing business.

"*Urra!*" The Russian shout rang through the woods. A submachine gun stuttered, somewhere off to Fujita's left. The Japanese preferred rifles because of their longer range. The Russians liked weapons that could fire rapidly at close quarters. A lot of the fighting in these woods was at very close quarters, because half the time you didn't see the other guy till you fell over him—or he fell over you.

"Advance toward the rear!" an officer shouted. The Japanese had no command for retreat. That one did the job, though. Hill 391 wouldn't fall today. Neither would the railroad line—not here, anyhow.

Chapter 2

Shanghai had seen better days. Pete McGill snorted when that piece of brilliance crossed his mind. It was a good thing he was a Marine corporal. He made a fine leatherneck. If he'd gone into the detective racket instead, his deductions wouldn't have put Sherlock Holmes out of business any time soon.

Of course Shanghai had seen better days. He couldn't think of one spot in China that hadn't seen better days, better years, probably better centuries. Peking, where he'd been stationed till just a little while before, sure as hell wasn't the same since the Japs occupied it.

Japan occupied Shanghai, too. The Japanese had dominated the area since the early 1930s, and threw the Chinese out in November '37, a year and a half ago now. The battle, not far outside of town, was supposed to have cost 300,000 Chinese casualties and 40,000 Japanese. The ratio said a lot about the quality of the two armies involved. That the Chinese stayed in the fight after taking such losses again and again said how much they hated the Japs.

The USA had pulled most of its Marines out of Peking to help protect

Americans in Shanghai, who were far more numerous than in the former capital. That was what the United States loudly proclaimed, anyhow. If you read between the lines, you saw that Marines in Peking were trapped. If trouble with Japan flared up, the garrison at the U.S. Legation would have to be written off. Shanghai was a port. Troops here had some kind of chance of getting on a ship and heading for Hong Kong or Manila or . . . somewhere.

McGill didn't worry about it. Worrying about foreign policy wasn't in a corporal's job description. He worried about making sergeant one of these days. He worried about the twenty bucks U.S. he'd lost in a poker game on the train down from Peking. He worried about finding a good, cheap whorehouse; he hadn't much cared for the couple of places he'd visited here. Till he found some suckers and won back what he'd lost— how often did you run into four sixes, for crying out loud?—cheap came first.

He didn't like worrying about the Japs anyway, so he did as little of it as he could. Like any Marine, he was convinced he was part of the best fighting outfit in the world. Back when Peking still belonged to China, he'd brawled with Japanese soldiers. He'd cheered the American baseball team against the Japanese nine.

But things weren't the same any more. Now that the Japs were at war with China, they didn't go in for friendly brawling. They'd mob you if you messed with them. It was an article of faith that one Marine was tougher than one Jap. One Marine sure as hell wasn't tougher than six or eight or ten slant-eyed little yellow monkeys, and that was how things worked out nowadays.

American, British, and French warships lay alongside Japanese naval vessels in the harbor. Their guns were supposed to give the Western powers bargaining strength against the Chinese and the Japs. They'd done the job against the Chinese . . . till the Chinese didn't hold Shanghai any more. Against Japan? Japan had far more firepower here than all the Western powers put together.

And Japan had fighters and bombers galore, which the Western powers here didn't. The crew of the American gunboat *Panay* could have preached a sermon about that. Japanese airplanes had sent her to the bottom of the Yangtze. Oh, the Japanese government apologized and paid an indemnity afterwards, but that didn't do the dead sailors a hell of a lot of good.

So Americans, and Westerners generally, had to watch themselves in Shanghai these days. But you could still have yourself a hell of a good time if you did watch yourself. Things cost more here than they did in Peking. With only a corporal's pay, Pete noticed the difference. Still, compared to Honolulu or even Manila, Shanghai remained a pretty good deal.

It had compensations Peking lacked, too. Most of the dance-hall hostesses at the clubs here were White Russians, refugees first from the Red takeover and then from the Japanese domination of what was now called Manchukuo. McGill couldn't remember the last time he'd danced with a white woman in Peking. He wasn't sure he ever had. Here, he could do it as much as he wanted, for anything from ten cents to a dollar Mex a dance, depending on how fancy the joint was. And some of the White Russian gals were real stunners, too.

Stunners or not, a lot of them were vampires who could put Bela Lugosi to shame. Their main goal was separating soldiers and sailors and businessmen from cash. Between dances, they wanted to drink. You ordered them champagne or wine or whiskey. They got ginger ale or apple or grape juice or weak tea. It went on the chit as booze, though. You paid—through the nose. Some of Pete's naïve buddies wondered how the girls could drink so much and never show it.

He knew better than that, anyhow. If the girl he was dancing with was pretty enough, he didn't care . . . too much. And Vera, tonight, was all that and then some. Her hair was the color of Jean Harlow's. If a peroxide bottle helped it along (as it was supposed to have done for Harlow), Pete didn't feel like fussing. She had big blue eyes, a button nose, and a mouth as red and sweet-looking as a strawberry. Moving south, she came equipped with everything else a girl needed, too.

And she could really dance. She danced well enough to make Pete, a man born with two left feet, feel like a good dancer himself. She also clung to him tighter than a coat of paint. If that wasn't inspiration, he didn't know what would be. She must have felt his hard-on bumping against her, but she didn't seem to mind. She let him kiss her, too. Her mouth turned out to be even sweeter than it looked.

They went on clinging to each other after the music stopped. A slinky Chinese gal in a dress slit up to there brought fresh drinks to the sweating Chinamen in black tie who played some pretty good hot jazz.

Somebody tapped Pete on the shoulder. Distracted, he half turned. There stood a buddy of his, a Marine named Puccinelli. Grinning, the dago said, "Why don't you make an honest woman out of that broad, man? You looked like you were gonna lay her right here on the dance floor."

"Why don't you get lost, Pooch?" McGill suggested sweetly. If he'd thought Vera would go for it . . . She might have been pouring down phony drinks, but Pete hadn't. He'd guzzled enough real whiskey to make it seem like fun, not craziness.

Vera tugged at his arm. "A little champagne?" she said. "Dancing makes you thirsty, yes?"

Dancing made Pete horny. "How's about you and me go off somewhere quiet, just the two of us?" he asked.

Even half in the bag, he watched the cash registers chinging behind the White Russian girl's big baby blues. He gave his own mental shrug. It wasn't as if he thought she was with him because of the charm of his own blunt, ruddy features. If you were looking for love, or even for a facsimile that seemed reasonable while it was going on, in places like this, you needed to keep your wallet in your hand.

"Sixty dollars Mex," Vera said.

That was four times the going rate for a Chinese girl in a Shanghai brothel. It was also fifteen bucks American, or a goodly part of a month's pay. But when John Henry started yelling . . . you really wished that asshole on the train hadn't had four of a kind. "Ouch," Pete said.

Vera considered. She wasn't like a whorehouse whore—she had some discretion about clients and prices. Her features softened a little. "All right, Yankee. For you, fifty Mex," she said.

She does like me—some, anyway, Pete thought. He also knew damn well she wouldn't come down twice. "Where can we go?" he asked.

She took his arm. "Follow me," she said. Right then, he would have followed her through ice or fire or a minefield. He didn't have to go that far: only to a little room over the dance hall.

It had a bare, dim light bulb hanging from the ceiling, a mattress on an iron bed frame, one cheap chair, and a nightstand with a pitcher and basin and a couple of folded towels on top. It was astringently clean and astringently neat, which made it stand out among the many whores' rooms Pete had visited.

"You like it?" Vera's mouth twisted as she slid out of her dress. "It is my palace."

"Sweetheart, any room with you in it is a palace," Pete said hoarsely. He might regret blowing so much jack tomorrow, but he sure didn't now. She looked even better naked than she had in the tight-fitting silk. He hadn't dreamt she could.

She gave him a wry smile. "An eager one like you, almost I forget I do this for money."

Pete wished she hadn't said *almost*. But, right this minute, he didn't care why she was doing it, as long as she was. He flicked off the light and reached for her. Even in the sudden darkness, he knew just where the bed lay.

LIEUTENANT COLONEL BORISOV GLOWERED at the assembled Red Air Force pilots and copilots. "You people have been sitting around on your asses too damn long," the squadron commander growled. "High time you went out and earned some of the rubles the workers and peasants of the Soviet Union are paying you."

Lieutenant Sergei Yaroslavsky stirred on his folding chair. That was monstrously unfair, and Borisov had to know it. It wasn't the flyers' fault that the unpaved Byelorussian airstrip turned to gluey mud in the spring thaw. *Everything* turned to mud during the fall and spring *rasputitsas*.

"Time to make the Poles sorry they climbed into the sack with that dog turd of a Fascist, Hitler," Borisov went on. "If they think they can get away with refusing the USSR's just demands, they'd better think twice."

Now Sergei nodded. That was more like it. Blame the enemy, not your own side.

Sitting next to him, Anastas Mouradian raised a thick, dark eyebrow. One of these days, the copilot and bomb-aimer aboard Sergei's SB-2 would end up in more trouble than he could hope to escape. An emotional Armenian, he couldn't keep what he was thinking off his face.

Enough propaganda. Just give us the mission and let us take care of it. Something like that had to be in Stas' mind. It was in Sergei's mind, too, but he had sense enough not to show it. What nobody saw wouldn't get reported to the NKVD.

Of course, the NKVD could haul you away and shoot you or chuck you into a camp north of the Arctic Circle with no excuse at all. But why make things easy for the Chekists? If you gave them a reason to jump on you, you were almost asking for it, like a girl in tight clothes that didn't cover enough of her.

"Our target is the railroad line that runs southeast from Wilno to Molodetschna," Colonel Borisov went on. Wilno to the Russians, Vilna to the Poles, Vilnius to the Lithuanians . . . one town with three names, depending on who was talking about it and who held it at any given moment. It was in Poland's hands now. Marshal Smigly-Ridz had refused to give it back to the USSR. The Lithuanians also wanted it again, though they hadn't ruled there for centuries.

Sergei didn't show annoyance, and he didn't show relief, either. Whether he showed it or not, he felt it. They weren't going to fly into East Prussia today. It wasn't that the Germans didn't have fighters and antiaircraft guns inside of Poland—they did. But they seemed much more serious about defending their own people than they did about protecting a bunch of Poles.

"Questions?" Borisov asked.

No one said anything. Borisov did not have a manner that encouraged queries. His face said, *Don't waste my time.* Not all questions did waste time, but the ones that didn't got asked no more than the ones that did.

After the meeting broke up, Sergeant Ivan Kuchkov asked his superiors, "Well, how are they going to fuck us over this time?"

"The railroad coming out of Wilno," Sergei answered.

"That won't be so bad," Kuchkov said. He was the bombardier, in charge of actually dropping the bombs on the enemy's head. It took brute strength, and he had plenty. He was short and squat and muscular. He was also one of the hairiest human beings Sergei had ever seen. People called him "the Chimp," but rarely to his face—you took your life in your hands if you did.

"I was thinking the same thing," Yaroslavsky said.

"I was hoping the same thing," Anastas Mouradian said, which sounded almost identical but meant something different.

Most of the winter whitewash had been scrubbed off their SB-2. What was left gave the Tupolev bomber's summer camouflage of brown and green an old, faded look. The SB-2 itself was starting to seem old and faded to Sergei. The two-engined machine had seemed a world-beater in the early days of the Spanish Civil War. It could outrun and outclimb the biplane fighters Marshal Sanjurjo's Fascists and their Italian and German allies threw against it.

But those days were long gone now. Sergei and his crewmates had fought as "volunteers" in Czechoslovakia. There, he'd made the unhappy discovery that the SB-2 was no match for the German Messerschmitt 109. Quite a few of his comrades who'd discovered the same thing didn't come back to the *Rodina*. Bf-109s had done far too many of the Motherland's flyers in this latest squabble with the Poles and Germans, too.

Better bombers were supposed to be on the way. Till they arrived, the SB-2 soldiered on. It was what the Soviet Union had. If losses ran high . . . Well, they did, that was all. Factories could crank out more planes, and *Osoaviakhim* flight schools could crank out more pilots.

Armorers wheeled bombs over to the plane. The carts didn't sink into the ground, a sure sign the *rasputitsa* was done at last. "Here's hoping they all land on the Hitlerites' cocks," Kuchkov said.

"And the Poles," Sergei added.

"Fuck the Poles. Fuck their mothers, fuck their daughters, fuck their sisters, and fuck their ugly old aunties, too," Ivan declared. He was, as Sergei had seen before, a man of limited vocabulary and strong opinions. "The Poles aren't worth shit. The fucking Germans, they're the ones we need to worry about."

He wasn't wrong. Sergei had seen enough of the Germans to alarm him, too. "They won't stop us," the pilot declared. Neither Kuchkov nor Mouradian tried to tell him any different.

Both big radial engines on the SB-2 thundered to life. Sergei ran through the checklist. Everything came up green. Other bombers were jouncing down the runway and flying west. When his turn came, Sergei joined them. Getting up in the air again felt good. Till the shooting started, he could remember what a joy flying was supposed to be.

But the shooting started all too soon. During the winter, Soviet troops had bitten off a disappointingly small chunk of northeastern Poland. A few of them fired at the westbound SB-2s, on the theory that anything in the air was bound to be dangerous. The Chimp's profanity echoed brassily through the speaking tube that connected the bomb bay and the cockpit.

And the Poles banged away at the bombers for all they were worth. Black puffs of smoke burst among the SB-2s. The antiaircraft fire was so quick and accurate, Sergei wondered if Germans were manning the guns down on the ground. One of the SB-2s had to turn back with smoke and flame coming from the starboard engine. Yaroslavsky hoped the crew got down safely.

That clang was a chunk of shrapnel biting into the fuselage. Sergei eyed the gauges. He tested all the controls. *"Khorosho?"* Mouradian asked.

"Da, khorosho," Sergei answered, and everything *did* seem fine. Part of him that only came out in times of stress wanted to thank God. The New Soviet Man who ruled his mind more often than not told that other part to shut up and go away.

There was the railroad line, stretching off toward Wilno. "Borisov didn't tell us where he wanted us to hit it, did he?" Mouradian said.

Sergei thought back. "No, I don't believe he did." That probably meant some Red Air Force higher-up hadn't told Borisov. Maybe none of the higher-ups had even stopped to worry about it. Since they figured one length of track was as good as another . . . "I'm going to start the bombing run."

He flew straight and level, changing course only as Mouradian aligned them more closely on the railway line. "Now, Ivan!" Mouradian bawled through the speaking tube, and the stick of bombs fell free.

As soon as they did, Yaroslavsky swung the bomber into a hard turn and mashed down the throttle. Even Polish fighters could outrun the SB-2, and if Messerschmitts were in the neighborhood . . .

Messerschmitts *were* in the neighborhood. The slab-sided fighters tore into the SB-2s that had pressed deeper into Poland. A blast from the dorsal machine-gun turret said one of them was thinking about coming after Sergei's plane. "Gutless whore!" Ivan yelled. "He's running like a prick with the clap!"

"Too bad!" Sergei said. He exchanged a look with Mouradian. They wore identical shaky grins. No matter how the Chimp felt, neither was sorry that German hadn't kept chasing them. *No, not a bit,* Sergei thought, and came down on the throttle even harder.

A GROUNDCREW MAN WALKED UP to Hans-Ulrich Rudel at what had been a French airstrip till the *Wehrmacht* overran it. These days, Stukas flew out of it to pummel the former owners and their English allies. "Excuse me, Lieutenant . . ." the enlisted man said, and stood there waiting.

"What's up, Franz?" Rudel asked. The mechanic had served in the trenches in the last war. He still recalled the strict and formal discipline of the Kaiser's army, which made him seem out of place in Germany's new, more easygoing military.

"Colonel Steinbrenner wants to see you right away, sir," Franz said.

"What kind of trouble am I in?" Hans-Ulrich assumed he was in one kind or another. He was a white crow in the squadron: a teetotaling minister's son didn't mix well with most of the hard-drinking, hard-wenching pilots. They teased him, and he shot back. There hadn't been any brawls yet, but it was bound to be only a matter of time. Even his rear gunner thought him a queer duck.

But Franz only shrugged. "Sir, you think a colonel tells me anything like that?"

Hans-Ulrich didn't. He walked over to the colonel's tent. Everything all around was green. The air was soft and sweet and mild with spring . . . if you didn't notice the faint death-reek that lay under the sweetness. Rudel's nose was used to it, so most of the time he didn't. This morning, for some reason, he did.

An unfamiliar *Kübelwagen* was parked next to the tent. The little utility vehicle was built on a *Volkswagen* chassis. Production of passenger cars, naturally, was on hold for the duration. A *Kübelwagen* could take four people almost anywhere, and carry a machine gun, too. If you didn't need armor plate or a cannon, what more could you want?

He ducked into the tent. "Rudel, sir, reporting as ordered."

"Yes, yes." Colonel Steinbrenner nodded to the two men standing next to the folding table that served as his desk. "These gentlemen have some questions they want to ask you."

The gentlemen in question didn't wear *Luftwaffe* blue-gray. Instead, their uniforms were somber black, with SS runs on one collar tab. The older SS man said, "So you're Rudel, are you?"

"That's right," Hans-Ulrich answered automatically.

"Good. Come with us," the blackshirt said.

"What's going on?" That was also an automatic yelp.

"Just come. We'll talk about it later," the SS man answered.

Numbly, Rudel went. Was this what Russian officers felt when somebody from the NKVD came for them? He didn't know; he'd never been a Russian. He did know people at the airstrip stared as he climbed into the *Kübelwagen* with Himmler's hounds. The younger one started up the machine. As it rolled away, Hans-Ulrich wondered if he'd ever come back.

After a little more than a kilometer, the driver pulled off the narrow, winding road and stopped. Everything was very quiet. A couple of black cows grazed in an emerald meadow. Off in the distance, a French farmer guided a horse-drawn plow. He probably would have used a tractor before the war, but where would he get gas for it now? The plow might have been sitting in the barn since his father put it there. But you did what you could with what you had.

What were the SS men going to do with him? The older one lit an Overstolz from a pack he took out of his breast pocket. When he held out the pack, Hans-Ulrich shook his head. "That's right," the blackshirt said, as if reminding himself. "You don't drink, either, do you?"

"What if I don't?" Rudel said. "Were you going to give me a cigarette before you put one between my eyes?"

The two big men in black looked at each other. Then, as if on cue, they threw back their heads and laughed like loons. A jackdaw flew out of a nearby tree, chattering in annoyance. "*That's* not what we brought you out here for," the younger one said. Tears leaked from the corners of his eyes. He dabbed at them with his sleeve before dissolving in giggles again. "Oh, dear!" He couldn't stop laughing—he was helpless as a baby.

And his partner wasn't in much better shape. Had Rudel needed to, he thought he could have disarmed them both without breaking a sweat. Evidently, though, he didn't need to. What he didn't understand was why he didn't need to. "Well, what *did* you bring me out here for?" he asked irritably.

"Nice to know our reputation goes ahead of us," the older one said. Did he mean it? Hans-Ulrich, already at sea, had trouble telling. The SS man gathered himself. He finally went on, "As a matter of fact, Rudel, we wanted to talk to you because you're known to be loyal."

"Huh?" Hans-Ulrich knew the uncouth noise made him sound like a moron, but it was what came out of his mouth.

"Because you're known to be loyal," the SS man repeated patiently. Maybe he had a small child at home, and didn't mind saying the same thing over and over again. Or maybe—since he didn't wear a wedding ring—he'd just done a devil of a lot of interrogations. "We want to root out disloyalty wherever we find it. People whose loyalty we trust can help us do that. This colonel in charge of your squadron, for instance . . . Has he ever done anything or said anything to make you think he's not doing all he can for the *Reich* and the *Führer*?"

"Colonel Steinbrenner? Never," Rudel said at once. Telling the truth was easy, and came as a relief.

"He's replacing somebody who wasn't reliable," the younger SS man said, tactfully reminding his superior of something he might have forgotten.

"*Ja, ja,*" the other blackshirt said, not so patiently this time. If he had forgotten, he wasn't about to admit it. "But so what? That doesn't mean he walks on water himself, not by a long shot."

"As far as I know, he's a good National Socialist," Hans-Ulrich said.

"*Wunderbar.* Maybe he does walk on water, then. What about the other people in your squadron?" the older man persisted. "Anybody saying rude things about the *Führer* because the offensive's slowed down a little bit?"

The offensive in France hadn't slowed down. It had stopped. No matter how German radio tried to disguise that, it was obvious to anyone who spent time at, or over, the front. The *Wehrmacht* hadn't taken Paris. It hadn't wheeled around behind the city from the north: the goal in 1914 and now again a generation later. It was scrambling to try to cover its long, weak southern flank against French counterattacks. It wasn't trench warfare of the sort that had murdered so many of the Kaiser's soldiers, but German troops weren't storming forward to glory right this minute, either.

Cautiously, Hans-Ulrich answered, "Nobody's very happy about it. I'm not very happy about it myself."

That last sentence made the older SS man close his mouth on a question. Rudel could guess what it was. He would have wanted to know exactly who was unhappy, and what the unhappy people had said. Easy to put a noose around someone's neck with testimony like that. But the blackshirt had to see Rudel wouldn't say anything worth hearing, not if he admitted he wished the war were going better.

"What about your crewmate, Sergeant What's-his-name . . . Dieselhorst?" the younger SS man said. "Some people have told us funny stuff about him."

"Then they're a pack of lying pigdogs," Hans-Ulrich answered hotly. "Nothing's wrong with Albert—not one single thing, you hear? If it weren't for him, I wouldn't have come back from a couple of missions. You want to listen to the *Scheisse* 'some people' come out with, you'd better haul me away, too."

He wondered if they would. Albert Dieselhorst loved Germany, but he didn't love the people who ran it these days. And he wasn't shy about saying so, which must have been why informers tipped these fellows off to him. If they had enough evidence, they'd know Rudel was protecting his sergeant. Then he and Dieselhorst would both catch it.

But the blackshirt said, "Take an even strain, buddy. We've got to check this stuff out, you know. It's our job. It's our duty." He nodded—he liked the sound of that better. It made him seem more like a soldier, less like the secret policeman he was.

"Take him back," the older SS man said. "He hasn't got anything good for us."

"Doesn't look that way," the fellow behind the wheel agreed. He started up the *Kübelwagen*, expertly turned around on the narrow road, and started east, toward the airstrip. Rudel couldn't let out the sigh of relief that wanted to explode from him. They might notice it and know it for what it was.

The older man did have the decency to say, "Good luck to you," when they dropped Hans-Ulrich off. The *Kübelwagen* chugged away. Ground-crew men and flyers stared at Rudel. If the SS arrested somebody right after this, he wouldn't be able to live it down. The gang would have to wait and see that everyone stayed safe before they trusted him again. Sooner or later, they would . . . he hoped.

SARAH GOLDMAN WALKED through the streets of Münster toward the only bakery in town that still served Jews. It was late afternoon: the only time Jews were allowed to shop. They got whatever was left after all the Aryans bought what *they* needed. It wasn't fair, of course. Nothing had been fair since the Nazis took over, more than six years ago now.

She'd only been twelve then. She hadn't understood all the reasons why her parents and her older brother were so upset. Well, she did now. No one who lived in Germany, Jew or Aryan, could fail to understand these days.

British bombers—or maybe they were French—had come over a few nights before. Nothing fell very close to the Goldmans' house, for which Sarah thanked the God in Whom she was having more and more trouble believing.

A labor gang worked to fill in a crater one of the bombs had blown in the street. A gray-haired man with only one arm shouted at the men to work harder. He was probably a sergeant mutilated in the last war. Some of the men were petty criminals. Some were too old to worry about getting conscripted. None seemed inclined to work any harder than he had to.

"Put your backs into it, you lugs!" the gang boss growled. "If you don't, they'll put you to work in a camp."

That made his charges speed up, at least for a little while. It made Sarah shudder as she walked by. She didn't know what happened to people who went to places like Mauthausen and Dachau. All she knew was, it wasn't good. No—she also knew they didn't come out again. Her imagination took it from there: took it all kinds of unpleasant places. She shuddered again.

"Hey, sweetheart!" one of the guys in the gang called. He waved to her and rocked his hips forward and back. His buddies laughed.

Sarah's spine stiffened. She walked on with her nose in the air. That only made the laborers laugh harder. She ignored them as best she could. She hadn't wanted to look at them at all. She was afraid she'd see her father sweating through pick-and-shovel work. Samuel Goldman, wounded war veteran, holder of the Iron Cross Second Class, professor of classics and ancient history . . . street repairer. It was the only work the Nazis would let him have.

Her brother had worked in a labor gang for a while, too. Saul was a footballer of near-professional quality. He exulted in the physical, where his father grudgingly acknowledged it. And, when his gang boss rode him and hit him once too often for being a Jew, he'd smashed in the nasty little man's head with a shovel.

He'd got away afterwards, too. Sarah didn't know how, but he had. His athletic training must have let him outrun everyone who chased him. And the police and the SS were still looking for him. A slow smile spread across Sarah's face. He'd found a hiding place they'd never think of.

How many of the people on the street at this time of day were Jews intent on getting whatever the hateful authorities would let them have? You couldn't tell by looking, not most of the time. Worried expressions and threadbare clothes meant nothing. During wartime, plenty of impeccably Aryan Germans were worried and shabby, too. And Sarah couldn't recognize Jews from the synagogue, either. Her family was secular, with mostly gentile friends; she couldn't remember the last time she'd gone to *shul.*

Her father had told her he felt more Jewish now, with the Nazis persecuting him, than he ever had before. If that wasn't irony, what was?

A young man in a *Wehrmacht* uniform, his left arm in a sling, smiled at her as she walked past. She didn't smile back. She thought she might have if she were an Aryan; he was nice-looking. Up till Hitler took over, she'd always thought of herself as more German than Jewish. Even with everything that was going on, her father and brother had tried to join up when the war started. They still wanted to be Germans. The recruiters wouldn't let them. It was all so monstrously unfair.

The Jewish grocer's shop and bakery sat across the street from each other. Before the war started, brownshirts had amused themselves by swearing at Jewish women who went in and out. They'd chucked a rock through the grocer's window, too. Naturally, the police only yawned. Now most of the brownshirts were carrying rifles. Sarah hoped the French and the English—yes, and the Russians, too—would shoot them.

She got some sad potatoes and turnips, some wilting greens, and a couple of wizened apples at the grocer's. It all cost too much and too many ration points. When she grumbled, Josef Stein only shrugged. "It's not like I can do anything about it," the proprietor said.

"I know." Sarah sighed. "But it's not easy for my family, either."

"You want easy, what are you doing here?" Stein said.

She walked across the street to the bakery. The bread was what the ration book called war bread. It was baked from rye and barley and potato flour. It was black and chewy. The alarming thing was that people who remembered the last war said it was better than what they ate then. That bread had been eked out with ground corn and lupine seeds—and, some people insisted, with sawdust, too.

The baker's son stood behind the counter. Isidor Bruck was only a couple of years older than Sarah. He'd played football with her brother, though he wasn't in Saul's class (but then, who was?). No doubt his parents had named him Isidor to keep from calling him Isaak. That kind of thing amused Sarah's father, who'd told her *Isidor* meant *gift of Isis*—not the sort of name a Jew ought to wear. She didn't think the Brucks had given it to him because of what it meant, but even so. . . .

"This is a pretty good batch," he said as he put the loaf in her cloth sack.

"You always say that," Sarah answered. "Or your father does, if he's back there instead."

"We always mean it, too. We do the best we can with what they let us have," Isidor said. "If they gave us more, we'd do better. You know what we were like before . . . before everything happened. We were the best bakery in town. Jews? *Goyim?* We were better than everybody."

"Sure, Isidor," Sarah said. As far as she could remember, he was right. Whenever the Goldmans wanted something special, they'd come to the Brucks' bakery. She remembered things as ordinary as white bread with a fond longing she wouldn't have imagined possible only a couple of years before.

She gave him money and more ration coupons. Just handling the coupons, printed with the Nazis' eagle holding a swastika in its claws, made her want to wash her hands. But she had to use them—she or her mother. If they didn't, the family wouldn't eat. It wouldn't eat well any which way. Aryans couldn't eat well under rationing, though they could keep body and soul together. Jews had trouble doing even that.

He handed her her change. Some of the bronze and aluminum coins also bore the eagle and swastika. She liked the older ones, from the Weimar Republic, better. They didn't make her wish she could be a traitor against the government, or at least that the country—*her* country, in spite of everything—had gone in a different direction.

"Take care," Isidor said as she turned to go. "Hope I see you again before too long."

"Sure," Sarah said, and then wondered if she should have. She could see his reflection in the front window as she walked to the door—neither brownshirts nor British bombs had broken this one. Yes, he was watching her. She had to ask herself how she felt about being watched. What would she do if he asked her to go walking in the botanical gardens, or through the park just south of them that held the zoo? (Those were the most exciting dates Jews could have these days. Even movie theaters were off-limits. Sarah didn't look especially Jewish, but Isidor did. The ticket seller would surely ask for his ID, and trouble would follow right away.)

A baker's son? In ordinary times, she would have laughed at the idea. These days, weren't all Jews equal in misery? And—a coldly pragmatic part of her mind whispered—if anybody kept food on the table, wouldn't a baker? The things you had to think about! She was glad when the door swung shut behind her.

Chapter 3

Up atop the U-30's conning tower, Lieutenant Josef Lemp imagined he could see forever. No land was in sight. Ireland lay off to the north, Cornwall to the east, but neither showed above the horizon. Gray-blue sky came down to meet green-blue sea in a perfect circle all around the boat. The eye couldn't judge how wide that circle was. Why *not* believe it stretched to infinity and beyond?

Why not? Only one reason: you'd get killed in a hurry if you did. Three petty officers on the conning tower with Lemp constantly scanned air and sea with Zeiss binoculars. The U-30 had almost circumnavigated the British Isles to reach this position. As far as the Royal Navy and the RAF were concerned, she made an unwelcome interloper. They had ways of letting her know it, too.

But the U-boat needed to be here. Convoys from the USA and Canada and Argentina came through these waters. Without the supplies they carried, England and her war effort would starve. And British troopships ferried Tommies and RAF pilots and the planes they flew to France. Sink them before they got there, and they wouldn't give *Landsers* and *Luftwaffe* flyers grief.

One of the petty officers' field glasses jerked. He'd spotted something up in the sky. Lemp got ready to bawl the order that would send everybody on the tower diving down the hatch and the U-30 diving deep into the sea. Then the binoculars steadied. The petty officer let out a sheepish chuckle. "Only a petrel," he said.

"That's all right, Rolf," Lemp said. "Better to jump at a bird than to miss an airplane."

Rolf nodded. "You bet, Skipper."

The surface navy was all spit and polish and formality. There was no room for that kind of crap aboard U-boats. The men who sailed in them laughed at it. They were a raffish lot, given to beards and dirty uniforms and speaking their minds. But when the time came to buckle down to business, nobody was more dangerous.

Lemp had his own binoculars on a strap around his neck. The conning tower also carried a massive pair on a metal pylon, for times when a skipper needed to trade field of view for magnification.

Rolf stiffened again, this time like a dog coming to the point. "Smoke!"

"Where away?" Lemp asked, grabbing for his field glasses.

"Bearing about 270," the petty officer answered. "You can make it out just above the horizon."

Back and forth, back and forth. Moving the binoculars that way was second nature for Lemp. And sure as hell, there was the smudge. "Well, let's see what we've got," he said, excitement tingling through him. "Go below, boys," Down the hatch they went, shoes clanging on iron rungs. Lemp, the last man there, dogged the hatch. "Take us to *Schnorkel* depth," he ordered as he descended.

The U-30 slid below the surface—but not far below. The tube mounted atop the submarine let the diesels keep breathing even so. Lemp was not enamored of the gadget, which didn't always work as advertised. The shipfitters back in Kiel wouldn't have installed the Dutch-invented device on his boat if he'd been in good odor with the powers that be. After sinking an American liner while believing it to be a big freighter, he wasn't. He was lucky they hadn't beached him—maybe lucky they hadn't shot him. No one who remembered the last war wanted to see the USA jump into this one.

Lemp turned to Gerhart Beilharz, the engineering officer who'd come with the *Schnorkel*. "Is the damned thing behaving?" he asked.

"Oh, yes, sir," Beilharz said enthusiastically. He was all for his new toy. Of course he was—he wouldn't have been messing with it if he weren't. Normally, an extra engineering officer on a U-boat—especially one two meters tall, who wore an infantry helmet to keep from smashing his head open on the overhead pipes and valves—was about as useful as an extra tail on a cat, but, if they were going to have the *Schnorkel* along, having somebody aboard who knew all about it seemed worthwhile.

It did have its uses. With it in action, the U-boat could make eight knots just below the surface—better than twice her submerged speed on batteries. And she could keep going indefinitely, instead of running out of juice inside a day. Best of all, with the *Schnorkel* the U-30 could charge the batteries for deep dives without surfacing. That was good for everybody's life expectancy . . . except the enemy's.

Lemp could have gone twice as fast in approaching the ship or ships making that distant smoke plume had he stayed surfaced. Maybe it was a lone freighter: a fat, tasty target. Maybe, sure, but the odds were against it. Freighters in these waters commonly convoyed and zigzagged. They commonly had destroyers escorting them. And destroyers loved U-boats the way dogs loved cats—even cats with two tails.

Better to be a cat o' nine tails, Lemp thought. With all the torpedoes the U-30 carried, he could flog England even worse than that. If he could keep England from flogging back, he'd bring the U-boat home so he could go out and try it again. *So the English have the chance to kill me again.* As he did every time that thought surfaced, he made it submerge once more.

He peered through the periscope. Nothing but smoke, not yet. Eight knots was a walk, even if it wasn't a crawl.

He could come closer to the enemy with the *Schnorkel* than he could staying on the surface. He did have to give it that. An alert lookout who'd spot a light gray U-boat hull even against a gray sky wouldn't notice the hollow pole that kept the diesels chugging. If he did spot it, he might think it was a piece of sea junk and keep his big mouth shut.

"What have we got, Skipper?" somebody asked. The first time he put the question, Lemp heard it without consciously noticing it. Whoever it was asked the same thing again.

This time, Lemp did notice. "Convoy. They're zigzagging—away from us, at the moment." Even tubby freighters could go as fast as the U-30 did on the *Schnorkel.*

"What kind of escorts?"

"Warships. Destroyers, corvettes, frigates . . . I can't make that out at this distance. I see two—bound to be more on the far side of the convoy." Lemp muttered to himself. If he was going to get close enough to fire at the enemy ships, either they'd have to swerve back toward him or he'd need to surface and close the gap before diving again. He didn't much want to do that; if he could see the enemy, they'd be able to see him after he came up. Trouble was, you couldn't fight a war doing only the things you wanted to do.

"Can we sneak up on them, sir?" That was Lieutenant Beilharz, both more formal and more optimistic than most of the submariners.

Unhappily, Lemp shook his head. "Afraid not," he said, and then, "Prepare to surface."

Beilharz grunted as if the skipper had elbowed him in the pit of the stomach. The youngster wanted his pet miracle-worker to solve every problem the sea presented. Well, no matter what he wanted, he wouldn't get all of it. Lemp wanted to be taller and skinnier than he was. He wanted his hairline to quit receding, too—actually, he wanted it never to have started. He wasn't going to get everything his heart desired, either.

Compressed air drove seawater out of the ballast tanks. Up came the U-30. Lemp scrambled up the ladder and opened the conning-tower hatch. As always, fresh air, air that didn't stink, hit him like a slug of champagne.

He knew he would have to dive again soon no matter what. British binoculars weren't as good as the ones Zeiss made, but even so. . . . And he had ratings scan the sky to make sure they spotted enemy airplanes before anyone aboard the planes saw them. How close could U-30 cut it? That was always the question.

Then one of the petty officers yelped. "Airplane!" he squawked, sounding as pained as a dog with a stepped-on paw.

"*Scheisse!*" Lemp said crisply. Well, that settled that. "Go below. We'll dive." He knew the U-30 had no other choice. Shooting it out on the surface was a fight the sub was bound to lose. And if machine-gun bullets holed the pressure hull, she couldn't dive at all. In that case, it was *auf wiedersehen, Vaterland.*

The ratings tumbled down the hole one after another. Again, Lemp came last and closed the hatch behind him. The U-boat dove deep and fast. He hoped the plane hadn't spotted it, but he wasn't about to bet his life.

Sure as the devil, that splash was a depth charge going into the water. The damned Englishmen had a good notion of what a Type VII U-boat could do—the ash can burst at just about the right depth. But it was too far off to do more than rattle the submariners' teeth.

"Well, we're home free now," Lieutenant Beilharz said gaily.

"Like hell we are." Lemp had more experience. And, before very long, one of the warships from the convoy came over and started pinging with its underwater echo-locater. Sometimes that newfangled piece of machinery gave a surface ship a good fix on a submerged target. Sometimes it didn't. You never could tell.

Splash! Splash! More depth charges started down. Unlike an airplane, a destroyer carried them by the dozen. One burst close enough to stagger Lemp. The light bulb above his head burst with a pop. Somebody shouted as he fell over. Someone else called, "We've got a little leak aft!"

Lemp didn't need to give orders about that. The men would handle it. He waited tensely, wondering if the Englishmen up there would drop more explosives on his head. They were waiting, too: waiting to see what their first salvo had done. Only a little more than a hundred meters separated hunter and hunted. It might as well have been the distance from the earth to the moon.

Splash! Splash! Those sounded farther away. Lemp hoped he was hearing with his ears, not his pounding heart. The bursts rocked the U-30, but they were also farther off. Lemp let out a soft sigh of relief. They were probably going to make it.

And they did, even if they had to wait till after dark to surface. By then, of course, the convoy was long gone. The English had won the round, but the U-30 stayed in the game.

VACLAV JEZEK POINTED to a loaf of bread. The French baker in Laon pointed to the price above it. The Czech soldier gave him money. The baker handed over the torpedo-shaped loaf. Jezek knew only a handful of French words, most of them vile. Sometimes you could make do without.

Off in the distance, German artillery rumbled. Vaclav started to flinch, then caught himself. If the Nazis were hitting Laon again, he would have heard shells screaming down before the boom of the guns reached his ears. They had plenty of other targets in these parts: a truth that didn't break his heart.

They hadn't got into Laon. Along with French, African, and English troops, most of a regiment's worth of Czech refugees helped keep them out. Vaclav had fought the Germans inside Czechoslovakia. He'd got interned in Poland, figuring that was a better bet than surrendering to the victorious *Wehrmacht*. And he'd gone to Romania and crossed the Mediterranean on the most rickety freighter ever built, just to get another chance to let the Germans kill him.

They hadn't managed that, either. He'd done some more damage to them, especially after he got his hands on an antitank rifle a Frenchman didn't need any more. The damned thing was almost as tall as he was. It weighed a tonne. But the rounds it fired, each as thick as a man's finger, really could pierce armor. Not all the time, but often enough. And what those rounds did to mere flesh and blood . . . Its bullets flew fast and flat, and they were accurate out past a kilometer and a half. Just the shock of impact could kill, even if the hit wasn't in a spot that would have been mortal to an ordinary rifle round.

The Germans hadn't got into Laon, but they'd knocked it about a good deal. Stukas had bombed the medieval cathedral to hell and gone. No using those towers as observation points, not any more. The Nazis had blasted the bejesus out of the ancient houses and winding streets up on the high ground, too. The lower, more modern, part of the city was in better shape—not that better meant good. Loaf under his arm, Vaclav trudged past a Citroën's burnt-out carcass.

He wore new French trousers, of a khaki not quite so dark as Czech uniforms used. His boots were also French, and better than the Czech clodhoppers he'd worn out. But his tunic, with its corporal's pips on his shoulder straps, remained Czech. And he liked his domed Czech helmet much better than the crested ones French troops wore: the steel seemed twice as thick.

He had the helmet strapped to his belt now. He didn't want that weight on his head unless he was up at the front. He smiled at a pretty girl coming past with a load of washing slung over her back in a bedsheet. She nodded with a small smile of her own, but only a small one. Vaclav was a tall, solid, fair man. When the French saw him, half the time they feared he was a German even if he did wear khaki. That he couldn't speak their language didn't help.

From behind Vaclav, someone did speak in French to the girl with the laundry. She sniffed, stuck her nose in the air, and stalked away. "Oh, well," the man said, this time in Czech, "they can't shoot me for trying. She was cute."

"She sure was, Sergeant," Jezek agreed.

Sergeant Benjamin Halévy was a Frenchman with parents from Czechoslovakia. Fluent in both languages, he served as liaison between the French and their allies. Parents from Czechoslovakia didn't exactly make him a Czech, though. His curly red hair and proud nose shouted his Jewishness to the world. Jew or not, he was a good soldier. Vaclav didn't love Jews, but he couldn't quarrel about that. And Halévy had even stronger reasons to hate the Nazis than he did himself.

Those German guns in the distance thundered again. Halévy frowned. "Wonder what the fuckers are up to," he said.

"They aren't shooting at me right now," Vaclav said. "As long as they aren't, they can do anything else they want."

"There you go. You're an old soldier, sure as shit," the sergeant said.

Other guns started barking: French 75s. Halévy listened to them with a curious twisted smile. "I wish we had more heavy guns around Laon. We could hit the Nazis hard. They've got this long southern flank just waiting for us to take a bite out of it."

"That would be good," Vaclav said. Hitting the Nazis hard always sounded good to him. If only he were doing it in Czechoslovakia.

"Of course, by the time the brass sees the obvious and moves part of what we need into place for a half-assed attack, the Germans will have seen the light, too, and they'll hand us our heads," Halévy said.

Vaclav wondered if the Jew had been that cynical before he became a noncom. Whether Halévy had or not, what he came out with sounded all too likely to the Czech. "Maybe we ought to move up without waiting for the brass," Jezek said.

Halévy laid a hand on his forehead. "Are you feverish? No real, proper old soldier *ever* wants to move up. The bastards in *Feldgrau* have guns, you know." The way he pronounced the German word said he could *sprechen Deutsch,* as Vaclav could.

"Best way I can see to throw the Germans out of Czechoslovakia is to start by throwing 'em out of France," Vaclav said.

"Well, when you put it like that . . ." Sergeant Halévy rubbed the side of his jaw. "Tell you what. Talk to your Czechs—see what they think. I'll go chin with a couple of French captains I know, find out if they'll go with it."

Jezek found his countrymen had as many opinions as soldiers. That didn't faze him; as far as he was concerned, Germans were the ones who marched and thought in lockstep. But most of the Czechs were ready to give the enemy one in the slats as long as the odds seemed decent. "I don't want to stick my arm in the meat grinder, that's all," one of them said.

"*Ano, ano.* Sure," Vaclav said. "If there's a chance, though . . . Let's see what the Jew tells me."

Halévy came over to the Czechs' tents a couple of hours later. "The French officers say they want to wait two days," he reported.

"How come?" Vaclav asked. "We're ready now, dammit."

"They say they really are bringing stuff up to Laon," the sergeant replied.

"Yeah. And then you wake up," Vaclav said.

Halévy spread his hands. "Do you want to attack without any French support?"

"Well . . . no," Vaclav admitted. No artillery, no flank cover—sure as hell, that was sticking your arm in the grinder.

"There you are, then," Halévy said.

"Uh-huh. Here I am. Here we are: stuck," Vaclav said. "I'll believe your captains when I see the stuff."

"Between you, me, and the wall, that's what I told 'em, too," the Jew said.

But trains rolled into Laon after the sun went down. Rattles and rumbles and clanks declared that tanks were coming off of them. When morning rolled round again, some of the metal monsters sat under trees, while camouflage nets hid—Vaclav hoped—the rest from prying German eyes.

He asked, "Now that they're here, why don't we attack today instead of waiting till tomorrow?"

Benjamin Halévy shrugged a very French shrug. "If I knew, I would tell you. Even going tomorrow is better than retreating."

"I suppose so," Vaclav said darkly. "But if we attack today, maybe we'll still be advancing tomorrow. If we don't go till tomorrow, we've got a better chance of retreating the day after."

"I'm a sergeant," Halévy said. "What do you want me to do about it?"

Vaclav had no answer for that. A corporal himself, he knew how much depended on officers' caprices. "Tomorrow, then." If he didn't sound enthusiastic, it was only because he wasn't.

The French dignitaries with the power to bind and loose set the attack for 0430: sunup, more or less. The Germans would be silhouetted against a bright sky for a while. That would help—not much, but a little.

At 0400, big guns in back of Laon started bellowing: more big guns than Vaclav had thought the French had in the neighborhood. Maybe they'd moved those up the day before, too. If they had, maybe they'd had good reason to delay the attack till now. Maybe, maybe, maybe . . . Big, clumsy antitank rifle slung on his back, Vaclav marched north and east, into the rising sun.

✳   ✳   ✳

WILLI DERNEN WAS SLEEPING the sleep of the just—or at least the sleep of the bloody tired—when the French barrage started. He'd dug a little cave (a bombproof, a veteran of the last war would have called it) into the forward wall of his foxhole. Now he scrambled into the shelter like a pair of ragged claws.

Shells kept raining down: 75s, 105s, 155s. He hadn't known the damned Frenchmen had moved so much heavy stuff into Laon. Life was full of surprises. The big blond private from Breslau could have done without this one.

Somebody not far away started screaming. The other *Landser* didn't sound hurt, just scared shitless. Willi wouldn't have blamed the other poor bastard if he was. He'd had to chuck his own drawers a couple of times. And he hated artillery fire worse than anything else war brought. While those packages kept coming in, you had no control over whether you lived or died. If one of them burst in your hole, you were strawberry jam, and it didn't matter one goddamn bit if you were the best soldier in your regiment. If you came up against a *poilu* with a rifle or even a bunch of *poilus* with rifles, well, hey, you had a rifle, too, and a chance. What kind of chance did you have against some arselick throwing hot brass at you from ten kilometers away? Damn all, that was what.

Poilus were coming. Willi was mournfully sure of that. The froggies wouldn't lay on a bombardment like this without following it up. They might not have been eager when this war started. Eager or not, they were fighting hard now. The Germans had done their damnedest to take France out in a hurry. Their damnedest hadn't been quite good enough. Now it looked like the Frenchies' turn.

Another voice shouted purposefully through the din: "Stand by to repel boarders!"

That had to be Corporal Arno Baatz's idea of a joke. Talk about arse-licks . . . Awful Arno didn't just qualify. He had to be in the running for the gold medal. Every soldier in Willi's section hated Baatz's guts. If the French were going to blow somebody sky-high, why couldn't it be him?

The barrage kept up for what seemed like a hundred years. In fact, it was half an hour. That crazy kike scientist who'd fled the *Reich* one jump ahead of National Socialist justice had a point of sorts. Everything *was* relative.

As soon as the artillery let up, Dernen popped out of his hole in the ground like a jack-in-the-box. Awful Arno might be—was—an arselick, but he was bound to be right. The French would be coming.

Willi wouldn't have been surprised if the drastically revised landscape in front of Laon slowed them down. He didn't fancy crossing terrain full of shell holes, some as small as a washtub, others large enough to swallow a truck. You had to pick your way through and past the obstacles. That gave the fellows who'd lived through the barrage a better chance to punch your ticket for you.

"Panzers!" The cry rang out all up and down the German line. Willi's mouth went dry just looking at the armored murder machines. He couldn't remember so many French panzers in the same place at the same time. Sure as the devil, the French high command had finally learned something from the way the Germans handled their armor.

Being on the receiving end of the lesson was an honor Willi could have done without. He nervously looked back over his shoulder. Where were the German panzers to stop this onslaught? They'd always been thin on the ground in this part of the front. The generals had concentrated them on the other wing. It almost worked, too . . . but *almost* was a word that got a lot of soldiers killed.

One of the French panzers started spraying machine-gun fire toward the German line. Idiotically, a couple of German MG-34s fired back. Their bullets spanged harmlessly from the panzers' thick iron hide. And, as soon as they showed themselves, other enemy panzers gave them cannon fire till they fell silent. It didn't take long.

Then flame spurted from the first French machine. It stopped short. Hatches flew open. The driver, radioman, and commander bailed out. One of them, his coveralls on fire, dove into a shell hole. The other two got shot before they could find cover. Willi didn't know for sure whether one of his bullets found the panzer crewmen. If not, though, it wasn't for lack of effort.

The German antitank gun knocked out another enemy machine a moment later. Then the surviving French panzers shelled it into silence. On they came, *poilus* loping along among and behind them. After snapping off a couple of more shots, Willi ducked for cover. He knew what was coming. And it came: a burst of machine-gun bullets cracked past less than a meter above his head.

Then he heard one of the sweetest noises ever. There were German panzers around here after all. One of them fired at the French machines. *Clang!* That was a hit. Willi thought it came from a 37mm gun, too. He *really* hadn't known there were any Panzer IIIs in the neighborhood.

Fire from the French panzers paused. They had to traverse their turrets to bear on the new threat. And their commander was also the loader and gunner. They couldn't shoot fast no matter how much they wanted to. The German Panzer I and II suffered from the same problem. Not the III. Commander, loader, and gunner all fit within its angular turret.

Because of that edge, the Panzer III knocked out two more French vehicles in quick succession. Its hull machine gun sprayed death at the advancing foot soldiers and made them sprawl for cover. But then the froggies started shooting back, damn them. Some of their panzers mounted 47mm cannon. The III was armored better than the I and II, but Willi didn't know of a panzer in the world that could stop 47mm AP rounds. The German machine showed smoke, and then flame. Willi hoped some of the crewmen got out.

A few Panzer Is and IIs still tried conclusions with the French armor. Willi could see how that would play out, even if it took a while. He didn't like the ending on the movie that ran in his mind. He didn't like retreating, either, but . . . He just hoped he could do it without getting shot in the back.

Then Corporal Baatz yelled, "Fall back through Etrepois!" That was the tiny village behind the stretch of line the section was holding. Willi had heard the Frenchies who lived there pronounce the name. Awful Arno made a horrible hash of it.

German artillery came to life then, pounding the ground in front of the line. That would make the *poilus* take cover if anything did. Trying not to think about short rounds, Willi scrambled out of his hole. He ran hunched-over and zigzagged. Maybe it did a little good, maybe not.

He dove into a crater a 155 round must have dug. A moment later, another *Landser* joined him. "Boy, this is fun," Wolfgang Storch panted. "Fun like getting all your teeth pulled out."

They'd gone through basic together. They still argued about who hated Awful Arno worse. Wolfgang was more apt to speak his mind than Willi, who usually had a sunnier disposition. But there wasn't anything to be sunny about, not right now there wasn't. "Fun. Yeah. Sure." Those were all the words Dernen had in him.

Storch fired a couple of rounds from his Mauser. "That'll make 'em keep their heads down," he said in some satisfaction. "C'mon. You ready to do some more moving?"

"I guess." Willi hoped he'd find reinforcements rushing up through Etrepois. He didn't. The village was only a few houses and a tavern marking a crossroads. Frenchwomen with impassive faces watched the Germans retreat. A few weeks earlier, their own men had been the ones giving ground.

The *Wehrmacht* was on the move then. Willi'd had his pecker up. Now . . . Now he was discovering what the Frenchies had known ever since December, when the German blow fell in the west. If you had the choice between advancing and retreating, advancing was better.

Now there was a profound bit of philosophy! Shaking his head, Willi left Etrepois behind him.

AFTER SO LONG on the Ebro front, Madrid was a different world for Chaim Weinberg. It was different for everybody in the Abraham Lincoln Battalion, for everybody in all the International Brigades.

That didn't make the embattled capital of Spain (though the Republican government had been operating out of Barcelona for quite a while now) an improvement over the trenches in the far northeast. Looking at the devastation all around him, Chaim said, "They had to destroy this place in order to save it, didn't they?"

Mike Carroll only grunted. The hand-rolled cigarette in the corner of his mouth twitched. "Fascists destroyed this fuckin' place to destroy it," he answered. "That's what Marshal Sanjurjo's assholes do."

He talked slow, like a foul-mouthed Gary Cooper. He looked a little like him, too: he was tall and fair and lean and rugged. Chaim, short and squat and dark, fit in fine in Spain. People stared at Mike, wondering if he was a German. Better to be thought a Gary Cooper lookalike. No one in Republican Spain loved Germans.

Grimacing, Chaim shook his head. That wasn't true. No one in Republican Spain admitted to loving Germans. That wasn't the same as the other. Just as Republicans had to lie low in land Sanjurjo's Nationalists held, so the jackals of Hitlerism needed to smile and pretend wherever the Republic still ruled. One side's firing squads or the other's took care of fools who slipped. As far as Chaim was concerned, the Nationalists massacred, while the Republic dealt out stern justice. That somebody on the other side might see things differently bothered him not a peseta's worth.

Somebody on the other side wouldn't have seen what the Fascists had done to Madrid. Spanish bombers—and those of their Italian and German allies—had been working the city over for two and a half years. Buildings looked as skeletal and battered as a bare-branched forest at the tag end of a hard winter. Spring would clothe the forest in green. Spring was here in Madrid, but this town still smelled like death. It would be a long time recovering, if it ever did.

Well, that was what the International Brigades were here for. They were the best fighters the Republic had. Chaim would tell people so, at any excuse or none. Few Spaniards seemed to want to argue with him. They knew they had no military skill to speak of. That shamed a lot of them. Maybe it should have made them proud instead—didn't it argue they were more civilized than most?

Many Internationals, including some of the Abe Lincolns, had fought in the last war. Chaim and Mike were both too young for that. But, like the rest of the Marxist-Leninists and fellow travelers who'd come to Spain to battle Fascism, they were motivated. They hadn't stood on the sidelines when reaction went on the march here. They'd come to do something about it.

"Funny, y'know," Chaim said, looking away from a skinny dog snapping at something disgusting in the gutter. "They were set to take us out of the line six months ago, when the big war fired up." He jerked a thumb toward the northeast toward the rest of Europe, the world beyond the Pyrenees.

"Yeah, well . . ." Mike paused to blow a smoke ring. He owned all kinds of casual, offhand talents like that. "Bastards back there finally figured out we knew what we were doing down here."

"Better believe it!" Weinberg had his full measure of the New York City Jew's passionate devotion to causes. How could you *not* be enthusiastic about putting a spike in Hitler's wheel? Plenty of folks, even Jews, seemed not to get excited about Fascism. *Dumb assholes,* Chaim thought scornfully.

Artillery rumbled, off to the northwest. The Nationalists were closest to the heart of the city there. In fact, they'd pushed into Madrid in the northwest. Most of the university lay in their hands. It had gone back and forth for the past couple of years. Whenever one side felt strong, it tried to shove out the other. Now it looked as if both sides had decided to shove at the same time, like a couple of rams banging heads. Only time would tell what sprang from that.

The university was less than two miles north of the royal palace. Chaim had been by the palace, just to see what it looked like. Marshal Sanjurjo had declared he would restore the King of Spain if his side won. That sure hadn't kept the Nationalists and Germans and Italians from knocking the snot out of Alfonso XIII's digs. If he ever came back, he could live in the ruins or in a tent like everybody else.

When Chaim said as much, Mike Carroll made a sour face. "If the reactionary son of a bitch comes back, that means we've lost."

"Yeah, well, if we do we probably won't have to worry about it any more," Chaim said. He didn't mean they would get over the border to France, either. The Nationalists didn't take many prisoners. Come to that, neither did the Republicans. Chaim didn't know which side had started shooting men who tried to give up. That didn't matter any more. The Spaniards might not make the world's greatest professional soldiers, but when they hated they didn't hate halfway.

He listened anxiously to find out whether any of the newly launched shells would gouge fresh holes in the rubble right around here. In that case, they might gouge holes in him, which was not something he eagerly anticipated. But the bursts were at least half a mile off. Nothing to get hot and bothered about—not for him, anyhow. If some poor damned Madrileños had just had their lives turned inside out and upside down . . . well, that was a damn shame, but they wouldn't be the first people in Spain whose luck had run out, nor the last.

Republican guns answered the Nationalist fire. Those were French 75s. The sound they made going off was as familiar to Chaim as a telephone ring. The Republicans had a lot of them: ancient models Spain had bought from France after the last war, and brand new ones the French had sent over the Pyrenees when the big European scrap started. All at once, the neutrality patrol turned to a supply spigot when the French and English realized Hitler was dangerous after all.

And then, after the *Wehrmacht* hit the Low Counties and France itself, the spigot to Spain dried up. The Republic would have been screwed, except Sanjurjo also had himself a supply drought: the Germans and Italians were using everything they made themselves.

One of the explosions from the 75s sounded uncommonly large and sharp. Weinberg and Carroll shared a wince. Chaim knew what that kind of blast meant. The French guns mostly fired locally made ammunition these days. And locally made ammo, not to put too fine a point on it, sucked. Chaim carried Mexican cartridges for his French rifle. He didn't trust Spanish rounds. German ammunition was better yet, but impossible to get these days except by plundering dead Nationalists.

A barmaid stepped out of a *cantina* and waved to the two Internationals. "*¿Vino?*" she called invitingly.

Chaim surprised himself by nodding. "C'mon," he told Mike. "We can hoist one for the poor sorry bastards at that gun."

"Suits," Carroll said. You rarely needed to ask him twice about a drink. Very often, you didn't need to ask him once.

The *cantina* was dark and gloomy inside. It would have been gloomier yet except for a big hole in the far wall. It smelled of smoke and booze and sweat and urine and hot cooking oil and, faintly, of vomit—like a *cantina*, in other words. Mike did order wine. Chaim told the barmaid, "*Cerveza.*" He tried to lisp like a Castilian.

She understood him, anyhow. Off she went, hips working. She brought back their drinks, then waited expectantly. Chaim crossed her palm with silver. That made her go away. He raised his mug. "Here's to 'em."

"Here's to what's left of 'em, anyway," Carroll said. They both drank. Mike screwed up his face. "Vinegar. How's yours?"

"Piss," Chaim answered. Sure as hell, the beer was thin and sour. But, save for a few bottles imported from Germany, he'd never had beer in Spain that wasn't. You could drink it. He did.

And Mike got outside his vinegary red. He raised his glass for a refill. The barmaid took care of him and Chaim. He paid this time. Outside, the not-distant-enough enemy guns started booming again. Again, nothing came down close enough to get excited about. That was good enough for Chaim. He'd go back up to the line PDQ. Till he did . . . What was that line? *Eat, drink, and be merry,* he thought, and deliberately forgot the rest of it.

Chapter 4

Peggy Druce positively hated Berlin. The Philadelphia socialite had visited the capital of Germany several times between the wars. She'd always had a fine old time then. If you couldn't have a fine old time in the Berlin of the vanished, longed-for days before Hitler took over, you were probably dead.

If you *could* have a fine old time in this miserable land of blackouts and rationing, something had to be wrong with you. Almost all civilian cars had vanished from the streets. Even the parked ones were in danger. One propaganda drive after another sent people out to scavenge rubber or scrap metal or batteries.

That didn't mean the streets were empty, though. Soldiers paraded hither and yon, jackboots thumping. When they passed by reviewing stands, they would break into the goose step. Otherwise, they just marched. The characteristic German stride looked impressive as hell—the Nazis sure thought so, anyhow—but it was wearing. Soldiers, even German soldiers, were practical men. They used the goose step where they got the most mileage from it: in front of their big shots, in other words. When the bosses weren't watching, they acted more like ordinary human beings.

Columns of trucks and half-tracks and panzers also rumbled up and down Berlin's broad boulevards. Peggy took a small, nasty satisfaction in noting that the treads on the tanks and half-tracks tore hell out of the paving. Repair crews often followed the armored columns, patching up the damage.

A Berlin cop—a middle-aged man with a beer belly and a limp he'd probably got in the last war—held out his hand to Peggy and snapped, *"Papieren, bitte!"*

"Jawohl," she replied. *Ja-fucking-wohl,* she thought as she fumbled in her purse. Her German had got a lot better than it was when she first arrived in Berlin. Getting stuck somewhere would do that to you. She found her American passport and pulled it out with a flourish. "Here," she said, or maybe, *"Hier."* The word sounded the same in English and *auf Deutsch.*

The cop blinked. He didn't see an eagle that wasn't holding a swastika every day. He examined the passport, then handed it back. "You are an American." He turned truth to accusation. He was a cop, all right.

"Ja." Peggy was proud of herself for leaving it right there. She damn near added *Nothing gets by you, does it?* or *Very good, Sherlock* or something else that would have landed her in hot water. Her husband always said she talked first and thought afterwards. Good old Herb! She missed him like anything. He knew her, all right.

"What is an American doing in Berlin?" the cop demanded. He took it for granted that, even though the USA was neutral, Americans wouldn't be pro-German. Maybe he wasn't so dumb after all.

And Peggy gave him the straight truth: "Trying to get the hell out of here and go home."

As soon as the words were out of her mouth, she wished she had them back. Too late, as usual. She'd given another cop the straight truth not too long ago, and he'd hauled her down to the station on account of it. If a desk sergeant with better sense hadn't realized pissing off the United States wasn't exactly Phi Beta Kappa for the *Reich,* she might have found out about concentration camps from the inside.

If this policeman was another hothead . . . If his desk sergeant was, too . . . You never wanted to get in trouble in Hitler's Germany. And, since the Germans themselves were walking on eggs after a failed coup against the *Führer,* you especially didn't want to get in trouble now.

The cop paused. He lit a Hoco. Like any other German cigarette these days, it smelled more like burning trash than tobacco. "If you don't want to be in Berlin to begin with, what are you doing here?" he asked reasonably.

"I was in Marianske Lazne when the war started," Peggy answered, using the Czech name with malice aforethought.

Sure as hell, the Berlin cop said, "You were where?" Give a kraut a Slavic place name, and he'd drown in three inches of water.

"Marienbad, it's also called," Peggy admitted.

Light dawned. "Oh! In the German Sudetenland!" the policeman exclaimed. "How lucky for you to be there when the *Führer's* forces justly reclaimed it for the *Reich.*"

"Well . . . no," Peggy said. For the first time, the cop's face clouded over. *See? Keep trying,* Peggy jeered at herself. *You'll stick your foot in it sooner or later.* Trying to extract the foot, she added, "I almost got killed."

For a wonder, it worked. "*Ach, ja.* In wartime, this can happen," the cop said, rough sympathy in his voice. Everything would have been fine if he hadn't added, "With those miserable, murderous Czech brutes all around, you should thank heaven you came through all right."

Peggy bit down hard on the inside of her lower lip to keep from blurting something that *would* have got her sent to Dachau or Buchenwald or some other interesting place. *Count to ten,* she thought frantically. *No. Count to twenty, in Czech!* The Czechs hadn't been the problem. The Germans had. Shelling and bombing Marianske Lazne was one thing—that was part of war. But the way the Nazis started in on the Jews who were taking the waters after overrunning the place . . . No, she didn't want to remember that.

None of it passed her lips. Herb would have been proud of her. Hell, she was proud of herself. The only thing she said was, "Can I go?"

"One moment." The Berlin cop was self-important, like most policemen the world around. "First tell me why you have not returned to the United States."

"I was supposed to go back on the *Athenia,* but it got sunk on the way east," Peggy said.

"*Ach, so.* The miserable British. They would do anything, no matter how vicious, to inflame relations between your country and mine." The policeman proved he could parrot every line Goebbels' Propaganda Ministry spewed forth.

Like almost everybody in the U.S. Embassy, Peggy figured it was much more likely that a German U-boat had screwed up and torpedoed the liner. Like Germany, England loudly denied sinking her. If anyone knew who'd really done it, he was keeping it a deep, dark secret. To Peggy, that also argued it was the Germans. Everything was secret around here, whether it needed to be or not.

"That was several months ago, though. Why have you not left since?" the policeman persisted.

"Because your government won't let me go unless I have full passage back to America, and that's not easy to arrange, not with a war on," Peggy said. The Nazis had come right out and said they were afraid she'd tell the British just what she thought of them if she stopped in the UK on the way home. She'd promised not to, but they didn't want to believe her.

Maybe they also weren't so dumb after all, dammit.

The cop scratched his head. "You may go," he said at last. "Your passport is in order. And you are lucky to be here instead of in one of the decadent democracies. Enjoy your stay." He gave her a stiff-armed salute and stumped away.

Peggy didn't burst into hysterical laughter behind him. That also proved she was winning self-control as she neared fifty. She walked down the street. When she stepped on a pebble, she felt it. Her soles were wearing out. Leather for cobblers was in short supply, and as stringently rationed as everything this side of dental floss. Some shoe repairs were made with horrible plastic junk that was as bad as all the other German ersatz materials. What passed for coffee these days tasted as if it were made from charred eraser scrapings.

She started to go into a café for lunch. Food these days was another exercise in masochism. The sign on the door—*Eintopftag*—stopped her, though. Sure as hell, Sunday was what the Master Race called One-Pot

Day. The only lunch available was a miserable stew, but you paid as if you'd ordered something fancy. The difference was supposed to go into Winter Relief. Peggy had heard it got spent on the military instead. That sounded like the kind of shabby trick the Nazis would pull. She was damned if she wanted to give Hitler her money when he'd use it to blow up more of France, a country she liked much better than this one.

She had some bread—war bread, and black, but tolerable once you got used to it—and apples back in her hotel room. She hadn't intended to eat them today, but she'd forgotten about *Eintopftag*. She wouldn't put an extra pfennig in the *Führer*'s war chest, and *Eintopf* was always swill, anyway.

Tomorrow? Tomorrow would take care of itself. She'd believed that ever since she was a little girl. If coming much too close to getting killed several times the past few months hadn't changed her mind, nothing less was likely to.

JOAQUIN DELGADILLO FLATTENED OUT behind a pile of broken bricks like a cat smashed by a tank. The Republican machine gun up ahead spat what seemed like an unending stream of bullets not nearly far enough above him.

"Stinking Communists," he muttered into the dirt. This machine gun happened to be French, not Russian. Joaquin couldn't have cared less. Like everybody in Marshal Sanjurjo's army, to the depths of his soul he was convinced the people on the other side took their orders straight from Stalin.

After all, weren't the International Brigades fighting in the ruins of Madrid's University City, too? And weren't the International Brigades a bunch of Reds who'd come to meddle in what was none of their damned business?

Germans and Italians fought on Marshal Sanjurjo's side. Joaquin didn't think of them as meddlers. They were allies. And they weren't spraying machine-gun rounds right over his head.

"*¡Maricones!*" someone from his side of the line shouted at the Internationals. Even groveling in the dirt the way he was, Joaquin giggled. Oh, it wasn't that he hadn't called the Republic's foreign mercenaries faggots along with anything and everything else he could think of. It was just that his own battalion CO, Major Uribe, was the biggest fairy who didn't have wings.

Most of the time, Joaquin would have had trouble understanding how a flaming queer could rise so high in the Nationalists' straitlaced army. Not with Bernardo Uribe. The major was, quite simply, the bravest man and the fiercest fighter he'd ever seen. The only miracle with Uribe was that he hadn't got his head blown off long since. As long as he stayed alive, nobody was going to care where he stuck his dick.

As abruptly as if someone had shut off a faucet, the machine gun fell silent. Major Uribe's high, sweet voice rang through the bruised silence: "Look alive, sweethearts! We're liable to have company for tea!"

The first time he came out with something like that, Joaquin's eyes almost bugged out of his head. The second time the major did it, Delgadillo nearly pissed himself laughing. Now he took it for granted.

So did Sergeant Carrasquel. Joaquin never laughed at him. Carrasquel was the kind of guy who'd tear off your head and then spit in the hole. He was a good sergeant, in other words. "Major's right," he rasped now. "Those fuckers'll hit us, sure as the devil. Don't let 'em push you back."

Joaquin ground his teeth. Something in his lower jaw twinged. One of these days—if he lived, if he ever got out of the line—he'd have to visit the dentist. He feared that worse than he feared facing the International Brigades. He'd seen a lot of war. He knew what it could do. He'd never been to the dentist. What you didn't know was always scary.

He did know that, if Sergeant Carrasquel ordered no retreat, somebody behind the line would be waiting to shoot him if he tried. Both sides gave troops that duty, to make sure people kept their minds on what they were supposed to be doing. The only trouble was that, while you could call the men in the International Brigades every filthy name in the book, anybody who'd ever bumped up against them—and Joaquin had, along the Ebro—knew they were damn good fighting men.

Between the Devil and a hard place. A rock and the deep blue sea. As Joaquin chambered a round in his old Mauser, he hardly noticed the phrases were all mixed up in his head. He didn't want to look out over the brick pile that had sheltered him from the enemy machine gun. If some rotten Red with a scope-sighted rifle was up on some high ground, waiting to blow his brains out . . .

A grenade burst, maybe fifty meters in front of him. Something clanged off his brick pile, flipped up in the air, and fell down a few centimeters from his face. It was a bent tenpenny nail. Along with grenades from every country in Europe, both sides used homemade models. A quarter-kilo of explosives, some nails or other metal junk, a tobacco tin if you had one, a blasting cap, a fuse . . . You could blow yourself up, too, of course, but you could also do that with a factory-made bomb.

Where grenades went off, men wouldn't be far behind. Grenades weren't like machine-gun bullets; they didn't fly very far. Joaquin popped up for a look—and a shot, if he had one. He hated to show himself. Yes, he wore a helmet: a Spanish one, almost identical to the German style. But it wouldn't keep out a rifle bullet. He'd seen much too much gruesome proof of that.

Sure as hell, there was an International, scrambling from one bit of maybe-cover to the next. The fellow had red hair and foxy features. Wherever he came from, he was no Spaniard. Catching sight of Joaquin, he started to bring his rifle to his shoulder.

Too late. Joaquin fired first. The foxy-faced man from God knew where clutched at himself and started to crumple. Joaquin didn't wait to find out whether he was dead or only wounded. Down he went again. Some other hard case from the middle of Europe or across the sea might be drawing a bead on him right now.

Most Spaniards on both sides were lousy shots. Without false modesty, Joaquin knew he wasn't. He had been, but Sergeant Carrasquel cured him of it. Carrasquel was a veteran of the fighting in Spanish Morocco. He knew how to make a rifle do what it was supposed to do: hit what you aimed at. All the survivors in his squad shot well.

And so did the Internationals. Some of them had learned soldiering a generation earlier, in a harsher, less forgiving school than even Spanish Morocco. The younger Reds had picked up their trade from the veterans— and anyone who lived through a few weeks of fighting made an infinitely better soldier than a raw recruit.

Joaquin wriggled like a lizard to find a fresh place from which to shoot. No one before had been watching the rubble pile from which he'd fired. Somebody would be now. He was grimly certain of that. You didn't want to give them two chances at you. For that matter, you didn't *want* to give them one chance at you. All too often, though, you had no choice.

He raised himself up high enough to see over his new pile of bricks. Once upon a time, this miserable wreckage had housed the department of agriculture. He'd seen a shattered sign that said so. The ruins had changed hands a lot of times since then, though.

Joaquin gasped. There squatted an International, not three meters away. The Red looked just as surprised—and just as horrified—as Joaquin felt. Neither man had had the faintest idea the other was around. They both fired at the same instant. They were both veterans, both experienced fighting men, both presumably good riflemen.

They both missed.

"Fuck!" Joaquin said fervently. He grabbed a broken brick and flung it at the International. The brick didn't miss. It thudded against the other man's ribs and kept him from working the bolt on his French rifle. The fellow said something hot and guttural. Then he jumped down behind Joaquin's rubble pile and tried to stick him with his bayonet.

With a desperate parry, Joaquin drove aside the long knife on the end of the other rifle. He'd learned bayonet fighting. Sergeant Carrasquel made sure you learned everything that had anything to do with soldiering. He'd learned it, but he'd never had to use it before. He knocked the International's feet out from under him with the barrel of his own rifle.

Then they were clawing and grappling and kneeing and gouging, there in the dirt. They were a couple of wild animals, snapping for each other's throats. One of them would get up again, the other wouldn't. It was as simple and mindless as that. In the end, what else did war come down to?

A rifle cracked. It wasn't Joaquin's. When he heard it, he figured it had to be the International's. And if it was, he had to be dead, and hearing the reverberations from the next world. He prayed he would rise to heaven, not sink down to hell.

But the foreigner was the one who groaned and went limp. Hardly believing he could, Joaquin shoved the man's suddenly limp body away from him. He bloodied his hands doing it—a human being held a shocking amount of gore.

There on the ground a couple of meters off to one side sprawled Sergeant Carrasquel, rifle in hand. "You had a little trouble there," he remarked.

"Only a little," Joaquin said, as coolly as he could with his heart threatening to bang its way out of his chest. After a moment, he managed to add, "*Gracias.*"

"*De nada,*" Carrasquel said. "If you would've shot the asshole in the first place, you wouldn't've had to dance with him."

"Dance? Some dance!" Joaquin laughed like a crazy man. Relief could do that to you. Then he lit a cigarette and waited for whatever horror came next.

LUC HARCOURT SEWED a second dark khaki hash mark onto the left sleeve of his tunic. He sewed much better now than he had before he got conscripted. Work with needle and thread wasn't something the French army taught you. It was something you needed to learn, though, unless you wanted your uniform to fall apart. You had to make repairs as best you could; the French quartermaster corps was unlikely to minister to your needs.

Sergeant Demange came by. Things were quiet in front of Beauvais, the way they had been on the border before the Germans made their big winter push. Luc wished that comparison hadn't occurred to him. He was proud that the *poilus* and Tommies had stopped the Nazis at Beauvais and not let them get around behind Paris the way they planned. He was even proud he'd made corporal, which surprised him: he sure hadn't cared a fart's worth about rank when the government gave him a khaki suit and a helmet.

The Gitane that always hung from the corner of Demange's mouth twitched when he saw what Luc was doing. "Sweet suffering Jesus!" he said. "They'll promote anything these days, won't they?"

"It must be so," Luc answered innocently. "You're a sergeant, after all."

You had to pick your spots when you razzed a superior. After he'd just razzed you was a good one. Demange wasn't just a superior, either. He was a professional, old enough to be Luc's father—old enough to have got wounded in 1918. He was a skinny little guy without a gram of extra fat. No matter how old he was, Luc, six or eight centimeters taller and ten kilos heavier, wouldn't have wanted to tangle with him. Demange had never heard of the rule book, and knew all kinds of evil tricks outside of it.

He grunted laughter now, even if it didn't light his eyes. "Funny man! You know what that two-centime piece of cloth is, don't you? It's all the thanks you're gonna get for not stopping a bullet yet."

"If they keep promoting me for that, I hope I'm a marshal of France by the time the war's over." Luc poked himself with the needle. *Nom d'un nom!*"

He made Demange laugh again, this time in real amusement. "The war may go on a long time, sonny, but it ain't gonna last *that* long."

"Well, maybe not." Luc chuckled, too. It wasn't a bad line, and a sergeant's jokes automatically seemed funny to the men he led.

German 105s started going off in the distance. Luc looked at his watch. Yes, it was half past two. Those shells would land on a road junction a kilometer and a half to the south. When the *Boches* weren't trying to pull the wool over your eyes, they could be as predictable as clockwork.

"Dumb *cons*," Sergeant Demange said with a contemptuous wiggle of his Gitane. "Like we're going to run anything through there at this time of day! What kind of jerks do they think we are?"

"The same kind they are, probably," Luc answered.

"Then they really are dumb," Demange said. "Maybe Englishmen wouldn't notice what they're up to, but we're French, by God! We've got two brain cells to rub together, eh?"

"Most of us do. I'm not so sure about our officers," Harcourt said.

That was safe enough. Any sergeant worth his miserable joke of a salary looked down his nose at the men set over him (privates looked at sergeants the same way, something sergeants tended to forget). And Demange had been a noncom a very long time. "Oh, officers!" he said. "You're right—officers can't find their ass with both hands half the time. But they'll have sergeants to keep 'em from making donkeys of themselves."

"Sure, Sergeant," Luc said, and left it right there. Yes, lieutenants and captains did need sergeants at their elbow. But that said more about their shortcomings than about any great virtues inherent in sergeants. So it seemed to a new-minted corporal, anyhow.

Demange stamped out his cigarette just before the coal singed his lips. Then he lit another one and strode off to inflict himself on somebody else in the platoon.

Luc lit a Gitane of his own. It wasn't as good as Gitanes had been before the war. Everything had gone down the crapper since then. Captured Germans loved French cigarettes, though. Luc knew why, too: their own were even worse. *Poor sorry bastards,* he thought, puffing away. And what they used for coffee! A dog would turn up its nose at that horrible stuff.

Almost as big as a light plane, a vulture glided down out of the sky and started pecking at something in the middle of the kilometer or so that separated the French and German lines right here. Maybe it was a dead cow or sheep. More likely, it was a dead man. If it was, Luc hoped it was a dead *Boche.* The Germans had been falling back in these parts, so the odds were decent it was.

Closer to him, blackbirds hopped across the torn-up, cratered dirt with their heads cocked to one side. Plenty of worms out there—and plenty of new worm food, too, even after the vultures ate their fill. The vultures and the blackbirds—and, no doubt, the worms—liked the war just fine.

You could walk around out in the open. Sergeant Demange was doing it. Odds were the Germans wouldn't open up on you. Luc didn't want to play the odds. It would be just his luck to have some eager German sniper itching to test his new telescopic sight right when he decided to take a stroll.

Peeking out of his foxhole, he could see Germans moving around in the distance. That had happened last fall, too. The *Boches* had stayed very quiet in the west while they were flattening Czechoslovakia. The French had advanced a few kilometers into Germany, skirmished lightly with the *Wehrmacht,* and then turned around, declared victory, and marched back across to their own side of the border.

When the *Wehrmacht* marched into France, it didn't dick around. If Luc never saw another Stuka—better yet, if no Stuka pilot ever spotted him again—he wouldn't shed a tear. And, if the war ever ended, he would happily buy drinks for all the Stuka pilots who hadn't spotted him.

Demange came back just before sunset. "Got a job for you, *Corporal* Harcourt." The stress he gave the rank convinced Luc it would be a dirty job. And it was: "When it gets good and dark, take a squad to the German lines, nab a couple of prisoners, and bring 'em back for questioning. The boys with the fancy kepis want to know what the damned *Boches* are up to."

"Thanks a bunch, Sergeant!" Luc exclaimed.

"Somebody's gotta do it. I figure you have a better chance to come back than most." After a moment, Demange added, "If it makes you feel any better, I'm coming along. I played these games in the trenches last time around."

Actually, it did make Luc feel better. The sergeant was a handy man to have around in a tight spot. Luc was damned if he'd admit it, though. He rounded up the men he'd been leading since he made PFC: a couple of veterans and the new fish just finding out what the water was like. The news thrilled them as much as it had him.

"Why us?" one of them whined.

"Because you'll get your miserable ass court-martialed if you try and wiggle out, that's why," Luc explained. "Maybe the Germans won't do for you. Your own side? You know damn well they will. Be ready an hour before midnight."

Nobody bugged out before the appointed hour. The French soldiers must have feared their own *gendarmerie* worse than the Nazis. Sergeant Demange said, "We'll get 'em at the latrine trenches. Easiest way I can think of to nab the sons of bitches. C'mon."

He made it sound easy. Of course, sounding easy didn't mean it was.

Luc had already had that lesson pounded into him. They had to make it across no-man's-land without any German sentries spotting them. The night was dark, but even so.... Then they had to get past the enemy's forward positions. Luc was sweating enough to let him smell his own fear.

Sergeant Demange, by contrast, took everything in stride. "This is too fucking simple," he whispered as the Frenchmen crawled past the German foxholes. "No ten-meter belts of wire, no continuous trench line ... Nothing to it." He sounded affronted, as if he'd expected the Germans to do a better job and wanted to ream them out for being sloppy. Luc wasn't so choosy.

Finding the latrine trenches proved easy enough. Something in the air gave them away. The Germans used lime chloride to keep the stench down, but even that couldn't kill it. Clutching their rifles, the Frenchmen waited in the bushes nearby.

They didn't have to wait long. A yawning *Boche* ambled over and squatted above a trench. Demange hissed at him in bad German. Luc thought he said he'd blow the Nazi a new asshole if he didn't get over here *right now.* That made the enemy soldier finish what he was doing a lot faster than he'd expected to. He didn't even try to clean himself. He just yanked up his trousers and followed orders.

"Amis! Amis!" he whispered in equally bad, very frightened French.

"We're no friends of yours. Shut up if you want to keep breathing." After a moment, Luc added, "You stink." Abstractly, he sympathized. He'd stunk worse than this a time or two.

He was just glad the prisoner didn't want to be a hero. That would have shortened everybody's life expectancy. A few minutes later, another German stood at the latrine trench and unbuttoned his fly. Sergeant Demange asked him if he felt like getting circumcised with a bullet. The *Boche* pissed all over his own boots. After that, he was amazingly cooperative.

"We need more than two?" Luc asked.

"Nah. They asked for a couple, and that's what we'll give 'em," Demange answered. "Now let's get the fuck out of here."

Luc had never heard an order he liked better. The German captives were at least as good at sneaking across broken ground as the *poilus* herding them along. They didn't let out a peep till they were inside the French lines. They seemed pathetically grateful still to be alive.

Luc knew exactly how they felt.

PARIS IS WORTH A SOMETHING. One French king or another had said that, or something like that, a hell of a long time ago. So much Alistair Walsh knew—so much, and not a farthing's worth more. The veteran underofficer had picked up bits and pieces of knowledge over the years, but too many of them remained just that: bits and pieces. They didn't fit together to make any kind of recognizable picture.

Staff Sergeant Walsh did know what Paris was worth to the Nazis, even if not to that long-ago and forgotten (at least by him) French king. It was worth everything. And, since they couldn't get their hands on it—no matter how bloody close they'd come—they were doing their goddamnedest to ruin it for everybody else.

He'd got leave at last—only a forty-eight-hour pass, but forty-eight hours were better than nothing. He could go back to the City of Light. He could drink himself blind. He could watch pretty girls dance and take off their clothes. He could visit a *maison de tolerance,* where a girl would take off her clothes just for him . . . if she happened to be wearing any when he walked into her upstairs room.

He could do all that—if he didn't mind taking the chance of getting blown up while he did it, or the almost equally unpleasant chance of spending big chunks of his precious, irreplaceable leave huddling in a cellar somewhere and praying no bomb scored a direct hit on the building overhead.

The *Luftwaffe* visited almost every night now. Ever since it became clear the French capital wouldn't fall into Germany's hands like a ripe plum, Hitler seemed to have decided to knock it flat instead. With so much of northern France under German occupation, his bombers didn't have to fly far to get there. They could carry full loads every night, drop them, and go back to bomb up again for a second trip before daybreak.

All of which made Paris the greatest show on earth. The circus just had to find itself a new slogan. Paris was every pinball machine and every fire-works display multiplied by a million. Searchlights darted everywhere, trying to pin bombers in their brilliant beams so the antiaircraft guns could shoot them down. Tracers from the guns scribed lines of red and gold and green across the sky's black velvet. Even the bursting bombs were beautiful—if you didn't happen to be too close to one when it went off.

Paris had already taken a lot of punishment. The Arc de Triomphe had a chunk bitten out of it. The Eiffel Tower was fifty feet shorter than it had been—and a meteorologist who'd been up at the top was never buried, because they couldn't find enough of him to put in a coffin. The Louvre had been hit. So had Notre Dame.

You needed to be determined, then, or maybe a little loopy, if you wanted to visit Paris. Some people said Hitler had vowed to wipe the cap-ital of Germany's great continental rival off the face of the earth. Others claimed he was trying to terrify the Parisians, and the French in general, into tossing in the sponge.

From what Walsh knew of the corporal who'd promoted himself field-marshal, and from what he knew of Germans, that last seemed likely to him. *Schrechlichkeit,* they called it—frightfulness. If you went into Paris with a forty-eight-hour pass, you had a respectable chance of not coming back. On the other hand, if you were anywhere near Paris with pass in hand and you didn't go in . . . well, you might never see another chance.

And so Walsh jumped into the back of a British lorry along with the other lucky sods who'd wangled a bit of leave. The lorry bounced over potholes the size of baby washtubs. Just outside of town, it got a flat. The passengers piled out to give the driver a hand. Changing a tire in the rapidly deepening dark was always an adventure. Walsh learned some bad language he'd never heard before. For a man who'd been a soldier for more than half a lifetime, that was almost worth the trip into town by it-self.

Hitler might hope to frighten the Parisians into surrendering, but he hadn't had much luck yet. The city was blacked out, of course, but it seemed noisier than ever. Touts stood in front of every establishment, shouting out the delights that lay beyond the black curtains. Quite a few of them used English; they knew a lot of Tommies would be here to blow off steam.

"Girls!" one of them yelled. "Beautiful girls! Wine! Whiskey!"

That all sounded good to Walsh. He pushed past the tout and into the dive. The glare of the electric lights inside almost blinded him. Loud jazz blared from a record. Before the war, there likely would have been a band. How many of the musicians were playing to amuse their buddies in the trenches right now?

Above the bar, a sign said PARIS CAN TAKE IT in English and what was bound to be the same thing in French. "Whiskey," Walsh told the barkeep, and slid a silver shilling across the zinc surface.

"Coming up," the fellow answered in tolerable English. He was graying at the temples; a black patch covered his left eye socket. He didn't look piratical—he looked tired and overworked. "Ice?"

"Why bother?" Walsh answered. With a shrug, the bartender gave him his drink. He hadn't asked for good whiskey. He hadn't got it, either. He consoled himself with the reflection that he probably also wouldn't have got it if he had asked for it. He made the drink disappear and put another shilling on the bar. "Why don't you fill that up again?"

"But of course." The bartender did. He nodded toward the stage. "The girls, they come on soon."

"Good enough, pal." Walsh knocked back the fresh drink. After a couple, good and bad didn't matter so much. Any which way, your tongue was stunned.

The girls weren't wearing much when they started their number. What they did have on sparkled and swirled transparently as they started gyrating on the little stage. They weren't so gorgeous as they would have been at the Folies Bergères—this was just a little place—but they weren't half bad. And they rapidly started shedding their minimal costumes. Walsh pounded the bar and whooped. So did other soldiers and flyers in a camouflaged rainbow of uniforms.

Just before the girls got down to their birthday suits, air-raid sirens started screaming. Polylingual profanity filled the air, burning it bluer than all the tobacco smoke already had.

After yelling through a megaphone in French, the bartender switched to English: "Cellar this way! Must go! Raids very bad!"

What no doubt propelled half the fellows in the joint down into the cellar was the hope that the naked cuties would come down with them. No such luck, though. The girls had somewhere else to hide. Some of the rowdier—read, younger and drunker—men started to go up and look for them. Then, even in the cellar, they heard the German bombs whistling down. That stopped that. No matter how rowdy you were, you didn't want to meet explosives head on.

Thunderous blasts staggered Walsh and everybody else. A few men screamed. Walsh didn't, but he didn't blame them, either. It wasn't as if he never had when he was under fire. Then the lights went out. More hoarse shouts rose. Walsh put his hand on his wallet, just in case. Sure as hell, before long another hand touched his, there in the pitch blackness. When he stomped, his boot came down on a toe. Somebody yelped. The hand jerked away in a hurry.

Eventually the lights came on again. The all-clear warbled. The crowd in the cellar trooped upstairs. The bartender started serving drinks. Somebody cranked up the gramophone. On came the girls. Except for ambulances and fire engines wailing outside, the raid might never have happened. Except.

Chapter 5

Behind Sergei Yaroslavsky's SB-2, columns of black smoke rose above Wilno. Some of the columns had surely come from the bombs his plane had dropped. "Well," he said in some satisfaction, "we're finally starting to get somewhere."

"Oh, yes." Anastas Mouradian nodded. If he was anywhere near as pleased as Sergei, he hadn't bothered telling his face about it. "Somewhere. But where?"

"We've got the Poles on the run." Sergei almost shouted, to make himself heard over the drone of the SB-2's twin radial engines. "It took a while, but now we do. A week from now, we won't just be bombing Wilno. We'll be shelling it—see if we won't. The Poles are brave, but that only helps so much when you haven't got the horses—or when the horses are all you've got."

Mouradian nodded again. He'd heard the same stories Sergei had: about how Polish cavalrymen, square-topped *csapkas* on their heads and drawn sabers gleaming in the sun, had charged Red Army tanks. You did have to be brave to do something like that. Didn't you also have to be out of your mind? Not many of the Poles who'd galloped forward galloped back again.

"All right. Fine. We have the Poles on the run. Now what?" Mouradian said after what seemed a pause for consideration. His Russian was fluent, but carried a throaty Armenian accent. He sounded a little like Stalin on the radio. Sergei thought so, anyhow, but Mouradian got offended when the Russian told him so. If you listened to Stas, Armenian and Georgian were nothing like each other. But, if you listened to him explaining that, he still sounded like Stalin.

He also took a perverse—a Caucasian?—pride in being difficult. "What do you mean, 'Now what?' " Sergei said. "We take back the chunk of Poland Pilsudski stole from us while we were fighting our civil war, that's what."

"And what do the Poles do then?" Anastas inquired. "Better yet, what do the Germans do then?"

The Germans couldn't do what Sergei suggested. Human beings weren't made that way. Mouradian chuckled indulgently, as he might have at a six-year-old showing off. Sergei went on, "But who cares what they do? If the Poles make peace with us, the Nazis have to get out of Poland, right?"

"They're good at marching into places. They aren't so good at marching out again," Stas said, which was bound to be true. He added, "Besides, they're still at war with us any which way. They have been since Czechoslovakia."

"Well, so what?" Sergei didn't like to think about Czechoslovakia. He and Stas and Ivan Kuchkov had come out again, which a lot of other "volunteers" hadn't. He'd first made the acquaintance of the Bf-109 there. If he never saw another angular German fighter, he wouldn't be sorry.

"So Hitler will find some other way to keep the fight going," Mouradian predicted. "He hates the Soviet Union worse than he hates France and England."

That held a nasty ring of truth. Yaroslavsky was glad to have to pay attention to his flying for a little while as he descended toward this new airstrip on what had been Polish soil. "He may hate us, but is he crazy?" he asked, leveling off again. "Does he *want* a two-front war?"

"Germany almost won the last one," Anastas answered, which was true even if unpalatable. "And it doesn't look like America's going to get into this one."

Sergei's grunt could have been taken as one of effort, because he was cranking down the landing gear. A hydraulic or electrical system would have been easier on the pilot. It also would have been more expensive and harder to build. He—and every other SB-2 pilot—went on working the crank.

Without American soldiers and munitions, France and England likely would have lost the World War—the First World War, it was now. That didn't make Soviet citizens love the USA. American troops in the north and the Far East had done their best to strangle the Russian Revolution in its cradle. They'd gone home, grudgingly, only after their best turned out not to be good enough.

The bomber set down roughly and taxied to a stop. Groundcrew men trotted up as the crew scrambled out of the plane. "How did it go, Comrades?" the chief maintenance sergeant asked.

"We put the bombs on target in Wilno," Sergei said. "Not much anti-aircraft fire. The Poles are wearing down."

"About time," the sergeant said. "I don't know why they got so excited over Wilno to begin with—or why we want it, come to that. Damn town is full of Litvaks and Jews." He spat in the dirt.

Before Sergei could answer that or even think about it much, Ivan Kuchkov stiffened like an animal taking a scent. He cocked his head to one side, listening intently. Then he said something worse than his usual *mat*-laced obscenities: "Messerschmitts! Heading this way!"

Sergei started running before he heard the planes himself. So did everybody else within earshot of the Chimp. Long before the pilot got to the trenches on one side of the runway, he did hear the hateful roar of the fighters' engines. That only made him run harder.

He didn't run hard enough to get to the trenches before the 109s' machine guns and cannon started stitching down the airstrip. Dust spurted up from the hits. Rounds slammed into the metal and doped fabric covering his SB-2. He didn't look back. He did a swan dive—if you could imagine a spastic swan—into the zigzagging trench.

That maintenance sergeant landed in the trench beside him. "Too god-damn close," Sergei said, panting. "I'm lucky I didn't break my ankle jumping down here."

The sergeant didn't answer. He wouldn't, either. A bullet—or, more likely, a 20mm round—had taken off the top of his head. Blood and brains soaked into the black dirt. One second, he'd been running for cover. The next? It was over. Lots of worse ways to go. Pilots found too many of them. If you got shot down, you were liable to have a lot of time to think before you finally smashed.

"*Bozhemoi!*" Anastas Mouradian said. "Poor bugger cashed in his chips all at once, didn't he?"

"I was thinking the same thing," Sergei answered as the Messerschmitts zoomed away at just above treetop height. Now he could smell the main-tenance man's blood, and the nastier smells that said his bowels and blad-der had let go when he stopped one.

"*Za Stalina,*" Mouradian added somberly. About every third Red Army tank and Red Air Force bomber had *For Stalin!* painted on its side. You fought for Stalin. And you died for Stalin, too. He looked after the 109s. They were long gone now. "You see? The Nazis haven't dried up and blown away."

"Well . . . no." Sergei didn't like to admit that. Oh, he knew Poles could kill him, too. But the Germans, damn them, were much too good at such things. He wondered what they'd done to his plane. It wasn't burning, anyhow. A couple of bullets through the engines sure wouldn't do it any good, though. Two of the tires on the landing gear were flat. That would make getting it out of the way for repairs even more fun than it would have been otherwise.

They'd have to do it, fun or not. They couldn't just leave the SB-2 in the middle of the runway. Not only did it clog Soviet air operations here, it sent the *Luftwaffe* an engraved invitation to come back.

"Planes . . . We can fight back against planes," Stas said, and Sergei made himself nod. It was true—to a point. The Bf-109 outdid anything the Red Air Force flew. Both biplane and blunt-nosed monoplane Po-likarpov fighters were last year's models—no, year before last's—next to it. New machines that could meet the fearsome Messerschmitts on even terms were supposed to be in the works. But the hot Soviet planes weren't here yet, and the Germans had theirs now. In a low voice, Mouradian went on, "What happens if the Nazis throw their panzers at us?"

Sergei took a deep breath, then immediately wished he hadn't. It wasn't just that he smelled the butcher-shop and outhouse reeks of the groundcrew man's sudden demise. But the damp-earth smell of the trench reminded him of a new-dug grave. He'd smelled that smell when they put his mother in the ground.

"Hitler wouldn't do that," he protested, remembering how stunned he'd been then. "He may be crazy, but he's not stupid. He'd really have a two-front war if he did."

"Well, maybe. I hope you're right," Mouradian said. "But so would we, and we didn't the last time around."

Only one thing was left for Sergei to do then: swear at the Japanese. He did it, with a flair and verve that made even the Chimp eye him in surprised admiration. With any luck at all, it would satisfy NKVD informers, too—assuming Ivan Kuchkov wasn't one.

SARAH GOLDMAN STARED at the rectangle of yellow cloth her mother held. It had crudely printed, fist-sized Stars of David on it. Each six-pointed star bore four black, Hebraic-looking letters: *Jude.* The Jews of Münster, the Jews of Germany, were going to have to put the stars on their clothes and announce to their Aryan neighbors what they were.

But that wasn't the worst part. Oh, no. The worst was that the Goldmans, like every other Jewish family in Germany, had to give up clothing ration points to get the cloth with which to mark themselves. Whoever'd come up with that masterpiece of bureaucratic *chutzpah* must have won himself a commendation from Himmler, or even from Hitler himself.

"They aren't just nasty," Sarah said. "They're *ugly.*" She tried to imagine wearing a yellow star on the breast of a jacket or blouse. She'd been shabby before—Jews got far fewer clothing points than Aryans. But her mother was good at mending and making do. Come to that, she wasn't bad herself. How were you supposed to make do with a star that shrieked JEW! at the world?

"I might have known it would happen. I should have known," her father said when he came back from his work on the labor gang that night. He was thinner than Sarah ever remembered seeing him; he did more than the food he got could support. Most nights, he fell asleep like a dead man right after supper. But he somehow seemed to limp less than usual, and his eyes were clear and bright.

"What do you mean, you should have known?" Hanna Goldman demanded. "Who do you think you are, Heydrich or somebody?"

"God forbid," Sarah's father answered. Sarah nodded and shivered at the same time. Heydrich might have been the scariest Nazi in business, not least because he looked like such a perfect Aryan. Samuel Goldman went on, "But when the *Wehrmacht* didn't roll into Paris, Hitler and Goebbels needed something to take people's minds off the war. Jews are perfect for that: the Nazis can jump all over us, and how are we going to hit back?"

No one said anything for some little while. The words held painfully obvious truth. Jews had always been scapegoats in Germany, the same way they had in Russia. When things went wrong somewhere else, you could set people banging on the kikes. Then you'd feel better, and the people would feel better, and if the Jews didn't feel better, well, who cared about *them*? Banging on Jews was the national equivalent of kicking your cat after a cop gave you a ticket.

While Sarah got the dishes as clean as she could with cold water, her mother cut out the yellow stars and started sewing them onto clothes. After Sarah got done washing and drying, she sat down to help. The radio blared out insipid music, and then stories about how German bombers were pulverizing Paris and the *Luftwaffe* was singlehandedly driving the Communist hordes out of Poland.

Pausing for a moment, Sarah's mother said, "If things were going as well as the newsmen say, we wouldn't be sitting here doing this."

"You think Father's right, then?" Sarah asked.

"Your father is right most of the time," Hanna Goldman answered. "The trouble is, he thinks that ought to do him some good."

Samuel Goldman had already headed for bed. Sarah shut up and went back to sewing. Her mother didn't usually sound so cynical; that was more her father's style. But people who'd been married a long time did have a way of growing together. And if sewing yellow Jewish stars onto clothes wasn't enough to turn a saint cynical, what would be? How could you sink lower than this?

Sarah found out how the next afternoon, when she went out shopping. It was a mild, even a balmy, spring day. She wore a white linen blouse, probably the best one she owned. Or it had been the best one, anyhow, till the yellow star with the big black letters went onto her left breast.

People stared at her as she walked by. Of course they did. She would have stared herself if someone else had put on anything that ugly. *It wasn't my idea!* she wanted to shout. *You're the ones who voted for the Nazis. You did this. Not me!* But that wouldn't have done her any good. Chances were it would have got her locked up. At least she had the sense to realize as much.

She saw a few other Jews out and about. They had to be, to get what they could in the scant time German regulations grudged them. Most looked as embarrassed as she felt. A few wore the star with dignity. And one or two might not have had it on, not by the way they acted. Sarah envied them their coolness, knowing she couldn't come within kilometers of matching it.

Nobody pointed at her and jeered. She didn't see Germans pointing and jeering at other Jews, either. She didn't hear anybody yelling *Lousy kike!* or something filthier yet. Had even the Aryans had all the anti-Semitic propaganda they could stomach? She wouldn't have imagined such a thing possible.

She wouldn't have imagined it, but maybe it was. A fiftyish man with a double chin—he looked like a mason, or perhaps a plumber—walked down the street toward her. As they passed, he gravely tipped his hat and went on.

She almost tripped over her own feet in astonishment. Had someone from the SS seen him do that, he might have wound up in a concentration camp. At the least, he would have got a stern talking-to. It hadn't stopped him. What was the world coming to? Sarah walked a little straighter after that.

Another man—this one an obvious veteran of the last war—tipped his hat to her before she got to the grocer's. She bought what vegetables she could and waited for the clerk to serve her. As long as any Aryans were in the shop, he was supposed to take care of them, even if they'd come in after she did.

But one of the women who had come in after her waved her forward, saying, "Go on, dear. You were next."

"Are you sure?" Sarah feared a trap. When ordinary politeness could scare you . . . you were a Jew in the Third *Reich*. But the *Hausfrau* took two steps back and waved her to the counter. The clerk took her money and her ration coupons. She got out of the grocery as fast as she could.

On the way home, a middle-aged man—another obvious veteran, with a bad limp and a scarred face—nodded to her and said, "Congratulations on your medal, sweetheart."

"Medal?" Sarah wished she hadn't echoed it. That only gave him the chance to let fly with whatever nastiness bubbled inside of him.

He pointed to the yellow star. "Your *Pour le sémite* there." He too tipped his hat, then stumped down the sidewalk.

Sarah needed a few seconds to get it. When she did, her jaw dropped. The highest German decoration in the last war—the equivalent of the modern Knight's Cross with oak leaves, swords, and diamonds—had the simple French name of *Pour le mérite*. For merit, it meant. And this stranger had punned off it, inventing a medal called *For the Semite*. That took brains. It also took nerve. Suppose someone other than a Jew had heard. What would have happened to him then? Nothing good.

To her amazement, at supper her father reported the same joke from his labor gang. "It must be all over town, then!" she exclaimed.

"All over the country, I'd guess," Father said. "Things like that, they spread faster than the grippe."

"Why bother with the stupid stars, then, if they only make people laugh at them and treat us better instead of worse?" Sarah said.

"You're asking the wrong person. You need to talk to the *Führer*, not me," Samuel Goldman said. "But one thing did occur to me."

"What's that?" Sarah wondered if she really wanted to know.

"If the Party ever decides it wants to round up as many Jews as it can, we're a lot easier to spot wearing our yellow stars."

"Oh." In a way, that made sense. In another . . . "Why would they want to do such a *meshuggineh* thing?" Sarah asked.

"Because they're Germans, and they're convinced we're not," her father said sadly. "If there's more bad news from the front, who knows what they'll do?"

No one knew. Even the Nazis didn't, not yet. That was the scariest part about it.

PETE McGILL WAS IN LOVE. This was his first time—the crushes he'd had on girls before he dropped out of high school to join the Corps didn't count. So what if she was a White Russian taxi dancer who'd turned tricks on the side before Pete got to know her? If anything, that only made him burn harder.

His Marine buddies in Shanghai thought he'd gone round the bend. "Hey, man, don't you think she still sleeps around for cash while you ain't looking?" Herman Szulc asked in what were no doubt intended for reasonable tones.

Whatever they were intended for, they didn't fly with Pete. "Watch your mouth, Shultzie, or I'll rearrange your face for you," he growled.

"You and who else?" Szulc didn't back down from anybody. He was a leatherneck, too.

More Marines had to grab them and hold them back, or they would have gone for each other. "This sucks," Pooch Puccinelli said. "I like drinking with both of you assholes, but now we can't go out together. Soon as we all try it, you'll have a couple and do your best to knock each other's brains out."

"He ain't got no brains," Szulc said.

"Fuck you, you dumb Polack," Pete said. "Fuck your—" Somebody clapped a hand over his mouth before he could come out with anything irrevocable.

He went to see Vera whenever he got off duty. When he couldn't see her, he thought about her. The touch of her, the scent of her, the taste of her . . . He had it bad, so bad he had no idea how bad it was. None so blind as he who will not see.

Vera, on the other hand, could see very clearly. She could see she had a meal ticket here. If things went the way she wanted them to, she wouldn't have to sell her time and her body any more. She didn't do it because she enjoyed it; she did it for the same reason a man built chairs: to make a living. She'd always hoped someone would fall for her so she wouldn't have to any more. She hadn't really expected it—it seemed like something out of a soppy movie. But she had hoped.

And now it had happened! A rich American, no less! (To Vera, all Americans were rich, even a Marine Corps corporal.) The rest of the girls at the Golden Lotus were madly jealous of her. In a different way, so was Sam Grynszpan, the Jew who owned the place. Like her, though for different reasons, he was what was bloodlessly called a stateless person. No rich American was likely to fall in love with him: he was short and squat and had a wide mouth and bulging eyes that made him look like a toad with five o'clock shadow.

Jealous or not, he gave good advice: "Don't let this one get away." His office was tiny and cramped and stank of stale cigar butts.

"Don't worry—I won't," Vera answered. She spoke Russian to him. He used a mix of Russian and Polish with her, flavored with Yiddish and French. They could both get along in six or eight different languages. Going around with Pete was doing wonders for her English.

She could have been polishing her Japanese just as easily. Tall, busty blond women fascinated Asians, as she had reason to know. To her, these days, men were men, regardless of where they came from. Well, almost. She'd never met even a Japanese major as open-handed as Pete McGill.

"You may really get to like him—who the hell knows?" Grynszpan said.

"Maybe." Vera left it right there. She knew Pete was nuts about her. She also knew exactly why: the sweaty athletics they performed together in her little upstairs room. He was a puppy. He didn't want anything fancy. He hardly knew there was anything fancy to want. For Vera, that made life easy. Well, easier.

She was made up and perfumed and wearing a blue silk dress—easy and cheap to do in Shanghai—when he came to the club to get her two days later. His eyes lit up as soon as he saw her. That was exactly what she'd had in mind. "Wow, babe! You look great!" he said, and kissed her on the cheek.

Most of the men she'd been with would have groped her, just to show everyone around that they could. She wondered if anybody'd kissed her on the cheek since she was ten years old. Offhand, she didn't think so. "What do we do? Where do we go?" she asked in English. That was the only language Pete knew, except for tiny bits of foul Chinese.

"We'll go to the Vienna Ballroom, and we won't dance," Pete declared.

That was one of the half-dozen fanciest cabarets in Shanghai. It put the Golden Lotus to shame. (So did plenty of clubs a lot less fancy than the one Pete named.) "What you do? Win lottery?" Vera asked. She meant it. She played the lottery herself. Ten dollars Mex could win half a million. Odds were long, but the lottery was legit. People did win, and did get paid when they won.

"I'm not that rich, but I didn't do bad. Had me four jacks when this other guy was mighty proud of his full house," Pete answered. He started to reach for his wallet, as if to show off how fat it was, but then stopped. You could land in all kinds of trouble if you flashed a roll in Shanghai—or in Dubuque, come to that.

The Vienna Ballroom sat at the corner of Majestic Road and Bubbling Well Road. The yellow brick building would have looked more at home in Vienna than it did in the Orient, but that was true of most of the International Settlement and the French Concession. Hard-faced guards with Lee-Enfield rifles stood outside the place. They were probably soldiers from one army or another who hadn't felt like leaving China when their tours were up. They only nodded to Pete and his lady. They were there to keep out the strife between Chinese and Japanese.

Inside, Celis' All-Star Orchestra blared away: second-rate jazz, with most of the tuxedoed musicians Chinese and the rest from all over the world. Pete wouldn't have been surprised if some of the white players were ex-soldiers, too. China got under some guys' skins the way Vera had got under his.

The maitre d' sized him up. A U.S. Marine in dress blues . . . two chevrons . . . not the best table. Expecting that, Pete slipped the guy a little something. Things improved: less than he would have liked, but enough to keep him from grousing out loud.

"Champagne, sir?" the fellow asked.

"You bet," Pete answered. He winked at Vera. "You get to drink the real stuff tonight, babe." She summoned up a blush.

He ordered steaks big enough to have come off the side of an elephant and rare enough to have still been mooing a couple of minutes earlier. Vera stared at hers in amazement but made it disappear as fast as Pete's. *Waste not, want not* had been drilled into her since she was a baby, when her mother and father made it to Manchuria one short jump ahead of the Reds. When the Japanese took Harbin, she'd made it to Shanghai the same way. If she jumped the right way now . . .

Some of the men out on the dance floor were European and American businessmen hanging on in Shanghai in spite of the widening war between China and Japan. Some were Japanese businessmen and officers. And some were sleek, plump Chinese collaborators in expensive suits, whirling their partners around as if Satchmo himself fronted the All-Star Orchestra.

Every single Oriental man danced with a white woman: almost all of them with a blonde or a redhead. Pete tried to guess which girls were hostesses here, which mistresses. Some danced better than others, but that was his only clue. The Japs and Chinamen all looked uncommonly smug. *See? We've got the West by the short hairs,* they might have been saying.

A Chinese man with gray at the temples came up to Vera and said, *"Willst du tanzen?"*

Even Pete could figure out that much German. "She's my friend," he said. "She doesn't work here."

He wasn't surprised when the Chinese fellow understood English; he'd assumed the man would. The Chinese eyed him, maybe wondering whether to make something out of it. Since Pete was half his age and twice his size, he decided not to: one of his smartest business decisions ever. He walked off, muttering what probably weren't compliments in Chinese.

A few minutes later, something big blew up a few blocks away. The lights flickered and went out for a couple of seconds. Celis' All-Star Orchestra discorded down into silence. A woman squealed. A man yelled, *"Merde!"* Then the power came on again. The master of ceremonies, a grin pasted onto his Eurasian face, called, "All part of life in Shanghai, folks! Next round on the house!"

That made people forget their jitters in a hurry. Pete grinned at Vera. "You know what, babe?"

"No. What?" she asked, as she knew she should.

"I've never had so much fun *not* dancing."

"Never?" she said innocently.

"Well, never with my clothes on, anyway," he answered, looking her up and down. She managed another blush. Pete waved for more bubbly.

WHEN THREE NAKED GERMANS JUMPED into their stream in northern France, turtles dove off rocks and frogs sprang away into the grass with horrified *"Freep!"*s. Theo Hossbach didn't give a damn. He had some violet-scented soap he'd liberated from an abandoned French farmhouse, and he wanted to get clean. He couldn't remember the last time he'd had a proper bath. The water was cold, but not too cold. You got used to it fast.

Adalbert Stoss and Heinz Naumann were scrubbing themselves, too. The panzer commander splashed Stoss and pointed toward their black coveralls, which all lay together on the bank. "You know, you're out of uniform, Adi," Naumann said.

Stoss splashed back. "What d'you mean? We're all out of uniform." He had soap bubbles in his hair.

"Not like that," Naumann said. "You ought to sew a yellow star on the front of your outfit." He laughed raucously.

"Oh, fuck off," Stoss said without much rancor. "So I had the operation when I was a kid. So what? Goddamn sheenies aren't the only ones who do, you know."

"Yeah, yeah." Naumann didn't push it any more. Sergeant or not, he might have had a fight on his hands if he had. Teasing somebody about looking like a Jew was one thing. Acting as if you really thought he was one was something else again—something that went way over the line.

Theo had known Adi was circumcised, too. You couldn't very well not know something like that, not when the two of you were part of the same panzer crew. He wasn't going to say anything about it, though. Sometimes—often—the best thing you could say was nothing. That was how it looked to him, anyhow. If Heinz thought otherwise . . . Well, Heinz was a sergeant. Sergeants got all kinds of funny ideas.

The other thing was, Theo wouldn't have wanted Adi Stoss pissed off at him. If Adi got mad, he was liable to go and rupture your spleen first, then feel bad about it afterwards. Theo wouldn't have wanted to take him on. Heinz Naumann thought he was a tough guy. He'd made that plain. If he thought he was tougher than his driver, he needed to think again.

They all started splashing one another and wrestling in the stream, skylarking like a bunch of schoolboys. Maybe by chance, maybe not, Adi held Naumann under water for a very long time. No, Theo wasn't surprised the sergeant couldn't break Stoss' hold. His struggles were beginning to weaken when Adi finally let him go.

"Jesus!" Naumann said, gulping in air till he went from a dusky red-purple back to pink. "You trying to drown me, asshole?"

"Sorry, Sergeant." Stoss sounded so sincere, he might have meant it. "I didn't know you'd turned quite that color."

"I thought I'd have to grow fins," Heinz said. "Save that shit for the Frenchies, huh?"

"You bet." Adi watched Naumann closely. Theo would have, too. If you beat somebody like that, he was liable to try to get his own back. But Heinz just walked out of the stream and started putting his uniform on again. Whatever he was going to do, he wouldn't do it right away.

With a shrug, Theo started for the bank, too. He didn't want his crew-mates squabbling. Taking a panzer into battle was hard enough when everybody got along. Another man might have tried to get them to make up. Theo was too withdrawn for that. He hoped they would be sensible enough to see the need without him. Adi seemed to have his head on pretty tight. Theo wasn't so sure about Heinz. The sergeant didn't just have his rank to worry about. He also owned a touchy sense of pride, more like a Frenchman or an Italian than your everyday German.

But the quarrel evaporated as soon as they got back to the encampment. It reminded Theo of nothing so much as an ants' nest stirred with a stick. People ran every which way. Theo watched two panzer crewmen bounce off each other, as if they were in a Chaplin film. *Something* had happened in the hour or so they'd spent in the stream.

He didn't need long to find out what. The company—well, never mind the company: the whole damned panzer division—was getting pulled out of the line. Where it was going, nobody seemed to know. Somewhere.

"What the hell do they think they're doing?" Heinz Naumann threw his hands in the air. "Are they going to break through without panzers? Not fucking likely!"

"Hey, come on, Sergeant—it's the General Staff," Adi said. "Just like the last war. My father used to tell stories about how the guys in the fancy shoulder straps screwed up half of what the *Landsers* did. More than half."

"Yeah, my old man goes on the same way." As soon as Stoss agreed with him, Heinz stopped being angry. That was good, anyhow. "But the *Führer* was supposed to clean up that kind of shit."

"What can you do?" Theo said. Both his crewmates looked at him in surprise. He didn't put his oar in the water very often.

What they could do was follow orders, and they did. Along with the rest of the company's machines, their Panzer II clanked back to Clermont, the nearest German-held railhead. Adalbert Stoss drove it up onto a flatcar. They chained the panzer into place, then boarded a jammed passenger car. Theo hated being surrounded by so many other people. He would rather have made the train trip inside the Panzer II. Expecting your superiors to care about what you would rather do, though, was like waiting for the Second Coming. It might happen, but not any time soon.

They rolled back through France, back through the Low Countries, and across Germany. Theo started to wonder if they would go all the way to Breslau.

They didn't. They went farther than that. The train stopped at the Polish border. Polish soldiers in uniforms of a dark, greenish khaki and domed helmets smoother in outline than the ones German foot soldiers wore waved to the men in the passenger cars. Some of the Germans waved back. Theo would have felt like an idiot, so he didn't.

After a delay of about an hour and a half, the train started moving again—into Poland. Adi whistled softly. "Well, now we know what's up," he said. "We're going to give the Russians a kick in the slats."

Nobody tried to tell him he was wrong. No wonder the Poles were waving and smiling! Here were Germans, coming to do their fighting for them! Theo wouldn't have wanted to be a Pole, forever stuck between bigger, meaner neighbors. Poland offered Germany a shield hundreds of kilometers wide against the Russians. If the Red Army started biting chunks out of that shield, didn't the *Reich* have to show Stalin that wasn't such a hot idea?

Evidently. And showing it with a panzer division—or more than one, for all Theo knew—would make sure the Reds remembered the lesson. Of course, that could also buy the *Reich* a much bigger war than it had now. Again, Theo wondered whether the *Führer* and the General Staff knew what the hell they were up to. Whether they did or not, he couldn't do anything about it but try to stay alive.

Poland sure looked like perfect panzer country: low and flat and mostly open. Every so often, the train would roll through a village or town. Some of them were full of bearded Jews, many wearing side curls. Theo glanced over at Adi Stoss, who happened to be spreading sausage paste—pork sausage paste—from a tinfoil ration tube onto a chunk of black bread. Circumcised or not, he didn't look like a Jew, and he didn't eat like a Jew, either.

Northeast to Bialystok—another town packed with them. Southeast to Grodno. Northeast again, through Lebeda to Lida. They detrained there. The grayish sky and chilly breeze said they'd come a long, long way from France. The distant thump of artillery said they hadn't come very far at all.

German and Polish officers shouted and waved at the panzer troops as they got their machines down off the flatcars. The Poles spoke German, but not a kind that made sense to Heinz or Adi. Theo had no trouble with it. Living in Breslau, he'd grown up around Poles doing their best in his language. Where he had to, he translated for his crewmates.

They went into bivouac outside of Lida. Polish infantrymen stared at the panzers with fearful respect. "They're glad we're going up against the Russians and not them," Adi remarked.

Theo hadn't thought of that, but it made sense as soon as he heard it. Sure as hell, the Poles were meat in a sandwich. Their best hope—their only hope—was that the slices of bread hated each other worse.

Chapter 6

"Hey, Sergeant!" Luc Harcourt called—quietly, so his voice wouldn't carry to the German line not too far away.

"Yeah?" Sergeant Demange said. "What d'you want?" He also kept his voice down, and didn't show himself. You never could tell when a German sniper had a bead on your foxhole. The bastards in field-gray were good at that stuff, damn them.

"What's up with the *Boches*?" Luc said. "They're laying barbed wire like it comes out of their asses." He didn't point toward the enemy, either.

"I wish it did. That'd make 'em think twice whenever they sat down, by Christ," Demange said. "You want to know what's going on, though? They've pulled a bunch of their tanks out, that's what. Now the foot soldiers have to hold the ground by themselves. They're digging in, the *cons*—digging like mad. In their boots, so would I."

Luc thought about it. Slowly, he nodded. He swigged *pinard* from his canteen. The rough red wine made the world seem easier to take. "How'd you find out? Where'd you hear it?" he asked. It sounded sensible, but in war that proved nothing, or maybe a little less.

"I was bullshitting with a radio operator. He told me," Demange answered. "Said we'd nicked some of their signals or something. And I haven't seen a tank over there for a couple of days. Unless they're trying to royally screw us, they really are moving their armor . . . somewhere. Where, I can't tell you."

"Tanks can flatten wire," Luc said. "Think we'll send ours in, and the infantry behind them?"

"I'll believe it when I see it. Swear to God, Harcourt, the high command still doesn't have its heart in the fight," Demange said, disgust in his voice. "Oh, when the Nazis tried to jump all over us we fought back, but who wouldn't? An offensive like that, though? In your dreams! In mine, too."

He wouldn't have talked to Luc that way before the fighting started. He would have told him to fuck off. Luc knew it. He was proud of himself for earning Demange's confidence, and more than a little revolted at being proud. Again, nothing in war made sense.

"So what do we do now? Wait for the Americans, the way we did in 1918?" Luc inquired with a certain amount of malice aforethought.

"Screw the Americans!" Yes, that was steam coming out of the sergeant's ears. "Cocksuckers were way late the last time. I don't think they're coming at all now."

"Here's hoping you're wrong," Luc said.

"Sure—here's hoping," Demange answered. "But don't hold your breath. Oh, and one more thing . . . Suppose we do send the tanks through the *Boches'* wire. How far do you think they'll get? How many mines have the fucking *Feldgraus* planted under there?"

That was another good question. *As many as they could* was the answer that occurred to Luc. Doubting the Germans' competence didn't pay. Luc knew he made a decent soldier now not least because the enemy was such a good teacher. If you lived, you learned.

Supper turned out to be something the cooks might have learned from the enemy: a stew of potatoes and cabbage and sausage that tasted like a mixture of stale bread and horsemeat. The only thing that suggested it hadn't come from a German field kitchen was a heavy dose of onions and garlic. Before the shooting started, Luc would have sneered at it. These days, he knew better. Anything that left him with a full belly and didn't give him the runs afterwards was not to be despised.

After supper, a private named Denis Boucher said, "Talk to you, Corporal, please?" He was a little round-faced fellow, maybe a year younger than Luc: a new conscript, just out of training, and in the line for the first time.

"What's up?" Luc asked.

Boucher looked at him the way he'd looked at Sergeant Demange when he was still a new fish. Luc still sometimes looked at Demange that way. To have somebody turn that kind of gaze on him . . . To the rookie, all noncoms were deities: some grander and more thunderous than others, no doubt, but all deities just the same.

"Well, Corporal . . . Can we talk someplace where nobody can hear us?" The kid fidgeted in what looked like acute embarrassment.

"Come on. Out with it. If we go off somewhere, people will wonder. If you talk to me right here, they'll think you're asking about cleaning your rifle or something," Luc said.

"You're so smart!" Boucher blurted. Luc didn't think he was trying to butter him up. That kind of thing hadn't occurred to him before. *I could get used to being the guy who knows stuff,* Luc thought. Then the little fellow in the unfaded khaki uniform went on, "It's about my girl. I'm afraid she's fooling around on me while I'm away. What can I do?"

Not even the guy who knew stuff had an automatic good answer for that one. Cautiously, Luc asked, "Why do you think she's messing around?" Some guys worried themselves sick over nothing.

And some guys didn't. "Marie's always been a flirt," Boucher said. "And we kind of had a fight before I had to go into the army."

That didn't sound so good. Luc spread his hands. "Don't know what to tell you except this: if she is messing around on you, she wasn't worth having to begin with."

"Easy for you to say! I love her!" Denis Boucher seemed as hot and bothered as a little round-faced guy could get.

"Well, if she's there for you when you get home, everything's great. And if she's not, you've got the rest of your life to pick up the pieces and find somebody else," Luc said. Sergeant Demange would have told the kid to shut the fuck up and soldier, which was also good advice. Luc wasn't so hardened. He also didn't point out that Denis was liable not to get home, or to come back so torn up that neither Marie nor anyone else in skirts was likely to want anything to do with him. No matter how true that was, it wasn't helpful.

True it was. The Germans might not have any tanks in the neighborhood of Beauvais any more, but they'd left behind plenty of artillery. It started working over the French lines in the middle of the night. It had them ranged to the centimeter, or so it seemed to Luc as he cowered in his hole. Nothing you could do about artillery fire but pray it didn't chop you up.

The barrage stopped as abruptly as it started. Wounded *poilus* shrieked. You could follow them by their screams as aid men took them to the rear. Luc grasped his rifle and stared wildly into the night, waiting for the fuckers with the coal-scuttle helmets to sweep down on the French trenches. Machine guns spat strip after strip of ammunition at the German lines to make the *Boches* think twice.

Maybe they'd already thought twice. They didn't come out of their foxholes and trenches. After a while, swearing and yawning, Luc curled up like a tired old dog and tried to sleep. No sooner had he closed his eyes, or so it seemed, than the artillery started up again.

It went on like that for the next several days: random shelling at all hours of the night and day. It wasn't anything like the usual methodical pattern of German fire. Maybe the regular German artillery commander had gone off with the tanks and left his halfwitted nephew in charge. If so, Junior was a damn pest.

And Denis Boucher went missing one morning. Luc glumly reported that to Sergeant Demange. "Maybe a German 105 blew him to kingdom come," he said. "But maybe he scooted off to see what was going on with his precious Marie."

"Well, if he did, he's not our worry any more," Demange said. "Let the military police get all hot and bothered about him. And if he does make it back to the mangy bitch, I hope she gives him the clap." The milk of human kindness ran thin and curdled in Demange's veins.

In Luc's, too, at the moment. He yawned till his jaw cracked like a knuckle. "I hope the *Boches'* artillery lets up during the day. I've got to grab some sleep."

"You get tired enough, you can sleep through a barrage. I did it myself, back in '18," Demange said.

"I believe you. I aim to try," Luc said. Maybe the generals should have sent armor surging forward to drive the invader from *la belle France*. Luc couldn't get excited about that, not right now. He went back to his hole and snuggled down in it. By now he was so used to sleeping on the ground, he'd decided mattresses were overrated. Exhaustion clouted him over the head with a padded blackjack. An hour and a half later, the German artillery started up again. Luc never knew it.

AS HE ALWAYS DID while he was atop the U-30's conning tower, Julius Lemp scanned. The sun was going down, far in the northwest. At this latitude and this season, it would rise again in the northeast in a very few hours. It wouldn't stay dark long, and it wouldn't get very dark; the sun wouldn't sink far enough below the horizon for that.

This stretch of North Atlantic between Iceland and Norway should have been deadly dangerous for a surfaced U-boat, then. And it would have been, had any Royal Navy ships been close enough to spot the U-30. The submarine lay almost two hundred kilometers north of the Faeroe Islands. The English had to figure no one in his right mind would care to visit this lonely stretch of sea.

Lemp thought the English had a point. You could die of boredom before you saw a freighter plowing across these waters. Even if you did, it would be flying a Danish or Swedish or Norwegian flag: a neutral, and so not a legitimate target. Lemp had already sunk one neutral. What Admiral Dönitz would do to him if he sank another did not bear thinking about.

Resolutely, then, Lemp didn't think about it. Or he tried not to. The thought kept making him notice it, like a chunk of gristle wedged between two back teeth. He longed for transcendental floss to make it go away.

The ratings up there with him were also peering through binoculars.

As a wave crest pushed the U-30 up a meter or two, one of them stiffened and pointed. "Smoke, Skipper!" he exclaimed.

"Where away?" Lemp asked, but he was already looking north, following the man's index finger. He needed to wait for another wave to lift the U-boat before he spied the plume himself. It was in the right quarter, but . . . He frowned. Diesels were supposed to make less smoke than turbines. That he'd seen this ship's exhaust before the masts came up over the horizon wasn't a good sign.

"Is it ours, or does it belong to the limeys?" asked the man who'd first noted the smudge in the sky.

"It had better be ours," Lemp answered. By the time they got close enough to be sure it wasn't, a Royal Navy ship would be pounding them to pieces. He waited for the ship itself to come into sight, then spoke to the bosun, who stood behind the signal lamp: "Give 'em the recognition signal, Matti."

"Aye aye." Matti Altmark clacked the louvers. Three Morse letters flashed out across the water.

A moment later, three came back. Lemp breathed a sigh of relief. That smoked, too—even heading into June, it was cold up here. You didn't want to fall into the sea. You'd last only minutes if you did. "Alles gut," Lemp said, noticing the sailors staring anxiously at him. They didn't know what the answer was supposed to be. Lemp did. "That's the *Admiral Scheer*, all right."

They grinned and gave him thumbs-up. He made himself smile as he returned the gesture. The pocket battleship was loose in the North Atlantic. With any luck at all, the Royal Navy didn't know it yet. Commerce raiders had kept England hopping in the last war. These armored cruisers and their eleven-inch guns were supposed to do even better this time around. The idea was that they could outfight anything they couldn't outrun and outrun anything they couldn't outfight.

By all their specs, they could do both those things. They could get the Royal Navy scrambling like eggs. They could disrupt commerce between the USA and England and between South America and England. They could. That didn't mean Julius Lemp thought much of them. He was a U-boat man from stem to stern, from top to bottom. Couldn't submarines do the same job as big, fancy surface raiders, do it better, and do it cheaper? Of course they could—if you asked a U-boat man.

On came the *Admiral Scheer*. She was a hell of a lot prettier than the cigar-shaped, rust-streaked U-30. Even Lemp had to admit that. She looked like a sword slicing through the waves. But so what? They didn't pay off on looks, not unless you were a chorus girl.

His men kept staring at the pocket battleship through their field glasses. "Everything is so clean," one of them murmured. "Every*body* is so clean." The submarine and its crew were anything but. They wore leather jackets to hide grease stains. They all smelled bad—you couldn't bathe properly in this cramped steel tube. Face fungus sprouted on their cheeks and chins and lower lips . . . and on Lemp's. The only thing that distinguished him from them was the white cloth cover on his officer's cap.

More signals flashed from the *Admiral Scheer*'s lamp. "Captain . . . will . . . repair . . . aboard," Matti said slowly.

"I read it," Lemp answered. "Tell them *Aye aye*." The U-boat's signal lamp clacked again.

The pocket battleship lowered a motor launch. It chugged across to the U-30. Feeling like a man entering a strange new world, Lemp boarded it. The petty officer in charge of the launch saluted him. He had to remind himself to return the gesture. There was no room for such nonsense in the submarine's cramped quarters.

Up on the bridge, Lemp did remember to salute Captain Patzig, the officer commanding the *Admiral Scheer,* as he should have. The middle-aged four-striper wore decorations from the last war on the chest of his spotless blue tunic. He eyed Lemp as if wondering whether the U-boat skipper would sneak off with silverware from the galley. But his voice was polite enough as he said, "Welcome aboard."

"Thank you, sir. You can see a long way from here, can't you?" Lemp wasn't used to being up so high.

Patzig glanced down toward the U-30. He smiled faintly. "We spot the enemy sooner."

"Yes, sir." That reminded Lemp of something else. "Sir, you should know we saw your smoke before we spotted your masts."

"You did?" Patzig rumbled ominously, as if warning Lemp to take it back. But Lemp only nodded—it was true. The older man frowned. "Well. I shall have to speak to my engineering officers about that." By the look on his face, it wouldn't be a pleasant conversation.

"What do you want with us, sir?" Lemp asked. "My orders say I am to cooperate with you in all regards." He didn't like them, but he had them.

"We're both out here for the same reason: to disrupt shipping between England and the Americas," Patzig said. "We would do better working together than separately."

"Sir?" Lemp said, and not another word. *Why does this shit always land on my head?* he wondered bitterly. But he knew the answer to that, knew it all too well. He got this assignment for the same reason that the U-30 got to test a *Schnorkel* under combat conditions. The powers that be didn't love him, and they had their reasons. Untested? Dangerous? Foolhardy? We'll send out U-30! If anything happens to her, it's no great loss.

Captain Patzig didn't seem to realize he was talking like an idiot. When you commanded a behemoth like this, a U-boat skipper was less than the dirt beneath your feet. "*Ja,*" he said. "Together. Your torpedoes will be useful in sinking ships we capture."

Lemp didn't explode. Holding himself in wasn't easy, but he did it. Carefully, he said, "Um, sir, is it not so that your *Panzerschiff* here also carries torpedoes?"

He knew damn well it was so. And he managed to embarrass Captain Patzig, at least a little. Color came into the older man's cheeks, which had been quite pale. "Well, yes," Patzig admitted, "but you submariners are the experts in their use, after all. With us, they are strictly auxiliary and emergency weapons."

And what was *that* supposed to mean? Had the *Admiral Scheer* tried to torpedo some luckless freighter and missed? It sounded that way to Lemp. He almost asked Captain Patzig. Had Patzig come aboard his boat, he would have. But surface-navy discipline stifled him here on the pocket battleship's spotless bridge.

"You can cruise at fourteen knots and keep station with us, *nicht wahr?*" Patzig said.

"Till we run out of fuel, yes," Lemp answered. "You've got much more range than we do."

The other skipper waved that aside. "We can refuel you," he said. And so they could—no doubt about it. The *Admiral Scheer's* diesels would gulp where the U-30 sipped, and the surface vessel would carry far more fuel, too. Patzig went on, "In case we encounter the Royal Navy, your presence would also be useful."

There he actually made sense. Enemy cruisers or destroyers going after the pocket battleship wouldn't expect her to have a U-boat tagging along. Lemp did say, "Once you run up to full speed, sir, you'll leave us behind. We may not be able to do you any good when you need us the most."

Patzig waved that aside. "We will do our best to lure the Englishmen straight into your path. The hunting will be good, Lieutenant. Return to your boat and prepare to conform to our movements."

No! You're out of your goddamn mind! No matter how much Lemp wanted to scream in the senior man's face, the words stuck in his throat. He saluted stiffly. *"Zu befehl, mein Herr!"* he said. *At your command, sir!* And it was at Patzig's command. Lemp wouldn't have done this on his own for every Reichsmark in Germany—no, not for every dollar in the USA. Military discipline was a strange and wondrous thing. Full of foreboding, he did a smart about-turn and walked away.

IT WAS . . . a railroad track. Had Hideki Fujita seen it somewhere in Japan or Manchukuo, he wouldn't have given it a second glance. The sergeant shook his head. No, that wasn't quite true. The two iron rails seemed uncommonly far apart. The Russians used a wider gauge than most of the rest of the world. Fujita had heard that was to keep invaders from the west from putting their rolling stock onto Russian tracks. He didn't know—or much care—whether that was true, but it seemed reasonable to him.

But watching Japanese engineers tear these tracks out of the ground and throw them into a roaring fire to bend the lengths of rail beyond repair was something else again. Wrecking the Trans-Siberian Railroad meant victory. No more trains would get through to Vladivostok. And, once the Soviet city on the Pacific was cut off and taken, the rest of the Russian Far East would drop into Japan's hands like a sweet, ripe persimmon.

The Russians understood that as well as the Japanese did. They'd fought like demons to keep the Kwantung Army from coming this far. Two engineers picked up a Russian corpse that lay on the tracks, one by the feet, the other by the arms. They tossed the body a couple of meters off to one side. The thump it made when it hit the dirt again sounded dreadfully final.

Fujita walked over to it. Russian boots were very fine—far more supple than Japanese issue. If this luckless fellow was anywhere close to his size . . . But the dead man wasn't. He was twenty centimeters taller than Fujita and twenty-five kilos heavier, and had feet to match his size. Large for a Russian, he would have made an enormous Japanese.

"*Shigata ga nai*," Fujita muttered—nothing to be done about it. But it wasn't as if this fellow were the only dead Russian close by. Oh, no. Fujita and his countrymen had plenty of corpses to strip.

And there were plenty of Japanese corpses to dispose of, too. The dead soldiers' souls would go to Yasukuni Shrine, where Japan would honor them for all eternity. That was a great deal . . . but somehow it didn't seem quite enough to Fujita right this minute. Maybe that was simple relief at coming through another fight unhurt. He hoped so. He wanted to give his fallen comrades all the respect they deserved.

But he didn't want to join them in death. And the Russians, even though pushed away from their precious railroad, hadn't given up. Artillery from back in the woods to the northeast started screaming in. Fujita stopped worrying about anyone else's boots and started worrying about getting blasted out of his. He jumped into the closest foxhole. A dead Russian already lay in there, crumpled like a broken doll. He rolled himself into a ball and hoped the shelling would let up soon.

It did, but then two or three Polikarpov biplane fighters strafed the Japanese at not much more than treetop height. They looked old-fashioned alongside the Japanese planes that fought them in the air, but they got the job done. One of the engineers who'd chucked the body off the tracks reeled away, clutching at his chest. He slumped to the muddy ground. Fujita feared he wouldn't get up again.

Japanese fighters showed up ten minutes after the Russians had zoomed away. Fujita watched them buzz around like angry bees looking for someone to sting. When they didn't find anybody, they flew away. "Bastards," he said. What were they good for if they came to the party late?

Sooner or later, the Reds would run out of gas for their planes and shells for their guns. That was the whole point to cutting the railroad. Sooner or later, yes, but not yet, dammit. Not yet.

Then Japanese bombers droned past, flying much higher than the fighters had. Fujita cocked his head, listening to the distant thunder of explosions from their bombs. Yes, those came from the general direction from which the Russian guns had been firing. Japanese flyers would presently claim they'd silenced those guns . . . till the artillery opened up again. Fujita was willing to admit the bomber pilots did try. He wasn't willing to admit anything more than that.

He needed to get rid of the dead Russian keeping company with him. The poor devil was just starting to stink, but that problem would get worse in a hurry. Grunting with effort, Fujita wrestled the body out of the hole.

He was about to drag it downwind when he noticed the dead man's boots. Damned if they weren't about his size. He wrestled one off the corpse and tried it on. It fit better than the boots his own country's quartermasters had given him. And the leather really was glove-flexible. He stripped off the Russian's other boot and put that on, too. As he walked around in the new pair, a broad smile spread across his face. He could kiss blisters good-bye!

The dead man didn't complain. He wasn't even wearing socks—just strips of cloth wrapped around his feet like puttees. Fujita had seen other Russians who did the same thing. They were welcome to the style, as far as he was concerned. *His* socks—*tabis*—were like mittens, with a separate space for his big toe on each foot. When the weather got warm, he could wear sandals with them. He wondered if the weather in Siberia ever got that warm. He wouldn't bet on it.

It was warm enough for mosquitoes right now. Siberian mosquitoes were numerous, savage, and *large*. A Japanese joke said one of them had landed at an airstrip, and groundcrew men pumped a hundred liters of gasoline into it before they realized what it was. Fujita thought it was a joke.

You didn't notice the bites when they happened. If you didn't feel the mosquito walking on your skin, or see it there, the damn thing would fly away happy. You'd feel it later, though—you'd itch for a week. Scratching only made things worse, too.

Back of the line, Japanese soldiers lit candles of camphor or citronella. You couldn't do it at the front. The scent, wafting on the wind, told the Russians where you were. They were like animals; they'd take clues a civilized man, a Japanese man, wouldn't even notice, and they'd use them to kill you.

An officer's whistle squealed like an angry shoat. "Advance!" Lieutenant Hanafusa shouted. "We have to push their guns away from the railroad line!"

Right now? Fujita wondered. A sergeant couldn't ask something like that out loud, not unless he wanted to get busted back to private—or, more likely, shot for cowardice. You'd disgrace your whole family if you did. Your father wouldn't be able to hold his head up at work. Your mother couldn't show her face at the vegetable market any more. Your little sister would never find a husband—or, maybe worse, she'd marry a latrine cleaner.

All that went through Fujita's head in less than a heartbeat. And so, instead of asking questions, he scrambled out of his hole, shouted, "My squad—advance!" and ran forward, clutching his rifle in hands whose palms were wet with fear-sweat.

Into the woods on the far side of the tracks. He wasn't alone. His squad—and the rest of the company—went in there with him. That made things a little easier. He didn't know whether misery loved company, but it *needed* company.

Were there Russians in the woods? Of course there were. There always were. Their damned machine guns started yammering right away. Cleverly hidden soldiers would let you run past, then shoot you in the back. They died after that, of course, but they didn't seem to care. They were so indifferent to death, Fujita wondered if they were human.

He got a flash of something moving, bounding away from the racket of combat as fast as it could. He started to bring his Arisaka up to his shoulder, then checked the motion, his jaw dropping in awe. "Damned if there aren't," he said softly.

"Aren't what, Sergeant?" asked a soldier at his elbow.

His cheeks heated; he hadn't meant to be overheard. "*Tora,*" he answered. "That was a tiger over there." He pointed. "I've seen a tiger, a live tiger."

"You should have killed it," the other soldier said. "That'd be a hell of a souvenir. A tiger's skin? I hope so! I wish I'd seen it." He sounded jealous and wistful.

But Fujita shook his head. "It was too beautiful. I couldn't." He'd seen too much of war, here and in Mongolia. War was ugly, the ugliest thing there was. And war, he was certain, had nothing to do with tigers.

"HELLO, PEGGY! How are you?" The receptionist at the U.S. embassy in Berlin greeted Peggy Druce with an all-American smile and a harsh Midwestern accent that would have set her teeth on edge back in the States but sounded heavenly here at the heart of the Third *Reich.*

"Hello, Lucinda. How's your daughter these days?" Peggy had been stuck in Berlin so long, she was on a first-name basis with everybody at the embassy and knew everybody's problems.

Lucinda's smile got wider. "She's much better, thanks. Those new pills, those waddayacallems, sulfas, fixed her up like magic—I just got a letter from her. *And* her husband finally has a job. He's riveting in an airplane factory that opened up a coupla miles from where they live."

"That does sound good," Peggy said. An airplane factory opening up in Omaha?—she thought it was Omaha. That sounded strange. Maybe FDR had decided the United States did need to be ready for trouble, just in case. Maybe he'd persuaded Congress that that might be a pretty decent idea. Having met war face-to-face, Peggy thought you had to be a jackass not to see it was a good idea. But when you were talking about Congressmen . . .

Lucinda continued, "And Mr. Jenkins is waiting for you. Go right on upstairs to his office." She chuckled. "Maybe you won't come around here all the time in a while. Maybe you'll be on your way home."

"Home." It sounded like a dream to Peggy—a receding dream, one she couldn't remember so well as she wished she could. She headed for the stairs, trying to drum up optimism inside herself, to believe she wasn't just going through the motions one more time. It wasn't easy. Nothing had been easy since German shells started falling on Marianske Lazne.

CONSTANTINE JENKINS—UNDERSECRETARY: gold-filled Roman-looking letters on a black nameplate on a door. At the moment, it was a closed door. Peggy fumed. It shouldn't have been. She was right on time, and Lucinda had said the undersecretary was ready. Peggy'd always been one to grab the bull by the horns. She knocked briskly.

The door opened. Constantine Jenkins looked out at her: mid-thirties, tall, thin, pale, almost handsome "Oh, yes," he said, his voice low and well-mannered. If he wasn't a queer, Peggy'd never seen one. "Give me five minutes, please. Something's come up."

Those five minutes stretched to fifteen. Peggy was ready to snarl, maybe to bite. Then the door opened again. Out came a short, trim, graying man with four gold stripes on the sleeves of his uniform. The naval attaché gave her a brusque nod and a murmured "Sorry about that," then hurried down the corridor.

"Come on in," Jenkins said.

Still a little irked—maybe more than a little—Peggy went on in. "What was that all about?" she snapped.

"Business I had to take care of," he answered, which told her exactly nothing. He held out a package of Chesterfields—they came from the States through Sweden and Switzerland, in diplomatic pouches. "Cigarette?"

"Oh, God, yes!" If anything could fix Peggy's mood in a hurry, real tobacco could. What you were able to buy in Germany got lousier by the day. She let him light the coffin nail for her—he had exquisite manners. Smooth, flavorful smoke filled her lungs. "Wow!" she said. "You put up with Junos for a while, you forget what the real stuff is like. And Junos are pretty good, at least next to the other German brands."

"So I've heard," he said coolly. With those diplomatic pouches, he didn't have to pollute his lungs with German tobacco, or whatever it was. After he got a Chesterfield of his own going, he asked, "What can I do for you today?"

"Tell me how to get to Stockholm or Geneva or Lisbon or anywhere else that'll let me get back to America," Peggy answered.

He sighed out smoke. "I'm sorry. I wish I could. Believe me, you aren't the only American who wants to be somewhere else." He paused. "I wouldn't recommend Lisbon, not when you have to cross Spain to get there."

"Okay. The hell with Lisbon. How about Copenhagen? Oslo? Athens, even, for crying out loud? Jesus, I'd take Belgrade right now. Anywhere but here!" Peggy said.

Jenkins spread well-manicured hands. "Difficult to arrange for anyone. More difficult for you, because you haven't so much as tried to hide how you feel about the Nazis."

"Wouldn't that make them want to get rid of me?" she demanded.

"Not when they fear what you'll say once you get to a neutral country," the undersecretary replied.

Peggy took a last angry puff on the Chesterfield and stubbed it out in a glass ashtray on Jenkins' desk. German officials had told her the same thing. She'd made them all kinds of promises. They hadn't believed her. Maybe they weren't so dumb as she wished they were.

"As it happens," Jenkins said, "I have two tickets for the opera tonight. My, ah, friend has come down sick. Would you care to go with me?"

She looked at him in surprise. Maybe he wasn't so queer as all that. No—she would have bet dollars to acorns his "friend" was a pointer, not a setter. And he was at least ten years younger than she was, probably fifteen. He couldn't be after getting her into bed. Even if he was, she was sure she could take care of herself. "Thanks!" she said. "Thanks very much. I *would* like that."

"Good enough," he said. "I'll come by your hotel about six, then. We can get some supper before the performance. It's Wagner."

"Surprise!" Peggy said. They both chuckled. Wagner was Hitler's favorite, of course. And what point to being *Führer* if you couldn't get your favorites up on stage? Hitler could, and he did.

Only after Peggy left the embassy did she realize the opera invitation had also let Constantine Jenkins get her out of his hair much faster than he would have otherwise. He might be a fairy, but he knew something about diplomacy.

She put on a blue silk gown that did nice things for her figure and played up her eyes. It was the fanciest one she had with her, which meant it was also the one she'd worn least. Jenkins showed up in the lobby at a quarter to six, looking dashing in black tie. Not even the blandness of a German dinner took the edge off things. Peggy drank schnapps to make sure nothing would. She was pleasantly buzzed when they walked over to the Staatsoper.

Berlin lay almost as far north as Edmonton, Alberta. You didn't think about that most of the time, but you did when you saw how long light lingered as spring neared summer. Even so, it would be dark when they came out. Getting back in the blackout might not be much fun.

The tickets were for the front row of the first balcony. Peggy peered down into the orchestra section as Nazi big wigs and their ladies took their seats. Jenkins handed her chromed opera glasses. "Goebbels and Göring are here," he said. "I don't see the *Führer* tonight."

Peggy wasn't disappointed. She did wonder about security. If someone up here pulled out a submachine gun instead of opera glasses . . . But nobody did.

Then the lights dimmed. The opera was *Tannhäuser*. It was early Wagner. It had raised a sensation when it was new, but it hadn't been new for a long time. It didn't beat you over the head with rocks, the way the later stuff did. So Peggy would have said, anyhow. A real Wagner lover might have had a different opinion—as if she cared.

She poured down champagne during intermission. That let her applaud more than she would have otherwise when the performance ended. The singers aimed their bows at the Party *Bonzen*, not the galleries. They knew who buttered their bread—not that anybody in Germany saw much butter these days.

"So how are we going to find the hotel?" she asked as she and Constantine Jenkins walked out into pitch blackness. Some Germans wore lapel buttons coated with phosphorescent paint so people wouldn't bump into them in the dark. She wished she had one.

"Here." Jenkins also went without. He took her hand, finding it unerringly despite the lack of light. "Stick with me. I'll get you home."

Damned if he didn't. Maybe he was part cat, to see in the dark, or part bloodhound, to sniff his way back. Getting back to the hotel so easily seemed worth celebrating with a drink in the bar. One drink in the bar became two. Two became several. When Peggy went up to the room at last, it seemed the most natural thing in the world that he should go up with her. He was a good deal steadier on his feet than she was on hers.

And when she woke up the next morning with him beside her smiling, she wondered what the hell she'd gone and done. She didn't wonder long, not when all she had on was her birthday suit. She sure wondered what she'd do next, though.

Chapter 7

Down roared the Stuka. The sirens in the landing-gear legs screamed. French troops scattered. Hans-Ulrich Rudel saw them through a red haze of acceleration, but see them he did. His thumb came down on the firing button. The forward machine gun hammered. A few of the running Frenchmen fell.

Some of the *poilus* had nerve. They stood there and fired at the Ju-87 as it roared by only a couple of hundred meters over their heads. You couldn't mistake muzzle flashes for anything else. Most of the time, they missed. The Stuka went mighty fast, and they wouldn't lead it enough. But all those bullets in the air were dangerous. Ground fire had brought down airplanes—not often, but it had.

Not today. Not this Stuka. It climbed again as Hans-Ulrich yanked back on the stick. "See any fighters?" he asked Albert Dieselhorst.

"None of ours," answered the noncom in the rear-facing seat. A moment later, he added, "None of theirs, either."

Theirs were the ones Hans-Ulrich worried about. Stukas were marvelous for shooting up and bombing enemy ground targets. When it came to air-to-air combat, they were too slow to run and too clumsy to dodge. A lot of good men had died before the *Luftwaffe* decided to admit that.

Although Hans-Ulrich had already been shot down once, he didn't intend to die like that. Unlike plenty of other cocky, cock-proud pilots, he didn't intend to be stabbed by a cuckolded husband, either. He aimed to have grandchildren and great-grandchildren gathered around his bed, so he could tell them something interesting and memorable as he went. He was a minister's son, all right.

He saw French panzers moving toward Clermont. He reported them by radio—that was all he could do. A Stuka had to score a direct hit with a bomb to harm a panzer, and a direct hit on a moving target was easier imagined than done.

On the way back to his airstrip, German flak opened up on him. He was tempted to strafe the idiots who'd started shooting. A Ju-87 was about the most recognizable plane in the world, for God's sake! Speaking of good men, how many were dead because their own friends murdered them? Too damned many—he knew that.

Even through the speaking tube, Sergeant Dieselhorst's voice sounded savage: "You ought to go back there and shoot those bastards up!"

"I thought about it," Rudel answered, "but at least they missed."

"That just makes them incompetent bastards," Dieselhorst said.

"Would you rather they'd shot us down?" Hans-Ulrich asked. Dieselhorst didn't answer, which was probably a good thing.

The landing wasn't smooth, but a Stuka was built to take it. Rudel went into Colonel Steinbrenner's tent to report. "We got your news about the panzers," Steinbrenner said. "Good job. The ground forces are doing what they can to stop the froggies."

"*Danke,* sir," Hans-Ulrich said. "Stuka pilots ought to be able to do more about panzers from the air. We're fine against soft-skinned vehicles, but armor . . . ?" He spread his hands, palms up, as if to say it was hopeless.

"I don't know what to tell you," the wing commander replied. "Machine guns aren't heavy enough, and you have to be lucky with bombs. You'd need to mount a cannon or something to do yourself any good."

By the way he said it, the idea was impossible. The more Rudel thought, the more he figured it wasn't. "You know, sir, we could do that," he said, excitement kindling in his voice. "You could mount a 37mm gun under each wing instead of the bomb that usually goes there. You'd need a magazine for the ammo instead of loading it round by round, and you'd want to use electrical firing, not contact fuses from the ground artillery. Once you had those, a Stuka would turn into a panzerbuster like nothing anybody's ever seen."

"You're serious," Steinbrenner said slowly, staring across the table with folding legs that did duty as his desk.

"Damn right I am, uh, sir." When Hans-Ulrich swore, he was very serious indeed. "I'd like to talk to the engineers and the armorers, see what they think of the idea."

"What if they say no?" the wing commander asked.

Hans-Ulrich only shrugged. "How am I worse off?"

Colonel Steinbrenner blinked, then started to laugh. "Well, you've got me there. Go ahead—talk to them. See what happens. Maybe they'll come up with something. Or maybe they'll tell you you're out of your tree. Who knows?"

Head full of his grand new idea, Rudel hurried away. The first person he talked to was Sergeant Dieselhorst. The rear gunner and radioman rubbed his chin. "That'd be a nice trick if they can do it," he said. "Can they?"

"I don't know," Hans-Ulrich said. "I sure want to find out, though."

He interrupted the armorers' skat game. They heard him out, then looked at one another. "That just might work," one of them said when he finished. "Mount the breech in a sheet-metal pod so it's more aerodynamic . . ."

That hadn't even occurred to Hans-Ulrich. "Wonderful!" he exclaimed. "Could you fellows rig up a gun like that?"

They looked at one another again. The fellow who'd spoken before—his name was Lothar—said, "Well, sir, that's not gonna be so easy. We're *Luftwaffe* guys, you know? How do we get our hands on a couple of infantry cannon?"

"Oh." That hadn't occurred to Hans-Ulrich, either. He wondered why not. Probably because he was so hot for the idea, he ignored problems. Other people didn't, though. He supposed that was good. Well, most of him did. Every once in a while, you wanted things to be easy.

"Talk to the engineers, sir," Lothar said. "They've got more pull than we do. If anybody can get hold of that kind of shit—uh, stuff—they're the guys."

So Rudel talked to the engineers. They visited forward airstrips every so often: they wanted to find out how the Stukas were doing in combat so they could get ideas for improving the planes the factories would turn out next month or next year. (A few weeks earlier, Hans-Ulrich wouldn't have believed that the war could still be going on next year. Now, however much he regretted it, he realized anything was possible.)

They heard him out. When he started, they listened with glazed eyes and fixed smiles, the way an adult might listen to an eight-year-old talking about how he intended to fly to the moon on an eagle's back. But he watched them come to life as he talked. When he finished, one of them said, "I will be damned. We could probably do that. And it sounds like it'd work if we did."

"It does," another engineer said. He might have been announcing miracles.

"You don't need to sound so surprised," Hans-Ulrich said sharply.

"Lieutenant, we hear schemes like this wherever we go. Well, not like this, but schemes." The second engineer corrected himself. "Most of them are crap, nothing else but. Somebody has a harebrained notion, and he doesn't see it's harebrained 'cause he's harebrained himself. And so he tries to ram it down our throats."

"And he gets pissed off when we tell him all the reasons it won't work," the first engineer added. "I mean really pissed off. A rear gunner took a swing at me when I told him we couldn't give a Stuka an electronic rangefinder—they're too big and too heavy for an airplane to carry. One of these days, maybe, but not yet."

"An electronic rangefinder?" Hans-Ulrich asked, intrigued in spite of himself.

"You don't know about those?" the engineer said. Rudel shook his head. The man looked—relieved? "In that case, forget I said anything. The fewer people who do know, the better."

Hans-Ulrich started to complain, then decided not to. Plenty of projects were secret. If the Frenchmen shot up his plane the next time he went out, and they made him bail out and captured him, the less he could tell them, the better off the *Reich* would be. The engineer was dead right about that. Hans-Ulrich did say, "But you think my idea *is* practical?"

"Hell with me if I don't," the man answered. Hans-Ulrich frowned; he didn't like other people's casual profanity. The engineer didn't care what he thought. The fellow went on, "The ammunition may get a little interesting, but that's the only hitch I see."

"We could adapt the firing mechanism from the 109's 20mm cannon," his colleague said.

"Hmm. Maybe we could," the other man said. Their technical colloquy made as little sense to Hans-Ulrich as if they'd suddenly started spouting Hindustani. But he understood the key point. They thought the panzer-busting gun would work, and they thought it was worth working on. He wondered how long they would need to come up with a prototype.

And he wondered if they would let him try it out.

"COME ON, damn you." Joaquin Delgadillo gestured with his rifle. "Get moving. If you were just a stinking Spanish traitor, by God, I'd shoot you right here."

The International sitting in the dirt glared at him. *He* wouldn't hold a rifle any time soon; a bullet had smashed his right hand. Blood soaked into the dirty bandage covering the wound. "What will you do to me instead?" he asked. Some kind of thick Central European accent clotted his Castilian. It wasn't German. Joaquin had heard German accents often enough to recognize them. But he couldn't have told a Czech from a Hungarian or a Pole.

"They'll want to question you," he answered.

"To torture me, you mean," the Red said.

Delgadillo shrugged. "Not my problem. If you don't start walking right now, I *will* shoot you. And I'll laugh at you while you die, too."

"Your leaders are fooling you. No matter what you think you're fighting for, you won't get it if that fat slob of a Sanjurjo wins," the International said. "All you'll get is—uh, are—tyranny and misery."

He came very close to dying then. Joaquin nearly shot him; the main thing that kept him from pulling the trigger was the thought that the Red's smashed hand made a good start on torture by itself. The interrogators could just knock it around a little, and the International would sing like a little yellow bird from the Canaries.

If the fellow hadn't got up when Delgadillo jerked the rifle again, he would have plugged him, and that would have been that. But the International did. He stumbled off toward the Nationalists' rear, Joaquin close enough behind him to fire if he tried anything cute. A wounded right hand? So what? He might be a lefty. You never could tell, especially with the Reds.

A bullet cracked past, a couple of meters over their heads. They both bent their knees to get farther away from it. "So you genuflect in that church, do you?" Joaquin said.

"Not many who don't," the International answered. "I want to live. Go ahead—call me a fool."

"If you wanted to live, you should have stayed away from Spain," Joaquin said. "This isn't your fight."

"Freedom is everybody's fight, or it ought to be," the Central European said. "If you don't have freedom, what are you? The *jefe's* donkey, that's what, with a load on your back and somebody walking beside you beating you with a stick."

That scream in the air was no ordinary bullet. "*¡Abajo!*" Delgadillo yelled as he hit the dirt.

The International flattened out, too. He yowled like a wildcat when he banged the wounded hand, but he didn't pop up again, the way a lot of men would have. The shell—it had to be a 155—burst less than a hundred meters away. Fragments whined viciously overhead. The Nationalists weren't going to take Madrid away from the Republic, not like this they weren't. In fact, the Republicans and their foreign friends had pushed Marshal Sanjurjo's men out of the university at the northwestern edge of town. It was embarrassing, to say nothing of infuriating.

Which only made the International luckier still that Joaquin hadn't shot him out of hand. Sergeant Carrasquel would have told him he was wasteful if he had. That was another good reason to hold back. No one in his right mind wanted a sergeant giving him a hard time.

When no more shells fell in the neighborhood, Joaquin cautiously rose. "Get up!" he snapped.

"What else am I going to do?" The Red pushed himself upright, using his left hand and both feet. Joaquin made him open the good hand—he might have hidden a rock in there. He might have, but he hadn't. A more clever man might have felt foolish at seeing that dirty palm. Delgadillo. didn't. Just one more chance he hadn't taken. You had to take too many any which way. Avoiding the ones you could made you more likely to live longer.

"Well, well! What have we here, sweetheart?" That was Major Uribe. That, in fact, couldn't very well have been anybody else. Uribe had been closer to where the 155 went off than Joaquin or his prisoner. Not a smudge, a stain, or a rumpled crease on his uniform suggested that he'd dove for cover. If he hadn't, wouldn't he be *ropa vieja* right now? (Even thinking of the stew of shredded beef—literally, old clothes—made Joaquin's stomach growl.) Maybe not. He had to be lucky as well as brave, or he would have died long since.

The International stared at him as if he couldn't believe his eyes. Chances were he couldn't. What were the odds of finding not just a faggot but an obvious—no, a flaming—faggot among the Nationalists' officers? Marshal Sanjurjo's whole campaign was about running such riffraff out of Spain, wasn't it? Of course it was—everybody on both sides knew that. But it was about running Reds out of Spain, too. Bernardo Uribe might want to stick it all kinds of places the priests didn't approve of (not that the priests didn't stick it into places like that, too), but he really and truly hated the Reds. Joaquin understood that, having seen him in action. The prisoner hadn't, and didn't.

"Yeah. What *have* we here, sweetheart?" With that miserable, ugly accent and a deep, rasping voice, the International couldn't coo the way Major Uribe did, but he gave it his best—or maybe his worst—shot.

Joaquin could have told him twitting the major wasn't the smartest thing to do. He could have, but he never got the chance. Uribe didn't even blink. He didn't waste a moment, either. "I'll show you what we have here, darling," he said, and drew his pistol. Raising it, he shot the captive in the face.

Red mist blew out of the back of the man's head. He fell over and scrabbled in the dirt. Uribe watched for a few seconds, then set the pistol by the International's ear and pulled the trigger again. The scrabbling stopped.

"*That's* what we have here, asshole," Uribe said, holstering the pistol once more.

"*¡Madre de Dios!*" Joaquin crossed himself. "Begging your pardon, sir, but I was taking him back for questioning."

"*¡Ai! ¡Qué lastima!*" Major Uribe exclaimed. And it *was* a pity—for the International, whose blood still soaked into the thirsty ground. "The One Who questions him now already knows all the answers. And when He gets through with this fellow—it won't take long—the fucker will wish what I did to him was all he got. But he'll have worse, for all eternity."

"Er—yes." Delgadillo also believed in hell. The Bible talked about it, so it had to be true. And he believed Internationals were bound to go there. All the same, he hadn't intended to give Satan this one right then. "I, uh, thought we ought to find out what he knew, *Señor.*"

Uribe flipped his hand, a gesture that magnificently mingled effeminacy and scorn. "I'll tell you what he didn't know, Joaquin: he didn't know how to keep a civil tongue in his head. And I'll tell you something else he didn't know, too: God forgives what you do in bed. He must, or He wouldn't have made it possible to do those things."

"Er," Joaquin said again. Something more seemed called for. "Yes, sir" seemed safe enough, so he tried that. How many priests would have apoplexy if they heard Major Uribe's doctrine? All of them, probably, clear on up to the Holy Father in Rome. If he told Uribe that . . . He tried not to shiver. He might end up lying in the dirt next to the dead International.

"Don't trouble your head about it, my dear," Uribe said. "Go back up and kill some more of these Communist monkeys. That's all you need to worry about."

"Yes, sir," Joaquin repeated, and he got out of there in a hurry. He'd often been more afraid of Sergeant Carrasquel than he was of the enemy. But Carrasquel would shoot him only if he tried to run away or something like that. The major might do it for the fun of watching him die. If that wasn't a bulge in Uribe's breeches, Joaquin had never seen one.

The Internationals might shoot him, too. He knew that. They'd come too close too often. But it was business for them, not sport. Killing for sport . . . He'd never been so glad to hurry to the front. Anything, as long as it got him away from Major Uribe.

"YOU! Dernen! What the hell do you think you're doing?" Arno Baatz shouted.

"Just working on my foxhole, Corporal," Willi replied. Maybe a soft answer would turn away wrath. If Awful Arno was on the rag—and he sure sounded that way—the odds were against it, though.

Sure as hell, he thought one lousy pip on each shoulder strap made him a little tin god. "Well, cut that crap out and do something useful instead," he snarled. "Go chop up some firewood."

Willi didn't think fixing up his hole so he was less likely to get killed—and so he could sleep without getting all muddy—was crap. Saying as much would only piss Corporal Baatz off worse than ever, if such a thing was possible. They did need firewood; Willi happened to know that. He didn't know how he'd drawn the short straw for chopping it, but that was just Baatz moving in mysterious ways, his wonders to perform.

"Right, Corporal," Willi said resignedly, and scrambled out of the foxhole. He had some wood in there, shoring up what would be his sleeping compartment. He kept his mouth shut about it, for fear Awful Arno would tell him to rip it out.

The Frenchies had left a lot of lumber behind when most of them cleared out of this village. Willi didn't particularly blame them for bailing. If his own small home town had got shelled and bombed first by one side and then by the other, he would have wanted to get the hell out of there, too.

They'd also left behind a really lovely axe: light, well balanced, sharp. It almost made chopping wood seem more sport than work. Almost. Imagining that fine steel edge coming down on Baatz's neck instead of blond oak livened up the job, too.

Awful Arno came by after a while to check on how Willi was doing. He eyed the pile of firewood, grunted, and went away again. From him, that was the equivalent of awarding the Knight's Cross with Oak Leaves, Swords, and Diamonds. If Baatz couldn't find anything to piss and moan about, there was nothing to find.

Quitting now, though, would only bring him back and give him the excuse he wanted to come down on Willi. Willi knew as much. He kept chopping for another twenty minutes. By then, the squad had enough wood for the next six months. It did if you listened to him tell it afterwards, anyhow.

He marveled that his palms weren't blistered when he did set down the axe. Part of that was the smooth, fine helve. And part of it was the thick calluses he'd acquired. Sure as the devil, soldiering toughened you up.

It also turned you into an accomplished thief. As soon as he got done, he started going through the houses in the village. Yeah, they'd already been picked over, but you never could tell what you'd find if you poked around a little. Some canned salmon, a little flask of what smelled like applejack, 250 francs somebody'd forgotten when he got out of town . . . A good scrounger could come up with all kinds of things other people had missed.

He'd share the salmon and the firewater. You didn't want to get greedy with stuff like that. Your buddies wouldn't stay buddies if you did. The French money went into a tunic pocket. You never could tell when that might come in handy. He came out into the late-afternoon sunshine, more than a little pleased with himself.

He came out into that sunshine at the exact moment a black Mercedes about as long as a light cruiser rumbled into the village. Two enormous men in black uniforms jumped out. Willi had been thinking soldiering toughened you. He might be tough, but he wouldn't have wanted to mess with either one of these SS behemoths. Something in the planes and angles of their faces said they not only knew all the dirty tricks but got off on them.

"You!" one of them rumbled, raising a hand roughly the size of a ham and pointing at him. "Come here!"

"What do you want?" Willi didn't move.

"To ask you some questions," the SS man said. "If you're lucky, we won't ask about your name or your pay number. Now get over here!"

Goddamn asphalt soldiers, Willi thought. The SS looked marvelous on parade. In the field . . . That was the *Wehrmacht*'s place. But the bastards with the runes on their collars were Hitler's fair-haired boys. Willi ambled over to this pair. If he didn't, they could make him disappear, and nobody would ever know where he'd gone. "Well, what is it?" he said. "You boys better watch yourselves around here, you know? French guns can reach this far, easy."

The big goons traded glances. But nobody was shooting at them right this minute. They could seem brave, even to themselves. One pulled out a notebook and flipped it open. "Do you know a certain, ah, Wolfgang Storch?" he asked, and rattled off Storch's pay number.

"Name sounds kind of familiar." Willi stopped right there. He'd see the SS men in hell before he ratted on a friend. Wolfgang and he had saved each other's bacon more times than he could count. They'd shared cigarettes and socks. They'd sworn at Awful Arno together. Would these clowns understand any of that? Not a chance in church. Willi eyed them. "How come you want to know?"

"We don't have to tell you that," said the goon with the notebook.

The other one tried to be subtle. He wasn't very good at it: "Have you ever heard this Storch make comments that reflect unfavorably on our beloved *Führer* or the National Socialist German Workers' Party?"

"Nope," Willi said at once. Everybody in the field always swore at the idiot politicians who'd put them in danger of getting their heads blown off. Would the SS men get *that*? Again, not a chance. *Nope* was safer.

Or so Willi thought, till the blackshirt with the notebook said, "If we can show that you are lying, the two of you will be judged guilty of conspiring against the *Reich*."

No talk of trials or anything like that. Just *You will be judged guilty*. And what would happen afterwards? Nothing good. Willi didn't need a road map or a compass to figure that out.

"You said it yourselves—everybody loves the *Führer*," Willi said. "Nobody has anything bad to say about him." Nobody did where somebody who might blab could hear, anyway. But if the SS men really believed all the Party bullshit, they might think Willi meant it.

By the way their faces hardened, he'd laid it on too thick. The one with the notebook said, "We have reliable reports that this Storch has delivered disloyal utterances on repeated occasions." He could talk that way without even realizing what a jackass he sounded like.

"Well, I never heard him do it," Willi said.

They didn't believe him. He could see it in their pale, merciless eyes. That meant his goose was cooked, too. Then he caught a break. French artillery really did open up on the village. Willi'd never dreamt he could be glad to get shelled, but he was now.

"Hit the dirt!" he yelled, and flattened out himself.

Because the SS men were greenhorns, they stayed on their feet longer than they should have. When shells started bursting and fragments screeched past, they got the message. "Hail, Mary, full of grace!" one of them gabbled as he got down. Whoever'd said there were no atheists in foxholes had a pretty good idea of what he was talking about.

Willi didn't like getting up in the middle of a barrage, but he didn't like getting hauled off to Dachau, either. He hurried toward the last place where he'd seen Wolfgang: a trench fifty meters or so south of where the houses petered out. Behind him, a 105 round turned the blackshirts' Mercedes into burning scrap metal. He laughed out loud.

"Where are you going?" one of the SS men called after him.

"To fight. You wouldn't know about that, would you?" he answered. And he even meant it. The froggies were liable to follow up the shelling with an attack. But he also had other things on his mind.

To his vast relief, he found Wolfgang right away and jumped into the trench beside him. "You trying to get yourself killed?" Storch asked.

"No. I'm trying not to get *you* killed. The SS wants your ass," Willi said. "I always told you you talked too goddamn much."

"Who squealed?" Wolfgang got right down to brass tacks.

"They didn't say, but my money's on Baatz. Doesn't matter now. Get the fuck out of here. Go across the line and surrender to the Frenchies. You can sit out the rest of the war in a POW camp."

"They're liable to shoot me if I do," Wolfgang said. Surrendering was always tricky. If the guys on the other side didn't like your looks or couldn't be bothered with you, you were dead meat.

"You've got a chance that way," Willi answered. "What kind of chance do you have with the blackshirts?"

Storch's unhappy expression told exactly what kind of chance he had. He pumped Willi's hand. "You're a good guy. Wish me luck." He scrambled out of the trench and crawled toward the enemy positions a few hundred meters away.

"Luck," Willi whispered. Most of the French shells were long. If Wolfgang really got lucky, they'd blow up the SS goons. Even as the thought crossed Willi's mind, he feared it was too much to hope for.

VACLAV JEZEK CAUTIOUSLY LIFTED his head. There was less to see than he'd hoped: the dust and smoke the bombardment had already kicked up obscured his view of later shell hits on the Nazi-held village. He ducked down again. "They're knocking the shit out of that place," he remarked.

"And so?" Benjamin Halévy didn't sound impressed. "Not like the German *mamzrim* don't have it coming."

A Czech fighting for his government-in-exile after the Nazis jumped on his country with both feet. A Jew fighting the regime that had been giving his people hell ever since it came to power. Who hated harder? They could argue about it. They did. They both despised the enemy enough for all ordinary purposes and then some.

Which didn't mean they didn't respect the soldiers in *Feldgrau*. Fierce in attack, the Germans were also stubborn in defense. They would have been less frightening if they weren't so good at what they did.

Vaclav popped up again. This time, he laid his antitank rifle on the dirt thrown up in front of the entrenchment. He didn't see any panzers, but the monster rifle made mincemeat—sometimes literally—of foot soldiers, too. "What's up?" Halévy asked him.

"Goddamn German crawling this way," Jezek answered. "I'm gonna ventilate the asshole." He took another quick look, then swore. The enemy soldier had disappeared behind a burnt-out armored car. No, here he came again. Vaclav swung the heavy rifle a hair to the right.

"Is it a real attack, or only the one guy?" the Jewish sergeant inquired. He raised his head, too. "I only see the one."

"Where you see one, there's usually a dozen you don't," Vaclav said. But he didn't pull the trigger. "This fucker isn't doing his best to hide, is he?"

"Nope. Maybe he's had enough of the war," Halévy said.

"I know I have. But he's a damn German," Vaclav said. Easier to think of the *Landsers* as mechanical men. You could break them, yes, but imagining them with mere human weaknesses came much harder.

It did for Vaclav, anyhow. But Halévy said, "Oh, they're people. They wouldn't be so scary if they weren't." The Czech wasn't sure of that: not even close. No matter whether he was or not, the Jew stuck his head above the trench lip again and yelled in German (which Vaclav hadn't known he spoke), "Throw away your rifle and get your sorry ass over here! You're vultures' meat if you don't!"

When Vaclav looked out, too, he saw that the *Landser* had tossed aside his Mauser. The fellow got to his feet and trotted toward the French trenches, his hands high and a shamed, kicked-dog grin on his face. "*Ja, komm! Mach schnell!*" Vaclav shouted. Talking to an enemy soldier the way he would to a waiter in a beer garden—or to a child or an animal—felt good.

The German made it snappy, all right. "I'm coming, I'm coming!" he said, as if he feared a bullet in the back. Maybe he did—and maybe he needed to. He let out what might have been a stifled sob as he jumped down into the trench. To make sure he didn't do anything stupid, Vaclav pointed the antitank rifle at his midsection. "Jesus!" the *Landser* yipped. "You shoot me with that thing, you can bury me in a coffee can afterwards."

"That's the idea," Halévy said from behind him. The Jew relieved him of the bayonet and potato-masher grenades on his belt, then added, "If you've got a holdout knife, hand it over. We find it on you, you'll never known what Red Cross food packages taste like." Slowly and carefully, the guy in field-gray pulled a slim blade from his left boot. Halévy took it. "That's all?"

"*Ja,*" the German said. "My name is Wolfgang Storch. I'm a private." He rattled off his pay number. "That's as much as I've got to say to you, right?"

"If you know anything that matters, pal, you'll spill it." Vaclav made the rifle twitch. It would have started twitching soon anyhow; the damn thing was heavy. "The French don't like you bastards much better than I do."

Storch seemed to notice the smooth lines of his domed helmet for the first time. "Oh. A Czech," he said. Then he took a longer look at Benjamin Halévy. He didn't need long to work out what Halévy was, either. "And—" He stopped, gulping.

"Yeah. And," Halévy agreed grimly. "Why don't you start by telling us what the hell you're doing here?"

"Damn blackshirts were going to grab me, that's what," the German answered. "A buddy of mine tipped me off. We figured maybe you guys wouldn't shoot me." He licked his lips. He still wasn't sure about that.

"Why would the SS want you?" Vaclav asked.

Storch shrugged. "I talk too much. Everybody says so. I must've said something dumb where some cocksucker heard me and squealed. There's this one corporal who's the biggest asshole in the world. Chances are it was him." His hands—dirty, scarred, broken-nailed, callused, just like Vaclav's—folded into fists.

"What d'you think?" Jezek asked Halévy in Czech.

"It could be," the Jew answered in the same tongue. Storch's eyes said he didn't follow it. Halévy went on, "Not our worry either way. We just have to deliver him and let the fellows behind the line put the pieces together."

"Fair enough." Vaclav went back to German: "All right, Storch—we'll take you back. First things first, though. Cough up your cash, and your watch if you've got one."

"I do. Here." The *Landser* was fumblingly eager to hand it over. Vaclav had seen that before. New prisoners figured they'd get killed if they didn't let themselves be robbed. They were usually right, too. Storch also emptied out his wallet. He thrust bills at the Czech. "This is all the money I've got."

Most of it was in Reichsmarks, which were too scratchy even to make good asswipes. But he also had some francs. Then Halévy patted him down and took another wad of bills from a tunic pocket. "Nice try," the Jew said dryly.

"I—I'm sorry," Storch stammered.

"Tell me another one," Halévy answered. If he'd plugged the German for holding out, Vaclav wouldn't have said boo. But he only gestured with his rifle. "Get it in gear. If your little friends don't shell us on the way back, you're a POW."

Vaclav slung the antitank rifle as they headed away from the front. That was easier than lugging it in his arms—not easy, but easier. The gun could do all kinds of things an ordinary rifle couldn't, but it weighed a tonne.

A couple of *poilus* eyed the procession as they zigzagged along a communications trench. One of them called a question in French. Halévy answered in the same language. The *poilu* snorted. Halévy switched to German: "He asked where we got you, Storch. I said we won you in a poker game."

"Wouldn't you rather have got fifty pfennigs?" the *Landser* asked. He took Vaclav completely by surprise. The Czech broke up. Damned if a human being *didn't* lurk under the beetling brow of the German *Stahlhelm*.

They eventually found a couple of military policemen who were happy enough to take charge of Wolfgang Storch. They'd be less happy when they found out Vaclav and Halévy had already picked the German clean, but that was their hard luck—and maybe Storch's as well.

"Now—we just have to do that another million times, and we've won .the fucking war," the Jew said as he and Vaclav started up toward the front-line trenches again.

"Should be easy," Jezek answered. He was damned if he'd let anybody outtry him.

Chapter 8

Airplane engines droned overhead. Chaim Weinberg looked up warily, ready to dive for cover if bombs started falling. The Condor Legion, the Italians, and Marshal Sanjurjo's Spanish pilots had already given Madrid a big dose of what Paris was catching now, and what Hitler no doubt wanted to visit on London as well.

But these were Republican planes: obsolescent bombers the French could pass on for use on a less challenging front. Chaim recognized the Fascists' Junkers and Capronis at a glance. The French planes were even uglier. He wouldn't have thought it possible, but there you were.

The Spaniards on the streets knew the bombers belonged to the Republic, too. They waved and blew kisses up toward the sky, though the pilots were too high up to see them. "Kill the traitors!" someone called, and several people clapped their hands.

Mike Carroll's smile had a sour twist. "Hell of a thing to say, isn't it?" he remarked in English. "In a civil war, everybody's a traitor to somebody."

Chaim hadn't thought of it like that. He nodded, but he said, "We aren't traitors. We're just lousy mercenaries—if you believe the Nationalists."

Mike mimed scratching his head and his armpits and the seams of his trousers. "I'm not lousy right now. Don't think I am, anyway."

"Yeah, me neither," Chaim said. Fighting in and around a big city had its advantages. When you weren't actually up there trying to murder the other bastards and to keep them from murdering you, you could come back and clean up and get your clothes baked and sprayed so you wouldn't be verminous . . . for a while.

Bomb blasts thudded off to the northwest. Chaim and the Madrileños on the street grinned at one another. Knowing the other guys were catching it for a change felt mighty good. *Do unto others as they've been doing unto you, only more so.* That might not make it into the Bible any time soon, but it was the Golden Rule of war.

"I'm gonna buy me a beer and celebrate," Mike declared, as if he thought Chaim would try to stop him.

If he did, he was out of his tree. "Sounds good," Chaim said. They didn't have to go more than half a block before they found a bar. About one business in three in Madrid seemed to sell something to help people forget their troubles. Well, people around here had a lot of troubles that needed forgetting.

No one in the dark little dive even blinked when two foreigners in ragged uniforms with rifles on their backs walked in. The skinny little guy behind the bar looked like a wall lizard with a Salvador Dali mustache. He raised one eyebrow a couple of millimeters by way of inquiring what the new patrons wanted.

"*Cerveza,*" Carroll said, doing his damnedest to give it a proper Castilian lisp: ther-VAY-tha.

"*Dos,*" Chaim added. His Spanish was bad, but not so bad that he couldn't get himself a beer with it.

Then the bartender said, "Okay, boys," in clear, American-accented English. As he poured, he went on, "I worked in Chicago for five years. I came back when the war started."

Chaim set coins on the bar. Mike nodded thanks. Chaim bought more often than not. The last thing he wanted was a reputation for being a cheap Jew. When the bartender started to make change, Chaim waved for him not to bother. Earlier in the war, the fellow probably would have given him his money, and a lecture to go with it. Tipping was seen as a leftover of class differences, and beneath a proper proletarian's dignity. That stern puritanism—always stronger in Barcelona than Madrid— had eased off now. The bartender nodded his thanks. He gave them the beers.

The glasses were none too clean. That would have bothered Chaim back in New York City. Not any more. Considering what all he'd eaten and drunk in the field, this was the least of his worries. He did note they were etched with the name of a German lager. That wasn't what they held now: nobody wanted to buy, or could buy, Fascist beer inside Republican territory. Fascists or not, the Germans brewed better than locals dreamt of doing. This tasted like horse piss.

But it was beer. Chaim raised his eye to the barman. "¡Salud!"

"Mud in your eye," the Spaniard said gravely. "If I didn't have to eat, I'd give 'em to you on the house. You're doing my job for me now."

Something in the way he said the last word made Chaim look at him in a different way. "Spent some time at the front, did you?"

"Uh-huh. I'd still be there, only I'm standing on a peg." The bartender shrugged microscopically. "I should count my blessings. I'm still here. Plenty of guys who caught ones that didn't look so bad, they're pushing daisies now."

Mike Carroll put down a couple of pesetas. "Buy yourself one, buddy."

"Thanks." The bartender could smile, most cynically. "I'd be on my ass if I poured down all the ones people buy me. I will this time, though." He poured his own beer. "¡Viva la República!"

"¡Viva!" Chaim and Carroll echoed. Chaim drained his glass. He dug in his pocket for more coins. "Let me have another one."

"Me, too," Mike said. He grabbed Chaim's money before the bartender could and gave it back to him. "I'll buy this time."

"Thanks." Chaim nodded. Fair was fair.

Along with the beers, the barman set out olives and crackers and pork sausage the color of a new copper penny. Chaim eyed the sausage warily. He liked the stuff: what wasn't pork was garlic and peppers. But it didn't like him. Every time he ate it, it gave him the runs. He stuck to the crackers and olives.

Mike started in on the sausage as if he thought they'd outlaw it tomorrow. Maybe his guts were made of stronger stuff than Chaim's. Or maybe he'd spend the next week being sorry. You never could tell.

Two more men walked into the bar. It got quieter than it had when the Americans came in. That made Chaim look around. They weren't Spaniards or even fellow Internationals—they were a pair of genuine Soviet officers, squat and hard-faced. You didn't see them very often any more. The Russian mission in the Republic was smaller than it had been before the bigger European war broke out. Some of the men had gone home to the motherland, while hardly anyone came out to replace them. Maybe getting from Russia to Spain was harder than getting back to Russia from Spain. Or, more likely, the Soviet government just had things to worry about in its own back yard.

These fellows might have been movie actors overplaying their roles. They stomped up to the bar, barely favoring Chaim and Mike with a glance. "You give us whiskey," one of them told the bartender, as if ordering him to assault Nationalist trenches.

"And something to eat," the other one added. Spanish with a Russian accent sounded as weird as German with a Spanish accent, which Chaim had also heard.

He eyed the Soviets. One was an obvious Russian. The other . . . Chaim would have bet they had more than accented Spanish in common. "*Nu*, friend, you understand me when I talk like this?" he asked in Yiddish.

"*Nu*, why shouldn't I?" the Soviet said. Like a lot of Jews Chaim knew, he looked clever—maybe too clever for his own good. "Where are you from?"

"New York. You?"

"Minsk."

"One of my grandmothers came from there. Maybe we're cousins."

"Maybe." The Soviet officer didn't seem impressed. Blood might be thicker than water, but ideology was thicker than blood. Jew or not, the officer knew what mattered to him: "How long have you been here? Where have you fought?"

Mike Carroll, the barman, and the Russian were all watching the two *Yehudim*. Chances were none of them could follow the Yiddish. Hell, they were liable to think it was German. Well, too goddamn bad if they did. "Almost two years," Chaim said, not without pride. "I've been on the Ebro front, and lately down here." He looked a challenge to the Soviet officer. "How about you?"

"Since 1936," the other Jew answered. That trumped Chaim's claim. It also meant the fellow had been here through the purges back home. Maybe that had saved him. Then again, who could say? Some of the Russians had gone back to almost certain arrest—but they'd gone. Soviet discipline, in its own way, was as formidable as the Prussian variety. The Jew went on, "I have fought here, and in the south, and on the Ebro, and now here again."

"And what do you think of it all?" Chaim asked.

"We are still fighting," the other man replied. He raised his glass. "Let us keep fighting!" He said it in Yiddish, and then in his strange Spanish. Everybody drank.

ONE OF THE SS MEN who'd come to grab Wolfgang Storch had taken an ugly leg wound. He was in a military hospital somewhere well behind the line. When he got out, he'd be able to wear a wound badge that would make him the envy of his deskbound friends. Willi Dernen wondered how much he'd care. Sometimes you paid more for things than they were really worth.

The one who was left was named Waldemar Zober. He thought Willi had something to do with Wolfgang's disappearance. He thought so, yes, but he couldn't prove a goddamn thing as long as Willi played dumb.

And Willi did. His old man had called him a goddamn dummy plenty of times. Back in the day, that had pissed Willi off. Now, for the first time, in came in handy. "No, I don't know what happened to him," he told Zober. "For all I know, he took a direct hit, and there wasn't enough of him left to bury. The Frenchies got kind of busy that day, you know."

Zober had the grace to look away. He knew how busy the French had been, all right. But he still suspected Willi. "You went running off to the trenches. Storch was already up there." It made perfect sense to the SS man. Well it might have, too. He only had to connect the dots.

But he didn't know for sure he had connected them. Willi had no intention of telling him. "I ran to the trenches to shoot at the enemy in case he followed up the shelling with an attack. That's what I get paid for, you know—and I don't get paid real well, either."

Waldemar Zober not only had rank—he had those SS runes on his collar tab. They made him Heinrich Himmler's fair-haired boy. They also meant he got more money than a *Wehrmacht* soldier of equivalent rank would have. And, most of the time, he never came unpleasantly close to shells or bullets. Life wasn't fair—not even close.

His lips were uncommonly red. He pushed out the lower one now, like a four-year-old about to throw a tantrum. You could spank a spoiled little brat. Nobody could wallop an SS man, no matter how much he deserved it.

"Interfering with an SS investigation is a crime with severe punishment attached," he growled.

"*Der Herr Jesus!*" Willi burst out. "I've been at the front ever since the fight in the West started. The Frenchies could blow my foot off any old time, same as they did with your buddy. They could blow my *balls* off, for Christ's sake! And you're going on about severe punishment? Give it a rest, why don't you?"

Zober's eyes might have been cut from blue and white glass, like the ones on an expensive mannequin. "You don't know what you're talking about," he said, and absolute assurance filled his voice. "You don't have the faintest idea. A week in our hands, and you'd beg to fight at the front, even in a punishment company."

Willi licked his lips. He knew about those. Officers and men who'd disgraced themselves by running away or otherwise fucking up got handed rifles and thrown in where the fighting was hottest. If they tried to run again, they got shot from behind. If they lived, they redeemed themselves . . . or maybe they just won the chance to put out another fire by smothering it with their bodies.

You're a tough guy when you're working over poor bastards who can't hit back, Willi thought. *How long would you last up here, though? Not long, I bet. If the bad guys didn't get you, somebody on your own side would arrange an "accident."* No one talked about that kind of thing, which didn't mean it didn't happen every once in a while.

You couldn't show thoughts like that, not unless you wanted to find out what camps were like from the inside out. Even if his father had called him a dummy, Willi wasn't that stupid. Wearily, he said, "Look, give it a rest, why don't you? I don't know what happened to Wolfgang, and I wish I did. We were friends. I miss him."

By the glint in Zober's glassy orbs, that was almost a ticket to Dachau all by itself. "He was a criminal. He was an enemy of the *Reich*, and of the *Führer*."

"He fucking *shot* enemies of the *Reich*," Willi answered. "He was a damn good soldier, and one of the best scroungers I've ever known. I'm still here answering your questions on account of him. The only good thing I can say about what happened to him is, he never knew what got him. I should be so lucky."

"If he did not desert to the enemy," Zober said implacably.

Willi stood up. "I know you're in the SS, sir. But if you say that to the soldiers who know Wolfgang, somebody's gonna punch you in the snoot." He walked out without waiting for leave from the blackshirt.

The funny thing was, he was dead right. Yes, Wolfgang *had* deserted. As far as Willi knew, though, he was the only guy on this side of the line who knew it. Anybody who didn't know wouldn't believe it. And anybody who heard it from a prick like Waldemar Zober *would* want to flatten his nose for him.

Only one thing was wrong with walking out on Zober: it didn't get Willi away from his problem. Arno Baatz was also convinced he had something to do with Wolfgang's going missing. Willi couldn't make Awful Arno feel inferior for not being a *Landser*. Baatz was one—maybe not a good soldier, but a soldier even so.

"You two clowns were asshole buddies," the corporal said. "Don't waste my time telling me you weren't, 'cause I know better. When the SS men told you they were looking for him, what would you do but squeal like a little pink piggy?"

"I didn't do anything like that, goddammit." Willi had told the same lie so many times by now, he was starting to believe it himself. He could feel himself getting angry, which was pretty funny when you thought about it. The anger might be ersatz, but it felt the same as the real thing. "All I did was go to the front line when the shelling started." He looked Awful Arno up and down. "I didn't see you there."

"Well, I was," Baatz said, which might have been true and might have been as big a whopper as any of the ones Willi had come out with. The noncom went on, "And sooner or later you'll tell me one I believe."

"Let's go talk to Captain Lammers," Willi said. "Either he'll jug me or he'll tell you to leave me the fuck alone. Either way, I'll be better off than I am listening to your bullshit all the time."

Baatz blinked. *His* eyes were dark, and reminded Willi of a mean dog's. Sometimes you could make a mean dog turn tail if you yelled at it and moved towards it instead of running. Sometimes you'd get bitten, though. Willi waited to see what would happen here. "You . . . want to talk to the captain?" Awful Arno said slowly.

"Bet your ass I do. If it'd get you and that blackshirt out of my hair, I'd talk to the general commanding the division." Willi wondered if he really meant that. Officers with fancy shoulder straps needed to listen to privates' troubles the way they needed getting their headquarters bombed.

But Arno Baatz was also imagining coming face-to-face with a general. By the look plastered across his ugly mug, he wasn't liking it much. He tried to hide that by jeering: "You think the division CO has time for piss-ants like you? Don't make me laugh!"

"The captain will," Willi said. "Let's go find him."

And Captain Lammers would. Awful Arno knew that as well as Willi did. He said something about Willi's mother. Had Willi popped him, they would have visited the captain on the corporal's terms. Willi just stood there. Baatz glowered as fearsomely as he knew how. Willi didn't blink "I've got my eye on you, Dernen," Awful Arno snarled, and he stomped away.

Five minutes later, Willi heard him screaming at some other private for having a dirty rifle. Willi smiled. If you beat up a little kid, he'd turn around and pound on some kid who was smaller yet to make himself feel better. Arno Baatz worked the same way.

Waldemar Zober summoned him one more time. "You'd better watch yourself, Dernen," the blackshirt said. If he'd worn a mustache, he would have twirled it like a villain in an old-time melodrama. "We've got our eye on you."

"Yes, sir," Willi said, in lieu of *We? You and your tapeworm?* But right after that, Zober went off to inflict himself on some other *Wehrmacht* men who were just doing their damnedest to win the war for their country.

Arno Baatz kept assigning Willi latrine duty and the other nastiest fatigues he could find. Then the gods of army luck reached down and tapped Willi on the shoulder. A promotion came through. All of a sudden, he found himself a *Gefreiter*, the lowest of the several grades between private and corporal. He got to wear a pip on his sleeve—not on his shoulder straps, but even so . . . And, as the rank's name implied, he was freed from the fatigue duties ordinary privates got stuck with. Baatz fumed, but he couldn't do anything about it.

One of these days, you son of a bitch, I'll rank you, Willi thought—a new idea, but a mighty tasty one. *See how you like it then. Yeah—just see.*

SERGEANT DEMANGE LOOKED DETERMINED and disgusted at the same time. "We are going to drive the Germans back," he declared. "That's what the officers say, and so that's what we're going to do." He spat out the microscopic butt of his latest Gitane, ground it into the grass under his bootheel, and lit another one.

The soldiers in his section listened: some eagerly, some impassively, some apprehensively. Luc Harcourt counted himself in the last group. He'd seen too much of the *Boches,* in defense and in attack. He was anything but thrilled about giving the blond boys in field-gray another chance to ventilate him. He knew Sergeant Demange felt exactly the same way. He also knew that did both of them exactly no good.

"What if the Germans are winding up to take a punch at us?" a soldier asked. The question was very much on Luc's mind, too, but he didn't come out of it. You couldn't ask such things so easily when you were a corporal. Luc didn't much like the responsibility that came with his small rank, but he accepted it.

Sergeant Demange folded both hands into fists and smacked them into each other. "*That's* what happens then, Louis," he answered. "But the brass doesn't think it'll go like that. They say the Germans have been shipping tanks and shit out of here. They aren't loading up for a punch of their own."

Louis had seen enough to realize the brass didn't know everything there was to know. "What if they're wrong, Sergeant?"

"Well, in that case, we get our nuts crunched. What else?" Demange said. "It happened often enough the last time around. A breakthrough? Of course the next offensive would give us one. Of fucking course. They haven't got a whole hell of a lot smarter since, have they?"

"What can we do, then?" Louis asked—a damn good question.

"When they tell us to go, we go. That's what we can do," Demange answered flatly. "Do anything else and your own side will scrag you. Matter of fact, for you I'll take care of it personally." He paused, his ferret face even fiercer than usual. "Any other stupid questions?"

No one said anything. Louis'd asked the one thing that really needed asking. Only as the knot of soldiers broke up did Luc say, "How hard are we gonna get fucked, Sergeant?"

Demange looked at him. "They won't kiss us—I'll tell you that. If they really have shipped out their tanks . . . Well, shit, what if they have? They'll know which way we're coming, and they'll have an antitank gun with every one of our tanks' names on it. But what can you do?"

Once you put on a uniform—once they drafted you and put a uniform on you—you couldn't do a goddamn thing except what they told you. You figured that out in a hurry. If you had trouble, if you were slow or stubborn, they rubbed your nose in it. Luc understood what was what, all right. "Ah, shit," he said.

"See? You're not so fucking dumb." Demange reached up and thumped him on the shoulder. Luc had to hold himself tight to keep from jumping. Even such rough affection from Demange was far, far out of the ordinary.

French tanks clanked up under cover of darkness. The people with fancy kepis were serious about this, anyway. How much that meant . . . The only way to find out was to see how many *poilus* turned into cat's-meat and how much ground they took doing it.

Dawn came early these days. Summer would be here soon. Luc hoped he would be here, too, so he could see it when it came. He waited for the balloon to go up, his mouth papery dry. He knew about all the barbed wire ahead. You could get hung up on the stuff, stuck like a fly on flypaper, waiting for machine-gun bullets to chew you up and leave you limp. How many French soldiers had died that way in the last war? How many more were about to? *Am I one of them?* That was the question you never wanted to ask yourself.

Behind him, the French artillery woke up early. 75s, 105s, 155s . . . They pounded away for all they were worth. The ground shook under his feet. He glanced back over his shoulder. All those muzzle flashes made it look as if the sun were rising in the west.

The Germans were *good,* damn them. It couldn't have been more than a couple of minutes after hell started coming down on their positions when their artillery started hitting the French forward trenches. Luc huddled there, trying to make himself as small as he could. Before long, he'd have to come out of the trench. He'd feel like an *escargot* without its shell. And the *Boches* had such sharp *escargot* forks!

An officer's whistle shrilled. The sound seemed small and lost in the middle of the thunderous artillery duel. Sergeant Demange let out a yell that cut through the explosions like a sharp knife through soft cheese: "Come on, you old *cons!* This is what you punched your time cards for!"

Luc would never have volunteered for this—which mattered not a sou's worth. He scrambled up the dirt steps that led out of the trench. His pack weighed him down, even stripped to the minimum as it was. It seemed heavy as an *escargot's* shell. But it didn't give him even that much protection.

As he went forward at a lumbering trot, he called fancy curses down on Denis Boucher's head. Maybe the little bastard was screwing his half-faithful Marie right now. Maybe the military police had caught him. Even that would be better than this. Anything would be better than this.

Clang-whang! That factory noise was an antitank round bouncing off a tank's armored carapace. If somebody inside the machine wasn't working his rosary beads, he was wasting a hell of a chance. Yes, the Germans were alert. When weren't they, damn them?

Clang! Blam! That factory noise was an antitank round penetrating a tank's steel hide and all the ammo inside going off at once. The turret blew three meters into the air and squashed a foot soldier when it came down. He didn't have time to scream. He probably didn't even have time to be surprised.

Machine guns rattled like malignant jackdaws. "Come on! Keep going!" Sergeant Demange shouted. "They aren't aimed at you!"

One of the things Luc had found out was that they didn't have to be aimed at you. They put out so many bullets, they could kill you any which way. But he couldn't flop down and start digging himself a foxhole, not when he had to mind a squad. He yelled "Keep going!" too. Once they smashed through the German line, things would—well, might—get easier.

Tanks really did mash down barbed wire, no matter how thickly the Germans laid it. And, if you went in right behind them, they shielded you from the fire directly ahead. Watching ricochets spark off the tank in front of him made Luc wonder how many of them would have nailed him if the tank weren't there. So what if its exhaust made him want to put on his gas mask? He might have been a Roman legionary advancing behind a big, fat shield.

This shield had weapons of its own. It stopped. So did Luc. Its cannon roared—once, twice. One of the machine guns that had been filling the air with death suddenly shut up. Even some of the new conscripts huddled behind the tank with Luc shouted happily. They knew every machine-gun nest that got ruined made them likelier to live.

The tank lurched forward—for about another fifteen meters. Then it hit a mine. That blew off its left track. It stopped. Hatches popped open. The crew jumped out. A tank that couldn't move was a tank an antitank gun would murder any minute now. The tank men carried only pistols. That made them useless in an infantry fight. Luc didn't know what they'd do now.

He didn't have time to worry about it, either. They were coming up on the Germans' foxholes and trenches. A *Boche* popped up with his hands high. *"Kamerad!"* he shouted hopefully.

Luc gestured with his rifle. The German climbed out of his hole, babbling thanks for not getting killed on the spot. Luc gestured again. The *Boche* stumbled back toward Beauvais. If he was lucky, no Frenchman would plug him before he got there. If he wasn't . . . Well, too bad, old man.

"Fuck me if I don't think we can do this after all!" Sergeant Demange yelled. Luc was starting to think the same thing. He hadn't seen any German tanks yet, and his own side still had plenty running. He tramped on toward the east.

"LET'S HAVE ONE MORE RADIO CHECK, Theo," Heinz Naumann said.

"Right, Sergeant," Theo Hossbach answered resignedly. The radio set had worked perfectly half an hour earlier. They hadn't moved since. What could have gone wrong? But Naumann had the prejump jitters. Nothing to do but humor him. Theo hooked in with the company, regimental, and divisional networks. The set still worked fine. *"Alles gut,"* he reported.

"Danke," Naumann said. "Won't be long now."

Theo didn't answer. The radioman's position in a Panzer II left him in a zone of no time and no place. He sat behind the turret and in front of the engine compartment. He couldn't see out unless he opened the hatch in the rear decking and stuck his head through it to look around. You didn't want to do that unless all your other choices were worse: cooking like a pork roast inside a burning panzer, for instance. No time and no place would do.

In an odd way, they even suited Theo. Some people who knew him called him self-sufficient. Rather more called him dreamy. All he knew was, most of the time the world within his head was more interesting than anything that went on outside. Being stuck in the bowels of all this complicated ironmongery bothered him much less than it would have troubled most other people.

Sometimes you couldn't ignore the outside world no matter how hard you tried. When hundreds of guns opened up behind you and thousands of shells crashed down in front of you, the world beyond the panzer's armored skin made you notice it. And the company commander bawled "Forward!" into his earphones.

"Forward!" Theo told Naumann.

"Forward!" The panzer commander passed the word to Adalbert Stoss.

"Forward!" The driver put the panzer in gear. The Polish plain could hardly have made better panzer country. The terrain was so smooth, they might almost have been rolling across a manicured practice ground. The only difference was, the Red Army wouldn't have been waiting at the edge of a practice ground.

Theo wondered how big that difference would turn out to be. All winter long, the Red Army had had a devil of a time beating the Poles. The Poles were brave—Theo had seen that in the couple of weeks since the panzer division traveled halfway across Europe. But the gear the Poles had . . .

He shook his head. Their army might have done all right in the last war. They had rifles and machine guns and field artillery. They also had cavalry regiments that went into battle with lances, as if the twentieth century—to say nothing of the nineteenth—had never happened. Their tanks were rusty French relics, and they didn't own very many. Panzer IIs could have run rings around them and shot them up with ease, and Theo knew the shortcomings of his own mechanical mount all too well.

Bang! Somebody might have smacked the panzer turret with a hammer. Or, much more likely, somebody might have taken a shot at Heinz Naumann, who, like any good panzer commander, rode head and shoulders out of the turret whenever he could. Theo didn't need to see out. Heinz damn well did.

He didn't need to get killed, though. When people started trying to blow your head off, you ducked back inside and used the vision ports. They didn't show much, but they were a hell of a lot better than getting shot. And, no sooner than Naumann had pulled himself inside his case-hardened steel cocoon, several more bullets spanged off the turret and the right side of the panzer.

"Halt!" he ordered, and Adi Stoss did. Heinz traversed the turret to the right. Then he stopped working the traversing gear and said "Forward!" again.

"What's up?" Stoss asked.

"Somebody else took out the foxhole before I could," Naumann answered. "*Those* Russians won't bother anybody from now on."

"Sounds good." The driver goosed the panzer again. They rattled on. In his mind, Theo pictured a map. Poland had a horn in the far northeast that separated the USSR from Lithuania. It *had* separated Russia from Lithuania, anyhow; with the Red Army in Wilno, the Soviets were going to border the little Baltic state. The Lithuanians were both furious because they wanted Wilno themselves (they called it Vilnius) and scared shitless because the Soviet Union was a thousand times their size. Now that Germany was jumping in with both feet, Lithuania might join the fight against Stalin. And if she did, Germany and Russia might notice.

Then Heinz said "Halt!" again. A moment later, he added, "Russian panzer!" He slewed the turret to the left for all he was worth.

Not being able to see out didn't usually bother Theo. At times like this, though . . . How fast was the enemy panzer's turret traversing? The sweat that dripped from his armpits had nothing to do with how hot it was inside the Panzer II. Fear made it foul and rank. Would a red-hot cannon round tear through the flimsy armor around him and set everything in here on fire? Or would it ricochet around inside and tear up the whole crew? All kinds of nice things to think about, and he couldn't do anything about any of them.

For that matter, how well could Heinz shoot? They'd all find out right about . . . *now.* The turret stopped traversing. Theo could see Naumann's left hand stab at the trigger on the elevating handwheel. The 20mm cannon barked—once, twice, three times. Heinz waited, then fired once more.

"You got him! He's burning!" Adi said excitedly.

"*Ja*," Heinz agreed. The coaxial machine gun's trigger was on the traverse handwheel, to his right. He squeezed off a couple of short bursts from the MG34, then grunted in satisfaction. "All right—we don't have to worry about the crew any more. Forward again, Adi."

"Forward," Stoss echoed. *"Jawohl!"* He hadn't sounded so respectful before Heinz killed his first enemy panzer. Theo could understand that. He was breathing easier, too.

Naumann squeezed off several more bursts from the machine gun. He didn't tell Adi to stop, or even to slow down. "Don't know if I got the damn Russians or not, but I sure as hell did make 'em duck," he said.

And that might be good enough. Foot soldiers who couldn't shoot back might as well not be there. And the German and Polish infantry advancing with and behind the panzers would soon make sure the Ivans weren't there any more. The Red Army might have seized Poland's northeastern horn, but it was about to get taken in the flank and cut off from its homeland. How would the Reds like that?

Not very much, Theo suspected. What could they do about it, though? How good were they, really? Before long, the *Wehrmacht* would find out.

A machine-gun burst rattled off the panzer's flank. Pebbles on a tin roof, the bullets might have been. They might have, but they weren't.

Huge blasts from somewhere up ahead made all the racket that had gone before them seem small. "Stukas, I hope," Theo said to Heinz.

"You'd better believe it," the panzer commander answered. "A whole bunch of Russians just went up in smoke. . . . Didn't get the panzers, though, dammit."

Theo didn't see how you could expect to wreck a panzer from the air. Only a direct hit would knock one out, and what were the odds of that?

When they stopped for the evening, Heinz said they'd come better than twenty kilometers. Theo believed it, though they might have been going round in circles for all he could prove. One stretch of Polish plain looked like another. That burnt-out Russian panzer hadn't been anywhere close by, though. Theo examined the hulk curiously.

The more he looked, the more formidable it seemed. It was almost the size of a Panzer III, and had a bigger gun than the III's 37mm. Instead of going straight up and down, the armor sloped to help deflect enemy fire. Theo glanced over at Heinz Naumann, who was also eyeing the Russian machine. "Did you kill one of these?"

"Uh-huh." Heinz sounded unwontedly thoughtful. "I wouldn't want to stop a round from that gun. What d'you think? Forty-five millimeters? Fifty?"

"Forty-five, I'd guess," Theo said.

"Smash through our plate like it was tinfoil either way," Heinz said. "Next question is, how many of these fuckers have the Ivans got?"

"Well," Theo answered, "we'll find out."

Chapter 9

Sometimes you got the best view of things from the air. Sergei Yaroslavsky had always thought the Soviet General Staff would have done better to get up in a plane every once in a while to look at the battlefield as if it were a chessboard. Russian chess players amazed the world. So, sometimes, did the Red Army, but not in such a happy way.

Sergei had been pleased with what he saw before. In spite of help from the *Luftwaffe,* the forces belonging to Marshal Smigly-Ridz's reactionary clique weren't going to be able to hang on to Wilno, or to the terrain that led towards it from the USSR. That would have brought the Soviet border right up to the edge of Lithuanian territory, and would have set another pack of semifascists to quivering in their polished boots.

The mere idea of an independent Lithuania offended Sergei. The locals had taken advantage of the Soviet Union's weakness right after the Revolution to break away. If you thought you could get away with something like that for long, you needed to think again. Or you had needed to think again, till yesterday morning. Now, with the *Wehrmacht* marching side by side with the damned Poles, everything was as much up in the air as he was himself.

Up in the air, Sergei looked down on . . . what? The neat analogy of a chessboard didn't really suggest itself. What he saw lay somewhere between chaos and hell on earth. Pieces that had been taken—no, tanks and infantry units that had been smashed—weren't neatly lifted from the board. They lay as they had died, some sideways, some upside down, some still sending up black, stinking smoke, ant-small human bodies motionless among the murdered machines.

Anastas Mouradian was seeing the same thing as Sergei, and liking it every bit as well. "Doesn't look so good, does it?" the Armenian said with what struck Sergei as commendable restraint.

"Well . . . no." Sergei admitted what he couldn't very well deny. Most of the tanks wrecked or burning down there were Soviet T-26s and BT-7s. Most of the ant-small corpses lying near the tanks wore Red Army khaki.

By contrast, most of the tanks still on the move were painted dark gray. Most of the men moving forward with them—moving forward like army ants, ferocious, seemingly unstoppable—wore German *Feldgrau*. On the Nazis' flanks, Polish troops in dark khaki also advanced: jackals fattening themselves as lions tore chunks out of beasts too big for the yapping scavengers.

Paying too much attention to the fight on the ground wouldn't do. Sergei had feared German Bf-109s before. He'd had good reason to fear them, too. Now he had better reason: far more of them sharked through the air. They weren't just helping the Poles any more. They were supporting their own countrymen, a job they took much more seriously. Yaroslavsky tried to look every which way at once. He wished some kindly quartermaster would have issued him eyes in the back of his head, and maybe one on top as well.

Mouradian pointed ahead, towards a clump of camouflaged tents whose long morning shadows revealed them for what they were. "That looks like a headquarters, don't you think?" he said. "Regimental, maybe divisional."

"*Da.*" Sergei nodded. "Shall we make the Germans jump and shout?"

He smiled at the idea of Nazis in monocles and caps with upswept crowns running for cover like ordinary mortals—and maybe finding out just how mortal they were.

When he shouted an alert through the speaking tube to Ivan Kuchkov, he found that the Chimp also liked the idea. "We'll bomb the living shit out of the fuckers," Kuchkov shouted back. He approved of any mayhem that didn't come down on his own head. Come to that, so did Sergei.

He flew straight toward the tent. Anastas Mouradian peered through the bombsight, giving minute course corrections with gestures. Then Mouradian also shouted to Kuchkov: "Now, Ivan!"

Down whistled the bombs. Without waiting to see what they'd done, Sergei wrestled the SB-2 around and got out of there at full throttle. The Germans wouldn't appreciate the visit he'd just paid them, and they had ways of making their displeasure known.

The wing's new airstrip lay well within what had been Polish territory, the better to keep pounding Wilno. Flying south against the Germans instead of west hadn't been what his superiors planned for, but the wing could do it when the situation required.

Getting back . . . Sergei hadn't worried about getting back. By all the signs, neither had anyone else on the Soviet side. That only went to show that the higher-ups didn't know what all they should have worried about. He watched two 109s hack an SB-2 out of the sky. No chutes came from the stricken bomber as it plunged to the ground. Three dead Soviet airmen, then. He ground his teeth. If they came after him next, there were liable to be three more.

But they didn't. They zoomed back to the south instead. The 109's only weakness he'd been able to find was its short range. If these fighters needed to gas up again . . . Sergei wouldn't complain. He knew a moment's pity for his countrymen who hadn't been so lucky.

When he got down, the airstrip was boiling like a pot of *shchi* forgotten over a roaring fire. Sergei hadn't even climbed down from the bomber's wing before a groundcrew man waved for him to get back into the cockpit. "What?" he said. "Why?"

"Because we're getting the fuck out of here, Comrade, that's why," the groundcrew man said.

"Why?" Sergei asked again, still not moving.

Before the groundcrew man could answer, the outside world did it for him: shells burst only a few hundred meters from the edge of the airstrip. "*That's* why, Comrade Pilot," the noncom said. "The German sons of bitches'll have the range on us any minute now. D'you *want* to get blown up?"

"They were nowhere near us when we took off," Sergei protested. He looked at his watch, pushing back fur-lined gloves and sleeves to see the face. No, it really hadn't been much more than an hour earlier.

"Yeah, well"—the groundcrew man shrugged—"the cocksuckers are fucking well near us now." He sounded almost as foul as the Chimp. "And if we don't haul ass right this minute, we'll get to meet 'em in person, like. So quit dicking around and head for the motherland, right?"

"Right," Sergei said dully, not knowing what else to do. He turned around—and almost bumped into Anastas Mouradian, who was right behind him. "Back in the plane, Stas. Back to Byelorussia."

"I heard," Mouradian said. "It's not so good, is it?" More shells screamed in. These burst closer than the ones in the last volley had. If the SB-2 didn't take off soon, it wouldn't get the chance.

Sergei thought about fighting the Nazis as an untrained infantryman. He thought about trying to get back to Byelorussia on foot—or, if he was very lucky, in the back of a truck. Much too easy to think about a German tank, or maybe a Stuka swooping down from above, pumping machine-gun bullets into the back of a truck.

Off to Byelorussia it was, then, and now, too. "Not so good, no," Sergei said. They returned to the cockpit and snapped their belts closed. Sergei had to tell Ivan Kuchkov what was going on.

"Happy motherfucking day," Kuchkov answered. "The stupid pricks who're supposed to be running things screwed it up royally this time, didn't they?"

"It could be better." Sergei left it right there. The engines, which had barely stopped, fired up again right away. That was something, anyhow—not much, but something. The SB-2 bounced down the runway and took off. It felt uncommonly agile; he couldn't remember the last time he'd gone up without a full bomb load.

He had to swing back to the east and come over the airstrip again to head for Soviet territory. Shells were dropping on the dirt runway by then. Any of the planes still hiding in revetments would have a devil of a time getting away. Sergei wondered if groundcrew men would have to set them on fire to keep the Germans from grabbing them. He also wondered whether any groundcrew men were hanging around to take care of such things. Trucks kicked up tall plumes of dust as they hightailed it toward the old border.

"Well, we're in it now," he said to Mouradian as he checked six to make sure he had no Bf-109s on his tail.

"No. The damned Germans are in it now, and they aren't screwing around the way they were before. That isn't good, either, especially with Japan jumping on us too," the Armenian replied.

"Not even slightly," Sergei agreed. "But what can we do except fight as hard as we know how?" Anastas Mouradian had no answers for him. Sergei wished Mouradian would have, because he had no answers of his own, either.

THE HORIZON WASN'T ENTIRELY EMPTY when Julius Lemp swung his binoculars around the horizon. But that smoke didn't come from a freighter bound for Britain. Nor did it rise from an enemy warship. There to the north sailed the *Admiral Scheer*. The pocket battleship was cruising the North Atlantic at fourteen knots, a pace the U-30 had no trouble matching.

A swell raised the U-boat, giving Lemp a glimpse of the *Admiral Scheer*'s angular profile. She could do a lot of damage if she got the chance. If . . . Lemp couldn't help wondering how many U-boats the *Kriegsmarine* could have built with all the steel and labor that went into the big armored cruiser, and how much more trouble they could have caused the British.

Well, too late for such questions now. There was the *Admiral Scheer*— and there, at the edge of visibility, was her signal lamp flashing urgent Morse. Lemp peered through the binoculars, but shook his head in frustration. "Can't make it out," he said, and then, to the bosun, who was up on the conning tower with him, "Tell them we need to approach, Matti. Let's see if they can read us."

"Aye aye, Skipper," Matti said, and the louvers on the sub's signal lamp clacked as they went up and down.

Lemp called down into the U-boat for a change of course. The boat swung north. He peered toward the *Admiral Scheer* through his field glasses again. With a wry snort, he said, "They say they can't make out what we're sending. They want us to come closer. Tell 'em we're doing it, for Christ's sake."

"Right you are," Matti answered. The louvers clacked some more. Lemp could read Morse by ear as well as by eye. The bosun said what needed saying as quickly and economically as anyone could want. He'd spent years in freighters before joining the German navy. He knew his onions, all right.

The pocket battleship's lamp flashed again. Word by word, Lemp read off the message: "Smoke . . . to . . . northwest. Several . . . ships."

"A convoy!" Matti exclaimed.

"That would be good," Lemp said. The other possibility would be several warships. The *Admiral Scheer* might fight off or escape from several British warships, especially with a sub on her side. All the same, freighters counted for more. Freighters fed England. Warships were nothing but nuisances: the dogs that kept sea wolves from feeding off the big, fat, slow sheep.

All the ratings up on the tower swung their glasses to the northwest. Closer to enemy shores, Lemp would have reproved them. An airplane could come out of nowhere and start shooting you up or bombing you before you even knew it was there. Not out in the middle of the Atlantic, though. Nothing that flew had the range to come out here and get back to land.

Back to land . . . What if one of those unknown ships out there was a carrier? Lemp spoke to the ratings after all. They resumed their usual scan. He peered intently toward the northwest, first with the binoculars on a strap around his neck, then with the more powerful pillar-mounted glasses each U-boat had.

He soon spied the smoke trails himself. He muttered to himself. If they were thick and black, he would have been sure they came from coal-fired steamers. Maybe they came from oil-burning freighters. Or maybe they poured from stacks that belonged to destroyers, cruisers, battlewagons—or a carrier.

No, probably not that last. The British would have seen the pocket battleship's smoke by now, too. If they had a carrier out here in the middle of the ocean, its planes would already be buzzing around the *Admiral Scheer* like so many stinging wasps. One or two of them might have found time for the U-30 as well.

More signals from the *Admiral Scheer*. "Commencing . . . firing," Lemp read. "Jesus Christ!" he added on his own. That answered all his questions. The *Panzerschiff* wouldn't have opened up on freighters at long range—she would have closed to make her kills sure. Those were warships out there.

Smoke and flame belched from the pocket battleship's six 280mm guns. Their thunder reached the U-30 several seconds later. It was still loud despite the kilometers between the pocket battleship and the submarine.

"They really mean it, don't they?" Matti said.

"You don't play skat with guns that size," Lemp agreed. The bosun chuckled.

But it was no joke, and the British weren't playing skat out there, either. Incoming shells splashed into the Atlantic several hundred meters short of the *Admiral Scheer*. They kicked up great columns of water: water dyed red, so the enemy officers would know which ship of theirs had fired them. A moment later, another salvo made green splashes. Lemp thought by the size of them that they came from cruisers rather than battleships. He thought so, yes, but he wasn't sure.

The *Admiral Scheer* fired again. She was fighting, not running. That also made Lemp believe she wasn't facing battleships. She wouldn't have lasted long slugging toe-to-toe against seagoing dinosaurs more heavily armed and far better armored than she was.

Off to the northwest, Lemp spied sudden heavy black smoke. "She's hit something!" he said, and the ratings up on the conning tower with him cheered and pumped their fists in the salt-smelling air.

But the Royal Navy hadn't quit. More shells came down around the pocket battleship. Around . . . Lemp ground his teeth. They'd straddled her. That meant they had the range. Sure as hell, one round from the next English salvo slammed into the German ship. More smoke spurted. The *Panzerschiff* kept on sailing and firing, though. Even if she wasn't armored like a battlewagon, one hit—*that* one hit, anyhow—wouldn't knock her out of action.

Distant across a much longer stretch of seawater, reports from the enemy's guns also reached Lemp's ears. And the *Admiral Scheer* sent another signal his way. "Turning . . . toward . . . you." The words came out one by one, maddeningly slow. "Surprise . . . unsuspecting . . . targets."

"*Donnerwetter!*" Lemp muttered. No doubt the order seemed easy to Captain Patzig—which only showed he didn't know much about how U-boats operated. Could the *Admiral Scheer* bring the enemy warships by on courses that would let the U-30 get a decent shot at them? Or would the U-boat turn into a harmless spectator the moment it submerged? Only one way to find out—and an order was an order. Lemp nodded to the bosun. "Send 'I shall conform to your movements,' Matti."

" 'I shall conform to your movements.' Aye aye, sir." Matti sounded much more serious than usual. *And well he might,* Lemp thought. The signal lamp's louvers clacked yet again.

Lemp wanted to stay on the surface as long as he could, to get the best notion of what course the Royal Navy ships were sailing. That would tell him what he could do—and whether he could do anything. The English skippers wouldn't notice him right away—he hoped. They'd focus all their attention on the *Admiral Scheer*—wouldn't they?

If he turned out to be wrong about either of those, he'd have a thin time of it. He wondered if that bothered spit-and-polish Captain Patzig, with all the gold braid on his sleeves. Lemp doubted it. To a surface officer, a U-boat was as much a service vessel as an oiler.

No help for it. Here came the pocket battleship, firing as she fell back from the enemy. What was going through the English captains' minds when they watched a stronger ship run from them? Contempt, probably. German U-boat commanders had an arrogant certainty that they were the best in the world. On the surface, that kind of pride had filled the Royal Navy since the eighteenth century.

Maybe it would come back to haunt them now. Their guns blazed as they pursued the *Admiral Scheer*. Like the *Panzerschiff*, they zigzagged over the sea to make themselves more difficult targets. They were firing faster than the German ship. Their guns were lighter, which made ammunition easier to handle. And they were English, damn them. Their ships undoubtedly had plenty of officers and sailors who'd fought in the last war. They had reason to be sure they were good.

Enough reason? Maybe not. Captain Patzig was doing a better job than Lemp had thought he would of leading the John Bulls onto the U-boat matador's hidden sword. *We might have good shots at them after all. I wouldn't have believed it, but we might.* All Lemp said out loud was, "Let's go below, men." He was last off the conning tower. As he dogged the hatch shut behind him, he called fresh orders: "*Schnorkel* depth! Up periscope! Ready forward torpedoes! Ready reloads!"

His men sprang into action without any fuss. Yes, they knew how good they were. He told the officers and chiefs what was up, and they passed the word to the ratings. The more you knew about what you were doing and why, the better you'd perform. That was U-boat gospel, anyhow. In the surface navy, the ideal still seemed to be turning men into blind, unthinking machines. It looked that way to Lemp, anyhow. He was willing to admit he was anything but unbiased.

He twisted dials on the gadget that helped him plan his shots. The targets would be at long range, and they were steaming ungodly fast. He didn't have time to wait and plan perfect shots, the way he might have with a lumbering freighter. He had to find something that would serve, then do it and hope for the best.

"What have we got up there, sir?" Gerhart Beilharz asked. The storklike engineering officer wore a *Stahlhelm* to keep overhead fittings from knocking him for a loop.

As long as he kept the *Schnorkel* behaving, Lemp didn't care what he wore. The gadget would give the U-30 twice the underwater speed it could get from battery power—if it worked. And the boat might need every bit of that and then some in the next few minutes. "Looks like two heavy cruisers, one light," Lemp answered absently. "Now shut up and get out of my hair."

"Aye aye, sir," Beilharz said.

Lemp hardly heard him. He felt the diesels surge through the soles of his feet as the U-30 went into her attack run. He steered her himself, his eyes on the the periscope. The first ship was coming into range. . . . "Torpedo one—*los!* Torpedo two—*los!*" he shouted.

Twin whooshes as the eels leaped free. Lemp forgot about them as soon as they were gone. He swung the U-boat to port, lining her up on the other heavy cruiser—or where the cruiser would be when the torpedo got there. If he had her range and speed right, if she didn't suddenly swerve, if, if, if . . .

"Torpedo three—*los!*" he said. Away the eel went. Lemp steered to port again. The light cruiser was trailing the other two warships and making more smoke than she should have. Battle damage from the *Admiral Scheer?* Lemp could hope so. "Torpedo four—*los!*" One more whoosh. "Reload forward torpedo tubes!"

That was backbreaking work—each torpedo weighed close to a tonne. Till it was done, though, the U-30 had only the single eel in her stern tube with which to fight. The "lords"—the junior ratings who bunked forward—would be happy when it was done, though. Now they'd have more room in which to sling their hammocks. Nobody'd have to sleep on top of a torpedo any more.

An explosion shook the U-30's hull. Sailors whooped. Lemp swung the periscope to starboard. The first English heavy cruiser lay dead in the water, though her guns kept firing. A few seconds later, another deep rumble rattled the submarine's crew like peas in a shaken pod.

People pounded Lemp on the back. "Two, skipper!" Matti bawled. "Way to go!"

Damned if he hadn't hit the second heavy cruiser. She was still moving, but down by the bow and slowing fast. Had he got the light cruiser, too? He waited for one more blast . . . waited and waited. It didn't come. He swore under his breath. When you did well, you wanted to do better.

With the light cruiser still among those present, he couldn't surface. She'd slaughter him if he did. Those 155mm guns weren't much for a surface ship to carry, but they made his lone 88mm deck gun look like a cap pistol by comparison.

Water spouts suddenly sprang up around the less damaged English heavy cruiser. The *Admiral Scheer* must have seen what the U-30 had done. Now the pocket battleship was coming back to finish off her crippled foes. Hits brought gouts of smoke and fire from the damaged warship.

The English light cruiser charged the *Panzerschiff*, guns blazing, doing her best to protect her wounded sisters. That was brave—even heroic. She scored hits, too. Then two rounds from the *Admiral Scheer*'s big guns slammed into her. She might have run headlong into a brick wall. Fire burst from her. She might almost have been broken in half.

"Skipper, we've got two eels in the tubes," the chief torpedoman reported.

"Good job, Bruno." Lemp hadn't expected them for another five minutes. "We are going to approach the enemy cruiser that has stopped, and we are going to sink her."

"Right," Bruno said. "They'll put a *Ritterkreuz* around your neck when we get home, too."

They would do no such thing, and Lemp knew it. Nobody who was in the brass' doghouse would win a Knight's Cross. No point wishing for one or thinking he'd earned it, because he wouldn't get it any which way. But he might get—partway—out of that damned doghouse.

Stubborn as any Englishmen, the sailors on the halted cruiser kept firing at the *Admiral Scheer* even as the pocket battleship teed off on a stationary target. Then the second torpedo from the U-30 slammed into her. This one broke her back. She had listed to starboard. Now she turned turtle and sank in a couple of minutes.

That left one Royal Navy ship still able to fight—but not for long. Even as Lemp turned toward her, a shell from the *Admiral Scheer* must have touched off her magazine. She went up with a roar that dwarfed the explosions from the torpedo hits.

"*Der Herr Gott im Himmel!*" Lemp said, shaken in spite of himself. How many men had gone up in that blast? How many more would struggle in the Atlantic—for a little while? The U-30 couldn't hope to pick up survivors; the boat was packed to the gills as things were. Would the *Admiral Scheer*?

A question from the bosun broke into Lemp's thoughts: "Uh, skipper, what just happened there?"

"Oh." Lemp remembered he was the only man in the U-boat who could see out. "That was the last British cruiser, not our ship." More cheers rang through the pressure hull.

He only half-heard them. If he commanded the pocket battleship, he wouldn't stick around. The Royal Navy would know exactly where this fight took place. Every warship within a couple of thousand kilometers would be hustling this way at flank speed. If the *Admiral Scheer* wanted to see home again, she'd have to get out without wasting time.

And that was just what she was doing. When Lemp turned his periscope on her, she was speeding northeast as fast as she could go. He nodded to himself. That was only sensible. The U-30 would have to run the Royal Navy's gauntlet to get back to the *Vaterland*, too, but it was easier for a sub.

Still, lingering here seemed the very worst of bad ideas. "Back to the surface," he ordered, "and then we'll shape course for Germany. Nobody can say we haven't done our job this cruise." The sailors cheered once more.

ONE OF THE PRIVATES in Alistair Walsh's section was reading the *International Herald-Tribune* with a long face. The *Herald-Trib* struck Walsh as annoyingly American, which didn't keep him from reading it, too. In France, it was one of the easiest ways to get your hands on news in English. If you didn't have a working wireless so you could hear the BBC, it was damn near the only way to get news in English.

"What's got you buggered up now, Jock?" Walsh said. "Something has, by the look on your mug."

"Damn Fritzes sank three of our ships, Sergeant," Jock answered in his broad North Country accent. Like several other men who'd joined the company at about the same time, he was from Yorkshire.

Walsh understood why he sounded so affronted. Everyone knew the Germans made good infantry. They'd proved that time and again. But when they took on the Royal Navy in what had been England's element for lifetime after lifetime . . . That was a bit much, or more than a bit.

Jock was still reading. "Says a fuckin' U-boat helped their bloody pocket battleship." For a moment, he seemed a little less irate. The Germans were good with U-boats not least because they couldn't match up on the surface. They hadn't in the last war, and their surface fleet was smaller this time: they'd had to start over from scratch once Hitler took over. Then Jock got mad again, mad enough to turn pink. Like a lot of Yorkshiremen, he was big and fair, which made his flush all the easier to see. "You ask me, it ain't cricket."

"We use planes and tanks to help infantry," Walsh said. "We do when we've got 'em, any road."

"That's different," Jock insisted. "It's not sneaky-like, the way a submarine is." *Soobmahreen*—the broad Yorkshire vowels turned the word into something that might have been found in a barn. (People who talked as if they were doing their best to sound like BBC newsreaders thought Walsh's Welsh vowels sounded pretty funny, too. Over the years, he'd had to punch a couple of them in the nose. If they didn't twit him too hard, though, he just ignored them.)

"I expect we'll sink the surface raider sooner or later, and we dealt with the U-boats in the last war. We can do it again," Walsh said.

"Aye—but the cost! All them drowned sailors!" Jock said. "Hundreds of men on a cruiser, and not many left alive after three went down."

"It's a bastard," Walsh agreed. It wasn't as big a bastard as Jock thought it was, though. England had taken 50,000 casualties on the first day of the Battle of the Somme, 20,000 dead . . . for a few square miles of cratered, poisoned mud that weren't worth having to begin with. Walsh hadn't been in the army yet in 1916. If he had, he probably would have been there. And if he'd been there, he probably wouldn't be here now.

"We've got to do something about them buggers, we do," Jock said, as if Walsh would know exactly what that something was. Maybe Jock thought he did. Common soldiers often seemed to think staff sergeants knew everything.

Staff sergeants sometimes thought they knew everything, too. When it came to dealing with common soldiers, they did, or near enough. When it came to setting Hitler's mustache on fire . . . "I'm open to suggestions," Walsh said dryly.

Before Jock could give him any, a German machine gun stuttered to hateful life. Things had been quiet lately. That made the short, professional bursts even scarier than they would have been otherwise. Three French machine guns started spraying the German lines a few seconds later. One of the froggies was also a professional: three rounds, pause, three rounds, pause, four rounds, pause. The other Frenchmen plainly didn't care how many gun barrels they burned through.

Walsh didn't get excited about the machine guns. He and Jock weren't out in the open. Machine guns could have kept banging away till doomsday without endangering them in the least. Then somebody threw a French grenade. Maybe a *poilu* saw Germans coming. Maybe he just imagined he did.

Any which way, the bursting grenade seemed to give the *Landsers* a kick in the arse the French machine guns hadn't. Something came down out of the sky with a whispering whistle and blew up with a bang much bigger than a hand grenade.

"Oh, bugger!" Walsh said. "*Down*, Jock!" He dove for the dirt himself. When the damned *Boches* started throwing mortars around, things stopped being fun. You could hide from machine guns. Not a thing you could do about mortars except pray one didn't land in your hole.

"I *am* down," Jock answered. So he was—he was flat as a swatted fly. The smell and taste of mud filled Walsh's mouth and nose. Mud was one of the characteristic smells of war, along with cordite, shit, and rotting meat.

French and English mortars answered the stubby little German guns. The French 75s behind the lines started tearing up the German trenches. Naturally, the Fritzes responded in kind. Both sides pounded away with everything they had.

"Fucking idiots!" Jock said. *Fooking idjits,* it came out, which made it sound all the more idiotic.

Walsh nodded without raising his head. Some bored German lieutenant had probably told the *Feldwebel* heading a machine-gun crew to squeeze off a couple of belts and make the fellows in the far trenches keep their heads down. And the *Feldwebel,* no doubt as bored as the officer, would have answered, *"Zu befehl, mein Herr!"* and told the *Gefreiter* who actually did the work to start shooting. And the *Gefreiter* would have said, *"Jawohl!"* and done as he was told, too.

And then, till somebody got tired of it, both sides would try their best to create hell on earth.

Their best, these days, was much too good. Nobody'd used gas yet, not so far as Walsh knew. That was the only thing from the last war's menu still missing in this one. Walsh peered out from behind the rubble of what had been some middle-class French family's house till a few months—perhaps a few weeks—before. He must have looked like a helmeted, submachine-gun-carrying khaki marmot popping out of its hole to make sure no helmeted, rifle-carrying field-gray wildcats were trying to sneak up on it. He didn't see any Germans scrambling forward. That only further convinced him the Fritzes hadn't had anything special in mind when they opened up with the MG-34. Just because you weren't looking for trouble didn't mean you wouldn't find any, of course.

While he spotted no enemy soldiers, he did see a skinny gray-and-white cat daintily picking its way through the wreckage where it must have lived till war turned everything inside out. It paused, staring at him with eyes green as verdigris. It still wore a bell on a collar, which couldn't have made hunting any easier. "Mrrow?" it said, and yawned, showing off needle teeth.

How did you call a cat in French? Walsh had no idea. He did what he would have done back in Blighty: he snapped his fingers, showed the cat his open hand palm-up, and went "Puss, puss, puss!" as persuasively as he could.

"Mrrow?" the cat said again. It might have been more suspicious if it were less hungry. It trotted toward him, stopping just out of reach. Walsh left his hand where it was. The cat stepped forward, sniffed, considered, and then rubbed against him. It started to purr. He'd passed whatever test it set him.

"Puss, puss, puss!" Walsh said again. He ducked down—he didn't want to give some sniper in a coal-scuttle helmet time enough to punch his ticket for him. The cat jumped into the hole with him and Jock.

Walsh scratched it behind the ears and under the chin. Purring louder, it stropped itself against his boot. "What'll you do with the sorry bugger?" asked Jock, he might have suddenly discovered Walsh was addicted to opium, or perhaps to unnatural vice.

"I'll give it something to eat. It looks like it could use a bite," the sergeant answered. "After that? Well, who knows? If it wants to stick around for a while, I don't mind. Why? Have you got something against cats?"

"Don't much fancy 'em," Jock said. Then he shrugged. A superior's vagaries weren't for the likes of him to question. "However you please, though."

"Let's see what it thinks of bully beef." Walsh opened a tin with his bayonet and put it on the ground in front of the cat.

Jock made a face. "Bugger has to be fuckin' starving if it'll stuff itself on that damned monkey meat."

Walsh smiled. *Monkey meat* was a straight translation of *singe:* what the Frenchies called tinned beef. Walsh wondered whether Jock knew that. He would have bet against it; even English often seemed a foreign language to the Yorkshireman.

As for the cat, it didn't care what you called the meat. It advanced, sniffed, and fell to without the slightest trace of feline fussiness. As it ate, it purred much louder than it had while Walsh scratched it. The tin held four ounces. By the way the cat emptied it, the beast might have disposed of four pounds of monkey meat just as eagerly.

"It must be hungry," said Walsh, whose opinion of bully beef was no higher than Jock's—or anyone else's.

After it had emptied the tin and got the inside shiny clean, the cat licked its chops. It licked its left front paw and meticulously washed its face. Then it cocked a hind leg in the air and started licking its privates. That deep, contented purr rose once more.

Jock gasped, half scandalized, half giggling. "Bugger me blind!" he said. "If I could do summat like that, damned if I'd go wasting my money on pussy half so often."

"You don't think you're wasting it while you spend it," Walsh said—it wasn't as if the same thing hadn't occurred to him.

"Too right I don't," Jock agreed ruefully.

"And I think you just named the creature, too," the staff sergeant added.

"I did?" Jock blinked. Then he got it, and started to laugh. He squatted and stroked the cat, which accepted the courtesy with regal condescension. "Nice Pussy," Jock said. Pussy purred.

Chapter 10

ans-Ulrich Rudel and Albert Dieselhorst both eyed their Stuka, then turned to each other with identical bemused smiles. No, not quite identical, because Dieselhorst could say something Hans-Ulrich couldn't. The sergeant not only could, he did: "Well, sir, this was your idea."

"I know," Hans-Ulrich answered. When he'd taken it to the armorers and then to the engineers, he'd been convinced it was a good one. So had they. They'd been so convinced, they'd gone ahead and given him exactly what he said he wanted. Now that he saw their handiwork in the flesh, so to speak, he wasn't so sure he wanted it any more. That said something about life; he also wasn't sure he wanted to know just what.

"You know what it looks like?" Dieselhorst said.

"Tell me," Rudel urged. "I didn't think it looked like anything."

"Oh, it does." Sergeant Dieselhorst looked at him the way a hard-bitten sergeant naturally tended to look at a minister's son. "It looks like our plane's got a hard-on, that's what. Two hard-ons, in fact."

"It—" Rudel started to tell him it looked like no such thing. The words clogged in his throat, because the Stuka *did* look as if it had seen a lady airplane it fancied. Mounted under the wings, the gun pods they'd fitted had barrels that stuck out almost as far as the prop. Each pod came equipped with a sheet-metal chute for ejecting spent 37mm cartridge cases. Sighing, Hans-Ulrich said, "You've got a filthy mind, Albert."

"Thank you, sir," Dieselhorst replied, which wasn't at all what Rudel had wanted to hear.

Since he hadn't wanted to hear it, he pretended he hadn't. "Now we get to find out how it flies with all that extra weight. It'll be a pig in the air—you wait and see."

Sergeant Dieselhorst nodded, but Rudel's forebodings didn't faze him. Again, he wasn't shy about explaining why: "Not to worry, sir. A Stuka's already an airpig." *Luftschwein* wasn't really a German word, which didn't mean Hans-Ulrich had any trouble understanding it.

Again, Rudel wanted to tell him he was wrong. Again, he couldn't, because Dieselhorst wasn't. Even the biplane Czech Avias had been dangerous to Ju-87s. Over England, the Stuka was nothing but a disaster. Hans-Ulrich knew he'd been lucky to make it back to the Continent from his handful of flights against the United Kingdom. The *Luftwaffe* had to pick targets carefully here in France, or too many dive-bombers wouldn't come back. For putting bombs right where you needed them, the Stuka couldn't be beat. For reaching the target and for getting away afterwards . . . Hans-Ulrich had managed so far—except once. And he and Dieselhorst were over German-held territory when they bailed out. So that didn't count—not to him, anyhow.

"We won't be pigs. We'll be wild boars," he said. "If this works the way it's supposed to, no panzer will be safe from us." He paused as a new thought struck him. "Do you suppose we could use the cannon to shoot down enemy planes, too?"

Dieselhorst gave him a crooked grin. "Don't know, sir. I'll tell you one thing, though—we'd only have to hit 'em once, that's for goddamn sure."

He was right yet again. The weapons the engineers had chosen for panzerbusting were antiaircraft guns. Their shells were supposed to knock out planes from the ground. No doubt they could knock them out from the air as well . . . if they hit. As the sergeant suggested, hitting would be the tough part.

Now that Rudel had his guns, he was wild to find out what they could do. No one tried to hold him back. Had his fellow flyers liked him better, they might have tried to restrain him from rushing out with untried weaponry. Nobody said a word. He didn't even think anyone might have. He didn't know how unpopular he was, and wouldn't have cared if he had known. He had his convictions, and the courage thereof.

As soon as he got the redone Stuka airborne, he realized he would need all the courage and conviction he could find. Sergeant Dieselhorst's prediction that the plane would be an airpig was, if anything, optimistic. The twin cannon and their pods weighed down the Ju-87 and loused up its aerodynamics.

"Keep your eyes peeled, Albert," Rudel said through the speaking tube.

"Why?" asked the veteran in the rear-facing seat. "We aren't fast enough to run away, and we can't maneuver for beans, either. Best chance we've got is if the bastards on the other side don't spot us."

Yet again, Hans-Ulrich couldn't argue even if he wished he could. He flew toward Paris. If the froggies and *Englanders* had massed panzers anywhere, they'd done it in front of the French capital. Rudel's right hand tightened on the stick. Had Paris fallen the way it was supposed to, the fighting might be over by now. Wouldn't that have knocked France out of the war? And how could England go on without a continental ally?

His hand tightened on the stick again, in a different way this time. Through the palm of his leather glove, he felt the wire that led up to the new firing button the engineers had mounted near the one on the stick that worked the Stuka's forward machine gun. If panzer-busting Ju-87s ever got manufactured from scratch, the installation would be neater. For now, this would do.

Contemplating purpose-built panzerbusters wasn't what made him squeeze the stick, though. Even if France went under and England made peace, the war wouldn't necessarily end. A thousand kilometers off to the east, or however far away it was, things were just starting to boil.

Hans-Ulrich nodded to himself. Russia was the real enemy, all right, Russia and Communism. If only the French and English would see what lay right in front of their noses, they could follow the *Reich* in a crusade against the godless Bolsheviks. Rudel remembered Red rabble-rousers from the days when he was a boy. They'd spewed their poison, their lies, all through Germany back then. The *Führer*'d taken care of that, but good. If he got half a chance, he'd take care of Russia, too, in spite of the stupid Western democracies.

First things first. Rudel suddenly stiffened in the cockpit. *There* were panzers, and those weren't German machines. Even from 3,000 meters, the difference in lines was unmistakable. "I'm going down, Albert," he said. "And I intend to come back up again, too." He tipped the Stuka into a dive.

"You'd better," Sergeant Dieselhorst answered. "Fly us into the ground and I'll be a long time forgiving you."

"Heh," Hans-Ulrich said as acceleration shoved him against the padding and armor in the back of his seat. The enemy panzers swelled before his eyes. *English machines, not French,* he thought. He'd decided he wanted to hit them from behind if he could. The armor over the engine compartment would be thinner than anywhere else. If he couldn't do that, he'd shoot them in the side.

Soon now. It should have been sooner still. Configured as a panzer-buster, the Stuka even dove slower than it had before. His forefinger found the new firing button. He pushed, hard.

That fired one round from each underwing gun. Shooting a pair of 37mm shells from a Ju-87 gave a whole new meaning to dive brakes. The recoil made the plane stagger, and almost seemed to stop it in midair. Machine guns were nothing beside it.

He hauled back on the stick, hard, to bring the Stuka's nose up again. "How'd we do?" he asked Dieselhorst, who could see where they'd just been.

"You got him!" the rear gunner said enthusiastically. "He's burning like billy-be-damned! It's easy—as long as there aren't any enemy fighters around, anyway."

"*Ja.*" That reminded Hans-Ulrich to look around once more to make sure he had no unwelcome company. He didn't see any. Since he didn't, he gave the dive bomber more throttle and climbed up into the sky. "Let's do it again."

"*Warum denn nicht?*" Dieselhorst said. Rudel couldn't think of any reason why not. Down roared the Stuka. He picked his target. Muzzle flashes on the ground meant the Tommies were shooting at him, too. They always did that. The dive-bomber's engine was as well armored as the cockpit. Small-arms fire was unlikely to hurt the plane.

Two 37mm cannon, on the other hand . . . *Blam!* The Stuka staggered in the air. He clawed for altitude. "How about it, Albert?"

"You killed another one! Jesus Christ, sir, this is fun!"

Rudel wouldn't have taken the Lord's name in vain. Well, he hoped he wouldn't have. He'd been known to slip in combat . . . and every now and then when he wasn't in combat, too. He hoped God would forgive him, although his father's stern Lutheran deity was longer on retribution than forgiveness.

And Dieselhorst proved right yet again. This was not only easy, it *was* fun. The enemy panzers couldn't hide, and they were even slower running away from him than he would have been trying to flee a Spitfire. Dive . . . *Blam!* . . . Climb . . . Dive . . . *Blam!* . . . Climb . . . Fish in a barrel . . .

After they'd smashed half a dozen machines, the rear gunner said, "Sir, maybe we'd better get back. If they come after us in the air . . . Mm, that's *not* my notion of fun."

"Mine, either," Hans-Ulrich admitted. He wanted to keep right on doing what he was doing. No matter what he wanted, pretty soon the Tommies or the French *would* scramble fighters. Best not to stick around till that happened. And he could report that the twin cannon worked— worked even better than he'd hoped they would, in fact.

Colonel Steinbrenner would be pleased. He'd probably be astonished, too. But so what? Hans-Ulrich was more than a little astonished himself. No more climbs and swoops, not now. Whistling in the cockpit, he flew off toward the northeast.

CHURCH BELLS PEALED in Münster, celebrating the *Admiral Scheer's* safe return to Kiel. Protestant, Catholic—it made no difference to the authorities. They wanted celebration. What the Nazis wanted, they ordered. What they ordered, they got. So it seemed to Sarah Goldman, anyhow.

The maddening thing was, most of the time the Nazis had little more use for pious Christians than they did for Jews. Believers had loyalties outside of the all-holy State, and the brownshirts and their grim, clever bosses hated that. Most Protestant ministers were so-called German Christians these days: Christians who leaned toward the *Reich* first, and only afterwards toward God. Catholics still looked to the Pope, but Pius was a long way off, the local *Gauleiter* very close.

Equally maddening was that her own family, like most Jews in Münster and throughout Germany, would have celebrated the *Panzerschiff*'s return, too, if only the Nazis had let them. Sarah knew her father would have. In spite of everything, he still insisted he was a German as well as a Jew.

Much good that did him, or any other Jew in the *Reich*. He wore the yellow Star of David on his ever more shabby clothes when he went out to his work gang every morning. He hadn't said any of the *goyim* in the gang gave him trouble on account of it. Just because he hadn't said it didn't mean it hadn't happened, though. Sarah knew Samuel Goldman kept all kinds of things to himself. She knew she didn't know all of them. By the very nature of that kind of conundrum, she couldn't, could she?

Trying not to borrow trouble—she didn't have enough already?—she helped her mother fix supper. It wasn't exciting: boiled potatoes and something the label on the package insisted was cheese. If the label hadn't insisted, Sarah would have guessed it was half-dried library paste. You could eat it. Sarah had, many times. It tasted more like paste than cheese, too. Her mother was a good cook, much better than Sarah was herself. Even Hanna Goldman couldn't make the nasty ersatz appetizing.

"I think the rations are getting worse," Sarah said as she cut a potato into quarters so it would boil faster.

"How can you tell?" her mother asked. That kind of tart comeback usually emerged from her father's mouth. When her mother said such things, the rations really were going to the dogs . . . except dogs wouldn't want to eat them, either.

But Sarah went on, "They really are, Mother. Not just for Jews, either. For everybody. Haven't you heard the *Hausfraus* complaining in the shops?"

Her mother only sniffed. "Some people don't know when they're well off." If that wasn't bound to be so, Sarah didn't know what would be.

Her father came in then. He looked exhausted—clearing bomb damage and repairing roads didn't come easy for a middle-aged professor of ancient history. But he also looked pleased with himself, which didn't happen every day. With the air of a magician pulling a coin from a spectator's ear, he reached under his coat and displayed a small package wrapped in stained butcher paper. "Look what I found," he said. It wasn't as dramatic as *Ta-da!*, but it would do.

"What is it?" Mother exclaimed. She tore the paper open. At first, Sarah thought it was a chicken. Then she realized it wasn't. "Oh! A rabbit!" her mother said.

Rabbits weren't kosher. They were cute, at least when they had their fur on. Sarah cared about none of that. Spit filled her mouth. "Hassenpfeffer!" she said.

"The guy who had it *said* it was a rabbit," Samuel Goldman said. "It may meow when you stick a fork in it, though. How fussy are you? I ate all kinds of things in the trenches, and times are pretty hard now, too."

He was still proud of his service in the Kaiser's army. And the wound he'd got and the Iron Cross he'd won meant the Goldmans had it better than most Jews in Münster—not much better, but a little. Sarah didn't need long to give him an answer: "Right now, I'd eat it even if I thought it was a rat."

"Me, too," her mother said.

"We didn't eat those," Father said. "We knew they ate us when they got the chance. Damned fat hateful things." He shuddered.

It wasn't hassenpfeffer Sarah's mother made. She cut up the rabbit and put it into the boiling water with the potatoes. The less fuel they used, the less trouble they would land in. The smell of cooking meat made Sarah even hungrier than she already was. She hadn't thought she could get hungrier, which only showed how little she knew. When was the last time the Goldmans ate meat? She couldn't remember. Some sausage earlier in the year, she thought.

"What did you pay for the rabbit?" Mother asked Father.

"Isn't it a nice day today? Sunshine all day long," he answered.

She sent him a look, but asked no more inconvenient questions. She did turn to Sarah, saying, "Why don't you put the shredded cheese in the icebox? As long as we've got the rabbit to go with the potatoes, we won't need it tonight."

"Sure." Sarah was glad to do that. The less she had to do with the horrible cheese, the happier she'd be. She would have liked to toss it in the trash instead of putting it in the icebox. But rabbits didn't fall out of the sky every day. *Too bad!* she thought. If another rabbit didn't appear tomorrow, they would need the cheese again. Wanting it was another story.

"That was *good,*" Samuel Goldman said when supper was over. From somewhere, he'd got himself a small leather tobacco pouch. He rolled himself a cigarette with casual aplomb. Sarah wondered where the tobacco came from. Right after they'd made Jews wear the yellow star, the Nazis had cut off the tobacco ration for them: one more way to make life unbearable. Was her father reduced to scrounging butts on the sidewalk and in the gutter? The idea was enough to make angry tears sting Sarah's eyes. Father was the very image of bourgeois dignity. He had to be dying inside whenever he bent to grab a dog-end. That evidently didn't stop him from doing it, though. Along with the smell, which she didn't like, all of a sudden Sarah had a new reason for being glad she didn't use tobacco.

When he'd smoked the handmade cigarette down to a small butt, he carefully unrolled it and put the few remaining shreds back into the pouch. That made Sarah sure he was getting his smokes from anywhere he could. When he noticed her watching him, he shrugged in faint embarrassment. "I have a habit," he said, as if he were talking about injecting himself with morphine. "I feed it as best I can."

"All right." Sarah wasn't sure whether it was or not. But if smoking meant so much to Father that he would let *goyim* laugh at him for guddling in the gutter, she didn't know what she could do about it. No, on second thought she did know: she couldn't do a thing.

Then she forgot about such trivial matters. Who would pound on the door right after supper? Fear lanced through her, because that was a question with an obvious answer. The *Gestapo* would. The *Gestapo* did whatever it pleased.

Someone out on the front porch shouted, "Open up, you stinking Jews, or we'll make you sorry!"

"Happy day. Something to settle supper," Samuel Goldman remarked as he got up and limped toward the front of the house.

He came back a moment later with three blackshirts in his wake. One of them pointed a pistol at him. They all leered at Sarah. She didn't look at them. Her father seemed as calm as if they were graduate students here to discuss a textual problem in Plutarch.

"Where's your murdering bastard of a son, Jew?" the one with the Luger snarled.

"I don't know," Father answered. That was a lie, but everything was fine as long as the Aryans didn't know it was a lie. Trying to show them how much they did know, he went on, "I'm sure you would have found out if we did. You must be keeping track of our mail and what we say on the telephone."

"Bet your ass," the *Gestapo* man said. "But somebody told us he might've gone and joined the *Wehrmacht*. Just what the *Reich* needs—a lousy kike lugging a rifle!" He rolled his eyes—blue, naturally—in disgust.

Fear made the unexpected feast churn in Sarah's belly. If Father felt it, too, he didn't show it. "You must have heard that Saul and I both tried to join up when the war started. Think what you please, sir, but we would have fought for Germany. I did in the last war, you know."

That blackshirt looked as if he'd found half a cockroach in his porridge. "*Ja, ja.* You were going to capture Paris all by yourself till they shot you. Damn shame they didn't blow your brains out."

"Anyway, this isn't about that," one of the other *Gestapo* men added. "Or we don't think it is. It's about after he smashed in that Aryan's head. He's a dangerous character, your kid."

Good! Sarah thought fiercely. She almost screamed it in the secret policeman's face. That wouldn't have been so good.

Her father only shrugged. "You know more than I do, I'm afraid. We haven't heard from Saul since ... since it happened."

"If we ever find out you're lying—" The *Gestapo* man glowered fearsomely. "You wait and see what you'll find out then. You'll wish you'd blabbed, and you can take that to church."

Both his friends thought that was the funniest thing they'd ever heard. The one who hadn't said anything was smoking a pipe. To Sarah, it stank like smoldering garbage. But it kept them from noticing the smell of Samuel Goldman's cigarette. Sarah didn't think gathering dog-ends was against the law for Jews. Anything could be against the law, though, if the *Gestapo* decided it was.

"Sir, I am very sorry for what my son did," Father said. "If the government had let him join the *Wehrmacht*, he would have fought the *Reich*'s foreign foes, as I did in the last war. But you must know I do not know where he is." A couple of things he didn't say hung in the air, at least to Sarah. One was *What have you done against the Reich's foreign foes?* None of the blackshirts looked old enough to have served under the Kaiser, and they obviously weren't at the front now. And the other was *If you thought I did know where Saul was, I'd be in Dachau now, and you'd be tearing out my toenails.*

The blackshirts got the second of those; fortunately, not the first. "Yeah, well, we got this report, and we had to check it out," said the one who did most of the talking.

"Wherever you got it, I think you should put it back," Samuel Goldman said. "Of all the places where my son might be, I'm sure the army is the least likely."

"So are we," the *Gestapo* man with the pipe said, taking it out of his mouth for the first time. He didn't notice Father hadn't said Saul *wasn't* in the *Wehrmacht*—and a good thing, too. He nodded to the other blackshirts. "We've done what we needed to do. We found out what we figured we would—diddly-squat. Let's blow."

To Sarah's relief, they blew. Her father's shoulders slumped. He let out a long, deep sigh. "Do we have any schnapps?" he asked Mother. "I could use a drink."

"I'll get you one." She hurried away.

"You were terrific!" Sarah exclaimed. "You—"

Before she could say anything more, Father shook his head and pointed to a lamp and to a picture on the wall. The Goldmans hadn't found any microphones in their house. Just because they hadn't found them didn't mean the microphones weren't there—the *Gestapo* certainly claimed they were. Even if they had found them, what could they have done? Breaking the gadgets would only have convinced the secret police they had something to hide. They did, but convincing the *Gestapo* of it they needed like a hole in the head.

Mother came back with not one but three little glasses of schnapps, carrying them on a brass tray. She set the tray on the table in front of the sofa. Everybody took a glass. Father pointed again to places where listening devices might lurk. Mother nodded. She raised her glass. "To peace!" she said.

"To peace!" Sarah choked a little on the fiery schnapps, but it felt good when it got to her stomach. Not even a Jew could get in trouble for toasting peace . . . she hoped.

PEGGY DRUCE HAD ALWAYS had a knack for complicating her life. She wouldn't have been in Marianske Lazne when the Nazis invaded if she hadn't. That wasn't the first time she'd done exactly what she wanted to do and worried about the consequences later. It wasn't the first time consequences got up on their hind legs and bit her in the ass, either.

But she'd never done anything like this before. She'd been married to Herb since before the War to End War—another wistful hope shot to hell. She'd gone plenty of places on her own in those years, too; she liked traveling more than Herb did. Plenty of men had tried to get her into bed with them. None had had any luck.

None . . . till Constantine Jenkins.

She had all kinds of excuses. She'd been away from home, away from Herb, an ungodly long time. She'd been drunk as a skunk. Christ! Had she ever! Her hangover the next morning almost called for a blindfold and a cigarette, not four aspirins and bad German ersatz coffee. And she'd been so sure the young American diplomat was queer. Even drunk she would have been more on guard if she weren't so sure.

Maybe he did like boys better than girls. But he was at least a switch hitter, as she had reason to know.

She muttered to herself, there in her hotel room. The young American diplomat . . . Her mouth twisted in rueful self-mockery. He wasn't young enough to be her son, not unless she'd started at an age that made people crack jokes about Mississippi and Alabama. He wasn't far from it, though. That had to be one more reason she hadn't had her guard up.

"Shit," she said distinctly. She could come up with all kinds of reasons, all kinds of excuses.

One of these days, she still expected to get back to the States. When she did, she expected a happy reunion with her husband. She hadn't written him about what the dog did in the nighttime—and it wasn't nothing, dammit. She didn't intend to. Lots of people (including several friends) carried on affairs that lasted for years without the other spouse's being any the wiser. She wondered how they managed. Maybe they'd had their consciences surgically extracted.

The Nazis probably had a medical center somewhere that did exactly that. Hitler would have been the first patient, followed by Himmler, Göring, and Goebbels. Everybody who'd joined the SS would have followed suit. Real heroes could get the job done without benefit of anesthesia.

Peggy shook her head. If she wasn't punch drunk . . . But that wasn't the problem. The problem was that she'd cheated on the man she'd loved for almost her entire adult life. And she hadn't had her conscience removed, no matter how convenient it would have been.

He'll never know. She'd been telling herself as much since she woke up next to Con Jenkins. Con . . . She shook her head again, even more ruefully. She hadn't known someone with such a formal—even formidable—name had that one-syllable nickname. She hadn't known all kinds of things about him. Oh, no!

But Con Jenkins wasn't the point, even if he'd given her the problem. Herb Druce was. And so was Peggy herself. *He'll never know* wasn't the point. *She* knew. She couldn't forget, and she couldn't forgive herself, either. She was going to have to deal with this, dammit.

She also couldn't drop Con like a live grenade. Had she done something stupid with one of the Germans who'd shown he was interested, she could have cut him out of her life from then on. That would have helped her get back her good opinion of herself.

But if anybody could help her go home at last, Constantine Jenkins was the man. If he got angry at her, how hard would he work to send her back to Philadelphia? And, now that she'd slept with him once—and, by all the signs, enjoyed it in a drunken way, even if she hardly remembered it now—how the hell was she supposed to tell him she didn't want to go to bed with him any more?

On the other hand, if she took him to bed again in the hope that that would make him move heaven and earth to get her out of Berlin, how was she different from the ladies of the evening who prowled the blacked-out nights, looking for anything in pants and looking to get the men they found out of their pants as fast as they could? *I'm classier,* she thought. As with *He'll never know,* it wasn't enough of an answer.

And something else occurred to her. If she kept laying the embassy undersecretary, how hard would he work to send her home? Wouldn't he have the best reason in the world—from a man's point of view, or at least from a stiff dick's, assuming there was any difference—for wanting to keep her available?

"I'm screwed if I screw him, and I'm screwed if I don't screw him," she blurted, and started to laugh. She could still she how ridiculous this all was, anyhow. If she were reading a novel, she'd keep turning pages like nobody's business. It was still funny in real life, but with a bitter edge no novel could match.

The telephone chose that moment to ring. Peggy jumped, then sprawled across the bed to pick it up. *"Bitte?"* she said.

"Hello, Peggy." Of course it was Constantine Jenkins. Who else would it be? *Just to drive me crazy,* she thought. *Um, crazier.* He went on, "I know you speak German pretty well."

"Fair," she said. "Better than when I got here. I know a lot more French—and much good *that* does me."

"As a matter of fact, so do I," he said. And he really was fluent *auf Deutsch,* while Peggy struggled to make herself understood and to follow what other people said to her. If he *did* speak French better . . . But he was after something else, because he asked her, "How well do you write German?"

"Write it?" Peggy could hear herself squeak in surprise. "I don't think I've tried since I was in high school. I'd make a horrible mess of the grammar—I'm sure of that. How come?"

"Because I want you to write a letter to Adolf Hitler," Jenkins answered. Whatever he thought of the *Führer*, it didn't show in his voice. Peggy had a good idea of his opinion. No *Gestapo* man tapping the phone line would, though. The blackshirt might wonder if he'd gone round the bend, of course.

And who could blame a hard-working blackshirt for that? Peggy wondered the same thing. She also wondered whether her own hearing had gone south. "You want . . . me . . . to write a letter . . . to Hitler? In German?"

"He doesn't read English, and I don't want his secretaries to sidetrack this. They may anyhow, but if it comes by way of the American embassy you have a chance of getting him to look at it," Constantine Jenkins said. "Sometimes you have to go straight to the top here, if you can do it."

"What should I say?" By now, Peggy was beyond flabbergasted.

"Tell him what you've been telling all the other Germans. You're a neutral, you're stuck here, and you'd appreciate it if he'd make it possible for you to go back to the USA and to your family. A couple of paragraphs should do it."

"You really think that will work?"

"I don't know. It may. Lots of leaders will do favors for little people because it makes them look good and doesn't cost anything much. And if he says no, how are you worse off?"

Peggy had no answer for that. Even though he couldn't see her, she nodded. "Okay, Con—I'll take a shot at it. I'll bring it by the embassy this afternoon."

She thought for a moment, then called the front desk. "A German-English dictionary?" said the clerk who answered. "*Ja*, we can supply one. Please wait. A bellboy will deliver it *sofort*." As Jenkins had before him, he hung up.

It didn't come immediately, but it didn't take long enough to annoy her. The bellboy was at least sixty-five, with a bushy white mustache and a limp. What had he stopped in the last war? She tipped him more than she would have if he were some kid. "*Danke,*" he said gravely, and brushed a forefinger against the brim of his cap.

She felt like cheering when she found the dictionary included a table of declensions, and another one for conjugations. She'd still write bad German, but it wouldn't be quite *so* bad.

Führer, she began—he wasn't *Mein Führer,* not to her. She set out her problem and what she wanted as simply as she could. As Jenkins had predicted, it didn't take much more than half a page. *I thank you very much for your help,* she finished, and signed her name.

She put the letter in an envelope but didn't seal it: Con Jenkins would want to look it over before it went out. Before it went to the *Führer.* She laughed again. Would Hitler see it? What were the odds? But, as Jenkins had also asked, if he didn't see it, or if he said no or just ignored it, how was she worse off?

She set the dictionary on the check-in counter as she left for the embassy. "I hope it was useful to you," the desk clerk said.

"It was. *Danke schön,*" Peggy answered.

Jenkins certainly didn't treat her like a lover when she got there. She had to cool her heels for half an hour before she could see him. Again, he was closeted with the gray-haired naval attaché. Well, that fellow probably had enough on his mind and then some. The whole business with the *Admiral Scheer* and the Royal Navy had played out right on the USA's front porch, so to speak.

"Let's see what you've got," the undersecretary said briskly when she made it into his office at last. She was just as happy to stay businesslike. She handed him the letter. He read it, then grinned at her. "Oh, this is fine, Peggy. Much better than I expected. You didn't give your German enough credit." She told him how she'd borrowed the dictionary. He clapped his hands. "Good for you, sweetheart!"

He didn't sound like a fairy being arch. He sounded like a lover praising his lover. Peggy wished he would have seemed more faggoty. At least he didn't say something like *I'll show up at your hotel tonight so you can thank me the right way.* Peggy asked, "How long do you think it will take before I know?"

"Hitler's staff will have the letter tonight," Jenkins said. "What they do with it, what he does with it—that's out of my hands."

"Okay," Peggy said. "Thanks again." She got out of there as fast as she could without being rude.

Three days later, the telephone in her room rang at a quarter to five in the morning. At first, muzzy with sleep, she thought it was the air-raid siren going off. When she realized it was the phone, she got good and pissed off. What asshole would call at this ungodly hour? It was getting light, but even so—! *"Bitte?"* she snarled.

"Sind Sie Frau Druce?" A man's voice.

"Yes, I'm Peggy Druce. Who the devil are you?"

"Adolf Hitler here," the voice answered. And it was. As soon as he said it, she knew it was. She'd heard him on the radio too often to have any doubt. "You are having trouble leaving my country?"

When Hitler said it was his country, he damn well meant it. "Uh, yes, sir," she managed.

"The trouble will end. Whatever neutral nation you wish to visit, you may. Never let it be said we keep anyone who does not wish to stay," the *Führer* told her.

"Uh—" Peggy kept saying that. She'd never expected a call from one of the two or three most powerful men in the world. She'd never expected anything to come of her letter, truth to tell. "Thank you very much, sir!"

"You are welcome. Have you any questions?" He spoke slowly and clearly, to make sure she could follow. Even over the telephone, the weight of his personality made her sag.

"Uh—" There it was again! "Why are you up so early?" she blurted.

He actually chuckled. How many people could say they'd made Hitler laugh? "I am not up early. I am up late. The enemies of the *Reich* do not sleep, and neither do I. Good-bye, Mrs. Druce. Finding a problem so easy to solve is a pleasure, believe me."

"Thank you." Peggy finally managed not to say *Uh,* but she was talking to a dead line.

Chapter 11

Down screamed the Stuka. Vaclav Jezek had never yet met a man who'd lived through a dive-bomber attack and didn't hate the German warplane with a fierce and deadly passion. Outside of a few luckless people down in Spain, no one had hated the Stuka like that longer than he had. He'd been dive-bombed on the very day the Nazis invaded Czechoslovakia, and more often than he cared to remember since.

"Get down!" he yelled to Benjamin Halévy, who was working his way across the field with him.

"I *am* down," the Jewish sergeant answered. So was Jezek. He lay flat as a flapjack. The smells of grass and dirt filled his nostrils.

That Stuka screeched like a soul tormented in hell. The sirens built into the landing gear were one more piece of German *Schrechlichkeit*. Vaclav sneaked a glance at it. It looked funny. What were those pods under its wings? Not bombs, surely.

The dive bomber couldn't have been more than fifty meters off the ground when fire blasted from the ends of the gun barrels projecting from the pods. That was when Vaclav realized they *were* gun barrels. Till then, he'd hardly noticed them—no great surprise, not when the Stuka was hurtling down at several hundred kilometers an hour.

As it pulled out of the dive and roared away, answering fire spurted from the rear decking of a French tank. The tank started to burn. The crew bailed out and ran for cover.

"Bastard's got big guns under there!" Halévy exclaimed.

"Tell me about it!" Vaclav answered. "What can we do to stop him?"

"Shoot him down," Benjamin Halévy said. "If you've got any other bright ideas, I'd love to hear them."

Vaclav didn't, however much he wished he did. He watched the Stuka climb high into the sky again, then dive at another French tank. He and Halévy both fired at the ugly, predatory warplane. If they hit it, they didn't harm it. At least one of the rounds it fired at the tank struck home—the motorized fort slewed to a stop, flame and smoke rising from the engine compartment. Again, the Stuka flew off at treetop height, then started to climb once more.

Another screaming dive. Another stricken French tank. "Jesus Christ!" Jezek said. "He can do that all day long!"

"Oh, I don't know," Halévy said. "Sooner or later, he's bound to run out of gas or ammo—unless we run out of tanks first."

"Happy day!" Vaclav sent him a reproachful look. "You really know how to cheer me up, don't you?"

"It could be worse," the Jew said.

"Oh, yeah? How?" Vaclav demanded.

"The Nazis could have a dozen Stukas armed like that, not just one," Halévy answered. "Looks like they're trying this out to see if it works. If it does, they'll put guns on more planes."

"Well, they will, on account of it damn well does," Jezek said. "Does it ever!" Three smashed tanks—three tanks smashed from an unexpected direction—had shot the Allied advance in this sector right behind the ear. Everyone was staring wildly into the sky, wondering if that Stuka would come back again.

And it did. This time, it had to dive through a storm of small-arms fire. But a dive-bomber was armored against nuisance bullets. The designers must have realized it would run into some. Letting them disable it didn't seem such a good idea, so the engineers made sure they wouldn't. *Germans*, Vaclav thought glumly. *They take care of those things.*

"Sure they do," Benjamin Halévy agreed when he said that out loud. "They wouldn't be so dangerous if they fucked up all the time, like a bunch of Magyars or Romanians."

"Well, you didn't say 'like a bunch of Slovaks,' anyway," Vaclav said.

"Or them," Halévy replied. "They're so fucked up, they jumped into bed with the Nazis, right?"

"Afraid so. When the Germans invaded us, I had this one Slovak in my squad, and I wasn't sure whether he'd shoot at them or try to shoot me." Vaclav grimaced and spat, remembering.

"So what did he end up doing?" the Jew asked in tones of clinical interest.

"Well, he didn't try and plug me straight off—I will say that for him," Jezek answered. "After that, fuck me if I know. We were right at the point of the bayonet, if you know what I mean, and things fell apart pretty fast. Maybe a Stuka blew him to kingdom come. Or maybe he surrendered to the Nazis. If he did, he's likely a sergeant in the Slovak army by now."

"In the Slovak army." By the way Halévy said it, it tasted bad in his mouth. Well, it tasted bad in Vaclav's mouth, too. Czechs no more believed Slovaks had a right to their own country than Germans believed Czechs had a right to theirs. Slovaks were bumpkins, country cousins, hillbillies who talked funny and drank too much and beat their wives. Only country cousins could take the Hlinka Guard and a fat windbag like Father Tiso seriously.

And now Slovakia *was* a country, with Father Tiso as its tinpot *Führer*, or whatever the devil they called him. The Hlinka Guard did its best half-assed imitation of the SS. And Bohemia and Moravia, the cradle of the Czech nation since time out of mind, had been bombed and shelled to kingdom come, and the German occupiers treated them exactly the way locusts treated a ripe wheatfield. Life could be a real son of a bitch sometimes.

Sometimes it could be a lot worse than that.

"You know what we ought to do?" Halévy's question derailed Vaclav's gloomy train of thought, which might have been just as well.

"What's that?" Vaclav asked. No, he wasn't sorry to think about something else.

"We ought to let our brass know the Germans have themselves a new toy," the sergeant said. "If those assholes can pull a stunt like that, we should be able to do the same thing, right?"

"Right," Jezek said, but his voice lacked conviction. The Germans were good at pulling new stuff out of the hat. That was part of what made them Germans, at least in a Czech's eyes. How good the French and English were at the same game . . . The war was a long way from new, but the French were just now figuring out that German tank tactics beat the snot out of their own half-bright ideas.

Benjamin Halévy gave him a crooked grin. "C'mon, man. We've got to try," the Jew said. "We keep our mouths shut, nobody with the clout to do anything about it will find out what's going on for another month and a half. You think the tankers'll tell?"

Vaclav considered that, but not for long. Tankers thought their big, clattering mounts were perfect. They wouldn't want to admit that the enemy had come up with a big new flyswatter. Sighing, Jezek said, "Let's go."

The next problem, of course, was getting an officer to listen to them. Two noncoms, one a Czech, the other a Czech *and* a Jew (naturally, the French thought of Halévy as a Czech, even if he'd been born in France— he spoke Czech, didn't he?), didn't have an easy time getting through to the fellows with fancy kepis. At last, though, a captain said, "Yes, I've already heard about this from other soldiers."

"And?" Halévy said. The captain looked at him. He turned red. "And . . . sir?" Even Vaclav, with his fractured French, followed that bit of byplay.

"I will do what I can," the captain said. "I don't know how much I can do. I am not in the air force, after all."

Sergeant Halévy translated that for Vaclav. Then he went back to French to inquire, "Sir, if no one says anything at all to the air force, what will happen then?" He also turned the question into Czech.

"*Rien,*" the officer replied. *Nothing* was a word Jezek followed with no trouble. The Frenchman went on, "But it could also be that the air force will do nothing just because the army is screaming at it to move."

"Those pilots don't want everybody in the army spitting at them, they'd better start treating German tanks the way the Nazis treated ours," Vaclav said. Sergeant Halévy did the honors with the translation. Vaclav thought it sounded better in Czech than it did in French.

"Yes, yes," the captain said impatiently. He looked from one grubby front-line soldier to the other. "Now, men, you have done your duty. You have done what you thought you had to do, and you have done it well. You can do no more in this regard—it is up to me to take it from here. I will do so. You had best return to your own positions, before the officers set over you start wondering where you are, and why."

Go away. Get lost. The message, once Halévy translated it, was unmistakable. And the Jew and Vaclav went. What else could they do? Maybe the officer would make some progress with his superiors and the air force; maybe not. But two foreign or half-foreign noncoms couldn't. *Back to the war,* Vaclav thought gloomily, and back to the war it was.

THE SPANISH NATIONALISTS HAD ALWAYS had more artillery, and better artillery, than the Republicans. Up on the Ebro front, Chaim Weinberg had got resigned to that. It was part of the war and something you had to deal with, like the endless factional strife between Communists and anarchists on the Republican side. Since the Soviet Union supplied Communist forces in Spain while the anarchists had to scrounge whatever they could wherever they could, the red flags had had a big advantage over the red and black.

Now nobody supplied anybody in Spain, not in any reliable way. Everyone was too busy with the bigger war off to the northeast. Both sides had forgotten about this particular brawl between progressive and reactionary forces—except for the people still doing the fighting and dying here.

The Nationalists still had the guns Hitler and Mussolini had lavished on Marshal Sanjurjo. What they didn't have any more were the endless crates of high-quality Italian and German ammunition. They'd already fired it off. So if they wanted to shoot at the Republicans defending Madrid, they had to use shells they made themselves.

Spanish factories didn't turn out nearly so much ammo as the ones in Germany and Italy. Not only that, Spanish artillery rounds, like Spanish small-arms ammunition, were junk.

Chaim didn't know why that should be so, but it was. At least half the shells the Nationalists threw at the Republicans lines just north of University City were duds. He would have liked to think the workers in the munitions plants were sabotaging their Fascist masters. He would have liked to, but he couldn't. The ammo that reached the Republicans from factories in Madrid and Barcelona was every bit as crappy. The workers on the Republican side should have had every incentive to do the best work they could. They *did* have every incentive, in fact, but the best work they could do wasn't very good.

"And what do you expect?" Mike Carroll asked when Chaim complained about that. "They're Spaniards, for Chrissake. They're brave. They'd give you their last bullet or their last cigarette or the shirt off their back. But they haven't heard about the twentieth century. Hell, they haven't heard much about the eighteenth century—and what they have heard, they don't like. As far as they're concerned, it's still 1492. They've cleaned out the Moors, and they're waiting to see what happens when that Columbus guy gets back."

As if to punctuate his words, another dud thudded in fifty meters away and buried itself in the hard brown dirt. That was too close for comfort; it would have been dangerous had it gone off. Chaim nodded—what Mike said held some truth. But only some, as he pointed out: "So how come the Republic won the election, then? The kind of progressive government Spain had—the kind our chunk's still got—doesn't come out of 1492. Not out of 1776, either."

"Think of it as a peasant uprising," Carroll said. "Spain was like Russia. It was one of the places where the jerks on top came down hardest on everybody under them. So of course it was the place where the reaction against oppression hit hardest. That's how the dialectic works, man."

More shells came in from the Nationalist gun pits off in the hills. Some of these burst, fortunately none too close to the arguing Internationals. Chaim peeped over the parapet to make sure Sanjurjo's soldiers weren't trying anything under cover of the barrage. He ducked down in a hurry:

no point letting snipers get a good look at him. Then he took out a pack of Gitanes and lit one.

"Can I bum a butt off you?" Mike asked eagerly. "I'm all out."

"Sure," Chaim answered without rancor, holding out the pack. Mike would do—had done—the same for him plenty of times.

The big blond American leaned close to Chaim for a light. "Thanks." Carroll took a drag. He made a face as he exhaled. "Fuck me if I know how the Frenchies smoke these goddamn things all the time."

"Better than nothing," Chaim said, which wasn't disagreement. He chuckled sourly. "See? This is what it really comes down to: shitty shells and shitty tobacco, not the dialectic."

"Oh, no." Mike stuck out his chin and looked stubborn. "*Oh,* no. Everything comes down to the dialectic in the end. Without the dialectic, the world makes no sense. And if the world makes no sense, who gives a rat's ass about shells and cigarettes?"

"If you don't, how come you keep working on your bombproof there?" Chaim retorted. "And who just scrounged that cigarette? Wasn't it some guy who looks a lot like you?"

With the evidence still sending up a thread of smoke from the corner of Carroll's mouth, he couldn't very well deny the charge. He did look exasperated. And he had his reasons, which he proceeded to spell out: "If a political officer hears you talking like that, you'll be lucky if you get off with public self-criticism. You could end up in a lot more trouble than that, and you know it."

Chaim did. He didn't like it. He took American-style freedom of speech for granted. He also took the revolution of the proletariat for granted. When one set of ideals ran headlong into the other like a couple of linemen on a football field, he ended up with a bad case of . . . what did the guy with the glasses and the chin beard call it at this one lecture he'd gone to?

"Cognitive dissonance!" he said happily.

"Huh?" Mike said. He could talk about the dialectic till everything turned blue, but if something wasn't in the Marxist-Leninist lexicon, he didn't know and didn't want to know. Chaim thought that made him narrow, but more Communists were made in his image than in Chaim's.

"Never mind," Weinberg said. Then, alert as a prairie dog at a rattlesnake convention, he sat up and pointed north. "What's that?" he asked, his voice rising in alarm.

"Airplanes!" Mike said. "Lots of airplanes!" Cigarettes and ammo might not trump the almighty dialectic, but airplanes did. Carroll wasted no more time discussing them. He dove into the bombproof Chaim had been teasing him about only a few minutes earlier.

Chaim had a bombproof, too, shored up with whatever bits of timber he could liberate. He didn't jump into it right away. He had a prairie dog's curiosity. It made him stare up at the swarm of Ju-52/3s and He-111s rumbling across the sky, all of them, it seemed, straight toward him. The Junkers trimotors were obsolete as bombers, except in Spain. The Heinkels still did their deadly work everywhere from England to the Soviet border.

Where were the Republican fighters that would have given this air armada a hard time? Wherever they were, they weren't here, and here was where they needed to be. When bombs started tumbling out of the enemy planes, Chaim dove for his burrow like any prairie dog that wanted to live to raise a new litter.

Air attack was even worse than artillery bombardment. Chaim thought so when he was being bombed, anyhow. When he was being shelled, his opinion changed. It changed again when machine guns tried chewing him to bits. Whatever was happening to you *right now* was the worst thing in the world . . . till something else happened.

This was plenty bad enough. Dirt trickled down between his bits of planking. It wasn't just that it got on the back of his neck as he huddled there. If one of those bombs set all the dirt above him crashing down, he would die without any direct enemy wound. *How* good had his carpentry been? One way or the other, he'd find out. No, he didn't want it to be *or the other.*

More and more bombs whistled down. Bombs were easy to make: impact fuses, explosives, and sheet metal. Even Spaniards had a tough time screwing up the combination. The Nationalists had it down solid. "Enough already, goddammit!" Chaim screamed. No one paid any attention to him.

Eventually, bombs started falling farther away. The drone from the bombers' engines faded, then disappeared. It was over—till the next time. Chaim crawled out. He nodded to Mike Carroll, who was emerging from his bombproof at the same time. Then he peered over the battered parapet, to make sure Sanjurjo's men weren't rushing forward to take advantage of the bombing run.

They weren't. German troops probably would have been. However brave Spaniards were—and both sides were, above and beyond the call of duty—they weren't what anyone would call efficient. The landscape had been drastically rearranged. Except for a few saplings leaning at odd angles, it might have come straight from the cratered moon.

Seeing he wouldn't need his rifle right away, Chaim set it down. He pulled another Gitane from the pack. He missed his mouth the first time he put it in, and he needed three or four tries before he could light a match.

Mike watched with knowing eyes. "I've been there," he said. "Give me another one, will you?"

"Sure," Chaim said. If the other International had teased him, he probably wouldn't have. But Mike had indeed been through the mill with him. They smoked together. Little by little, Chaim stopped shaking. Cigarettes helped as much as anything, except maybe brandy. Trouble was, nothing helped much.

"WATCH YOURSELF, PETE," Herman Szulc warned. "Here come the Japs."

"I see 'em," Pete McGill answered. They'd patched things up, after a fashion. And on Shanghai's mad, crowded streets, missing Japanese soldiers was harder than seeing them. The Japs were the only people who behaved as if all the Chinese frantically hawking this, that, and the other thing—and the Europeans who livened up the throngs—weren't there at all. They marched straight ahead. If you didn't clear out, they'd knock you down with rifle butts (or just shoot you, if they happened to be in a lousy mood) and then walk over you. You couldn't do anything about it. Shanghai was theirs.

Pete got out of the way, along with his Marine buddies. They stood out in the crowd, not just because they were white but because they stood a head taller than most of the Chinese around them. Pete met the eyes of a noncom. He nodded first, with respect but without fear. Respect would do. The Jap nodded back, as if to say, *Maybe some other time, but not now.* Then he shouted at his men. They were already stiff as robots. They got stiffer yet.

"Goddamn monkeys think they're as good as white people," Szulc muttered.

"Watch it, Herman," Sergeant Larry Koenig snapped. "Too many folks here savvy some English."

"Yeah, yeah," Szulc said. They weren't on duty; he didn't have to kowtow to Koenig because the sergeant had those three stripes on his sleeve.

"You better watch it, Herman." Pete still enjoyed sticking the needle in. "Way you go on, you figure Polacks are as good as white people."

"Ah, your mother," Szulc said. If he'd been drunk they might well have started banging away at each other right there. But it was still morning. Nobody'd got potted . . . yet.

Another company of Japanese soldiers marched by. They *did* think they were as good as white men. Their faces were hard and impassive, but every line of their bodies shouted their pride. *We beat the crap out of the Russians once, and now we're doing it again,* they might have yelled. *And if you Yankees want to fuck around with us, step right up. We'll knock your ass over teakettle, too.*

They couldn't have been more different from the Chinese who scrambled away from them. The Chinese knew they were licked. Everybody knocked them around. They couldn't do a damn thing about it, any more than a wife stuck in a rotten marriage could when her husband beat her up for the hell of it. She might hate. Hell, she had to hate all the more when she had no hope. Hate or not, though, she was stuck. She had to take it. So did the Chinese.

"Good thing the Japs don't know you got yourself that White Russian girlfriend," Herman Szulc said with a leer. "They'd probably figure she was radioing everything you tell her straight to old Joe Stalin."

"Jesus Christ, Herman, shut the fuck up!" Pete said. "You open your big dumb mouth any wider, you'll fall right in."

"Who you callin' dumb?" Szulc growled. Some dumb guys didn't have a hint that they weren't the brightest bulbs in the chandelier. Others were uneasily aware that their candlepower left something to be desired. You really pissed them off when you called them stupid, because down deep they feared you knew what you were talking about. Szulc was one of those. He folded his hands into rocklike fists.

"Knock if off, Herman," Sergeant Koenig told him. "You got him, so he got you back."

"He called me a Polack first," Szulc said. Sometimes the Marine Corps looked a lot like third-grade recess.

Koenig only laughed. "Yeah? So? What are you, a sheeny like Weinstein?"

"Not me!" Szulc crossed himself. "He ain't just a yid, neither. He's a fuckin' Red. If anybody's sending shit to Stalin, he's the guy."

It was a good thing Max wasn't there, or he would have tried to clean Szulc's clock for him. It wasn't that he wasn't a Red. But he didn't let anybody rag on him for being a Jew. There weren't many Jewish leathernecks. The handful Pete had known were uncommonly tough, even for the Corps.

Before anything else could happen, the clock in the tower of the new Customs House chimed the hour. Pete checked his watch. It was a few minutes fast, so he adjusted it. "Hurray for Big Ching," he said. It wasn't Big Ben, but it was halfway around the world from London.

"Lottery ticket?" a woman screeched in the Marines' faces.

"No wantchee," Pete said, shaking his head. He'd picked up a bit of pidgin English since coming to Shanghai. It wasn't used much in Peking. There, the locals either knew English or, much more often, they didn't. Here, pidgin seemed a halfway house between English and Chinese. People who'd been here longer than he had said it held bits of Portuguese, too, and a mostly Chinese way of putting words together.

"My no savvy," the woman said.

"You savvy plenty good," Koenig told her. "Get lost." That wasn't proper pidgin, but she understood it anyhow. She said something in Chinese that sounded like a cat getting its tail stepped on. Koenig only laughed. "Good thing I don't know what that meant, or I'd have to do something about it," he said.

Then the woman spoke two words of perfectly clear English—"Fuck you!"—and accompanied them with the appropriate gesture. Pete wondered whether she'd learned that from a leatherneck or an English Marine. She'd got it down solid, wherever she'd found it.

And Larry Koenig went nuts. "No slanty-eyed cunt's gonna give me the finger!" he yelled, and started after her with intent to maim, or maybe to murder. Pete and Herman Szulc looked at each other for a split second. Then they both grabbed the sergeant and held on for dear life.

"Take it easy, man!" Pete said. "You'll set all the Chinks off!" Sure enough, the small, golden-skinned men and women were pointing and giggling at the spectacle of two white men trying to hold back a third.

"Like I give a shit! Let me go, goddammit!" Koenig tried something Pete had last seen from a dirty-fighting coach before he went overseas.

He still remembered what to do about it—remembered without thinking, the knowledge literally beaten into him. He jerked, twisted . . . and Koenig gasped in pain. "I'll break your wrist if you try any more of that," Pete said, and the other man had to know he meant it. "Now calm down, okay?"

What Koenig said then would have made a Marine sergeant blush— except he was one. "C'mon, man—take an even strain," Szulc advised, also not letting go. "Just an old Chinese broad. She's gone now anyway." So she was; the crowd had swallowed her up.

"I'll find her. I'll wring her scrawny neck when I do, too," Koenig ground out. He surged against the Marines who held him—but he didn't try anything else cute.

"You and McGill've been in China too long. You're both going Asiatic yourself," Szulc opined. "You want to clobber this gal for nothing, and he's all mushy over that gold-digging taxi dancer. This place'll drive anybody nuts if he stays long enough."

If Pete hadn't been hanging on to Koenig for all he was worth, he would have taken a swing at Szulc himself. Then the Chinese would have been treated to the spectacle of three Americans, each trying to beat the crap out of the other two. Even Japanese soldiers would have laughed at that. When the people who hated you fought among themselves, how could you lose?

Simple. You couldn't. And so Pete didn't clobber Herman Szulc, no matter how much Herman deserved it. And Koenig did eventually calm down—enough so they could let go of him, anyhow. And they walked on through Shanghai just as if it were their town after all.

NORTH. The front faced north. To Hideki Fujita, that meant one thing and one thing only: the Kwantung Army stood firmly astride the Trans-Siberian Railway. If the Russians wanted to do anything about it, they would have to come to the Japanese. He didn't think they would have an easy time doing that. His own countrymen had attacked the railroad in other places, too. Japanese radio claimed all kinds of breakthroughs against the Red Army, but Fujita had seen enough to understand that not everything the radio said was exactly true. You needed to impress the foreigners who were bound to be listening.

He did know what was happening behind him. Japanese engineers were systematically tearing up the railroad track and mining the ground on which it had lain. The Russians wouldn't have an easy time putting the Trans-Siberian Railway back together even if they did drive off the Kwantung Army.

And, without the railroad, Vladivostok would starve. Bombers from Japanese aircraft carriers and from bases in Manchukuo already pounded the town. The Russians were hunkering down for a siege. Well, they'd done the same thing at Port Arthur. It hadn't saved them then. Fujita didn't think it would save them now.

He pictured a map in his mind. Would the Emperor take Vladivostok for Japan, or would he say it was territory redeemed for Manchukuo? It didn't really matter one way or the other. Japanese influence would predominate no matter which flag flew there.

Then Russian artillery opened up. The Reds hadn't gone away, even if Fujita wished they would have. He cocked his head to one side, gauging the flight of the shells by the way they snarled through the air. He relaxed. Nothing aimed at him—not this time.

He lit an Aeroplane. Smoke helped when you couldn't take a drink. Everything around you seemed a little less important while you had a cigarette going. It was as if . . . as if you were laying down a smoke screen against the outside world.

He liked that well enough to say it out loud. Shinjiro Hayashi grinned and dipped his head. "Oh, very good, Sergeant-*san!*" he said.

If Hayashi, with his education, appreciated the joke, that meant it was a good one . . . didn't it? Fujita wished he wouldn't have had the afterthought. He remembered the days when he was a private himself. Any stupid joke the sergeant cracked was funny, for no other reason than that he was a sergeant. If you didn't laugh, he'd thump you like a drum. Of course sergeants slapped privates around; that was what privates were for. If you didn't keep your sergeant greased, the army would get even more miserable than it already was for a private.

Now Fujita had a thin gold stripe and two stars on his red collar tabs. Now he was the one who expected the sorry bastards under him to laugh at whatever came out of his mouth. And they did. Oh, they did. They knew where their rice came from, all right. But that meant he couldn't trust them. They would laugh even if he said something stupid—no, especially if he said something stupid. He remembered doing that. What was sweeter than laughing at a puffed-up sergeant who was playing the fool and didn't even know it?

Nothing, for a private. All the more reason for a sergeant to watch himself. Privates were unreliable, officers thought they were little tin gods. . . . You had to take care of yourself. Nobody would do it for you.

That also applied when the Russians came. Some of the people you led wouldn't be sorry to see you dead. If they got the chance to arrange that in a way that wouldn't land them in trouble, they were liable to do it.

Those were thoughts Fujita wished he hadn't had when Lieutenant Hanafusa came up to him and said, "You've done well since you got here, Sergeant. I wondered about you, because you didn't have much experience fighting in forests. But nobody can say you haven't picked it up in a hurry."

"Thank you very much, sir." Fujita wondered what Hanafusa had in mind. He also wondered if he would have done better to stay on Manchukuo's Mongolian frontier, where only sandstorms kept you from seeing for kilometers every which way and where any tree was a prodigy.

And so he heard the platoon commander's next words with a mournful lack of surprise: "We need some prisoners for interrogation. Take your squad forward and get me a couple. Try not to make too much of a fuss while you're doing it."

"Yes, sir," Fujita said—the only thing he could say. He did ask, "Right now, sir, or may we wait till after dark?"

Lieutenant Hanafusa looked surprised, as if the possibility had never crossed his mind. It probably hadn't. He'd got the order from above, and hadn't thought twice about it. After a few seconds, he said, "I suppose it will keep that long."

"Yes, sir," Fujita repeated. He couldn't say *Thank you* again; he would have meant it this time. Scooting forward at night, he and his men had at least a chance of coming back in one piece.

It started raining before the squad set out. Fujita didn't know whether to take that for good luck or bad. It would make finding Russians harder. But it would also make it harder for the Reds to hear his men coming. Nothing he could do about it either way. He just had to hope for the best.

"Stick close together," he told the Japanese. "We'll grab the first couple of men we catch and head on back." He made it sound easy. Whether it would be . . .

He had a compass that glowed in the dark. Without it, he probably would have blundered around in circles. Even by daylight, you couldn't see very far in these woods. At night, in the rain . . . He wondered what Lieutenant Hanafusa would say if he came back and told him the squad couldn't find any Russians. Nothing good. He was sure of that.

He walked right into a tree. "*Zakennayo!*" he snarled. It would have been worse if he weren't wearing his helmet. He would have mashed his nose instead of scratching his cheek. Muffled—and sometimes not so muffled—curses from his men said they were having their troubles, too.

How were you supposed to walk straight when you couldn't see where you were putting your feet? Only luck nobody sprained an ankle, or maybe broke one. And the lieutenant was back somewhere warm and dry. Of course he was. He was an officer.

Then somebody bumped into him. Before he could call his own man a clumsy idiot, the other fellow growled, "*Metyeryebyets!*"

Fujita didn't quite know what the endearment meant. He did know it wasn't in Japanese. "Grab him, boys!" he said happily.

The Red Army man didn't want to get grabbed. Fujita hit him in the side of the head with his entrenching tool. The Russian was wearing a helmet, but it rang his bell anyhow. If he hadn't had the helmet, Fujita might have smashed in his skull. That would have been a waste of some good luck.

Hanafusa wanted a couple of prisoners. If they didn't nab somebody else . . . *Maybe I can blame it on the rain,* Fujita thought. Or maybe not. Officers looked for results. If you didn't give them what they told you to get, whom would they blame? Themselves, for giving idiotic orders? Fat chance!

And than Senior Private Hayashi whooped, "I've got another one!" By the shouts and scuffle that followed, who had whom wasn't obvious. The Russians must have sent out their own patrol, and it had blundered straight into Fujita's. Sometimes luck counted more than skill. The Japanese snagged the second Red Army man.

A Russian opened up with a submachine gun, but none of the bullets came anywhere close to the the Japanese. The Red was firing blind. "Let's get out of here!" Fujita said. He'd never had an order obeyed with such alacrity.

Japanese sentries almost fired on the patrol before Fujita convinced them he was on their side. He hadn't come in where he thought, and had to make his way back to Lieutenant Hanafusa. "All right—you got them," Hanafusa said, eyeing the battered, unshaven, miserable-looking Russian captives. "Not so bad, *neh?*"

If Fujita used the entrenching tool on Hanafusa's skull, they'd kill him a millimeter at a time. He knew that, but his hand twitched all the same. He made it hold still. "No, sir," he said expressionlessly.

Chapter 12

Photographs and posters made Marshal Sanjurjo look tall and stern and heroic. He always wore splendid uniforms. Joaquin Delgadillo liked that. If you were somebody, you should look as if you were.

In the flesh, Sanjurjo was less imposing. He had a lot of flesh—were those three chins or four? He was shorter and wider than the posters made him out to be. He was also at least fifteen years older. He looked like a village druggist just on the point of retiring.

He still wore a fancy uniform. And, whether he was a hero or not, he had *cojones* enough to come up to the front on the northwestern outskirts of Madrid. If some traitor—and there were always traitors—had let the Republicans know he was coming, they could smash up these trenches with mortar bombs and cut off the Nationalist state's head. Or a lucky sniper could take care of it. The enemy's trenches lay almost a kilometer off, but even so. . . .

Sanjurjo eyed Sergeant Carrasquel, who stood at stiff attention. A slow smile spread across the marshal's face. He set a hand on Carrasquel's shoulder. He knew what kind of creature he had before him. "So tell me,

Sergeant, how are things here? Tell me the truth," he said. *Dígame la ver-dad.* He made the last three words a caressing invitation.

"It's fucked up, sir. But it's always fucked up, so what can you do?" the sergeant answered. "The Republicans are as stubborn as we are, and the Internationals over yonder, they're damn good troops. We need more of everything if we're gonna shift 'em."

"You get what we have," Sanjurjo said, no anger in his voice.

"Yes, sir. But we don't have enough," the sergeant said. "Just so you know, the rations suck, too." The look in his eye said he'd noticed San-jurjo wasn't missing any meals. Not even Carrasquel seemed ready to come out with that, though.

"You said it—things are fucked up." The crude phrase sounded much more elegant in Marshal Sanjurjo's mouth. The marshal turned to Del-gadillo. "Is this a good man, Sergeant?"

"I've got plenty worse, sir," Carrasquel replied.

That was the kindest thing he'd ever said about Joaquin. Sanjurjo's pouchy eyes were clever, also like a village druggist's. "How is it with you, soldier?" he asked. "Speak freely. I didn't come here to listen to polite *bull-shit.*" He used the English word with a certain sour relish. Delgadillo had heard it from the Republicans often enough to know what it meant.

"It's war, sir," he said. "How is it supposed to be?"

"That's a fair question, son," Sanjurjo said. "It's supposed to be a lot like this. Sometimes it's worse, eh, Sergeant?"

"It can always get worse." Carrasquel spoke with deep conviction. "I was in Morocco, fighting against the Rifs. If it gets much worse than that, I don't want to know about it, by God!"

"That was bad," Sanjurjo agreed. "Maybe the Western Front in the last war was worse. So much slaughter, and for nothing. But maybe it wasn't worse, too. When you fought the Rifs, you knew they really meant it."

Sergeant Carrasquel nodded. "Oh, are you ever right there, sir!"

All Delgadillo knew about the Rifs was that they were savages and the Spanish army had beaten them. He'd been a little kid when that fight ended. So Carrasquel had been in Morocco, then, had he? He didn't look old enough. Maybe vipers aged slower than ordinary human beings.

"I hoped our friends would go on supplying us after the European war started, but"—Sanjurjo spread his plump palms—"*así es la vida*. The Republicans have the same worries. We can still beat them. We *will* still beat them, eh?"

"*Absolutamente,* your Excellency!" Delgadillo said quickly. Was he going to tell the marshal the Nationalists would lose? Not likely! Sergeant Carrasquel might be convinced he was a dope, but he wasn't that big a dope.

"*Bueno,*" Sanjurjo said, and stumped down the trench. A gaggle of aides in almost equally gaudy uniforms followed him. They ignored Joaquin but edged away from Sergeant Carrasquel. They knew a dangerous man when they saw one.

"Well, kid, you can tell your grandchildren you talked with a big shot once upon a time," Carrasquel said gruffly.

"Yeah. How about that?" Joaquin said. "The *Caudillo*." It wasn't quite so strong a title as *Führer* or *Duce,* but it was plenty strong enough.

Carrasquel glanced after Sanjurjo's henchmen. When he decided they'd got out of earshot, he went on, "You know what else you can tell your grandkids?"

"What, Sergeant?" Delgadillo asked, as he was obviously meant to do.

"Tell 'em Sanjurjo's shit stinks just like yours," the older man growled.

Joaquin blinked. He'd expected something different. He looked around, too, to make sure no one could overhear. Satisfied, he spoke in a low voice: "If you feel that way, how come your aren't fighting for the Republic?"

"*Chinga* the Republic." Carrasquel spat. "Those assholes think workers' shit doesn't stink, just on account of they're workers. *Everybody's* shit stinks, God damn it to hell. Everybody's. You get down to the bottom of it, it's all shit."

If he'd been on the other side of the line when the fighting started, would he be cussing out the Nationalists now? Delgadillo couldn't ask; he'd said too much already. But he wouldn't have been surprised. Carrasquel needed to fight *somebody*. Who probably didn't matter much.

And, after some of the things Joaquin had seen, he had a devil of a time thinking the sergeant was wrong. Shit and rotten meat and maggots: things did end up like that, all right. What you did before then mattered, though . . . didn't it? *If it does, what am I doing here?*

What was Joaquin doing here? They'd drafted him. They'd made sure he couldn't run away, and they'd beaten the stuffing out of a couple of luckless lugs who tried. They'd shoot him if he deserted at the front, and they wouldn't even waste a cigarette on him before they did. In spite of everything, they'd made a soldier out of him. Turning into a soldier gave him the best chance to live.

A Republic machine gun growled to malign life. One of Marshal Sanjurjo's aides, a tall, gangly man whose head must have stuck up above the rim of the trench, let out a choking moan and crumpled, clutching at himself. Medics rushed over to him. Delgadillo wondered how long *he* would have had to lie there if he'd got hit. A hell of a lot longer than that, he was sourly sure. The medics carried the groaning officer past him on a stretcher.

"How bad?" Carrasquel asked in tones of professional interest.

"Scalp wound. He's bleeding like a pig, but he ought to make it," a medic answered. "A few centimeters lower, and . . ." He shook his head.

"Madonna, it hurts!" the officer said.

"I gave you morphine, *Señor*," the medic told him. "It'll make you easier soon." He and his comrades lugged the man away.

"It could have been the *Caudillo*," Joaquin said.

"Not unless he really was as big as his pictures make him out to be," Carrasquel said, so Delgadillo wasn't the only one who'd had that thought.

The rest of Sanjurjo's aides plainly thought they'd seen as much of the front as they wanted to, and more besides. Sanjurjo himself took the wounding, and the firing that went on afterwards, in stride. His attitude declared he'd known worse. He had nerve—that much of what they said about him to make him look good was true, anyhow.

Major Uribe's shrill voice rang out: "Come on, my dears! We have to let them know they can't get away with being so rude!"

Joaquin fired a few shots toward the Republican lines. He saw no good targets, but fired anyway. A bullet *might* do something. The one that creased the aide's head sure had. Beside him, Sergeant Carrasquel was doing the same thing. So were Nationalist soldiers all along the line. One of their machine guns opened up, and then another. Another Republican murder mill responded. It was getting dangerous out, whichever side you were on.

As Joaquin Delgadillo put a fresh clip on his rifle, he glanced toward Sanjurjo. What did the marshal make of his *maricón* battalion commander? By his smile, he already knew about Bernardo Uribe. If you were a good enough soldier, you could get away with almost anything that didn't hurt the way you fought. Uribe was, and then some.

How many times had Joaquin yelled "*¡Maricón!*" at the Republicans? And now he had a fairy giving him orders! War was a crazy business, all right. He shouldered the reloaded piece and squeezed off another shot at the enemy.

"MOSCOW SPEAKING." The newsreader's familiar voice came out of the radio at the Byelorussian airstrip. Sergei Yaroslavsky drank from a glass of strong, sweet tea as he listened to the morning report. Another pilot walked over to the battered samovar bubbling in a corner of the tent and poured a glass for himself. He already had a *papiros* sticking up at a jaunty angle from the corner of his mouth, as if he were Franklin D. Roosevelt. Tobacco and tea—how could you run a war without them?

On vodka, that's how, Sergei thought. The Russians had run on vodka long before they'd ever heard of tea or cigarettes, and on beer and mead and wine before they knew about vodka. That was all very well for a foot soldier. He thought about flying his SB-2 smashed out of his skull. He grimaced. No, not a pretty picture.

"Comrade Stalin reports heavy fighting on the frontier between the peace-loving Soviet Union and the regime of Hitler's jackal, Marshal Smigly-Ridz," the newsreader said. That was code of sorts, if you knew how to read between the lines. *Fierce fighting* and *stubborn fighting* weren't so bad. When they started talking about *heavy fighting,* the Devil's grandmother had spilled the pisspot into the borscht.

Well, that was nothing he didn't already know. If things were going well, would he have had to get out of Poland while German shells cratered the runway from which he'd been flying?

Across the table from him, Anastas Mouradian raised one dark eyebrow a few millimeters. The Armenian had no trouble understanding news reports, either. Sergei sometimes thought Armenians and Jews and people like that were born reading between the lines. He wondered why Russians weren't. Some Russians didn't even seem to know there were lines to read between.

"Despite the Red Army's displays of heroism, the campaign in the area illegally occupied by the Polish junta has not necessarily gone to the Soviet Union's advantage in all respects, due to the Nazis' treacherous intervention in a fight where they had no true interest." The radio newsreader paused portentously. "Accordingly, Comrade Stalin finds that the situation has changed."

He paused again, making sure he had everyone's attention. He did—all the officers waking up in the tent stared toward the radio. Curls of smoke rose from *papirosi* being smoked or held between index and middle fingers. Changed. In the middle of a war, there were few more ominous words. Changed *how*?

The newsreader had the answer, straight from the General Secretary's lips: "Up till this time, our dispute with the vile Polish clique has concerned only the border region they unjustly occupied. But, now that the jackals have invited the deadly German viper into their filthy burrow, they make it only too clear that they are a danger to all lovers of peace. This being so, we are no longer concerned with the border region alone. We shall punish the Smigly-Ridz regime as it deserves. Its very existence is a product of our unfortunate weakness during the civil wars following the glorious Soviet revolution. We shall make Poland—all of Poland—pay for its brazen effrontery."

He went on to talk about the war in the Far East. He also described the fighting there as heavy, which wasn't good news. But Sergei listened with only half an ear. He and Stas Mouradian weren't the only men who exchanged glances of what looked much too much like consternation. No one said anything; people naïve or stupid enough to do that had been weeded out by a process of brutal Darwinian selection. Even expressions could endanger, though. Somebody in here was bound to report to the NKVD.

Then again, maybe the local Chekist, whoever he was, also wore a look of consternation. Who wouldn't? If what the newsreader said meant what it sounded like, the USSR intended to attack, or more likely was attacking, Poland up and down their long frontier. The Red Army was much bigger than its Polish opposite number. If it was much better, it hadn't shown it yet.

And that was only half the problem—the smaller half, at that. So far, Hitler had been fighting a limited war against the Soviet Union. If Stalin widened that war, wouldn't the *Führer* do the same? The Red Army was bigger than the *Wehrmacht,* too. Better? Anybody who said so . . . probably spewed out propaganda for the radio and the newspapers.

Widening the war would have been adventurous enough without the fight in the Far East. With it? Sergei was reminded of a dinosaur like *Brontosaurus.* If it was looking forward when something bit it at the end of the tail, how long would it take to notice the trouble back there?

He shook his head as he lit a *papiros* of his own and stuck the end of the paper holder into his mouth. He had to watch himself. The USSR was a progressive state—the most progressive state in the world, as a matter of fact. You'd better not think of it as a dinosaur. If you did, you were liable to say something like that out loud. And if you did open your big mouth, it would be a camp or a bullet in the back of the head for you. Darwinian selection, all right!

The news ended. Music as syrupy-sweet as Crimean champagne poured out of the radio. No one turned it off even so. If you didn't want to listen to what the state wanted you to hear, weren't you subtly anti-Soviet? Somebody was liable to think you were, anyhow, and that would be all it took.

But you didn't have to pay attention to the music, the way you did with the news. "Well, well," someone ventured.

"How about that?" someone else added.

"We can whip the Poles," Sergei said. That was only a kopek out of his ruble of thought, but it was the kopek he could spend in public.

"Sure we can!" Three or four men said the same thing at the same time.

They all sounded relieved to be able to come out with something safe. Well, Sergei was relieved to come out with something safe himself.

"I wish Hitler didn't have panzers in Poland," Anastas Mouradian remarked.

No one responded to that, not for a little while. Stas liked to sail close to the wind, and everybody knew it. Who in the tent didn't wish there were no Germans in Poland? The Poles were easier to beat. Mouradian hadn't criticized anyone. Still, even mentioning those panzers seemed faintly indecent.

"Well, maybe it won't be so bad," Sergei said. You couldn't get in trouble for optimism (though he did wish he could have that *maybe* back).

"Maybe the Nazis will see we're serious about this Polish business and clear out," another flyer put in. "They've got their own troubles on their other frontier."

"We don't, of course," Mouradian said dryly. He was no *Brontosaurus;* he could contemplate wounded head and wounded tail at the same time.

"Not like theirs," the other flyer insisted.

He wasn't wrong. How much did being right matter, though? "They only fought for four years on two fronts last time," Mouradian said. This wasn't the first time he'd brought up that inconvenient truth.

"They lost," Sergei said. His crewmate sent him an *Et tu, Brute?* look.

Before Mouradian could say anything, the other pilot ran to the conversational ball and booted it far down the pitch: "That's right! And they'll lose this time, too! The historical dialectic makes it inevitable."

The dialectic! Heavy artillery! You could blow anybody out of the water when you trotted out the dialectic. But Anastas Mouradian didn't stay there to be blown to rhetorical smithereens. He nodded politely. "No doubt, Comrade. But how far will the cause of Socialism be set back by the conflict? How many farms and cities and little children will go up in smoke?"

"A fine question for the fellow who aims the bombs to ask," the pilot sneered.

"I serve the Soviet Union," Mouradian said. "I do try to serve the Soviet Union intelligently."

There was another one nobody wanted to touch. Sergei was far from sure serving the Soviet Union intelligently was what the apparatchiks who ran the country wanted. You got a command. You carried it out. You had no business wondering about it. That wasn't your responsibility.

But were you a man or were you a sheep? Which way were you more valuable to the state? If you were a man, weren't you safer pretending to grow wool? Sergei knew damn well you were. How much baaing had he already done? How much more would he have to do?

THE POWER TO BIND. The power to loose. St. Peter had it, if you took Jesus seriously. Whether you took Jesus seriously or not, Adolf Hitler had it—inside the borders of the Third *Reich,* anyhow. Peggy Druce found that out in a hurry.

Once the *Führer* said she could leave Germany, the mountains that had stood in her way for so long all at once turned into molehills. Konrad Hoppe came to her hotel room and affixed an exit visa to her passport as exactingly as if he were working with gold leaf. The scrawny Foreign Ministry official had met with her once before, to explain why she couldn't get out. *Because we don't want you to, that's why,* was what it boiled down to.

Peggy couldn't resist saying, "Nice of you to change your mind."

Hoppe didn't notice the sarcasm—or, if he did, he was armored against it like a battleship. "My superiors have given me my orders, *Frau* Druce. I follow them."

They'd given him different orders not so long before. He'd followed those, too. What did Jerome K. Jerome call the German attitude toward civic responsibility? Peggy smiled, remembering. *Blind obedience to everything in buttons*—that was it. And the Englishman, writing at the very end of the nineteenth century, had gone on to say *Hitherto, the German has had the blessed fortune to be exceptionally well governed; if this continues, it will go well with him. When his troubles will begin will be when by any chance something goes wrong with the governing machine.*

Had Jerome K. Jerome had a crystal ball, or maybe one of H.G. Wells' time machines, to look into the future and see just what would happen next? If he could see it, why couldn't everybody else? Hell, why couldn't anybody else? Why couldn't the Germans see it themselves?

Blind obedience to everything in buttons, dammit.

She realized she'd missed some pearl of wisdom falling from *Herr* Hoppe's lips. "I'm sorry?"

"I *said*"—he rolled his eyes at Anglo-Saxon lightmindedness—"the train to Copenhagen departs each afternoon at half past three. Shall I secure you a Pullman berth on today's train?"

Now they couldn't get rid of her fast enough. "Yes, please," she said, and even unbent enough to add, "Thank you very much." Then she decided to press her luck a little: "Can you send me a cab, so I can bring my suitcase along easier?" She would have gone without it—Lord, she would have gone naked if she had to!—but why not see what she could get away with?

Konrad Hoppe didn't even blink. "*Aber natürlich.* The cab will be here at half past two, precisely." Taxis in wartime, fuel-starved Berlin were almost as scarce as Nazi big shots with Jewish wives, but the *Führer* had ordered the machinery to give Peggy what she wanted, and Hoppe was one of those smoothly turning gears. He did say, "Please remember to be punctual."

"*Jawohl!*" Peggy said. Mussolini boasted that he made the trains in Italy run on time, but he lied. Everything in Germany ran on time. As far as Peggy could see, nobody had to make it do that; it just did. Half past two wouldn't mean 2:29 or 2:31. It would be 2:30 on the dot. And she would be in the lobby waiting.

"Very well, then." Hoppe clicked his heels. "If you will excuse me, dear lady . . ." With a nod that was almost a bow, he made his getaway.

I'll make mine, too, Peggy thought, almost delirious with glee. But she had to attend to one more thing, no matter how little she wanted to. She picked up the telephone in her room. When the hotel operator asked whom she wanted to call, she sighed and said, "The American embassy, please."

"One moment," the German woman said primly. It took more than a moment, but Peggy had known it would. Like every other part of civilian life, the telephone system was neglected these days. Well, all except one part of it: somebody from the *Gestapo* or the SD would be listening to her conversation. She was as sure of that as she was of her own name. What could you do, though?

The embassy operator came on the line. The hotel operator put Peggy through. She gave her name and asked to speak to Constantine Jenkins. "One moment," the embassy operator said, only in English, not German. "He may be in a meeting."

If he was, Peggy could get out of Berlin with a clear conscience. She laughed a sour internal laugh. Would she ever have a clear conscience again? It seemed painfully improbable, but she would have done her best here. No, it wasn't the same thing, goddammit.

The operator came back on the line. "I can connect you to him."

"Thank you," Peggy said, not without wincing. She'd been connected to the undersecretary, all right! Hadn't she just?

"Hello, Mrs. Druce." Jenkins sounded properly formal. No doubt he also knew the Nazis would be tapping the telephone lines.

"Hi. I just wanted to let you know they've got a place for me on the train to Copenhagen this afternoon," Peggy said. "And I wanted to thank you for all your help."

"It was my pleasure, believe me," Jenkins answered. Did he sound all male and knowing there for a moment, or was that only Peggy reading between the lines? She couldn't very well ask him.

"If you hadn't suggested that I write to the *Führer* with my problem, I don't know if it ever would have got fixed," Peggy said. Not only was that true, but it reminded the lurking listeners Hitler was on her side. *Can't hurt,* she thought.

"Nothing else was working. I figured you should go straight to the top and try your luck there," he said. Peggy found herself nodding. Blind obedience to everything in buttons, sure as hell. Jenkins spoke again, on a different note this time: "And I hope everything else is all right?"

"Oh, yes!" Peggy said quickly. She'd got her period—and what the Germans used for pads these days was a shame and a disgrace. Wouldn't *that* have been fun? She couldn't have brought a visible sign of her shame home to Herb. But how she could have found a discreet German doctor without opening herself up to *Gestapo* blackmail forever was beyond her. One thing she didn't need to worry about, anyhow. Those things made a dismayingly short list these days.

"Well, that's good," Jenkins said. "Believe me, we like to do everything we can for Americans in Germany. Too often, it's less than we'd want. I hope everything goes very well for you, and I hope to see you again one day after everything settles down, if it ever does."

"Thanks again," Peggy said. "So long." She hung up. *I hope to see you again*? If that didn't mean *I hope to lay you again,* what did it mean? She was damned if she'd ever get drunk with a diplomat again.

She lugged her suitcase down the hall to the elevator at ten after two. It was heavy and clumsy. Why didn't it have wheels and a handle with more reach? But that was a side issue. She wouldn't be late here, not for nothin'.

The elevator operator was a woman. A gray-haired man had had the job, but something—war work? conscription? trouble with the *Gestapo*?—had pulled him away from it. The war was biting more and more people these days.

Peggy checked out and settled down to wait. She watched traffic go by on the street outside. There wasn't much to watch: buses, military vehicles, a doctor's car (a placard taped to the door proclaimed what that one was).

Right at 2:30, a taxi pulled up in front of the hotel. Peggy hauled her suitcase out onto the sidewalk. "Let me take that for you," the driver said. His left hand was artificial, but his right arm was plenty strong. Into the trunk the suitcase went. "The train station, yes?"

"Yes!" Peggy said. He opened the door for her, then got in himself. He used his right hand to clamp the thumb and fingers of the left onto the wheel. That left the good hand free to shift gears, and to help the other as needed.

Maybe he saw Peggy's eye on him, for he said, "It's clumsy, but it works. And I've had plenty of practice since the last war. Only one accident in all that time, and it wasn't my fault. The police court said so."

"Good for you," Peggy said. She gave him a big tip when they got to the station. He took her suitcase out of the trunk as easily as he'd put it in, but she didn't let him carry it to the ticket counter. Enough was enough. She could manage, and she did.

Her ticket was waiting. She'd had paranoid fantasies that it wouldn't be, that the Nazis were still playing cat-and-mouse games with her. But no. Here it was, in her hands. The conductor gravely examined it when she walked up to the train. "I am required to ask you to show me an exit visa," he said.

"Here you go." Peggy was proud to show it off.

"*Sehr gut. Danke schön,*" he said, touching the brim of his cap. "All is in order. You may board."

You may board! If those weren't the three most beautiful words in the German language, Peggy didn't know what could top them. She found her berth. It had to be the best one on the train. The Germans were laying it on thick, all right. About time, too! Peggy settled in with a sigh of pleasure.

At 3:30—not 3:29, not 3:31—the train jerked into motion. "Yippee!" Peggy said. No one heard her. It wouldn't have mattered if someone had. You couldn't translate *Yippee!* into German. But she was on her way home at last.

HANS-ULRICH RUDEL ALWAYS WONDERED what would happen when Colonel Steinbrenner summoned him to the tent that did duty as squadron HQ. Showing you were worried was only likely to make things worse, though. "Reporting as ordered, sir," he said, drawing himself up to stiff attention.

"At ease," Steinbrenner said. "You're not in trouble this time, *Oberleutnant* Rudel."

"*Oberleutnant?*" Hans-Ulrich squeaked in surprised. He'd just got promoted. "Thank you very much, sir!"

"You're welcome. You earned it." Steinbrenner opened a box that sat on the card table serving as a desk. "You earned this, too." He took out a large Iron Cross on a red-white-and-black ribbon.

"A *Ritterkreuz!*" Rudel said, all breath and no voice—he was beyond even squeaking now.

"That's right. You've got the first Knight's Cross in the squadron. Not the last, I hope, but the first. Congratulations!" Medal in hand, Colonel Steinbrenner stood up. He came up and handed it to Hans-Ulrich. "You wear it around your neck."

"Yes, sir. I know," Hans-Ulrich said dazedly. Too much was happening too fast. He managed to put it on without dropping it. If you had to have a shield for your Adam's apple, where could you find a better one?

"I've got the gold pips for your shoulder straps and the new collar patches with two chickens on them, too," Steinbrenner said. "I figured you'd rather put the *Ritterkreuz* on first, though."

"Uh, yes, sir," Rudel managed.

Something besides the medal sat in the box, too: a piece of paper. Unfolding it, Steinbrenner read, " 'In recognition of Lieutenant Rudel's cleverness in suggesting the installation of antipanzer cannon on the Ju-87, and in recognition of his gallantry in personally testing the new weapons system against the enemy.' That's not a bad citation. No, not half bad." He stuck out his hand.

Hans-Ulrich shook it. "I never expected any of this," he muttered.

"Well, you've got it. Enjoy it." Steinbrenner's eyes twinkled. "And you get to buy everybody drinks twice—once for the promotion, and once for the Knight's Cross."

"Oh, joy." Now Hans-Ulrich's voice sounded distinctly hollow. That was an honor he could have done without. He'd be the only sober guy at a party—no, two parties—full of rowdy drunks. They'd get rowdy on his Reichsmarks, too, and it wasn't as if he were rolling in them.

"You could even unbend a little yourself," the squadron commander said. "It's not as if you haven't got a good excuse."

"I don't care to do that, sir, thank you." Rudel stayed within military discipline. He also stayed stubborn.

"Well, have it your way. You've earned the right this time." Colonel Steinbrenner, for once, didn't feel like arguing or teasing.

Hans-Ulrich could be stubborn about several things at the same time: a Renaissance man, of sorts. "You need to give Albert something, too," he said. "If we'd got hit, he'd be roast meat just like me."

Steinbrenner tapped another box on the table with the nail of his index finger. "Iron Cross, First Class. Does that suit you, your Excellency?"

Sarcasm went over Rudel's head as often as not. This time, his ears burned. "Yes, sir," he mumbled.

"Well, good. Now get out of here so I can pin it on him. He's due in"—Steinbrenner glanced at his watch—"six minutes."

Thus encouraged, Hans-Ulrich got. Sergeant Dieselhorst wasn't coming yet, which was good. If he saw the Knight's Cross, he'd figure he was in line for a medal, too. This way, it would be a surprise—and the nice kind of surprise, at that.

Several groundcrew men walked out of a revetment where they'd been working on a damaged Stuka. As usual, their chatter was two parts technical jargon, one part filth. One of them waved to Hans-Ulrich: not much spit and polish on a working air base. The wave came to a jerky stop when he saw the new medal at Rudel's throat. *"Heilige Scheisse!"* he said. "That's a *Ritterkreuz!"*

The noncoms in greasy coveralls swarmed over Hans-Ulrich, pumping his hand and pounding him on the back. Then, before he could do more than squawk, they hoisted him onto their shoulder and carried him back to the airstrip. "Look!" one of them yelled. "He's flying!" The others thought that was so funny, they almost dropped him.

Pilots came out of their tents to see what the fuss was about. They started yelling and beating on Hans-Ulrich, too. "You've got balls, you little squirt," one of them said—he was twenty-five, a whole two years older than Rudel. "Now if you only had some brains."

"Hey, he thought up those antipanzer guns," another flyer said. "Maybe he's not as dumb as he looks."

"Maybe he's not as homely as he looks, either, but I wouldn't bet on it," the first man said. They all laughed like lunatics. Hans-Ulrich didn't think he was particularly homely, but nobody cared what he thought. The first flyer went on, "We ought to find out what the French girls think."

Everybody cheered—everybody but Rudel. Several of the local girls could be friendly . . . for a price. Being friendly with them came with a price, too. Several flyers had come down with drippy faucets. The medics had some brand-new pills that could actually cure the clap, but Colonel Steinbrenner wasn't amused any which way.

As for Hans-Ulrich, he said, "Spare me, please." The other Germans laughed, some of them not so good-naturedly now. What kind of pilot was he if he didn't want to drink or to screw? It wasn't that he didn't have animal urges of his own, either. He did—did he ever! But he didn't feel like wasting them on French popsies who probably smelled like garlic.

"We weren't asking what you thought of the girls, Rudel," the twenty-five-year-old said. "We want to know what they'll think of you."

"I don't care." Hans-Ulrich started to kick in earnest. "And put me down, for heaven's sake!"

They did, none too gently. He was just working his way through the *Luftwaffe* pack when Sergeant Dieselhorst came back from Steinbrenner's headquarters tent, his new decoration prominent on the left breast of his tunic. That took some of the heat off Hans-Ulrich, because people had to congratulate—and to thump—Dieselhorst, too.

Eventually, the two men from the Stuka crew managed to shake hands with each other. "Well, sir, here's another fine mess you got me into," Dieselhorst said, sounding like a Laurel and Hardy film.

"As long as we keep getting out of them," Rudel answered.

"I'll drink to that," Dieselhorst said, and everybody cheered—not least because everybody knew Hans-Ulrich wouldn't. The sergeant went on, "The old man told me you got promoted, too. You can watch us get plowed on your cash—twice."

That put the focus back on Rudel. *Thanks a lot, Albert,* he thought. The flyers and groundcrew men bayed like wolves, anticipating their sprees. They teased Hans-Ulrich about not joining in. "If you're wasted, too, you won't give a rat's ass about what it costs," someone said. Half a dozen men roared agreement.

"Not then," Rudel said.

"Why worry about afterwards?" another pilot asked. "Afterwards, the enemy's liable to smoke us. Don't you want something fun to remember while you're going down in flames?" Rudel didn't answer, and a lot of the good cheer drained out of the gathering. Some questions cut too close to the bone.

Chapter 13

Theo Hossbach, Heinz Naumann, and Adalbert Stoss sat at the north-easternmost corner of Poland. A scrawny chicken roasted above a fire. Naumann reached out to turn the stick on which the bird was spitted. "Well, we're here," the panzer commander said morosely. "We did what they brought us to Poland to do. Hot damn!" He gave the chicken another turn.

"Hot damn," Stoss echoed. Theo, as usual, kept his mouth shut. It wasn't that he disagreed with his crewmates; he just didn't feel like talking.

With some help from the Poles, the German panzers had smashed through the Red Army and cut a hell of a lot of Russians in this invaded chunk of Poland off from their homeland. Now German and Polish troops were methodically mopping them up.

That was all very well. It would have been better than all very well if only the Russians hadn't just poured across the rest of the Polish border. How hard could the Poles fight? If the Russians cut a couple of railroad lines . . . Theo glanced over at their Panzer II, an angular shadow in the long, slowly deepening northern twilight. In spite of the surprising Soviet panzers, it had come a long way and done a lot of hard fighting without taking much damage in return.

But it ran on gasoline. If the gasoline couldn't get through, the machine was nothing but nine tonnes of scrap metal. A dead turtle, a shell without legs. And, in that case, Theo and Heinz and Adi were nothing but three foot soldiers. The only problem with that was, they didn't have rifles and they didn't have helmets. Well, if you were going to piss and moan about every little thing . . .

"So what's going through your thick head now, Theo?" Naumann asked. Like Ludwig Rothe before him, he recognized Theo wouldn't say much on his own. Unlike the late Ludwig, he kept trying to get answers anyway.

"Gasoline." Theo doled out a word.

"Now why would you worry about something like that?" Adalbert Stoss said. "It's not like we need it or anything."

"Heh," Naumann said, sounding as laconic as Theo usually did. The panzer commander looked around. There wasn't much to see, nor would there have been on a sunny noon: a burnt-out farmhouse and a barn (that was where the chicken must have come from), some crops growing out in the fields, and a couple of dead Russians just starting to bloat and stink a hundred meters or so past the barn. Heinz shook his head. "If the world ever needed an enema, you'd plug it in right here, by God."

Somewhere a couple of kilometers away, a machine gun opened up. All three panzer men leaned toward the noise. "Russian piece," Stoss said.

"We might have captured it," Naumann said. And so the Germans might have; you used anything you could get your hands on. Theo had seen that in France. If it could hurt the other guy, you grabbed it, turned it around, and started shooting it at him.

Another machine gun spoke up to answer: an unmistakable German MG-34. "They might have captured it," Adi Stoss said, grinning.

Heinz didn't grin back. He made a sour face instead. Theo didn't like that. The rivalry between driver and panzer commander hadn't gone away after Adi ducked Heinz in that French creek. Naumann had the rank, and maybe the meanness. But, while he was no weakling, he wasn't in Stoss' league for muscle. Theo hoped trouble wouldn't come of it. He wished he could do something, but had no idea what to do. Working with artillery fuses was nothing next to this.

"We'll sleep in shifts tonight," Naumann decreed. "We all sack out at once, we're liable to wake up with our throats cut." He glared a challenge at Adi Stoss. Adi only nodded back; what the sergeant said made obvious sense. Heinz muttered to himself. Yes, he wanted an excuse to come down on the driver. If he didn't find one, chances were he'd go and invent one.

Theo drew the first watch. The panzer crew had long since doused the fire. Blankets would do on a mild summer night, and why advertise where you were? Theo held on to his pistol. If some Russian sneaked inside of thirty meters before trying to pot him with a Mosin-Nagant, he could defend himself with some hope of hitting back. Otherwise . . . Well, the weight in his hand was comforting, anyhow.

The moon, swelling toward full, spilled pale light from low in the south. Moonshadows stretched long. They looked black as the inside of whatever Satan used in place of a soul. Anything could hide in them, anything at all.

Not that the Russians needed such advantages. They could hide in places where most people wouldn't even find places. Then they'd wait till you went by and shoot you in the back. They carried next to no food—only ammo and grenades and sometimes vodka. If they wanted to eat, they had to scavenge from the countryside. And they did. Theo's stomach growled, reminding him of the chunk of chicken in there. But the Reds were the prize chicken thieves.

Here and there, off in the distance, rifle shots and occasional bursts of machine-gun fire marred the night's stillness. The Russians were supposed to have been cleared out of this stretch of Poland, no matter what was going on farther south. Some of them hadn't got the word, though. They didn't fight with a great deal of skill, but they had no quit in them.

In due course, Theo woke Adi Stoss. He jumped back in a hurry, because Adi came awake with a trench knife in his hand. "Oh. It's you," the driver said then, and made the knife disappear.

"Me," Theo agreed.

Adi yawned and sat up. "Anything going on?"

"Nothing close."

"That's all that matters," Stoss said.

"*Ja.*" Theo hesitated. He thought he had a better chance talking to the driver than to the panzer commander . . . and Naumann lay a few meters away, snoring like a sawmill. "You ought to take it easy on Heinz. He doesn't like it when you give him grief."

"You think I have fun when he rides me?" Stoss returned.

"He's a sergeant," Theo said, as if that explained everything. If you'd been in the army for even a little while, it damn well did.

"I don't care if he's a fucking field marshal," Adi answered. "Nobody's going to call me a kike."

So that still rankled, did it? Theo didn't suppose he should have been surprised. "He didn't mean anything by it," he said.

"Ha!" One syllable carried a tonne's weight of disbelief.

Theo gave it up. He didn't know what else he could do. "Just be careful," he said.

"*Ja, Mutti,*" Adi answered indulgently. *Yes, Mommy* chased Theo under his blanket, as Stoss had no doubt intended it to do.

Dawn came early. Black bread spread with butter from a tinfoil tube and ersatz coffee made a breakfast of sorts. Heinz Naumann, who'd had the last watch, turned to Theo and said, "See if we've got any new orders. Or are they just going to have us sit here with our thumbs up our asses?"

"I'll find out," Theo said. Climbing back into the panzer felt good. So did putting on the earphones and hooking into the radio net. Like anyone else, Theo enjoyed doing things he was good at, and *Wehrmacht* training made damn sure he was damn good at using the panzer's radio set.

When he stuck his head out of the hatch in front of the engine compartment, Heinz barked, "Well?"

"We're ordered to motor back to the railhead at Molodetschna," Theo reported. "Further orders when we get there."

"*Himmeldonnerwetter!*" Naumann burst out. "Why'd we come all the way up here, then? A round trip to fucking nowhere, with the chance of getting shot or blown up thrown in for a bonus!"

"Gasoline at the railhead?" Stoss put in. "We've got enough to get there—I think so, anyhow—but not much more than that."

"*Wunderbar,*" Heinz said sourly. "What do we do if we run dry? Hoof it?"

"See if we can get a tow, if we're close," Adi answered. "If we can't . . . Well, d'you want to stick around?"

"Here? Christ, no!" Heinz said. Theo felt the same way. There were stories about what the Reds did to Germans they caught. Theo didn't know if those stories were true, and he didn't want to find out, either. He slid back into the Panzer II. The other crewmen also came aboard. The reliable little Maybach engine fired up right away. Off they went, back in the direction they'd come from.

THE FRENCH LIEUTENANT EYED VACLAV JEZEK with what might have been sympathy. He gargled something in his own language. Vaclav looked back blankly. He didn't understand a word. Even if he had, he wouldn't have let on.

Benjamin Halévy turned French into Czech: "He wants your antitank rifle. They're obsolete, he says. They don't penetrate the armor of the latest German tanks."

"Tell him no," Vaclav said at once. The heavy weight on his right shoulder, the recoil bruises that never got a chance to heal up, had become a part of him.

More French from the lieutenant. He couldn't just demand; Vaclav was a foreign ally, not somebody under his direct command. "He wants to know why you're so enamored of an outmoded weapon."

"Why I'm so what?" Vaclav scratched his head.

"Why you like it so much."

"Why didn't you say so in the first place? Tell him the Germans still have plenty of old tanks and armored cars, and my beast'll do for them. Tell him I've got a decent chance of killing a man from a kilometer and a half away with this baby, too."

Sergeant Halévy spoke in French. So did the French officer. Halévy translated: "He says it wasn't intended as a sniper's rifle."

"I don't give a fuck what it was intended for. It works," Vaclav declared.

He and the lieutenant stared at each other in perfect mutual incomprehension. To the logical Frenchman, that antitank rifle was made to destroy tanks. If it couldn't do the job for which it was made, it was useless. Vaclav had found it could do other things better than the ordinary rifle he'd carried till he took the big piece from a casualty.

"It will be your responsibility." The lieutenant sounded grave even when Vaclav couldn't understand him. After Halévy translated, the French officer seemed more like Pilate washing his hands.

"That's fine," Vaclav said at once. What was wrong with these people? He had less trouble understanding Germans. He hated their guts, but at least he could see what made them tick. Something else occurred to him. He rudely pointed at the young lieutenant. "You're discontinuing these rifles, right?"

"*Oui.*" The Frenchman couldn't have been haughtier. "That is what I am trying to explain to you."

"Yeah, yeah. That means you're going to shitcan all the rounds that go with it, too, aren't you?"

Sergeant Halévy raised a gingery eyebrow. "Hey, boy, I see where you're going." He translated for the lieutenant yet again.

"*Mais certainement,*" the French officer replied. Again, to him, if the rounds couldn't kill tanks, they couldn't do anything.

Vaclav had a different idea. "Don't throw 'em out. Give 'em to me. I'll be the—waddayacallit?—the official obsolete rifle-toter, and I'll get the guys in my squad to lug what I can't. They know what this baby can do." *Even if you don't, asshole.* He affectionately patted the antitank rifle's padded stock. With a bit of luck, he wouldn't have to quarrel with stuck-up French quartermaster sergeants any more.

With a bit of luck . . . How much would the nasty little gods in charge of war dole out? Have to wait and see.

"This is most irregular," the French officer said after the Jew translated one more time.

"Fine. It's irregular," Vaclav said. "But if it's *officially* irregular . . ." Maybe that would get through to the lieutenant.

The fellow eyed him. "You go out of your way to be difficult, *n'est-ce pas?*"

"To the Nazis, sure. Not to anybody else." Vaclav lied without hesitation. He was difficult with anybody who got in his way. The jerks on your own side would screw you over worse than the enemy if you gave 'em half a chance.

After more back-and-forth between Halévy and the Frenchman, the lieutenant threw his hands in the air and strode off. "He says, have it your own way," Halévy reported. "He'll see that you get the ammo. He'll probably see that you end up ass-deep in it—he's not real happy with you."

"I'd rather have too much than not enough," Jezek said.

He wondered if he meant that when he got two truckloads of wooden crates full of the thumb-sized cartridges the antitank rifle fire. No, he couldn't very well burden the Czechs in his squad with that load. Each man's share would have squashed him flat.

That meant dealing with a quartermaster sergeant after all. Fortunately, this wasn't the guy he'd almost murdered a few months earlier. Benjamin Halévy sweetened up the French noncom, and the fellow seemed amazingly willing to hang on to most of the ammo and issue it as needed.

"What did you say to him?" Vaclav asked.

"I asked him how he'd like to be the *official*"—Halévy bore down on the word—"keeper of what's left of the antitank-rifle ammunition. He jumped at the chance."

Vaclav laughed. "Swell! You know more about dealing with these people than I do, that's for sure." He sent the quartermaster sergeant a suspicious stare. "Now, will he turn loose of the stuff when I need it, or will he decide he has to keep it because it's too important to fire off?"

Halévy spoke more French. The supply sergeant raised his right hand, as if taking an oath. "He says he'll be good," the Jew reported. Vaclav decided he'd have to take that—it was as good as he'd get. And if the Frenchman turned out to be lying, threatening to blow a hole in him with the antitank rifle ought to get his attention.

Now that Vaclav had enough ammunition for months if not years, he found that he had little to do with it. The Germans had pulled most of their armor out of this sector. They were digging in for all they were worth; it might have been 1916 over again. The French kept promising offensives, then stopping in their tracks whenever the boys in field-gray shot back at them.

Without tanks and armored cars to shoot at, he started doing just what he'd told the snooty young French lieutenant he'd do: he sniped at the Germans from long range. Behind their lines, the *Wehrmacht* men moved around pretty freely. They didn't think anyone could hit them from the Allies' positions. One careful round at a time, Vaclav taught them they were wrong.

"Congratulations," Benjamin Halévy told him one day.

"How come?" Jezek asked.

"Prisoners say the Nazis really want the son of a bitch with the elephant gun dead," Halévy answered.

It was a compliment of sorts, but it was one Vaclav could have lived without. He hoped he could go on living with it. He was a careful sniper. He never fired from the same place twice in a row. He didn't move from one favorite spot to another. As often as not, he didn't know whether he'd shift to the left or right till he tossed a coin to tell him. If he couldn't guess, the Germans wouldn't be able to, either. He made sure nothing on his ratty uniform shone or sparkled (that was easy enough). He fastened leafy branches to his helmet with a strip of rubber cut from an inner tube to break up its outline.

German bullets started cracking past him more often than they should have even so. Regretfully, he decided the prisoners had known what they were talking about. When one of those bullets knocked a sprig off his helmet camouflage, he realized the Germans had to have a sniper of their own hunting him.

That made for a new kind of game, one he wasn't even slightly sure he liked. It wasn't army against army any more. The Germans didn't think of him as one more interchangeable part in an enormous military machine. They wanted him dead, him in particular. This was personal. He could have done without the honor.

When he complained, Sergeant Halévy said, "All you have to do is put down the antitank rifle and go back to being an ordinary soldier."

"I'm killing a lot more Germans than the ordinary soldiers are," Vaclav said.

"Then you'd better figure they'll do their goddamnedest to kill you," Halévy replied.

Vaclav started hunting the German sniper. He found a brass telescope in an abandoned farmhouse (it wasn't as if the officers on his side would give him field glasses—perish the thought!) and painted it a muddy brown so it wouldn't betray him. He also had to be careful not to let the sun flash off the objective lens and give him away.

The German was good. Jezek might have known he would be. Well, he wasn't so bad himself. That he still prowled and hunted proved it. He took shots at other Nazis as he got the chance. Somewhere over there, a German with some kind of fancy rifle of his own was waiting for a mistake. If Vaclav made one, he wouldn't have to worry about making two— or about anything else ever again.

JULIUS LEMP STUDIED HIS ORDERS. He turned to his executive officer. "Well, Klaus, what do you think of these?"

Klaus Hammerstein blinked. He'd served on the U-30 with Lemp since before the war started, but as a lowly *Leutnant zur See* till the previous exec got tapped for a command of his own. Now, newly promoted to *Oberleutnant zur See,* and to second in the chain of command, Hammerstein had to deal with his skipper in a whole new way. "They're interesting, that's for sure," he ventured.

"Interesting. *Ja.*" There was barely room for two people in Lemp's curtained-off little excuse for a cabin. You worked with what you had, on the boat and with the crew. "What do these orders make you wonder?" Lemp pressed. If Klaus didn't have what it took to swing it as the executive officer, they both needed to find out right away.

The kid studied them again. "How many other boats are getting orders just like these right now?" he said after a pause only a little longer than it should have been.

And Lemp nodded, pleased. "There you go! That's exactly what I'd like to find out." Naval high command wouldn't tell him, of course. Anything he didn't urgently need to know was something he shouldn't know. What he didn't know, he couldn't spill if things went wrong and he got captured.

"I could ask around," Klaus said.

"Don't," Lemp told him, not without regret. "Anybody who told you would be breaking security. Better not to tempt somebody—and better not to give the *Gestapo* an excuse to come down on us."

"Oh," Hammerstein said, and then, "Right." Lemp's head went up and down once more, crisply this time. Things went better when you didn't need to worry about looking over your own shoulder . . . quite so much, anyhow.

Two days later, the U-30 chugged out into the North Sea. The men ate like pigs. You had to get rid of the fresh food first, because it wouldn't keep. They'd go back to sausage and tinned sauerkraut and hard-baked bread soon enough—too soon, really. Boiled beef, stewed chicken, fresh cabbage, even some peaches . . . Lemp gobbled down his share. He might have eaten a little more than his share. He was the skipper, after all. But his pants still fit all right, so he couldn't have been too much of a greedyguts.

Gerhart Beilharz put the *Schnorkel* through its paces. Lemp was less nervous about the gadget than he had been when it first got installed. It hadn't misbehaved too badly, and it did come in handy every now and then. Lemp still would have liked it better if the brass had given it to him as a reward rather than a punishment.

The tall engineer said, "It's working the way it's supposed to, Skipper."

"All right." Lemp hoped it was. He was also more willing to believe Beilharz than he had been when the beanpole came aboard with the *Schnorkel.* Beilharz had to be two meters if he was a centimeter. He needed his *Stahlhelm,* all right. U-boats weren't built with people his size in mind.

This was a different kind of patrol. Instead of telling him to go out into the Atlantic to torpedo freighters traveling between the Americas and England, the orders over which he and Klaus had puzzled instructed him to stay in the North Sea and patrol north and south between two fixed parallels of latitude. He was to sink anything he saw, and to be especially alert for Royal Navy warships.

That codicil kept him scratching his chin. The Royal Navy wasn't in the habit of pushing into the North Sea. As long as it could keep German surface vessels bottled up—which it hadn't managed with the *Admiral Scheer*—it kept its distance, leery not only of U-boats but also of land-based airplanes.

So why did his orders talk about enemy warships as if expecting them to rush into the path of his patrol? It made for a nice strategic question, one that gave both officers and ratings something to chew on. Lemp had his own opinion—or rather, his own suspicion. He didn't voice it; even on a U-boat, people were often reluctant to contradict the skipper. He was amused to discover he wasn't the only one to arrive at that suspicion. Amused, yes, but not surprised. If you could read a map and thought a little about how and where the war was going, it was one of the things that seemed likely.

Likely, of course, didn't have to mean true. It might prove nothing but so much moonshine. Lemp knew how much he didn't know. The ratings sounded much more confident than he did. They didn't worry about what they didn't know. From his days in school, Lemp remembered Socrates going on about such things.

Socrates had got sunk for his trouble. Lemp intended to be on the other end of the bargain. At the moment, though, it looked like no bargain at all. No Royal Navy battleships or carriers, destroyers or corvettes—hell, no Royal Navy tugs or garbage scows—showed themselves in his patrol zone. From what the radio operator could pick up, things were also quiet elsewhere.

No freighters bound from Norway to England or the other way lumbered past, either. Petrels skimmed by the U-30. One landed on the radio aerial atop the conning tower. It seemed surprised to find an island in the middle of the sea. After a minute or two, it flew off.

One of the ratings on watch up there let his binoculars down onto his chest and grinned at Lemp. "Do we sink the sea birds, Skipper?" he asked. "They're the only things in the neighborhood."

"Bad luck!" another sailor said, and everybody else nodded. You didn't hurt petrels, not for anything.

"I was only kidding," the first man protested.

"Don't worry about it, Erich," Lemp said. "We know you didn't mean anything by it." By their expressions, not all the ratings agreed, but they let it lie—for now. Lemp wondered if Erich would get himself a set of lumps after he went below. He hoped the others wouldn't rack the sailor up to the point where he couldn't carry out his duties. A U-boat needed every man it carried.

He was also willing to bet that, as long as Erich was still able to walk, he wouldn't let out a peep about what had happened to him. Officers didn't need to know—and certainly didn't need to notice—everything that went on aboard a warship.

Or maybe the rating escaped his expected fate, because the very next day a sailor fishing from the conning tower caught an enormous cod. If that wasn't good luck, Lemp didn't know what would be. The sailors gutted the big fish and threw the offal overboard.

"Now what do we do with it?" somebody wondered.

"I know how to make codfish balls," another sailor said.

A wit piped up: "What do we do with the rest?"

"Funny, Michael," Lemp said amidst groans. "You should take it on the stage—or anywhere else a long way from here."

But, for lack of other suggestions, they let the volunteer have his way. And the codfish balls, eked out with flour, proved surprisingly good. Lemp put a commendation in the log. It might earn the amateur cook a promotion when the U-30 came home.

In the meantime, they patrolled. They saw ocean, and more ocean, and more ocean still. They saw petrels. Some were gray. Some were black. Some were gray and black. A birdwatcher probably would have gone into ecstasies about them. Lemp took them for granted, as long as no one talked about doing them in.

Still no freighters. No Royal Navy ships, either. Only long days and short, light nights. Twilight never quite left the northern sky, and the dimmer stars remained unseen. The weather was good—as good as it ever got in the North Sea, anyhow. It might almost have been a pleasure jaunt. *If only the accommodations were fancier,* Lemp thought. *The Strength through Joy cruises do a better job.*

It didn't take long for the patrolling to get to be first routine, then dull routine. Lemp fought that as best he could. Taking things for granted was one of the easiest ways to get yourself killed.

No ships. No planes. No suspicious smoke smudges on the horizon. No stalking a quarry. No crash dives when someone came stalking you, either. Back and forth. Back and forth again. Nothing. Lots of nothing. Lemp got bored, too. He worked all the harder on account of it. He made sure the crew did, too.

The U-30 didn't travel very far. It could stay at sea as long as it had fuel and food. No orders to do anything else came over the radio. Back and forth one more time, and then one more time after that.

ARNO BAATZ GLOWERED at Willi Dernen. "I've got my eye on you," the corporal warned. "You may have fooled that SS fellow, but I know damn well you had something to do with Storch lighting out for the tall timber."

Awful Arno was right. So was a stopped clock, twice a day. Most days, that put it two up on Baatz. "I don't know what happened to Wolfgang," Willi said, for what had to be the hundredth time. "Maybe he did light out, but he was always a good soldier till people started giving him grief. Or maybe a shell came down right on top of him. We were catching hell from the Frenchies that day, remember. Sometimes there's nothing left to bury, you know?" He eyed his squad leader. "It could have happened to you."

"And you would have been happy if it did?"

"You said that. I didn't. I don't mean it, either." Willi didn't aim to let Awful Arno pin an insubordination rap on him. He also didn't particularly hope Baatz would get blown to nothingness on the instant. That would be too quick, too easy. If the sniper with the monster rifle nailed Awful Arno right in the knee, though . . .

A German sniper prowled the lines these days, too, hunting the Frenchman or Czech or whatever he was. A rifle made for knocking out panzers did horrid things to flesh and bone. Sometimes a hit on the arm or leg would kill just from the shock of the impact. The sooner the expert with the scope-sighted rifle—he was an *Oberfeldwebel* named Helmut Fegelein, a grizzled veteran of the last war—disposed of the bastard with the big rifle, the happier everybody would be.

Everybody except the enemy sniper, of course. But Willi wasted no sympathy on him. Every so often, that big, distinctive *boom!* would echo from the trenches off in the distance. And then, as often as not, some German who'd been careless or naïve would fall over screaming—or sometimes just twitching.

"Fucker's good," Fegelein allowed, spooning up a stew of cabbage and sausage and potatoes from his mess tin. "I've got a couple of shots at him, but he's still in business."

"How come you missed?" Awful Arno asked.

Fegelein looked through him. The senior noncom didn't have to put up with Baatz's bullshit the way Willi did. "You try it, sonny boy," he said. "You got a split second at extreme long range, and maybe you hit and maybe you don't. He stays well back, too—that antipanzer rifle's got more reach reach than a Mauser."

Willi smiled at his corporal. Sonny boy, was it? He liked that, and liked it all the better because Awful Arno obviously didn't. "You ought to get closer, then—that's all I've got to say," Baatz remarked.

"If that's all you've got to say, keep your big fat dumb mouth shut," Fegelein answered. "I didn't come here to get my head blown off, either. This guy hasn't been doing it for long, or I never would have got a shot at him at all. But he's sharp. He keeps learning. I haven't got a glimpse of him for a day and a half. If I were talking to most people, I'd tell 'em to keep their heads down till I nail him."

"But not me?" Baatz reddened with anger. "Why not?"

"Because you don't have enough brains in there to worry about getting 'em blown out," the sniper answered. "If he shoots you in the ass, though, you're liable to end up with a concussion."

Somebody behind Awful Arno guffawed. Willi would have, if he were sitting where Baatz couldn't see him doing it. And Baatz couldn't even round on the miscreant, not with Fegelein's cold gray gaze pinning him down. People talked about sniper's eyes. Willi hadn't seen any examples of that unfailing, scary watchfulness before. But the *Oberfeldwebel* had it in spades.

"Were you a sniper in 1918, too?" Willi asked him as they washed out their tins side by side.

"*Nein.*" Fegelein shook his head and lit a small, stinky cigar. "I was an assault trooper. I carried a machine pistol and a big sack of grenades. I started this business in one of the *Freikorps* after the war. I'd had it up to here with fighting the other guys at twenty meters. They don't have to be good to kill you at that range—just lucky. I figured I'd give myself better odds. I got into the *Reichswehr* in . . . was it '21 or '22? Anyway, I've been doing this ever since."

"Makes sense to me," Willi said. "The farther away the enemy stays, the better I like it."

That chilly stare appraised him for a moment. Sure as hell, Willi felt as if he were in the crosshairs. Then Fegelein gave him a smile—a thin smile, but a smile. "Yeah, I've heard a lot of guys go on like that," the sniper said. "Half the time, it's right before they do something that gets 'em a *Ritterkreuz.*"

"I don't want one," Willi said with great sincerity.

Helmut Fegelein only shrugged. "Sometimes you want the medal, sometimes the medal wants you. When the time comes, you'll know what needs doing. That piece of crap you've got for a corporal, now . . ."

Willi laughed out loud. "You mean Awful Arno?" Sure as hell, Fegelein was a keen judge of character.

The veteran chuckled. "Is that what you call him?"

Belatedly, Willi realized he might have stuck his foot in it. An *Oberfeldwebel* could land a *Gefreiter* in all kinds of trouble for badmouthing another noncom senior to him. "Well . . ." Willi said reluctantly.

"That's what you call him when you don't think anybody'll gig you for it," Fegelein said, which was perfectly true. The sniper reached into his pocket and pulled out the stogies again. He offered Willi one. "Here you go. I don't blab. I remember what I called the jerks who ordered me around."

Next morning, the son of a bitch with the antipanzer rifle potted a captain—knocked him off a motorcycle, in fact. And that evening, as darkness descended, Fegelein did go out into the no-man's-land between the lines. "About time," Arno Baatz said—but not where the *Oberfeldwebel* could hear him.

Willi didn't see Awful Arno volunteering to go out there. He couldn't say that, but thought it very loudly. Baatz strutted off to do some of the important things corporals did. One of those things was to make sure Willi stood sentry in the middle of the night and broke up his sleep. As always, Willi appreciated it.

Come morning, he saw no sign of Helmut Fegelein. The sniper was out there somewhere, sprawled in a shell hole or under one piece of wreckage or another. He had his rifle and he had a hunter's patience. Somewhere farther off, the enemy sniper had the same patience and an even nastier weapon.

The antipanzer rifle thundered, its report distinctive even though it came from a long way northwest of the trench in which Willi waited. Fegelein's piece stayed silent. Either he didn't spot the enemy or he had no chance to hit him from wherever he hid.

Fegelein came in after dark. He slipped past the German pickets, which was bound to raise officers' blood pressure. If all the Frenchmen out there were as good as he was, they could do it, too. And if cows pissed gasoline, the *Reich* wouldn't have to worry about running low on fuel.

Some time in the middle of the night, the sniper vanished again. Maybe he was going back to the same hidey-hole, or maybe he changed his lair daily like a hunted wolf. Willi thought he would have if he were doing that job. He thanked heaven he wasn't.

No sign of the *Oberfeldwebel* when the sun came up. He'd be waiting—or, for all Willi knew, he'd be sound asleep right now. Who was going to tell him he couldn't do that if he felt like it?

Sweat ran down Willi's face. Summer was coming in, all right. When he pushed his way through the Ardennes in the middle of winter, he'd thought the war would be over by now. "Shows what I knew," he muttered.

Then the antipanzer rifle spoke again, seemingly right in front of him.

A split second later, a Mauser in no-man's-land answered. Willi's ears told him about where the shot came from, but he still couldn't spot Fegelein.

He couldn't, but the enemy sniper could. That goddamn elephant gun fired once more, as soon as it could have after the man using it worked the bolt. Silence returned, punctuated only by the skrawks of frightened crows.

Helmut Fegelein didn't come back for supper after sundown. Willi guessed he wasn't hungry any more, and never would be again.

Chapter 14

Pussy didn't like tanks, not even a little bit. Alistair Walsh wasn't surprised. The cat had come to take gunfire for granted. Animals sometimes got used to things more easily than people did. Pussy couldn't know what bullets and shell fragments did to soft, vulnerable flesh. She didn't know how lucky she was to be ignorant, either.

Tanks were a whole different business, though. She didn't just hear them rattle and clank. She could see them move. Here was something bigger than an elephant that could—and might want to—squash her flat. Tanks smelled funny, too. No wonder the cat disappeared into the smallest hole she could find.

Regardless of Pussy's opinion, Walsh liked tanks in the neighborhood fine. These Mark I Cruisers seemed a vast improvement over the poor Matildas that had tried to hold off German panzers the winter before. The Matildas mounted nothing more than a machine gun, and a running man could easily keep up with them. They did have thick armor . . . and they needed it.

These cruisers were a different business. Their turrets packed a two-pounder cannon and a machine gun, while they mounted two more MGs in the front of the hull, one on each side of the driver's position. It was probably crowded as all get-out up there, but enemy infantry in front of them would be very unhappy.

And they could *move*. They were as fast as anything the Germans had. More than once during the retreat from the Low Countries, English tankers had had to bail out of Matildas, set them on fire, and go back on foot or in a lorry when enemy thrusts outflanked and overran them. If they hadn't, they would have been cut off and killed or captured. In fact, Walsh had seen a Matilda or two in German service, with a prominent cross painted on either side. He suspected he would have seen more if the Nazis liked the clunky little machines better.

Jock's reaction to the Mark I Cruisers was more like Pussy's. "Ah wish the bloody things'd go somewhere else," the Yorkshireman grumbled.

"Why's that?" Walsh asked. "Now that they're here, we can give the Fritzes one right in the slats."

"That's why," Jock said morosely. "Long as we sit tight here, we're safe enough. Oh, not safe, Christ knows, but safe enough. With them buggers around, though, they'll tell us to go forward again, damn their black hearts. Bad things happen when you go forward, by God."

Half a lifetime ago, Walsh had been eager to go over the top—once. Living through that first assault cured him of eagerness forevermore. He was much happier staying in the trenches and letting the Germans come to him after that. Bad things *did* happen when you went forward. There you were, out in the open, with nothing to protect you but a lousy tin hat that wouldn't keep bullets out anyhow. All these years later, his leg wound still bothered him.

Which meant nothing when the brass hats told you to advance. The Fritzes might rack you up. You own side assuredly would if you didn't follow orders. He was part of that machinery himself. If you didn't go forward because you were battle-wild, you'd damn well go forward because bad things would happen to you if you stayed behind.

"No help for it, Jock," he said, not without sympathy. No, he wasn't eager, either.

Jock nodded. "Oh, Ah know. What'll we do about Pussy, though? Can't take her along—she wouldn't fancy riding in your pack or on your shoulder like a bloody pirate's parrot."

Walsh chuckled. "Chances are she wouldn't," he agreed. "Somebody else will take care of her once we push on, though. Or she'll shift for herself. Cats are good at that, you know. Plenty of birds, plenty of bugs. Plenty of mice, too, with no one setting out traps to keep them down."

"Maybe." Jock still looked gloomy—he often did. "She was mighty peaked when we first started feeding her, though. Mighty peaked."

"We can't bring her along. You said so yourself," Walsh pointed out.

"Ah knows, Sergeant. Don't mean Ah like it," Jock said.

More and more Mark Is came in. Had Walsh been running the show, he would have kept them hidden till the attack went in. Surprise counted. The high foreheads actually in charge of things sent a few of the cruisers forward to see how they did against the German positions most of a mile away.

And the high foreheads learned some things they hadn't known before. Matildas couldn't get out of their own way and sadly lacked firepower, but they laughed at antitank rifles. The Mark Is weren't laughing. Those big bullets pierced their armor with the greatest of ease: not only in the hull sides, but even in the turret, which was supposed to have more metal than any other part of the tank.

The Fritzes had some 37mm antitank guns in their defensive positions, too. A Matilda might even live through a hit from one of those. The cruisers looked far more modern. They had better engines and more firepower. But they burned so easily, the English soldiers started calling them Ronsons. One shot, and they lit.

"What bloody fool designed 'em?" Jock demanded, watching two of the hopeful machines send up black columns of smoke from the fields ahead. The way he said *bloody*, it had the same long *oo* as *fool*. It sounded even more accusing that way. "They won't hold out anything tougher than a rifle round."

"Doesn't look that way, does it?" Walsh said glumly.

"We're supposed to go forward with tanks, eh?" Jock said. "How do we do that if all the tanks blow up afore they get to the Fritzes' trenches?"

"Good question," the sergeant answered. In the last war, the order to advance would have gone out anyway. Tanks not up to snuff? Too bad. The infantry would handle things. That was what it was there for, wasn't it?

Things were supposed to be different this time around. No one wanted another catastrophe like the Somme. With brilliant plans like that, no wonder people started calling generals the Donkeys.

But, just because things were supposed to be different, that didn't mean they would be. Driving the Germans farther away from Paris was high on everybody's list. The French had had an even closer call this time than in 1914. The more frantic they got about dealing with that, the more frantic they made their allies across the Channel.

Walsh did wonder how enthusiastic Neville Chamberlain was about the war. He'd done everything he could to hold it off, even flying to Germany to try to talk Hitler out of jumping all over Czechoslovakia. He might have pulled it off, too, if that Czech maniac hadn't gunned down Konrad Henlein, the Sudeten Germans' vest-pocket *Führer*.

Then again, it was hard to tell how enthusiastic Chamberlain was about anything. He looked like a constipated stork, and he didn't sound much different. Winston Churchill might be a voice crying in the wilderness of party disfavor, but he was a voice crying in impassioned, exciting sentences. Walsh thought that kind of thing went a long way in wartime. As if anyone gave a damn what a staff sergeant thought!

The order to storm forward got pushed back forty-eight hours. To celebrate, Jock fed Pussy a whole tin of steak-and-kidney pie, the best ration England issued. In Alistair Walsh's biased opinion, it was better than anything the froggies or the Fritzes made, too. Pussy daintily fed, then washed up the sides of her face with a well-licked paw. "She even goes behind her ears," Jock said.

"When was the last time you did?" Walsh asked.

"Beats me," the soldier said. Walsh couldn't remember the last time he'd washed behind the ears, either. Out in the field, you stopped worrying about dirt. What difference did it make? He patted the cat. She rewarded him with a purr. When he stopped, she twisted her head and started licking the man-scent off her fur. *How can I catch mice,* she seemed to say, *if I smell like a gamy old sergeant?*

Before the two days were up, the order to advance got postponed indefinitely. No one said it had anything to do with the Mark I Cruiser's deficiencies, but no one had trouble reading between the lines. Jock shared some milk-smooth cognac with Walsh to celebrate.

"Here's to stayin' put!" the Yorkshireman said.

"Here's to," Walsh agreed. He wasn't sorry not to leave this ruined village. It wasn't home, but it also wasn't bad—no, not half. Pussy ambled up, willing to be stroked and begging for a treat. His hand caressed the cat's warm, soft fur. Pussy purred.

LITTLE BY LITTLE, Sarah Goldman got used to wearing the yellow star whenever she went outside. She hardly noticed. Hardly anyone else in Münster seemed to notice, either. The Nazis might have wanted to turn Jews into a spectacle, but they hadn't done it.

Aryans were entitled to cut in front of Jews in a queue at any shop. Shopkeepers were supposed to serve Aryans ahead of Jews, which was doubly unfair because Jews had limited hours in which they could go out. The yellow star was designed, among other things, to make that easier.

It didn't happen, not right away. German women took their places behind Sarah when they got into line after she did. No shopkeeper followed the rules to the letter. That surprised her; she knew how orderly the folk of whom she'd once thought herself a part were.

It must have surprised the Nazis, too. A flood of new edicts came from Berlin. No one was to extend Jews any courtesies, no matter what. *These people are the enemies of the* Reich, *and must not be treated softly,* newspapers thundered. *Always remember—the Jews are our misfortune!*

"What did we ever do to them?" Sarah complained over a miserable supper that night. "What they've done to us . . . But what did we do to them?"

"Nothing," her mother said. "We don't do anything to anybody. All we try to do is stay alive. They don't even like that, and a *choleriyeh* on them."

"*You* haven't done anything to them," Father said. He was weary, but contrived to look amused even so. "I haven't done enough—nowhere near so much as I wish I had. But Einstein and Freud and Schoenberg . . . They've done plenty. They've tried to drag Germany kicking and screaming into the twentieth century. 'Jewish physics! Jewish psychology! Jewish music!' " He did his best to sound like a Nazi plug-ugly bellowing on the radio. His best was alarmingly good. He didn't have a red face and a roll of fat at the back of his neck, but you would never have guessed as much from his voice.

"But what if Einstein's right even though he's Jewish?" Sarah said. "Then Germany will miss out on . . . on whatever he was talking about." She knew more about the theory of relativity than she did about Zulu, but not much more.

"That's the chance they take," Samuel Goldman said, not without relish. "I don't pretend to understand Einstein, but I'd think twice before I bet against him."

Sarah always thought of her father as knowing everything. So hearing him admit ignorance always came as a surprise. Of course, Socrates hadn't just admitted ignorance—he'd professed it (being a scholar of ancient history's daughter, she knew such things herself). But that was different. Socrates had been—what did the card-players call it? He'd been sandbagging: that was the word. When Father said he didn't understand Einstein, Sarah thought he meant it.

"Jewish physics? What can Jewish physics do that German physics can't?" Sarah picked the wildest thing she could think of: "Blow up the world? That would serve the Nazis right, wouldn't it?"

"It would." Father sighed. "I don't think things are quite so simple, though. It would be nice if they were, but . . ." He spread his hands. His palms weren't blistered, the way they had been when he first joined the labor gang. Now ridges of hard yellow callus crossed them. He was in better physical shape than Sarah remembered his being—but he slept whenever he wasn't working or eating. How long before he started to break down? And what would happen then?

She didn't want to think about that. Father anchored the world. Without him, everything would be adrift, topsy-turvy. Which, she had to admit, didn't mean such a thing couldn't happen. In the Third *Reich*, anything could happen to Jews, anything at all. If you didn't understand that, you didn't understand anything.

One of the things that could happen to Jews could also happen to Aryans. A little past midnight, air-raid sirens began to wail. Berlin and other places in the east were safe from bombs during short summer nights: the bombers that had to deliver them would still be flying and vulnerable when light came back to the sky. Not Münster. It lay too close to the French border to enjoy such protection.

"Not fair!" Sarah groaned as she hurried downstairs to huddle under the heavy dining-room table. She wasn't thinking only of geography. Father would have to go out to the labor gang tomorrow morning even if he'd had his sleep shattered. Well, plenty of others would be in the same boat.

That a bomb might land on top of the house never crossed her mind. She'd been in plenty of raids before, and no bombs had hit here yet. That had to mean none could. The logic was perfect . . . at least till she met a counterexample.

Her parents joined her under there a moment later. Her mother was grumbling because she'd stubbed a toe on the stairs. "Miserable air pirates," Father said. He'd lifted the phrase straight from the Nazi papers. Sarah wondered if he realized what had just come out of his mouth.

Before she could ask him, bombs began whistling down. Even when you knew—or thought you knew—one wouldn't hit here, the sound was scary. Then the bombs started going off. The noise was horrendous. Feeling the ground shake under you was worse. Sarah had never been in an earthquake, but now she had a notion of what they were like.

Antiaircraft guns added their own crashes to the racket. Through it all, Father said, "I think those must be French planes. The engines sound different from the ones the RAF uses."

Sarah hadn't noticed. Even when it was pointed out to her, she couldn't hear any difference. She wouldn't have cared if she could. She just wanted this to be over.

Then several bombs burst much closer than any had before. She screamed. She couldn't help herself. The house shook like a rat in a terrier's jaws. For a second, she thought everything would come down on top of the table. Windows blew in with a tinkle of glass. All of a sudden, she could smell cool, moist outside air—and the smoke it carried.

The raid seemed to last forever. They often felt that way while they were going on. At last, the enemy planes flew off to England or France or wherever they'd come from. Not long afterwards, the all-clear sounded. Father said, "I'd better see if the neighbors are all right."

"Would they do the same for us?" Sarah asked sourly.

"Some of them would," he answered, and she supposed that was so. He went on, "Even my bathrobe has a yellow star, so I won't get into trouble on account of that."

"Oh, joy," Sarah and her mother said at the same time. They both started to laugh. Why not? What other choice did you have but pounding your head against a table leg?

Father's voice joined the shouting outside. Sarah didn't hear anyone screaming. That had to be good. The Nazi government was tormenting Jews. She should have hoped the RAF or the French would knock it flat. But bombs didn't fall on a government. Bombs fell on people. And, even though a lot of those people must have voted for the Nazis back before elections turned into farces, most of them were just . . . people. They weren't so bad.

After a while, Father came back in. His slippers scraped on broken glass. (What would they do about that? Worry about it after dawn, that was what.) "All right here," he reported. "Those big ones came down a couple of blocks away, thank God." Bells and sirens told of fire engines and ambulances rushing where they were needed most.

"You may as well go back to bed," Mother said. "Nothing else to do now."

After the first couple of air strikes against Münster, Sarah would have laughed at that. Now she nodded. As life since the Nazis took over showed, you could get used to anything. If you were still tired after the bombs stopped falling, you grabbed some more sleep. She heard Father yawn. He'd need every minute he could get. Come morning, he'd be even more overworked than usual.

He'd just trudged out the door when someone started pounding on it. Sarah and her mother exchanged looks of alarm. That sounded like the

SS. What could the blackshirts want so early? All sorts of evil possibilities crossed her mind. Would they claim the Goldmans were showing lights to guide the enemy bombers? That was ridiculous—or would be if the SS weren't saying it.

Feet dragging, Sarah went to the door and reluctantly opened it. Her jaw dropped. "Isidor!" she blurted. "What are you doing here?"

"I rode over to make sure you folks were safe," Isidor Bruck answered. Sure enough, a beat-up bicycle stood behind the baker's son. He managed a shy smile. "I'm glad you are."

"Yes, we're fine," Sarah managed. She didn't know what else to say. Obviously, Isidor hadn't ridden across town to check on her mother and father. What were they to him but customers? She'd thought she was something more. Till this moment, she hadn't realized she might be a lot more. She took a deep breath and, without thinking about it, ran a hand through her hair. "Are your kin all right?"

He nodded. "Nothing came down real close to us. But I heard this part of town got hit hard, so I thought I'd better check."

"Thanks . . . Thanks very much. That was sweet of you," Sarah said, which made Isidor turn red. She added, "It's nice to know somebody—anybody—cares."

Isidor nodded again. "I know what you mean," he said. "We have to take care of ourselves these days. Nobody else will do it for us—that's for sure. To us, maybe, but not for us." As his mouth tightened, he suddenly looked fifteen years older. He touched the brim of his cloth cap. "Well, I'd better get back. The work doesn't go away."

"I'm sure," Sarah said. "Come again, though." He bobbed his head and rode away. Surely it was only her imagination that the bicycle tires floated several centimeters above the sidewalk.

CHAIM WEINBERG LOOKED AROUND the battered streets of Madrid. "You know what's missing here?" he asked.

Mike Carroll also considered the vista. "Damn near everything," he answered after due contemplation. "What have you got in mind?"

They were both speaking English. Madrileños walking by grinned at them. Even more than their ragged uniforms, the foreign language showed they were Internationals. Internationals were still heroes in Madrid—at least to the majority that didn't secretly favor the Fascists. And most of the locals didn't speak English, which gave at least the hope of privacy.

"I'll tell you what's missing here," Chaim said. "A *shul*'s missing, that's what."

"In case you didn't notice, it's a Catholic country," Mike said, as if to an idiot child. "And, in case you hadn't noticed, the Republic isn't pro-religion. It's not supposed to be, either."

By that, he meant *The Republic does things the same way as the Soviet Union*. And so it did. Both had broken the priesthood's long-entrenched power in their respective countries. Even so, Chaim said, "There's a difference between Spain and Russia."

"Oh, yeah? Like what?" Carroll didn't quite say *Tell me another one*, but he might as well have.

Even so, Chaim had an answer for him. Two answers, in fact: "For one thing, the opposition in Russian's been broken. You can't very well say that here." His wave swept over the ruins, all created by the ever-so-Catholic Nationalists. "And for another, Spain discriminates against Jews. You can't say the Soviet Union does, not when so many of the Old Bolsheviks are *Yehudim*."

"Yeah, well . . ." This time, Mike paused in faint embarrassment. And, after a couple of seconds, Chaim understood why. A whole great swarm of the Old Bolsheviks convicted in Moscow's show trials were Jews, too.

"It's still discrimination. Discrimination's still wrong," Chaim said stubbornly. "Before the Republic, it was fucking illegal to be a Jew in Spain. It still is, in Nationalist country. If that's not why we're fighting, what *are* we doing here?"

"Stopping Hitler and Mussolini and Sanjurjo?" Mike suggested.

"Stopping them from doing what? Screwing over people they don't happen to like, that's what!" Weinberg answered his own question.

Mike Carroll looked at him. "When was the last time you were in a— what did you call it?—a *shul*?"

"It's been a while," Chaim admitted. His folks had made him get bar-mitzvahed. He'd quit going right after that. As far as he was concerned, action counted for more than prayer. But the right to prayer was a different story. He stuck out his chin as far as it would go (which wasn't as far as he would have wished). "All the more reason to have one now."

"How do you figure that?"

"Because it's been a hell of a lot longer since any of the Spaniards have been. Because the ones who're still Jews have to pretend they're Catholics when anybody's looking. Because that's wrong, dammit," Chaim said.

"Let me buy you a drink or two, okay?" Mike said. "You need something to wind you down—that's for goddamn sure."

Chaim looked around. He blinked in surprise. "Trust you to go on about buying drinks when there's not a cantina in sight for miles."

"We'll find one. Come on." Carroll turned to a Madrileño. "*¿Donde está una cantina?*"

He got elaborate, voluble directions, complete with gestures. The Spanish was much too fast to follow, though. The local soon saw as much. He grabbed Mike with one hand and Chaim with the other and took them where they needed to go. Yes, Spaniards would give you the shirt off their back. The problem was, not enough of them had shirts to give.

And were they proud! Mike tried to buy this fellow a drink, but the local wouldn't let him. He hadn't brought them here for a reward, but because he was grateful to the International Brigades. That was what Chaim thought he was saying, anyhow. The Madrileño saluted and bowed and left.

Mike did buy Chaim a drink, and then another one. Chaim bought a couple of rounds, too; Jews had their own kind of pride. After four shots of rotgut, Chaim wobbled when he walked. He was no less determined than he had been sober, though. If anything, he was more so.

"You'll get in trouble," Matt said blearily.

Chaim's laugh was raucous enough to make heads swing his way. "Yeah? What'll they do to me? Send me back to the front?"

"They'll throw you in a Spanish jail, that's what they'll do," Carroll answered. "Those joints are worse than the front, you ask me."

He had a point. Chaim was too stubborn and too plastered to acknowledge it. "I'm going to talk to Brigadier Kossuth," he declared.

"On your head be it," Mike said. "And it will be."

Kossuth wasn't the brigadier's real name. Chaim had heard that once, but couldn't come within miles of pronouncing it; it sounded like a horse sneezing. But the real Kossuth had also been a Hungarian rebel against the status quo. The modern one had glassy black eyes and a tongue he flicked in and out like a lizard. He spoke several languages, and sounded like Bela Lugosi doing Dracula in every damn one of them.

English, though, wasn't one of those several. He understood Chaim's Yiddish, and Chaim could mostly follow his throaty German. "A *shul*?" Kossuth said. One of his elegantly combed eyebrows climbed. "Well, there's something out of the ordinary, anyhow."

Plainly, he didn't mean that as a compliment. "Why not?" Chaim said. "It's part of the freedom we're fighting for, right?"

Flick. Flick. Chaim wondered whether Kossuth caught flies with that tongue. "More likely, Comrade, it's part of the trouble you enjoy causing."

"Me?" If Weinberg were as innocent as he sounded, he never would have heard of the facts of life, let alone practiced them as assiduously as he could.

Brigadier Kossuth ignored the melodramatics. "You." His voice was hard and flat. "Americans are an undisciplined lot—and you, Weinberg, are undisciplined for an American. Your reputation precedes you."

"So I'm not a Prussian. So sue me," Chaim said. That made Kossuth show his yellow teeth. Prussian discipline was anathema in the International Brigades. They had their own kind, which was at least as harsh but which they—mostly—accepted of their own free will. "I am a Jew. Can't I act like one once in a while?"

"You want to offend the Spaniards." Kossuth probably didn't catch flies with his tongue—there sure weren't any on him.

But Chaim had an answer for him. And when did Chaim not have an answer? "The ones who favor the Republic's ideals won't be offended."

"Oh, of course they will. They don't like Jews any better than anyone else here does. Do you know what a *narigón* is?" Kossuth said.

Literally, the Spanish word meant somebody with a big nose. But that wasn't what Kossuth had in mind. "A kike," Chaim said.

He wasn't surprised when the Magyar did know that bit of English.

Kossuth nodded. "Just so," the brigadier said. "And you want to draw extra attention to yourself here?"

"It's not about extra attention," Chaim said, which held . . . some truth. "It's about rights and freedoms. Why am I in Spain, if not for those?"

"I don't know. Why are you in Spain? Because you can raise more hell here than back home, I suspect." Kossuth drummed his fingers on the tabletop in front of him. His nails, Chaim noticed, were elegantly manicured. "Even if you do found this *shul*, how much would you care to wager that you will not attend services for longer than a month—six weeks at the outside?"

That might well have held more than some truth. "All the same," Chaim said.

To his surprise, Brigadier Kossuth's chuckle didn't emit puffs of dust. "Well, go on, then," Kossuth said. "I doubt you can lose our struggle against the forces of reaction all by yourself—though not, I am sure, for lack of effort. Now get out." Thus encouraged, if that was the word, Chaim got.

LUC HARCOURT EYED THE THREE REPLACEMENTS who'd just joined his squad with a distinctly jaundiced eye. "Look, boys, try to keep your heads down till you start figuring things out, eh?" he said. "You don't keep them down, the *Boches*'ll blow 'em off—and you won't learn much after that, by God. Right?"

"Right, Corporal," they chorused. One was Louis, one was Marc, and the other, poor devil, was Napoléon. At least he didn't stick his hand between two of the buttons on his tunic. He wasn't especially short, either. Or especially bright—he said, "But we want to kill Germans, Corporal."

"You'll get your chance," Luc promised. "Don't forget, though—they have a chance at you, too. That's not so much fun. Bet your ass it's not."

He stood back from himself, as it were, listening to what came out of his mouth. Damned if he didn't sound like a slightly smoother copy of Sergeant Demange. He hadn't been sanding his throat with Gitanes as long or as enthusiastically as Demange had, but the attitude was there. He didn't like Demange—he didn't think anyone *could* like Demange, or that the sergeant would acknowledge it if anyone did. But he'd learned how to take charge of other men from him. The method wasn't pretty, but it worked.

Off in the distance—*far* off in the distance: a couple of kilometers away, at least—a machine gun stuttered. Louis and Marc and even the bellicose Napoléon suddenly looked apprehensive. Yes, things could go wrong up here. This wasn't basic training any more.

Luc grinned at them: a sneering, acrid grin, also modeled on Sergeant Demange's. "That was one of ours, my dears," he said. "That won't kill you . . . except by accident, of course." The grin got nastier yet. He cocked his head to one side, listening and waiting. Sure as hell, the Germans didn't let the French burst go unanswered. An MG-34 fired back. Luc raised an index finger. "There! That's one of theirs!"

"But they both sound the same," Marc protested.

"You'd better learn the difference pretty goddamn quick, that's all I've got to tell you," Luc said. "Make a mistake there and you won't get a chance to make a whole lot more."

"What *is* the difference?" Louis asked—he couldn't hear it, either.

"Theirs fires faster," Luc answered. "They can change belts faster than we can change strips, too."

"It sounds like you're saying their guns are better than ours." Napoléon sounded as scandalized as a society matron at an indecent proposal.

"Damn straight they are," Luc said. "Look, the *Boche* is a bastard. He does all kinds of horrible shit, and he does it in France. But you'll only get killed for nothing if you think he's a stupid bastard. He knows what he's doing in the field, and his engineers know their business just as well."

The new fish gaped at him as if they'd caught an archbishop celebrating a Black Mass. "But—they're the enemy!" Louis sputtered.

"Very good. Nothing gets by you, does it?" Luc sure did sound like Sergeant Demange, and he didn't have to step away from himself to hear it now. "But they're not the stupid buffoons the papers make them out to be. They wouldn't be so fucking dangerous if they were. You get that, sonny?"

"I . . . think so, Corporal," the raw private answered.

"You'd better. All of you had better. Otherwise, somebody in the Ministry of War will send your family a wire no one wants to get. And you, you'll be a black-bordered photo gathering dust on the mantel, and you'll never suck on your girlfriend's titties any more or try to talk her into jerking you off. Do you get *that*?"

Louis nodded. So did Marc and Napoléon. Their eyes were big and round as gumdrops. They looked as if he'd hit them where they lived. He hoped he had. He wanted them to live. He also wanted them to learn the ropes as fast as they could. Troops new to the front did stupid things. That could get them killed in a hurry, and it could bring trouble down on the more experienced men who had to keep company with them. Luc didn't want to get killed for no better reason than that Marc, say, was an idiot.

Come to that, he didn't want to get killed at all.

He gave the new men a last once-over, as withering as he could make it. Louis flinched, so he didn't do too bad. Sergeant Demange would have had every one of them trembling in his clodhoppers. Well, they'd meet the sergeant soon enough—too soon to suit them, Luc was sure. "Let's go, you lugs," he said. "Keep your heads down. Don't let the Germans see you moving. They've got mortars and artillery zeroed in about every ten meters. If they start shooting at you, they can hit you. They can hit me, too."

He wished he could have the last handful of words back. He didn't want them to realize he could get jumpy himself. They heard the words, but they didn't hear the tone that informed them. They probably thought he'd give them all a kick in the slats if he got wounded. They didn't know a wounded man just lay there and thrashed and screamed and bled. Well, they'd find out.

Luc led them through trenches to the ruins of a village. Digging like moles, damming like beavers, the Frenchmen had done a lot to improve the ruins. Unless you were very tall, you could move around freely without worrying about sniper fire. There were underground galleries where you could eat and sleep and shelter from artillery fire. It wasn't the Maginot Line, but Luc had been in plenty of worse places.

Half a kilometer to the east, the German lines boasted about as many comforts. If you weren't advancing or retreating, you settled down and made yourself at home.

The new fish exclaimed at what the soldiers dug in here had done. Luc enjoyed eating well and sleeping soft, too. Unlike Napoléon and Louis and Marc, he knew too well that these good times wouldn't last. The Nazis had almost knocked France out of the war with their winter on-slaught. They'd grabbed more of the country this time than they did in 1914, and made it harder for England to send help across the Channel. And, unlike Germany, France hadn't had its heart in the war from the beginning.

It did now. Getting your whole northeast occupied would do that to you. And the Germans were fighting Russia now. A lot of Frenchmen with Red leanings had seen the whole war as a struggle between two sets of oppressive imperialists: as none of their business, in other words. But if Hitler threatened the Soviet Union, the font of world revolution, obviously he was a monster who needed suppressing. The Communists were singing the Popular Front song again, as loud as they could.

So, eventually, there would be big pushes forward. They'd leave this place behind. The people who lived here would come back and try to put the pieces together again. None of the offensives yet had been the real thing. But it was coming. And all the horrors that went with a war of movement would come with it.

"Sweet suffering Jesus, Harcourt, why didn't you wipe your ass before you came back here? Look at the dingleberries you brought with you." Sergeant Demange eyed the replacements as if he'd never seen anything so disgusting in his life. The twitching Gitane in the corner of his mouth only amplified his scorn.

"This is Sergeant Demange, men," Luc said. "He commands the section. You'd better listen to him, or—"

"Or I'll fucking well whale the shit out of you," Demange broke in. "Well, you syphilitic scuts, what do they call you?" One by one, the new men hesitantly named themselves. Demange clapped a hand to his forehead. "Napoléon? *Merde alors!* Well, I won't forget that—unless you get killed quick. Go round up canteens and fill 'em at the well. Go on—move! You never want me to have to tell you something more than once. Believe it, punk. You don't."

Thus encouraged, Napoléon moved. Marc and Louis gaped till Demange found fatigues for them, too. Luc smiled. He'd been on the other end of those growls not so long ago. This was better. Oh, yes. Much, much better.

Chapter 15

Pete McGill had never figured he would walk into a shop that sold carved jade and other jewels. Then again, he'd never figured he would fall in love with a White Russian taxi dancer. Life was full of surprises. He was enjoying this one a hell of a lot more than, say, getting stomped by half a dozen Japanese soldiers with hobnailed boots.

All the same, he'd come to the Jade Tree Maker out on Yates Road by himself. If he'd had any of his buddies along, they would have told him he was pussy-whipped. They might even have been right. But that would have made him more likely to try to punch them out, not less.

A Eurasian man in a sharp silk suit stood behind the counter. "Good day," he said in smooth English. The way he dipped his head was almost a bow. "How may I help you today, sir?"

"Right now I'm only looking," Pete said.

"Of course." The proprietor or clerk or whatever he was pretended the American Marine didn't exist. He was good at it. A white man would have kept sneaking glances Pete's way. This fellow didn't. He had the Oriental knack for not seeing what lay right under his nose. You needed that knack if you were going to live in the crowded warrens of Peking or Shanghai without going nuts.

If Pete tried to heist something, now . . . The man in the suit would turn out to have been watching all along. Understanding as much, Pete kept his hands to himself as he examined the merchandise.

Jade trees, sure enough. They came in all sizes from three inches to three feet tall, all qualities of jade—jadeite was a much more brilliant green than the cheaper nephrite—and all degrees of elaboration in the carving. Prices started at a few dollars Mex and went straight up like a mortar bomb.

He thought—he hoped—Vera would like a jade tree. He had cash in his pocket. A corporal's pay was nothing back in the States; in Shanghai, it made him well-off. He had nothing to spend his money on but cigarettes and booze—both cheap—and his lady love. Spend he would.

He picked up a jade tree: not a very big one, but full of detailwork in the carving of branches and leaves, and of peasants and cattle on the base. When he took it over to the counter, the Eurasian man dipped his head again. "You are a man of taste," he said.

Which meant the dicker would be harder. "How much do you want for it?" he asked.

"The price is on the tag here." The man in the silk suit tapped it with his forefinger. "One hundred twenty-five dollars Mex."

That was about forty bucks U.S.—a month's pay, more or less. The exchange rate went up and down, often wildly. Pete didn't get mad or storm out. He'd played these games before. "I know that's what the price tag says," he said patiently. "But how much do you really want for it?"

"You are an American," the Eurasian said. *You've got lots of cash. Why do you care about getting gouged?* Everybody in Shanghai thought that way, and with some reason. But only some. Even Vera thought that way. Pete might be head over heels, but he wasn't blind. He didn't think so, anyhow.

He stayed patient now. "I'm not an American general—I'm an American corporal. A hundred and a quarter Mex is too steep for me."

"What a pity," the man behind the counter murmured. For a moment, Pete thought there'd be no haggle after all. But then the fellow's narrow shoulders shifted as he sighed. "Perhaps, from an American corporal, I might take a hundred and ten."

Pete ended up getting it for seventy-five dollars Mex. He'd hoped to beat the Eurasian down to half the price on the tag, but this wasn't bad. The man swaddled the jade tree in cotton batting and wrapped it in newspapers full of incomprehensible Chinese hentracks. "Much obliged," Pete said. It wouldn't look like anything special as he carried it down the street. In a town where thievery was as much a sport as a crime, that mattered.

"Not at all, sir. A pleasure matching wits with such a good bargainer," the Eurasian replied. Of course he'd still made a profit at the price Pete paid—he wasn't in business for the fun of it. How much had he made? Was that a polite *You sucker!*? His face gave away nothing. Pete was glad not to have to face him across a poker table.

Bauble in hand, he walked down Yates Road. He knew where he was going next, and 332 was on the other side of the street from 343. Crossing meant risking his life, but he made it. KEN KEE—EMBROIDERY AND UNDERWEAR, the sign over the door said, with a picture of a lofty pagoda next to the words and some Chinese above them. Pete drew himself up straight before going in, as if advancing on an enemy trench. If you wanted something fancy in the way of lingerie, he'd heard, this was the place that had it.

The shopgirl who greeted him with a bright smile could have made a mint dancing in any of Shanghai's fancy clubs. She was tiny and gorgeous. "Yes, sir?" she said, her voice ringing like silver bells.

"Just looking," Pete mumbled again. This was harder than going up against a trench full of Japs. They just scared you; they didn't embarrass you.

He'd never bought lingerie before. He'd never dreamt he might want to buy lingerie. But when you found yourself with a gorgeous girlfriend, didn't you want to make her even gorgeouser? (The English teachers who'd rapped his knuckles at every mistake and helped encourage him to drop out of high school and join the Marines would have flinched, but not a goddamn one of them was within 5,000 miles of Shanghai.)

He nervously eyed a gown. He'd also never dreamt even silk could be so transparent. You could see the more substantial blue thing behind it right through the fabric. He wanted to touch it, but didn't dare. It looked as if it would tear if you breathed on it. When he thought about seeing Vera through that fabric, he had to turn away from the salesgirl till his hard-on went down.

When he swung toward her again, he coughed a couple of times and asked, "Um—how much for, uh, this one?" He pointed.

"Let me see, sir." She walked over and looked at the tag. "A hundred dollars Mex, even."

"Ouch!" Pete exclaimed. "That's more than I can afford."

"It's very fine quality." She didn't add *And your girlfriend had better be, if she's going to put it on,* but he could hear it in her chiming voice. She cocked her head to one said, studying him. "Well, what can you afford?"

No matter what the tags said, there weren't many fixed prices in Shanghai. "I was thinking, oh, fifty," Pete answered. Coming back with half the asking price was a standard opening move—a conservative one, but the place intimidated him too much to let him go any lower.

She nodded and came down a little. Pete moved up. He felt less confident than he had haggling with the Eurasian who sold jade trees. Thinking about jade trees didn't make him horny. Thinking about this gown . . . He almost had to turn away from the shopgirl again.

He ended up paying eighty dollars Mex, more than the carved tree had cost. So much cash, for something that was hardly there! Well, that was the point, wasn't it?

When the girl wrapped up the gown, it seemed to take up no space at all. It didn't weigh anything, either. Maybe it wasn't silk after all. Maybe some clever Chinaman had figured out how to curdle air, just a little.

Pete got out of Ken Kee's as if the place had caught fire behind him. The salesgirl didn't laugh at his retreat, but he could feel her amused eyes on his back. How many guys had she seen sneaking out of there? It wasn't as if he were buying dirty pictures, dammit. He paused out on the sidewalk on Yates Road. Dirty pictures only promised. This nightgown would deliver. Boy, would it ever!

But he wasn't completely stupid. The next time he saw Vera, he gave her the jade tree first. "Got something for you, babe," he said, as casually as he could.

"*Chto?*" That meant *What?* When you caught her by surprise, she still sometimes came out with Russian without thinking. He'd got some real wrapping paper from a clerk at the consulate, so the tree looked nicer now than it had when he took it out of the shop. Vera's quick, clever fingers stripped off the paper and the cotton wool. "Ahh," she said. "It is very pretty, Pete." Chances were she could guess to the penny what he'd paid for it, too. By the warmth of the kiss she gave him, she approved. "We go out now?"

They went out. He was throwing away money like a drunken sailor— like a drunken Marine—but he didn't care. Not while he was with Vera he didn't, anyhow.

They ate. They drank. They danced. They drank. By the time they went back to her little chamber, he *was* a drunken Marine. Not too drunk, though. He hoped.

With an air of suddenly remembering, he pulled the smaller package from an inside pocket. "This is for you, too," he said. If she didn't like it . . . Would dying on the spot or wishing he were dead be worse?

She wasn't quite so deft unwrapping this one; she'd also been knocking them back. "Ahh," she said once more, this time on a different note. She unfolded the gown and held it up. It still might as well have not been there. She gave him a slow sidelong smile. "For myself, darling, I would not buy this. I would not wear this. For you . . . Do you want me to?"

"Jesus, do I!" he said hoarsely. "Do you gotta ask?"

Asking was part of the game. Vera understood that, even if Pete didn't. She also understood enough to walk behind him and say, "Not to turn around until I am telling you." A pause. Faint rustlings. "Okay now."

He turned. She looked even better than he'd imagined, and he hadn't thought such a thing possible. He took her in his arms. Somehow, the silk also made her feel more like a woman than she ever had before, and she'd always felt about as much like a woman as a woman could feel.

And he wasn't *too* drunk. Oh, no. That turned out to be better than ever, too. One more time, he hadn't dreamt it could.

*   *   *

SERGEANT CARRASQUEL GLOWERED in the direction of downtown Madrid, only a few kilometers away but as unreachable as the bottom of the sea or the mountains of the moon. "Stupid bastards," he snarled at no one in particular. "They brought us here to take the capital away from the Republic, but we're farther away than we were right after we came up from Gibraltar."

"It's those damned Internationals, Sergeant." Joaquin Delgadillo knew he had to soften up the underofficer before Carrasquel started throwing around extra duty or dangerous assignments. "If they hadn't got between us and the city, we might be in there by now."

"That's what *she* said," Carrasquel retorted. "Just shows the brass has its head up its ass, that's all."

"You didn't say things like that when Marshal Sanjurjo came up to look things over," Joaquin said slyly.

"I said plenty. What good would more have done?" Carrasquel replied. "He *is* a marshal. He talked nice to me, but to the likes of him a sergeant isn't even a squashed turd on the sole of his boot." He looked around. "I won't go on about taking things up the ass where Major Uribe can hear me, either. He'd think it was a good idea."

Joaquin giggled, deliciously scandalized. "He's got *cojones*," he said in what might or might not have been reproof.

"Sure he does," the sergeant agreed. "And he'd like 'em to be slapping the backside of some pretty little boy—or he'd like some big manly fellow's *cojones* slapping *his* backside. Or maybe both?"

"Both?" The straitlaced private hadn't thought of that. Could you both do and be done by? He supposed you could, but . . . "¡*Madre de Dios!*"

"She hasn't got any *cojones*. I'm sure of that. Hell, she didn't even get Joseph's," Carrasquel said.

This time, Delgadillo didn't answer right away. He was scandalized all over again, and not so deliciously this time. At last, stiffly, he said, "If you're going to make filthy jokes about the Virgin, you really *should* fight for the Republic." Everybody knew the people on the other side hated God—and He hated them, too.

"God understands me," Carrasquel said. "If a snot-nosed private doesn't, I won't lose sleep over it."

Major Uribe had said that God forgave his love life. Everybody seemed to think God would be soft on him in particular, even if all the other sinners running around loose would roast on Satan's grill forever, with demons sticking pitchforks into them every so often to turn them and make sure they cooked evenly on all sides. Joaquin didn't think God worked that way. It wasn't as if God had told him He didn't—God didn't waste time talking to a snot-nosed private. But that was how it looked to him.

"Go liberate some firewood." Sergeant Carrasquel talked to him, all right. "If you've got the time to jaw with me, you've got the time to do some real work." With a martyred sigh, Joaquin started scrounging. He'd tried to keep Carrasquel sweet-tempered, and look what he got for it! Nobody else would sympathize, either. The rest of the guys would just be glad he was busting his butt and they weren't.

To add injury to insult, Major Uribe chose him to join a raiding party that night. "We need some prisoners, sweethearts," Uribe lisped. "We always need prisoners. Have to keep track of what the dirty Reds are up to. They're going straight to hell, and you can count on it." He crossed himself.

So did Delgadillo. He also started working the beads on his rosary. How many prayers would he need to stay safe in a trench raid? The probable number struck him as unpleasantly large. He worked the beads harder. *Hail, Mary, full of grace. Don't listen to the foul-mouthed sergeant.* That wasn't your standard *Ave Maria*, but it came from the bottom of his heart.

After he got done with the rosary, Joaquin fixed the bayonet on his rifle—something he hardly ever did—and sharpened one edge of the blade on his entrenching tool. Trench raiding was close-quarters fighting at its nastiest. A couple of the men in the raiding party carried machine pistols, to fill the air around them with lead. Major Uribe had a sword—not an officer's ceremonial sword, but a shorter, fatter blade, almost a pirate's cutlass. Christ only knew where he'd found it. By the way he made it *wheep!* through the air as he limbered up in the Nationalist trenches, he knew what to do with it. And it went without saying that he would lead the party himself. No matter how queer he was, he never sent men where he wouldn't go himself.

No moon tonight. That was good. Light wouldn't betray the raiders as they crawled toward the Republican lines. A few hundred meters away, some of the other soldiers in the Nationalist trenches started shooting at the enemy. As Major Uribe had hoped, the Republicans fired back. With luck, the racket would cover any little noises the raiding party made.

With luck! What beautiful words those were! Joaquin had thought about that before, usually when artillery dropped too close. It crossed his mind again as he scrambled out of the trench and slithered forward.

Somewhere not far away, a cricket chirped. It fell silent as the Nationalist soldiers went by. "*Mierda*," Joaquin muttered under his breath. An alert Republican sentry might wonder why the bug suddenly shut up.

He couldn't do anything about that. All he could do was go on. The Republicans had barbed wire in front of their positions, damn them. Most wiring in Spain was halfhearted: a few strands, easy to cut through and to get through. Not here. The Internationals took war seriously. Damn them, too, in spades.

"No worries," Major Uribe said. He had wire cutters. The lengths twanged as they parted one by one. The noise seemed very loud to Joaquin, but the enemy didn't start shooting. Maybe the Mother of God *was* watching over him. The major hissed in the darkness. "Come along, lambs. All clear now."

On they went, mostly on their bellies. There was the parapet. In. Grab. Out. It would be easy. It could be easy.

"At my count of three, we rush," Uribe whispered. "*Uno . . . Dos . . .*"

He never got to *tres*. All hell broke loose. Internationals popped up along the parapet and started blasting away with everything they had. The Nationalists shrieked in despair. Major Uribe ran forward, sword drawn. Starlight glittered on the blade—for a moment. Then a bullet caught him. He groaned and fell. The sword flew from his hand.

Another bullet grazed Joaquin's shoulder. "*Aii!*" he howled, and then clapped both hands to his mouth. The more noise he made, the easier the target he gave the enemy. Well, a slug had found him anyhow. Blood dripped warm down his arm.

The firing eased for a moment. From the trench, someone called out in accented Spanish: "Surrender! Come in now! We'll take prisoners if you do. If you don't, you're dead. First chance, last chance, only chance. Now!"

How many meters back to his own lines? Too many. Joaquin was sure of that. Maybe they *would* take prisoners. His side had wanted some, after all. "I'm coming!" he said. Two or three other men also gave up. The others, he decided, would never move again, not in this life.

He slid down into the trench. An International frisked him in the dark. The fellow took everything that would have done him any good in a fight, and his wallet, too. That was a joke—he had all of seven pesetas in there. He didn't say anything. The foreigner would find out this wasn't even chicken feed.

"Get moving," the guy said in bad Spanish. "Not to do anything stupid, or I shoot you in the back. *¿Comprende?*"

"*Sí*," Joaquin said miserably, and then, "Where are you from?"

"*Estados Unidos. Nueva Iorque*," the International answered as they started toward Madrid.

"Why did you come here?" If Joaquin kept the guy talking, maybe he wouldn't shoot him for the fun of it. Maybe.

"For freedom," the American said. "Why do you want to fight for a *puto* like Marshal Sanjurjo?"

"For my country," Joaquin replied. The American—was he a Jew? wasn't everybody from New York a Jew? Joaquin had never talked with a Jew before—laughed at him. He would have laughed at the other fellow's so-called freedom, if only he were the one holding the rifle. But he wasn't. Head down, he shambled off into captivity.

NIGHT IN THE SIBERIAN WOODS. Hideki Fujita sat in a foxhole, slapping at mosquitoes. Daytime, nighttime . . . The mosquitoes didn't care. They bit whenever they found bare skin. Fujita had itchy welts all over. The damn mosquitoes had bitten him right through his puttees. He wouldn't have believed they could do that till he got here, but he did now.

"Hayashi!" he called.

"What is it, Sergeant-*san*?" the superior private asked.

"What's the name of that bloodsucking demon in the American movie?"

"Ah! He's called Dracula, Sergeant-*san*," Shinjiro Hayashi answered. Fujita could hear the relief in his voice. He'd figured Fujita wanted something harder, something more dangerous. Whatever a sergeant wanted, a private had to give it to him.

"*Hai!* Dracula!" Fujita said, and slapped again. "The night tonight is full of Draculas. You hear them buzzing, *neh*?"

"That's right," Hayashi said. Not even a private with an education would ever tell a sergeant he was wrong. If he did, he'd get an education of a brand-new kind, but not one he'd want.

Fujita wanted a cigarette. He didn't light up. Who could guess where a Russian sniper might be lurking? Like any other hairy animals, the Russians were at home among the trees. A bullet might fly out of nowhere if he struck a match. Or even the smell of burning tobacco might guide a sniper toward him. Who could say how Russians knew what they knew?

They didn't know how to give up. Though the Kwantung Army had cut the Trans-Siberian Railroad, Red Army counterattacks showed that the enemy would keep trying to restore the lifeline to Vladivostok.

A buzz in the air . . . Fujita paused with his hand raised to swat at something. This was no mosquito: this was a deeper sound, almost a rumble. Japanese bombers flew by at night to pound Russian positions farther north. And sometimes the Russians returned the favor. These sounded like Russian machines, sure as hell. Their note was different from those of Japanese airplanes. To Fujita, it seemed more guttural, like the incomprehensible Russian language compared to his own.

"Bombers!" someone yelled in perfectly comprehensible Japanese.

Just before the bombs started whistling down, Fujita did stick a cigarette in his mouth and light it. Why not? It would make him feel a tiny bit better—and, if there were Russian snipers in the neighborhood, they'd be scared out of their wits, too. Those planes were dropping by dead reckoning, dropping blind. Bombers, as Fujita had found, were none too accurate even when they could see their targets. When they couldn't . . . Any Russian snipers faced at least as much danger as the Japanese on whom they preyed.

The first crashing explosions came from a couple of kilometers behind the trench line. Fujita breathed easier. Let the quartermasters and cooks and the rest of the useless people get a taste of what war was like for a change! How would they like it? Not very much, not if he was any judge.

Then he said, "Uh-oh." That didn't seem enough. "*Zakennayo!*" he added. The bombs were coming closer. He'd seen that happen before. After the lead plane dropped, the others would use his bursts as an aiming point. But they wouldn't want to stick around any longer than they had to. They'd drop too soon, and the ones behind them sooner still, and . . .

And Hideki Fujita cowered in his hole as the explosions crept nearer and nearer. "Mother!" someone wailed. "Oh, Mother!" That wasn't a wounded man's scream—it was just terror. Fujita had a hard time condemning the frightened soldier. He was about to shit himself, too.

He almost tore down his trousers so as not to foul them. Only one thing stopped him: the thought that the mosquitoes would feast on his bare backside if he did. He hadn't got bitten too badly there. He clamped down as hard as he could and hoped for the best.

Crump! That one was close. *CRUMP!* That one was closer—much closer. The ground shook, as if in a big earthquake. Fujita knew more about earthquakes than he'd ever wanted to learn. To their sorrow, most Japanese did.

But earthquakes didn't throw razor-sharp, red-hot shards of steel through the air. Several of them wheeped and snarled by above Fujita's head. Dirt kicked up by the explosions arced down on him. Blast tore at his ears and his lungs. He breathed out as hard as he could. It might not do much good, but he didn't think it could hurt.

Then the bombs started going off farther away. Some of them had to be landing on Red Army positions. Instead of exultation, Fujita felt a kind of exhausted pity for the Russians huddling in their trenches. It wasn't as if his own side hadn't also tried to kill him.

Did blasts murder mosquitoes? He hoped so, but was inclined to doubt it. Nothing else did much good against the droning pests.

He couldn't hear them now. Someone was shouting something. He had trouble making that out, too. Yes, the near miss had messed up his ears. It wasn't the first time. He wondered how long they would need to come back to normal. Time would tell.

The shout came again, more urgent but no more understandable. *"Nan desu-ka?"* Fujita shouted back. *What is it?* He heard a little something the next time, but not enough to make sense of what the yelling soldier was saying. "*What* about Lieutenant Hanafusa?" he demanded.

"He's dead." This time, the key word came through very clearly. The other man added something else. Fujita caught the last part of it: "—left but his boots."

The sergeant's stomach did a slow lurch. He knew what happened to men who ended up in the wrong place at the wrong time. Lieutenant Hanafusa's spirit would join the rest of Japan's heroic dead at Yasukuni Shrine in Tokyo. His body . . . His body was probably splashed over half a square kilometer.

Somebody out there in the night said something else, something with Sergeant Fujita's name in it. "I'm here," Fujita called. "What was that? So sorry, but my ears are ringing like a bell."

Ringing or not, he got the answer very clearly: "You're in command of the platoon till we get a new officer. Sergeant Jojima got his hand blown off, and Sergeant Iwamura's hurt, too. So you're the senior noncom."

"What do we need to do now?" Fujita asked. But the other soldier couldn't tell him that. Only an officer could. And if any officers were left in the neighborhood, he wouldn't find himself in charge of the platoon. So he had to figure it out for himself. One thing looked blindingly obvious: if he ordered the men to retreat, somebody would hang him. "Hold tight!" he yelled as loud as he could. "If the Russians come, drive them back."

That sounded brave—braver than it was, probably. With any luck, the round-eyed barbarians would no more be able to attack than the Japanese were to defend.

So it proved. The rest of the night passed with hardly a shot fired by either side. When morning came, Fujita could see what a mess the bombs had made of the platoon's position and order his men to start setting things to rights. He didn't need to be an officer to see that that needed doing. How much *did* you need to be an officer to see? Not for the first time, he suspected it was less than officers claimed.

IF COPENHAGEN WASN'T A MIRACLE, Peggy Druce couldn't imagine what one would look like. The lights were on. Cars ran through the streets amidst the swarms of Danes on bicycles. Somehow, nobody seemed to get clobbered. No one looked shabby. No one seemed to have even heard of rationing, let alone suffered under it. You could buy all the gas you wanted, and all the clothes you wanted, too.

And the food! My God, the food! Peggy gorged on white bread and butter, on fine Danish ham, on pickled herring—on everything she wanted. She poured down good Carlsberg beer. The only things with which she didn't stuff herself were potatoes, turnips, and cabbage. She'd had enough of those in Germany to last her about three lifetimes.

She did her best not to think of Constantine Jenkins. She was back in touch with Herb. All the cable lines between America and Europe passed through England, and the English allowed no traffic with the continental enemy. But Denmark was a neutral, just like the USA. She and her husband could catch up on what had happened since last October.

On most of it, anyhow. Of course Peggy wouldn't put anything about the embassy undersecretary in a wire, or even a letter. She didn't think she'd ever be able even to talk about what happened with him. *I was drunk,* she told herself, over and over. And she had been. But she'd been horny, too, or she wouldn't have gone to bed with him no matter how drunk she was.

That wasn't the worst of it, either. Would Herb have got horny, too, there across the Atlantic? Sure he would; Herb was one of the most reliably horny guys she'd ever known. What would he have done about it, with her away for so long? What wasn't he putting into his telegrams and letters? What wouldn't he want to talk about after she got home?

Every time that crossed her mind, she muttered to herself. It wasn't that she'd mind—too much—if he'd laid some round-heeled popsy. But not being able to talk about things with him . . . That wasn't good. That was about as bad as it could get, in fact. They'd always been able to talk about everything. If they had to put up walls against each other, something precious would have gone out of their marriage—part of the whole point of being married, in fact.

Before long, she'd have the chance to find out about all that. Travel between Denmark and the UK was more complicated than it had been before the war. Because of mines and U-boats, few ships cared to cross the North Sea. Airplanes flew between one country and the other, but they carried far fewer passengers. Peggy couldn't book a flight to London any sooner than three weeks after she got to Copenhagen.

In the meantime . . . In the meantime, she made like a tourist. She rented a bicycle herself, relying on the polite Danish drivers not to run her down. She shopped. You could buy things in Copenhagen! The shop windows weren't mocking lies, the way they were in Berlin. If you saw it on display, you could lay down your money, and the shopkeeper would hand it to you. He'd even gift-wrap it for you if you asked him to. Quite a few Danes knew enough English to get by. A lot of the ones who didn't could manage in German. Peggy wasn't fond of the language, but she could use it, too.

Danish radios picked up not only Dr. Goebbels' rants but also the BBC. The *International Herald-Tribune* reported both sides' war bulletins. After so long with only the German point of view dinning in her ears, that seemed almost unnatural to Peggy. She presumed Danish papers did the same thing, but she couldn't read those.

The Danes might publish both sides' war news, but they didn't seem the least bit military themselves. She saw very few soldiers. Like so many other things, that reminded her she wasn't in Berlin any more. At the heart of the Third *Reich,* more men wore uniforms than civilian clothes. And she had trouble imagining German soldiers pedaling along on bicycles, waving to pretty girls as they passed. German soldiers always looked as if they meant business. The Danes seemed more like play-acting kids in uniform.

At Amalienborg, off Bredgade, the royal guard changed every day at noon. The soldiers there looked a little more serious, but only a little. The cut of their tunics and trousers and the funny flare of their helmets still kept them from being as intimidating as their German counterparts. Or maybe that was because Peggy had seen *Wehrmacht* men in action, while only the oldest of old men remembered the last time Denmark fought a war.

Between two and half past five every afternoon, young people promenaded from Frederiksbergggade past the best shops to Kongens Nytorv, near the palace. Peggy found the parade oddly charming. It was something she would have expected in Madrid (before Spain went to hell, anyhow) or Lisbon, not Scandinavia.

Days slid off the calendar, one by one. Getting her exit visa from Denmark and an entry visa cost some money, but not a speck of stomach lining. Examining the Czechoslovak and German stamps, the minor official at the British embassy who issued the entry visa remarked, "Seems as though you've had a bit of a lively time, what?"

If that wasn't a prime bit of British understatement, Peggy had never heard one. "Oh, you might say so," she answered—damned if she'd let the American side down.

She wondered if the functionary would ask her about what things were like in the enemy nation, but he didn't. He took her money, plied his rubber stamp with might and main, and used mucilage to affix the visa in her passport. "Safe journey," he told her.

"Much obliged," Peggy said. The phrase was a polite commonplace. Suddenly, though, she felt the words' true meaning. "I *am* much obliged to you—everybody who's finally helping me get home."

"I am here to assist travelers, ma'am," the official said, a trifle stiffly.

"Yes. I know. That's why I'm obliged to you," Peggy replied. He didn't get it. He was an Englishman, but maybe the war and all the accompanying madness seemed no more real to him than they did to the Danes. How long had he worked here?

Well, it didn't matter. All that mattered was that she had the documents she needed. Nothing would keep her off that airplane. Nothing!

She sent a wire to Herb: EVERYTHING SET. FIRST ENGLAND, THEN USA. WHOOPEE! LOVE, PEGGY. The clerk at the telegraph office had to ask her how to spell *Whoopee.* She was happy to tell him.

Herb's answer was waiting at the hotel when she finished spending money for the day: WHOOPEE IS RIGHT, BABE. SEE YOU SOON! LOVE, ME. She smiled. He always signed telegrams to her like that. And, like her, he'd stayed under the ten-word minimum-rate limit. They were nowhere near poor. When you'd been through the Depression, though, you watched every penny from habit. When you weren't shopping, of course. Well, sometimes even then, but not always.

She ate another splendid Danish breakfast the next morning. One day to go. She was all packed. The only thing she'd have to do tomorrow would be to put the clothes she had on now into her suitcase. What she'd wear then was already draped over a chair in her room. She intended to go to the airport very, very early. She didn't care how bored she'd get waiting for the plane. As with the train out of Germany, she wasn't going to miss it. She wasn't, she *wasn't,* she *WASN'T!*

She had lunch at the Yacht Pavilion. A guidebook called it delightful, and she agreed. She could see the statue of the Little Mermaid staring out into the sound. The smorrebrod was good, the aquavit even better.

Men started getting off a couple of freighters in the harbor and forming up in long columns on the piers. Peggy's eye passed over them, then snapped back. "No," she whispered. But yes. She'd never mistake the color those men were wearing. She grabbed a passing waiter by the arm and pointed across the almost waveless water. "Those are German soldiers! You're being invaded!"

He looked at her, at the troops in *Feldgrau* and beetling *Stahlhelms,* back to her again. Laughing, he shook his head. "No. It cannot be. Someone is making a film, that's all."

Briskly, the German soldiers marched off the piers and into Copenhagen. They looked as if they were heading straight for the royal palace. Well, where else would they be going?

A few rifle shots rang out, then a sharp burst of machine-gun fire. Faint in the distance, Peggy heard screams. Blood drained from the waiter's face, leaving him pale as vanilla ice cream. All over the Yacht

Pavilion, people started exclaiming. "But it cahn't be!" someone said in clear British English.

More gunfire. More screams. It could be, all right. And it damn well was. That plane wouldn't fly to England tomorrow, or anywhere else. Peggy burst into tears.

Chapter 16

Julius Lemp felt happier about the world, or at least about how his little part of it worked. Now the U-boat skipper understood his orders. And he was pleased with himself, because he'd had a pretty good notion of what they were about even before the balloon went up.

If the *Reich* had decided to forestall the Western democracies by occupying Denmark and Norway before they could, of course France and especially England would try to do something about it. And one of the things they would try to do would be to rush as many warships as they could to Scandinavian waters. If they did that, they'd likely storm right through Lemp's patrol zone.

No sooner had the thought crossed his mind than one of the ratings on watch sang out: "Smoke to the southwest, Skipper!"

"Ha!" Lemp swung his own binoculars in that direction. "Now the game starts!" He peered and studied. "Looks like . . . three plumes."

"I think so, too," the sailor said, and then, after a moment, "They've got wings on their feet, don't they?"

"*Ja.*" Lemp nodded. "Destroyers. They have to be. Nothing else will go that fast." By now, England had to know Germany was using her warships to move troops into southern Norway and fight the coastal forts. Destroyers could get to the battle in a hurry, and their crews were practiced with both guns and torpedoes. They were also quick and cheap to build, which made them more readily expendable than bigger, slower ships.

"Can we get to them?" another rating asked.

"We're going to try," Lemp answered. They couldn't make a surface approach, not unless they wanted to get blown out of the water long before their could loose their own eels. "Go below," he added. "We'll see how much help the *Schnorkel* can give us." He followed the men off the conning tower. As he slammed the hatch behind him and dogged it, he called, "Dive! *Schnorkel* depth! Change course to"—he calculated in his head— "to 195."

"Diving to *Schnorkel* depth. Changing course to 195," the helmsman said. Nothing flustered Peter. That was one of the reasons he was at the helm.

Lieutenant Beilharz appeared. The matte-black paint on his helmet had a fresh, shiny scratch. He really needed the protection to keep his skull from being gashed. Lemp pointed at him. "Just the man I'm looking for, by God! If we go all-out with your infernal device, how fast can we manage underwater?"

"They say thirteen knots, Skipper," the *Schnorkel* expert answered. "Everything shakes and rattles like it's coming to pieces, though."

"We'll try it anyway," Lemp declared. "Three destroyers are heading east as fast as they can go. Without the snort, we don't have a prayer of getting into firing range before they're past us. With it . . . Well, we've got a prayer. I think. We'll give it our best shot, any which way. You keep the damned gadget working the way it's supposed to, you hear?"

"*Jawohl!*" Beilharz said. Lemp had to hope he could deliver. The device was still experimental. And experimental devices had a way of going haywire just when you needed them most.

All he could do was try. He spoke into the voice tube to the engine room: "Give me thirteen knots."

"*Thirteen*, Skipper?" The brassy response didn't come right out and ask *Are you out of your bloody mind?*, but it might as well have.

"Thirteen," Lemp repeated firmly. "If that's more than we can take, we'll back it down. But our targets are making better than twice that. If we want to meet them, we have to give it everything we've got. Thirteen." He said it one more time.

"Aye aye, Skipper." The men who minded the diesels would do what you told them to. What happened afterwards wasn't their worry . . . unless, of course, it turned out to be everybody's worry.

They'd done eight knots submerged plenty of times, ten or eleven often enough. Above that, Beilharz had been reluctant to go. War sometimes forced you to do what you'd be reluctant to try in peacetime, though. If the U-30 could knock out one of those destroyers, how many soldiers' lives might that save? Hundreds? Thousands? No telling for sure.

The diesels surged. They had to work hard to push the U-boat through the resisting water. Lemp felt the power through the soles of his feet as he looked through the periscope. Without taking his eyes off the destroyers the optics displayed, he said, "You there, Klaus?"

"Sure am, Skipper," Klaus Hammerstein answered. Lemp hadn't expected anything else. Hammerstein might be a pup, but he was a well-trained pup. The exec's place in an attack run was at the captain's elbow. He'd have to do most of the calculating . . . if they could get close enough to the destroyers for it to matter.

Lemp fed him speed and range. He had to shout to make himself heard. As Beilharz had warned, everything inside the U-30 rattled as if it were getting massaged by an electric cake mixer. Lemp hoped his fillings wouldn't fall out. And that was no idle worry; every U-boat sailor dreaded a pharmacist mate's amateur dentistry.

"Skipper, there's no good solution if the numbers you fed me are anywhere close to right," Hammerstein said. "They're going to get past us before we close within three kilometers."

"*Scheisse!*" Lemp exclaimed. "Are you sure?" Here he'd done everything but tear his boat to pieces, and it hadn't done him a goddamn bit of good? That wasn't fair. That wasn't how life was supposed to work.

But sometimes life worked that way anyhow. The destroyers were making better than thirty knots. As Hammerstein had said, they raced past the U-30 before the sub could approach near enough to launch with any hope of success. You wanted to get inside of a kilometer if you could. Even the exec's three seemed optimistic.

"*Scheisse,*" Lemp said again, resignedly this time. He spoke to the engine room again: "You did all you could, but we can't catch them. Bring us back down to six knots."

"Six knots. Aye aye." Even through the long metal tube, the skipper could hear the relief in the answer. All the same, the *Schnorkel* had paid its dues. Without it, he wouldn't even have tried the attack run: it would have been obviously hopeless.

"What do we do now?" Hammerstein asked, his voice falling as the boat stopped trying to come to bits around him.

"We stay submerged till those Royal Navy ships get farther away—I don't want them turning around and coming after us," Lemp said. "Then we surface and radio their position and speed to the *Vaterland.* We aren't the only U-boat in the sea. And the *Kriegsmarine* and the *Luftwaffe* will have planes flying out of Germany—out of Denmark, too, by now, I suppose. Someone may pay them a call."

"All right." The exec still sounded unhappy, and explained why a moment later: "I still wish we could have done the job ourselves."

"So do I. If we could have made twenty knots submerged, we would have got them. But you can imagine what the boat would have been like at twenty knots. I don't think I've got the nerve to try thirteen again," Lemp said.

He went into his tiny cabin to prepare the encoded message he would send when the boat surfaced. The machine that filled most of his safe gave him the groups he needed. Experts assured him the code the machine generated was unbreakable, as long as the other side didn't get its hands on one of these machines. His orders were to sacrifice anything, including his own life, before he let that happen. He hoped—he prayed—he never had to make the choice.

He carefully scanned the whole horizon through the periscope before surfacing. As soon as he could, he sent off his carefully composed code groups. Then he ordered the boat down to *Schnorkel* depth again. However little he'd wanted to at first, he'd come to rely on the long, ugly stovepipe. It did what the Dutchmen who'd invented it said it would do. You couldn't ask for more.

Or could you? A U-boat that would make twenty knots submerged . . . That would be a weapon the likes of which the world had never known. With U-boats like that running around, how long could a surface navy survive? Days—weeks at most. .

But how would you get such a weapon? Better streamlining came to mind right away. The U-30 wasn't made for high-speed underwater travel. The engineers who'd designed the boat had assumed such a thing was impossible. And it was—when they'd designed the boat. Was it now, with the *Schnorkel* and whatever other clever notions the boys with thick glasses could come up with?

"Not even slightly," Lemp murmured. "No, not even." He retreated to his cabin again. Once he got there, he started sketching and making notes. After a few minutes, he shut the curtain that gave him more privacy than anyone else on the boat enjoyed. He didn't want his men to think he'd gone round the bend.

A TRAIN HAULED ALISTAIR WALSH and God only knew how many other English soldiers towards a port on the Atlantic or the western side of the English Channel. He didn't know exactly where he was going. He did wonder whether the officers who'd dragged him and his comrades away from the line in front of Paris knew where they were sending them.

Inside a cat carrier improvised from a lady's fancy hatbox, Pussy meowed. "Hush, there," Walsh said, and fed the cat a bit of bully beef. Pussy loved the stuff, which, to Walsh's way of thinking, only proved the little beast didn't have the brains God gave a flatiron or a General Staff colonel.

Rank had its privileges. Had Jock or Alonzo tried to bring a cat along when they got transferred to . . . somewhere, some officious corporal would have made sure it never got on the train. But a staff sergeant was allowed his little eccentricities.

And Pussy entertained the rest of the smelly, dirty, khaki-clad men shoehorned into the compartment with him. They vied with one another at finding little delicacies for her. And their weary, badly shaved faces softened when they stroked her. She wasn't a woman, but she was warm and soft—the next best thing, you might say. They laughed when she chased a bit of string over their forest of knees, and hardly swore at all if she slipped and dug claws into a leg to keep from falling.

They didn't know where they were going, either. Some guessed Russia. More plumped for Norway. "Me, Ah don't much care," Jock said. "Put a goddamn Fritz in front of me, and Ah'll shoot the bugger." When he came out with that, the rest of the men solemnly nodded. How could you sum things up better?

One fellow kept insisting they wouldn't see any more Fritzes—they'd done their bit, he insisted, and were going back to Blighty for good. The other soldiers humored him, as they would have humored any harmless maniac. Like them, Walsh would have loved to believe it. Like them, he couldn't. Once the army got hold of you, it didn't turn you loose till the war ended—which didn't look like happening any time soon—or till it used you up.

In Brest (which turned out to be their destination), they filed aboard what was called a troopship. By the way it smelled, it had hauled more cattle, or maybe sheep, than soldiers. Pussy found the symphony of stinks fascinating. Walsh lit a Navy Cut to blunt what it did to his nostrils. On that ship, he would have lit a Gitane, and he thought they smelled like smoldering asphalt.

They made it back to England without meeting a U-boat. He heartily approved of that. They came into port just after sunup, and got served huge helpings of bangers and mash and properly brewed tea. After British army rations, French army rations, and a lot of whatever he could scavenge, he approved of that, too.

"You see?" said the chap who was convinced they were going to be discharged. "They wouldn't feed us like this if they meant to keep us on." For the first time, Walsh began to wonder. That did fit in with the way the army mind worked.

Whether it did or not, it turned out not to be true. A captain with a really splendid red mustache stood up on a barrel and addressed the soldiers just returned to their native soil: "Well, lads, we'll be entraining you soon. Then it's Scotland, and then another little pleasure cruise." His wry grin said he knew what the troopship had been like. Maybe he'd been on it, though an officer would have had better accommodations than other ranks. He went on, "After that, it's Norway. If Adolf thinks we'll just sit by whilst he gobbles it up, he'd best think again, what?"

"Norway?" That astonished, dismayed bleat came from the luckless private who'd been so sure he would soon be set at liberty.

"Norway," the captain repeated. "The Norwegians are tough fighters—there just aren't enough of them to hold back the Fritzes on their own." His smile suddenly went broad and lickerish. "And the girls there are mighty pretty, and they'll be mighty glad to see the blokes who're helping to keep 'em free."

That might turn out to be true, and it might not. Most likely, it would be part truth, part stretcher. Some Frenchwomen enjoyed spitting in an English soldier's eye, while others were complaisant as could be.

Lorries growled up to take the troops from the dockside to the train station. Had the Germans sneaked a few bombers across the Channel, they could have worked a fearful slaughter. But everything went off smoothly. No one seemed to give a damn about Pussy. Walsh was probably breaking all kinds of laws by bringing her into the country, but he didn't care.

The train proved less crowded than the one in France that had hauled him away from the fighting there. Tinned rations were passed out. He sighed. They'd keep him full, which didn't mean he loved them.

As the train rattled through the north of England, Jock nudged him and asked, "You won't mind if me and my mates 'op it here, will you, Sergeant?" The Yorkshireman's grin said he didn't expect to be taken seriously.

"Oh, right," Walsh answered. "Desertion in wartime—they'll pin a medal on you for that, they will." He glanced over to make sure the private understood exactly what officialdom would do if he and his mates took off. The twinkle in Jock's eyes showed he did. Walsh gave him a cigarette and fired up one of his own. They smoked in companionable silence.

Scotland. Walsh had expected Edinburgh, but the train pounded on, north and east. "Aberdeen," guessed someone whose clotted accent said he knew the local geography pretty well. It made sense. Norway was pretty far north, and they wouldn't be sailing toward the part the Germans had already grabbed. Walsh hoped like blazes they wouldn't, anyhow.

Aberdeen seemed to come out of nowhere. It was a gray granite city, as if the bones of the countryside were carved into churches and shops and houses and blocks of flats. The North Sea lay beyond. Walsh hadn't seen it before. It looked colder and generally grimmer than the Channel. Who would have imagined anything could?

More khaki lorries waited at the station as the soldiers got off their trains. Some of the drivers smoked. One or two nipped from flasks unlikely to hold water. A raw wind blew down out of the north. Summer? Gray Aberdeen scoffed at summer. What would Norway be like? Walsh half wished he hadn't thought to wonder.

He clumped up the gangplank onto a freighter that had seen better days but didn't reek of livestock, Pussy still in her hatbox. As soon as he found his assigned place, he let her scurry around for a while. The cat had been very good about staying cooped up—she'd slept most of the way north. But she needed to get out while she could.

She rewarded him by dropping a dead mouse on his bunk. *Aren't you proud of me?* the green eyes asked. *Isn't it a lovely present? Will you eat it right now or save it for later?* Walsh took it by the tail and tossed it in a dustbin. He made much of Pussy afterwards and chucked her under the chin, but he could tell she was disappointed.

A small convoy pulled out of the harbor: troopships escorted by a destroyer and a pair of smaller warships. Frigates? Corvettes? Walsh was no sailor; he didn't know their right names. He did know he was glad to have them along.

A name began to drift through the freighter. Trondheim. It was somewhere up the Norwegian coast. Just where, Walsh couldn't have said. How far away from the place were the Germans? Somebody in the convoy probably knew. Walsh hoped so. Nobody admitted anything about it where he could hear, though. He did notice that abandon-ship drills came more often and were more thorough than any he'd seen before. He didn't take that for a good sign.

Daylight lingered long, and got longer as the ships zigzagged north-east. Walsh didn't take that for a good sign, either. U-boats and enemy airplanes had most of the clock's face in which to prowl. A sailor told him the last run in to Trondheim was planned for the brief hours of darkness. He hoped that would be long enough to shield them from prying eyes. Past hoping, he couldn't do anything about it but worry.

As twilight neared, an angular biplane with floats under the wings buzzed toward the convoy from the east. The warships opened up on it right away. It flew past them and dropped a small bomb that just missed one of the lumbering freighters. Then it sprayed that troopship with machine-gun bullets and went back the way it had come.

Two more German biplanes attacked the convoy an hour later. Gathering darkness or dumb luck kept them from doing much harm. All the ships made it to Trondheim. As he had before, Walsh filed off the freighter. Pussy meowed inside her makeshift carrier. Off in the distance, artillery rumbled. That answered one thing. The Germans weren't very far away after all.

EVERYONE ON HIS SIDE had told Joaquin Delgadillo he would march into Madrid in triumph. Well, here he was, but not the way he'd had in mind. He'd heard the Republicans shot prisoners. That didn't seem to be true: he was still breathing. Maybe they thought he was too insignificant to be worth a bullet. If they did, he didn't want to change their minds for them.

He wasn't even in a proper jail. They housed him and their other prisoners in a barbed-wire enclosure in a park. They gave the captives tents of such surpassing rattiness that he would have thought it a deliberate insult had he not known they used equally ratty ones themselves (so did his side).

They fed him beans and cabbage and occasional chopped-up potatoes. It wasn't very good, and he always craved more than he got. But he wouldn't starve on these rations—not soon, anyhow. He'd been hungry often enough—too often—in the field to get excited about this.

Most of the Republican guards were men recovering from wounds. They couldn't move fast. But they carried submachine guns. If anyone tried to escape, they could send a hell of a lot of bullets after him.

Joaquin wasn't going anywhere, not right away. He was just glad to say alive after the disastrous raid on the Internationals. He was even more relieved to find himself untortured after being taken prisoner. Little by little, he started to realize not everything his superiors had told him about the Republicans was the gospel truth.

He didn't do anything about the realization, not yet. For one thing, it was still a newly sprouted seed pushing up through dead leaves and chunks of bark toward the light. For another, he was in no position to do anything about anything. He ate. He slept. He mooched around the camp, taking care not to get too close to the wire. Coming too close—or anything else out of the ordinary—would have made the guards open up on him without warning.

When flights of bombers droned over his foxhole to drop their deadly cargo on Madrid, he'd cheered. How not? Those bombs were falling on the enemy's heads. Well, so they were. One thing that hadn't occurred to him before he got captured was that those bombs were also liable to come down on the heads of prisoners of war.

The only spades the Republicans allowed inside the wire perimeter were the ones the captives used to lengthen their latrine trenches and shovel lime into them to fight the stink. The guards counted the spades before they doled them out, and made sure they got them all back every time. Joaquin had no trouble seeing why: they didn't want the prisoners tunneling under the barbed wire. But it meant the captured Nationalists had nothing but a few mugs and tin mess kits to dig scrapes in which to shelter when the bombers came by.

Joaquin had borne up when Republican planes bombed his positions. He'd always consoled himself by thinking his side had more planes with which to punish the godless foe. And he'd been right. The Nationalists did have more bombers . . . and they concentrated them against Madrid.

He'd always thought of bombing as a pinpoint business. That wasn't how Marshal Sanjurjo's flyers went about it. Madrid belonged to the Republicans. As far as the Nationalists were concerned, they could put their bombs anywhere and still hurt their opponents.

They could—and they did. Maybe they didn't aim as well as Joaquin thought they could. Or maybe they just didn't care. With antiaircraft guns shooting at them from the ground, with Republican fighters sometimes tearing into them, the pilots and bombardiers wanted nothing more than to get back to their airstrips in one piece.

Either they didn't know the camp for their comrades lay right in the middle of the city they were flattening or they didn't care. Joaquin would have bet on the latter.

You could watch the bombs fall from the planes' bellies. You could watch them swell as they grew nearer. You could listen to the rising whistle as they clove the air on their way down. You could watch fire and smoke and dust leap up and out as they burst.

You could, yes—if you were stupid enough. You could get smashed or chopped by flying fragments and rubble, too. Artillery fire and those earlier bombings from the Republicans had rammed one lesson into Joaquin: when things started blowing up, you got as low and as flat as you could. Even that might not be enough, but it gave you your best chance.

Most of the prisoners knew as much. They lay down in whatever tiny dips in the ground they could find. Those who had anything to dig with scraped at the hard, dry dirt as fiercely as they could. Some of those who didn't broke fingernails and tore fingertips in the animal urge to burrow.

Joaquin screamed when bombs went off nearby. That was as much instinct as the prisoners' frantic scrabbling at the dirt. Odds were the thunderous explosions kept other men from hearing his cries. And odds were his weren't the only shrieks rising up to the uncaring sky.

Were the guards on the other side of the wire screaming, too? Of course they were. Terror conquered Nationalists and Republicans with equal ease. And if some of the Republicans weren't calling out to their mothers or to God, Joaquin would have been amazed. You could tear the cassock off a priest or torch a church, but tearing the beliefs you grew up with out of your heart wasn't so easy.

Then two bombs smashed down inside the perimeter, and Joaquin stopped caring about anything but staying alive longer than the next few seconds. He got picked up and slammed down, as if by a wrestler the size of a building. Blood dribbled from his nose; iron and salt filled his mouth. He spat, praying the blast hadn't shredded his lungs. Were his ears also bleeding? He wouldn't have been surprised.

More bombs burst—mercifully, farther away. As if from a long way off, he heard screams full of anguish, not fear. He knew the difference; he'd heard both kinds too often. Whoever was making noises like that wouldn't keep making them very long—not if God showed even a little kindness, he wouldn't.

If the bombs had blown a hole in the barbed wire, the camp might empty like a cracked basin. Then again, it might not. The thought flickered through Joaquin and then blew out. He was too stunned to do anything but lie there with his sleeve pressed to his face to try to stanch the flood from his nose. How many others in here would be in much better shape?

The guards wouldn't, either. . . . That thought also flickered and blew out. To try to escape, Joaquin would have needed more resolution than he owned right this minute. He imagined running this way and that, trying to find a gap in the perimeter. Imagining was easy. Doing wouldn't be. Even telling his rosary beads took as much as he had in him.

Guards came into the prisoners' enclosure to take away men who'd been killed or wounded. They didn't seem to treat the injured Nationalists any worse than stretcher-bearers and medics who fought for Marshal Sanjurjo would have. Seeing that, Joaquin decided the Republicans weren't just fattening him for the slaughter, so to speak.

He got another surprise a few days later: the International who'd captured him came to see how he was doing. He wouldn't have known the man by sight, not when the ill-fated raid came off in the middle of the night. But the fellow's slow, bad Spanish and the timbre of his voice were familiar. "Here I am!" Joaquin called from his side of the wire.

"*Bueno*." The International—the American, the Jew, he'd said he was—nodded back. "They treat you all right?"

Joaquin considered. "Not too bad. Could be worse." Lord knew that was true. They might have decided to see how many small chunks they could tear off him before he died. He'd feared they would do exactly that. And they still might, if he annoyed them enough.

"Here. Catch." The International tossed an almost-full pack of Gitanes over the barbed wire. Joaquin grabbed it eagerly. He could smoke some of the harsh cigarettes and trade the rest for . . . well, for anything you could get here. On this side of the wire, cigarettes were as good as pesetas, maybe better.

"*Muchas gracias,*" he said. "You didn't have to do this. You must be a gentleman."

To his amazement, he saw he'd flustered the fellow from the other side. The Jew was ordinary, or a little homelier than that: short, kind of pudgy, with a big nose and not a whole lot of chin. "I don't want to be a gentleman," he said. "I don't want anybody to be a gentleman. Everybody ought to be equal, *sí*?"

"Then how does anyone decide what needs doing?" Joaquin asked. "Once he does decide, how does he get them to go along?"

"Ah!" The International leaned forward till he almost pricked that formidable nose on the barbed wire's fangs. "Here's how . . ." Like an airplane climbing from a runway, the talk took off from there.

MIKE CARROLL EYED CHAIM WEINBERG in mingled amusement and scorn. "You came here to fight the fucking Fascists, man. You didn't come here to convert 'em."

"Bite me," Chaim answered. "The more of those guys we win over, the better."

"You know what Mencken said about that kind of shit," Mike persisted. He quoted with relish: " 'I detest converts almost as much as I do missionaries.' "

Chaim didn't want to listen, especially since Mike hardly ever read anything that didn't follow the Party line. Why now? "Who cares what a reactionary says?"

"He may be a reactionary, but he's a damn fine writer." The other American sounded a little defensive, or more than a little.

"For an enemy of the people." Chaim trotted out the heavy artillery.

Mike breathed heavily through his nose. "Okay. Fine. Have it your way. But if you're back at that camp blabbing about dialectical materialism when you're supposed to be up here fighting, Brigadier Kossuth'll skin you alive. He'll call it desertion, not conversion."

He was right, which didn't make Chaim any happier with him. If anything, Chaim only got angrier. "Hey, you know better than that. When did I ever miss action?"

"That time just after you got here, over near the Ebro."

"Oh, give me a break! I was down with dysentery, for cryin' out loud. You never got a case of the galloping shits?"

"Not to where I couldn't grab my rifle."

"Terrific," Chaim said. "Grab it and shove it up your ass—bayonet first." He was ready for a brawl. Mike was bigger than he was, and looked to have more muscles, but all that mattered only so much. Land a guy one in the pit of the stomach or in the nuts and all the muscles in the world wouldn't do him a goddamn bit of good.

But instead of pissing off the other American, Chaim made him laugh. "All right, already," Carroll said, as if he were a *Landsman* himself. "But watch yourself, okay? You really are making like this one Nationalist is more important than the rest of the struggle."

"Nah," Chaim said, even if Mike was right, or nearly right, again. He'd come to see the effort to reeducate Joaquin as a representation of the larger fight against Fascism. He realized that, just because he saw it that way, other people wouldn't necessarily do the same thing. Some of those other people were officers who could tell him what to do and land him in hot water if he didn't do it or if he wasn't around to do it.

"What do you see in the guy, anyhow?" Mike pressed. "He's nothing but a dumb kid off the farm. If he came from the States, he'd be a hayseed from Arkansas or Oklahoma or somewhere like that. He'd be a hardshell Baptist, too, instead of a Catholic."

Chaim's knowledge of Arkansas and Oklahoma was purely theoretical. So was his knowledge of the differences between one brand of Christianity and another. Catholics went to fancier churches, and their bishops dressed the way rabbis would if rabbis were crazy faggots. What more did you need to know?

(Thinking of rabbis reminded him of his brief fling with starting a *shul*. Just as Kossuth had predicted, he hadn't stuck with it. Now he had this new cause instead. Always something, but never the same thing for very long.)

Besides, he was sick of soldiering. He'd seen enough, done enough, lived through enough, to have its measure. If the Internationals needed someone with a rifle to get up on a firing step and shoot at Sanjurjo's men, the Republican equivalent of a fellow like Joaquin Delgadillo would do. Chaim had discovered the joys of . . . well, of preaching. If it was a smaller moment than the one St. Paul had on the road to Damascus, the difference was of degree, not of kind.

He might have preached better with more fluent Spanish. But he might not have. He had to keep his ideas simple and direct, because he couldn't say anything fancy or highfalutin. Even staying simple, he fumbled for words and verb endings. Joaquin—and, soon, other Nationalist prisoners who'd started listening to him for no better reason than to pass the time of day—threw him a line whenever he needed one. If anything, that made him more effective. His audience was, and felt itself to be, part of the show.

And changing minds—winning converts—turned out not to be that hard, no matter how little H. L. Mencken might have cared for the process. Chaim had a solid grounding in the doctrines of Marx and Lenin. The men to whom he preached seemed to have no ideology at all.

"Well, why did you keep fighting for Sanjurjo, then?" he asked a Spaniard who wore a patch over his right eye socket. He knew the fellow would have fought with desperate courage, too. The Nationalists might serve a vile cause, but they served it bravely.

"Why, *Señor*?" A Spanish shrug was less comic, more resigned, than its French equivalent. "I was in the army. We had an enemy. What else was there to do but fight?"

"You were oppressed, in other words. That's why you fought," Chaim said. No matter how lousy his Spanish as a whole was, he knew words like *oppressed*. "How do you get rid of oppression?" He answered his own question: "You have to struggle against it, not for it."

"But how, *Señor*?" the soldier asked. "If we didn't do what our officers told us, they would have shot us. And if we tried to come across the line, chances are you Republicans would have shot us. It is a bad bargain."

It *was* a bad bargain. The natives on the two sides hated each other too much for it to be anything else. Their higher-ups did, anyhow. Ordinary soldiers sometimes had a more sympathetic understanding for the poor sorry bastards who filled out the ranks on the other side. Sometimes.

"Officers who oppress can have accidents," Chaim said. "Officers who oppress ought to have accidents. They deserve them."

The Nationalists listened to him without surprise. Things like that had happened in every army since the Egyptians went to war against the Assyrians. Anybody who made his own men despise him needed eyes in the back of his head. Even those weren't always enough to save him.

"Your real problem was, you never wondered if Sanjurjo's officers had the right to give you orders," Chaim said. "Who set them over you? God?" He smiled crookedly. "They want you to think so."

"Who makes officers for the Republicans?" Joaquin asked.

"Mostly, the men choose them. We do in the Abraham Lincoln Battalion," Chaim answered. "Just about all the Spanish Republican units do the same thing." He told the truth—for the most part. Sometimes the Party wanted certain men in certain slots . . . but the will of the Party was the will of the people. Wasn't it?

The Nationalist prisoners muttered among themselves. Finally, one of them asked, "But what if these men make bad leaders?"

"Then we get new ones," Chaim replied. "What if *your* officers make bad leaders?" None of the prisoners tried to give him an answer. He and they all knew what the answer was. If a Nationalist officer made a bad leader, his men were stuck with him. Most armies worked that way. Chaim pressed the advantage: "You see how much better the Republican way is?"

They didn't say no. They weren't in an ideal position to say no, but Chaim didn't let that worry him.

Neither did his own superiors. As Mike had prophesied, he got a summons from Brigadier Kossuth. The Magyar eyed him impassively. "So," he said. "Now you are a propagandist instead of a soldier?"

"No. And a soldier," Chaim said, wondering how much trouble he was in.

Kossuth's lizardy tongue flicked in and out. "Soldiers we can always find," he observed. "Propagandists are harder to come by. Do you want to go on reeducating the Nationalist prisoners? That might be useful."

By which he could only mean *You'd better want to go on reeducating them.* Since Chaim did, he answered, "If that would help the Republic, sure I'll do it."

"Good. We understand each other." Kossuth was dry as usual. Chaim wondered what would have happened to him had he said he'd rather stay at the front. Nothing he would have enjoyed: he was sure of that. The brigadier seemed surprised to find him still standing there. "Dismissed," he said, and Chaim beat it. Moscow or Barcelona might replace Kossuth, but an ordinary lug could only obey him. Maybe Chaim wasn't so different from the Nationalists who needed reeducating after all.

Chapter 17

"Moscow speaking," the radio said importantly.

Sergei Yaroslavsky yawned as he listened. He was drinking a glass of strong, sweet tea and smoking a cigarette, but it was still six in the morning. Had he had any choice, he would have stayed rolled in his blanket.

A thick slab of roast pork, glistening with fat at the edges, sat on the tin plate in front of him. Had he had any choice, he wouldn't have picked something like that for breakfast. It would fill him up better than black bread; he couldn't deny that. But it would also make him want to go back to sleep . . . wouldn't it?

He sawed away with knife and fork. Methodically, he chewed and swallowed. As soon as he got up in the air, he wouldn't be sleepy any more. He was sure of that. Sleep and terror blended like vodka and castor oil.

Several flyers were fortifying their tea with healthy shots of vodka: the ration was a hundred grams a day. Others were swigging the vodka and ignoring the tea. Sergei preferred not to do that. You might be bolder in the cockpit once you'd got outside with some antifreeze, but you'd surely be slower. Against German fighter planes, against skilled, sober German pilots, slower wasn't a good idea.

"The liberation of Poland from the clutches of the semifascist Smigly-Ridz clique and their Nazi henchmen continues to gather momentum," the newscaster declared. "Advances on a broad front accelerate. Polish soldiers surrender in growing numbers, recognizing the hopelessness of their cause and the justice behind the Red Army's struggle against the lawless hyenas who have led them to destruction."

"He doesn't say anything about the fucking Germans surrendering," remarked a pilot who was knocking back vodka as if afraid it would be outlawed tomorrow—not likely, not in the hard-drinking Soviet Union.

"Hush," three people said at the same time. The only good thing about fighting Germans was that there weren't many of them in Poland. As Sergei had seen in Czechoslovakia, the *Wehrmacht* and *Luftwaffe* were dauntingly good at what they did.

The brief byplay made him miss the newsman's latest recital of towns taken and towns bombed from the air. The voice on the radio might have been broadcasting a football match. If he was, he was definitely the home team's announcer. If you listened to him, you had to believe the Red Army and Air Force could do no wrong.

Then he switched to a match in a different league: "The Fascist occupation of Denmark appears to be all but unchallenged. The Danes have chosen not even to fight. If they hope for mercy from the Nazi jackals, they are doomed to disappointment. Combat does continue in Norway. England and France claim to be flooding men into the country to help the Norwegians resist the Hitlerite jackals. Oslo and the south, however, seem already to be in German hands. Whether counterattacks can be effective remains to be seen. The Fascists claim to have inflicted heavy losses on the Royal Navy."

He talked about the fighting in France. There wasn't much. Then, at last, with the air of a prim matron discussing the facts of life, he talked about the war in the Far East. He kept going on about how heavy the fighting there was.

Across the table from Sergei, Anastas Mouradian raised an eyebrow.

Yaroslavsky nodded back. They didn't mean to speak; speaking would have endangered them. But *heavy fighting* was never good news.

Sure enough, the broadcaster went on, "High-ranking officers in the combat zone are no longer completely certain that Vladivostok's resistance against the Japanese brigands can continue indefinitely."

Vladivostok would fall. That was what he meant. He didn't want to come right out and say so—and who could blame him? With the Trans-Siberian Railway cut, the Japanese were nipping off the USSR's main window on the Pacific. The only word for that was disaster.

Not everybody would be able to understand exactly what the newsreader meant. Most people, very likely, would think Vladivostok could still hold out for a long time, even if not forever. But why mention that it might fall if you weren't getting ready to admit that it would fall, or even that it had fallen?

He wanted to sigh with relief when the announcer shifted to the over-fulfillment of the steel quota and then gave forth with the gory details of a train collision down in the Ukraine. "One of the engineers is suspected of being drunk on the job," the newsreader said portentously. "The General Secretary of the Communist Party of the USSR finds this most unfortunate."

The fellow said no more about that, nor did he need to. If Stalin didn't like it . . . Well, anything could happen after that. Sergei had thought a program of prohibition impossible in his homeland. The Tsars had tried one during the last war, and it failed miserably—Russians drank like swine. But if Stalin wanted to do the same thing, who would stop him? Nobody.

The pilots who'd already started drinking drank faster than ever. Maybe the stuff really would be outlawed tomorrow. Maybe . . . but Sergei still wouldn't believe it till he saw it.

"Molodetschna," Colonel Borisov said. "We hit Molodetschna again. We have to keep the Nazis from getting through and getting away."

Anastas Mouradian raised a hand. Frowning, the squadron commander nodded his way. "Comrade Colonel, is it not likely that as many Germans as could get through the miserable place have already done it?" the Armenian asked.

It was more than likely: it was as near certain as made no difference. They'd been pounding Molodetschna since the war widened. Too many SB-2s had gone down in flames to Bf-109s and the heavy concentration of antiaircraft guns around the place. They'd watched panzers and infantry units entrain and head elsewhere. Colonel Borisov had flown over Molodetschna. He knew what was and wasn't going on there, too—or he should have.

But he also knew something else. "I have my orders, Mouradian," he said heavily. "We have our orders. We will carry them out. Is that clear?"

"I serve the Soviet Union!" Mouradian said. That was always the right answer.

Ivan Kuchkov also knew about the new orders. Maybe he'd had a separate briefing from someone less exalted than the squadron leader. Or maybe, being a sergeant, he'd found out about them before Borisov or any of the other officers. He wasn't worried about coming out with what he thought of things, either: "Only way the cunts don't fucking murder us is if they don't care about the place any more."

Sergei set a hand on his shoulder. "It's nice, the way you try to cheer us up," he said. The squat, muscular bombardier eyed him suspiciously. The Chimp was a stranger to irony, and a hostile stranger at that.

The SB-2 lumbered into the air. Sergei remembered how proud of his "fighting bomber" he'd been while serving as a "volunteer" in Czechoslovakia. Against the biplane fighters they'd seen in Spain, SB-2s were fine. Against the deadly German Messerschmitts . . . well, they lumbered.

Through the engines' din, Mouradian said, "What if the Red Army's already taken Molodetschna? Are we supposed to bomb our own men?"

There was an interesting question. It all but defined *Damned if you do and damned if you don't*. You could get shot for dropping bombs on your own side. But you could also get shot—you could very easily get shot—for not following orders. "Let's see what it looks like," Sergei said, and left it there. If he didn't have to make up his mind right now, he wouldn't.

When he saw black puffs of smoke ahead, he nodded to himself. The Germans still held the town. Soviet flak wouldn't have been anywhere near so intense. Yaroslavsky was a good patriot, but he knew what his own people could and couldn't do.

Now—where was the train station? He had a devil of a time spotting it. Either Red Army artillery had set Molodetschna ablaze or the Nazis had fired the town on purpose to give themselves a smoke screen. If he thought of it, they could, too, and they were more than ruthless enough to do it once they thought of it.

There! He pointed through the gray-black billows. "See it, Stas?"

"*Da*," Mouradian said. "Straight and slow, if you please." He shouted into the speaking tube to the bomb bay: "Ready, Ivan?"

"Ready!" The answer came back at once.

A burst too close for comfort jolted the plane. Sergei flew straight and slow all the same. "Now!" Mouradian yelled.

Bombs whistled down. Sergei wrestled the SB-2 around and started flying back to the Motherland at full throttle. He hadn't seen any German fighters this time. He didn't miss them, either. And it wasn't as if he wouldn't see them again—all too likely, much sooner than he wanted to.

A FRENCH CAPTAIN CAME UP to Vaclav Jezek and started shouting and waving his arms. Whatever he had to say, he was excited about it. The Czech with the antitank rifle understood not a word. Why the fellow started bothering him when he was trying to spoon up some mutton stew . . . He looked around for Sergeant Halévy. No sign of the Jew, though. "Sorry, but I don't speak your language," Vaclav said in what he hoped was French.

The captain went right on yelling and carrying on. Vaclav didn't know why he was all excited. He also didn't care. He just wanted the Frenchman to leave him alone.

With a sudden evil grin, he decided he knew exactly how to get what he wanted. Spreading his hands in apology, he said, "*Entschuldigen Sie mich, Herr Hauptmann, abe ich spreche Französisch nicht. Sprechen Sie Deutsch, vielleicht?*"

He'd had to speak German to get a Pole to understand him after the Nazis overran his country. He figured a Frenchman would sooner cough up a lung than admit to knowing the enemy's language.

Which only went to show you never could tell. The captain answered,

"*Ach! Sie sprechen Deutsch! Wunderbar! Ich kann es auch sprechen, aber nicht so gut.*"

Vaclav didn't care whether the Frenchman couldn't speak German very well. Now that they had a language in common, he had to pay attention to the son of a bitch. Resignedly, he said, "What do you want with me, sir?" To show just how interested he was, he shoveled in another big spoonful of stew and made a point of chewing with his mouth open.

He didn't faze the captain. The fellow's patched, faded uniform said he'd seen some real action; he wasn't a staff officer coming up to the front to make trouble. He said, "You have been shooting German soldiers. Sharpshooting. Sniping." On the third try, he found the word he wanted.

"*Jawohl, Herr Hauptmann.*" Vaclav made his voice as sarcastic as he could. "The last I looked, there was a war on."

"Yes, yes," the French captain said impatiently. "But the damned Nazis have imported a sniper of their own."

"I know that. I potted the stinking pigdog, by God!" Now Jezek sounded proud of himself. And well he might have. The German could have killed him, too. The bastard had been too goddamn good at what he did.

"Another one," the Frenchman said. Vaclav hadn't thought of that. When you'd gone and killed the dragon, you could live happily ever after, couldn't you? At least for a little while? Maybe not. Evidently not—the captain went on, "Another one, without a doubt. He put one through Colonel Laplace's head more than half a kilometer behind the line."

"Did he?" Vaclav said tonelessly. That was a good shot, all right. A very good shot, if he was using a Mauser. It was a good rifle—a very good infantry rifle, as far as accuracy went. But it was only an infantry rifle, not an elephant gun like the one Vaclav lugged around.

"He did," the captain said, in the *how dare you question me?* tone French officers were so good at using. "And he bagged a captain and two lieutenants as well, these past three days. He likes officers, you see." He raised an eyebrow at Vaclav. "I daresay he would like you, too. I believe he is here because you have annoyed the *Boches* to such a degree." *Boches* stuck out in the middle of his slow, pause-filled German, but Vaclav couldn't very well pretend he didn't get it. The captain's eyebrow lifted again. "Since you have caused the problem, so to speak, it is up to you to solve it."

"*Danke sehr, Herr Hauptmann.*" *Thanks a bunch.*

"*Bitte schön.*" *You're very welcome.* God scorch him black as a potato forgotten in the oven, the captain could be sarcastic, too. "I expect you to deal with the problem . . . one way or another." What that meant was unmistakable, too. If Vaclav punctured the new Nazi sniper, that would be all right. And if the German put one through *his* head at better than half a kilometer, the shitheel would likely be satisfied and go torment some different stretch of the front for a while. That would also content the captain and the people who were telling him what to do. If it was hard luck for one Vaclav Jezek . . . well, who cared about a lousy Czech corporal who insisted on hanging on to an obsolete rifle?

With a last nod, the captain loped away. Benjamin Halévy chose that moment to show up. Vaclav unleashed a torrent of the nastiest Czech he knew. Halévy heard him out. (Later, Vaclav wondered whether he would have shown so much patience for the Jew.) When he finally ran down, Halévy said, "Be careful. If they did send a second man after you, he'll be better than the first one was."

"Yes, I worked that out for myself, thanks," Vaclav said bitterly. "I could do without the honor, you know."

"I didn't do it," Halévy said. "I didn't even ask the Frenchman if he spoke German."

"Oh, fuck off," Vaclav snarled. "How was I supposed to know the cocksucker really would?"

"Chance you take," the Jewish noncom said. "Maybe he was going to be a scientist or a historian before the army got him." The trade Vaclav proposed for the captain would not have required any knowledge of German. Benjamin Halévy only laughed.

Vaclav started hunting again. He didn't poke his head up at any place he'd used lately. He didn't know just when this new German hotshot had got here. If the German had any brains, he would have scouted the area before he started sniping. And, while Germans had all kinds of noxious deficiencies, you'd regret it in a hurry if you figured them for stupid.

He carried an ordinary piece when he did his scouting, not the antitank rifle. He also wore a French Adrian helmet instead of his Czech model. The Czech helmet was of better, thicker steel, but neither mark would keep out a bullet. And not looking like a Czech sniper counted, in case the Nazi with the scope-sighted Mauser happened to notice him.

The Nazi was doing *his* job. The French captain came back, complaining in uvular German about two more officers struck down. "Why have you not shot him?" the captain demanded.

"Because I haven't seen him yet." Vaclav made as if to thrust the anti-tank rifle at the Frenchman. "If you are so hot to kill him, *Herr Hauptmann,* here is the weapon to do it with."

"You are the specialist. It is for you to take care of." The captain walked away. He might have been an apartment dweller complaining that a plumber hadn't made his sink quit backing up. Vaclav said something in Czech the captain assuredly wouldn't understand. He *was* a military plumber, dammit. Unless the Germans swarmed forward again with tanks, which didn't look likely, he had to find some other use for his big, ugly gun.

"Can I do something to help?" Benjamin Halévy asked.

"Sure. Put on a French major's uniform and walk around where the asshole can see you," Vaclav answered. "Only trouble is, you won't be able to keep at it very long. He knows what he's doing, damn him."

"He's a German," Halévy said morosely. "Well, if you get any bright ideas, let me know, all right?"

"Brightest idea I've got is to shack up with a French broad with big jugs and about ten liters of cognac," Vaclav said. The Jew snorted. After a moment, so did Vaclav. "Well, you asked," he pointed out.

"Tell you what," Halévy said. "Nail that German, and I'll see that the Frenchmen give you a free one at an officers' brothel and all you can drink. How's that?"

"Better than anything else I'm likely to get," Jezek answered. Halévy snorted again and clapped him on the back.

The next morning, still wearing the Adrian helmet, Vaclav put his Czech pot on the end of a stick and held it up above the edge of the trench he was traveling. A shot rang out from the German lines. The helmet rang and spun. Two neat 7.92mm holes pierced it, six or eight centimeters from the top. "Holy Jesus!" Vaclav said. He'd wear the crested French helmet from now on.

Now—exactly where had that shot come from? And was the German sniper enough of a creature of habit to visit that place again? The last fellow had been, and it cost him. This guy? Time would tell. Vaclav resolved not to check from right here, though.

One other question crossed his mind. If he'd get himself a throw with a fancy whore and all he could drink for punching the enemy sniper's ticket, what did the Nazi bastard stand to win by eliminating him?

HEINZ NAUMANN GRUNTED in what might as easily have been satisfaction or annoyance. His bare arms were greasy to the elbow; Theo Hossbach would have rolled up the sleeves on his coveralls to mess around inside the engine compartment, too. The panzer commander held up a wrench in triumph. "There," he said. "Goddamn carb won't give us any more trouble."

"Till the next time," Adi Stoss put in.

Naumann glared. *Oh, Lord, they're going to bite pieces off each other again,* Theo thought. Sure as hell, Naumann said, "Yeah, well, I didn't see you fix it, *Herr Doktor Professor* Mechanical Genius."

"It's a piece of crap," Stoss answered. "Nobody's going to fix it so it stays fixed. We just have to keep the valves clean, and to clean 'em out when they clog up in spite of us."

He was right, which made Naumann no happier. Theo wished he could get between them and stop them from rubbing on each other so roughly. But that wasn't his way. When people locked horns, he didn't try to separate them. He backed away and watched them in something not far from horror.

"Well, anyway, the old beast will keep running a while longer," Heinz said. To Theo's relief, Adi seemed willing to leave that alone.

Other panzer crews also tinkered with their machines. If you didn't tinker with your panzer whenever you could, it would break down when you needed it most. More often than not, you wouldn't get the chance to tinker with it after that. Somebody would plant you where you'd fallen, with a fence picket to mark the grave. You wouldn't even get a helmet on top of the picket, the way a dead infantryman would.

A hooded crow, black and gray, hopped up to Theo, looking for a handout. The birds were beggars, but they weren't so thieving as their smaller jackdaw cousins. Theo tore off a bit of black bread and tossed it to the crow. The bird seized the prize in its strong bill and flew off toward the closest tree to eat it.

"Now you'll have twenty of them scrounging from you," Heinz said. "Lousy things are as bad as the packs of Jew beggars we get around here. They even dress like 'em." He laughed at his own wit. He wasn't so far wrong, either. The Jews who filled a lot of villages in these parts did mostly wear black, with lighter shirts and blouses for relief. Laughing again, Naumann added, "Bills are about the same, too."

Theo also laughed, nervously. The way things were these days, you took a chance if you didn't laugh when somebody made fun of Jews. He got paid to take chances against the *Reich*'s enemies. Nobody gave him a pfennig to take chances against his own side.

Adi Stoss chuckled, too. "Where I come from, the crows are black all over," he said. "They don't have the gray hoods they grow here."

"So they're niggers instead of kikes, huh?" Heinz said. "Only matters to the lady crows, I guess."

"One of these days, Sergeant, you'll open your mouth so wide, you'll fall right in," Stoss said.

"What's that supposed to mean?" Naumann tossed the wrench in the air and caught it in his callused hand. "You want to make something of it?"

That went too far for even Theo to take—the more so since he was sure Adi wouldn't back down. "Enough, both of you," the radioman said. Naumann and Stoss both looked at him in surprise, as they did whenever he spoke up. He went on, "Haven't we got enough to worry about with the Ivans?"

Neither crewmate answered that. What could you say? Off in the distance, a Russian machine gun stammered out death. Another gun replied a moment later. Theo cocked his head, listening. That one sounded French, which meant it had to belong to the Poles. They made some of their own stuff, but scrounged the rest from whoever was selling on any given Tuesday.

"Our allies," Heinz said scornfully, so he'd also figured out to whom the second machine gun belonged.

"Would you rather fight them along with the Russians?" Stoss asked.

"What I'd *rather*, Private, is that you keep your big mouth shut," Naumann snapped. "So try it, hey?"

Stoss didn't say another word, but if that wasn't murder in his eyes, Theo had never seen it. A panzer crew was supposed to work together. Theory was wonderful. This particular crew had as many clogs and hitches as the much-maligned carburetor.

The company commander was a bright young first lieutenant named Schmidt. The captain who had been in charge went up in flames with his Panzer II. There wasn't enough of him left to bury, with or without a helmet over his grave. Schmidt was trying his best to do a good job. He came around every evening, as the captain had before him. "*Alles gut?*" he asked.

"*Jawohl, Herr Oberleutnant,*" Heinz answered. "Carb is working the way it's supposed to again." He said nothing about whether the crew was working the way it was supposed to. Maybe he didn't even worry about it. From his perspective, from a commander's perspective, Adi might have been no more than a bit of grit in the works. He might have been, but Theo didn't believe it for a minute.

"Well, all right," Schmidt said. "The push southwest goes on tomorrow. If everything works the way it's supposed to, we'll link up with more *Wehrmacht* units in the afternoon. They aren't far away."

"That's good, sir," Heinz said. Theo found himself nodding. He saw Adalbert Stoss doing the same thing. They'd wedged their way through the swarming Russians this long. Maybe they wouldn't have to do it any more. Maybe there'd be a real front again soon. The Red Army wasn't as good at blitzkrieg as the *Wehrmacht*. All the same, being on the wrong end of it wasn't much fun.

"All right," Lieutenant Schmidt repeated. "We move at dawn—the sooner we give the Reds one in the teeth, the better for us." He ambled off to talk to the next panzer's crew.

Dawn came later than it would have a month before. Summer was going, autumn on the way. What would winter be like around here? Worse than the last one in the Low Countries and France—Theo was sure of that.

He ducked down into the back of the panzer with relief. On the move, the crew would talk about business, and that would be that. The radio net was full of traffic. Some of it was in unintelligible Polish and Russian, but most came from the Germans moving south to cut off the Russians who'd moved west to cut off the Germans moving north to cut off the earlier wave of Russians moving west. War could get complicated.

Down in what was now "independent" Slovakia, more German divisions were on the move, these heading north into Poland. Had they been attacking the Poles, the country would have fallen in a couple of weeks. But the Poles were Germany's friends . . . for the moment.

The first hint Theo had that things weren't going perfectly was the machine-gun bullets slamming into the Panzer II's armored side. "Panzer halt!" Heinz shouted. Adi hit the brakes. Heinz traversed the turret and fired a long burst from the machine gun and several rounds from the 20mm cannon. "That'll shift the Red arselicks," he said. "Go on now." The panzer clanked forward again.

Despite the earphones, Theo heard more gunfire outside. A rifle round smacked the panzer. Theo tensed. Anything bigger than a rifle round would punch right through. He'd bailed out of one burning machine. That was why he had nine and a half fingers now. He didn't want to find out what he'd be missing if he had to do it again.

Naumann stuck his head and shoulders out of the turret. Without a decent cupola, you needed to do that every so often if you wanted to know what was going on. French turrets had proper cupolas. So did Panzer IIIs. For that matter, so did the very latest Panzer IIs. But not this one . . .

Naumann let out a sound halfway between grunt and groan. He slumped back into the turret. Theo needed no more than a heartbeat to realize he was dead. The twin stinks of blood and shit told the story even before the radioman saw the red-gray ruin that had been the side of the panzer commander's head.

He ripped off the earphones and tried to get Naumann's corpse out of the way so he could serve the cannon and machine gun himself. Like it or not, he had to command the panzer now. "Heinz caught one," he shouted into the speaking tube up to the driver's compartment.

"*Scheisse*," Adalbert Stoss said. "Bad?"

"Dead," Theo answered succinctly.

"Well, you're it, then," Adi said. "Tell me what to do."

"Just keep going for now," Theo said. Before long, he'd have to stick *his* head out of the blood-dripping hatch. That was part of what a panzer commander did. Heinz was still bleeding onto the floor of the fighting compartment. That had nothing to do with anything, either.

Absently, he wondered what the new commander would be like. He also wondered whether they'd ever be able to wash out the inside of the Panzer II. Then he wondered if he'd live long enough to find out about either of the other two. Doing his job was the best way to make the answer to that yes. The best way, sure—but no guarantee.

HANS-ULRICH RUDEL SOON DISCOVERED wearing the *Ritterkreuz* at his throat changed his life very little. Oh, some jackass reporters from the Propaganda Ministry talked with him about panzer-busting with a Stuka. A photographer snapped his picture with the Knight's Cross. But that was about it. The reporters and photographer couldn't very well fly with him. And when he was airborne he had only two concerns: finishing the mission and getting home in one piece.

"We could take 'em along under the wings," Sergeant Dieselhorst suggested. "We drop 'em on the frogs or the Tommies, they'll make bigger booms than a thousand-kilo bomb."

In spite of himself, Rudel laughed. "They would, wouldn't they? They're nothing but a bunch of blowhards, so of course they'll be blow-up-hards."

"Damn straight," Dieselhorst said. "What I wonder is, how come they aren't in real uniforms instead of their fancy ones? They've got to have connections. Otherwise, they'd need to work for a living like honest people. They'll go back to Berlin and drink like fish and screw like there's no tomorrow—you wait."

"And you'll stay here and drink like a fish and screw like there's no tomorrow," Hans-Ulrich said—with, he hoped, not too much reproof in his voice. He didn't take his fun that way, but he didn't want to come down on his rear gunner. Dieselhorst was much more inclined to worry about this world than his hope of the next one.

The sergeant grinned. "More fun than anything else I can think of. You ought to try it yourself once, so you know what you're missing the rest of the time."

"No, thanks," Hans-Ulrich said. "I'll leave you alone if you do the same for me."

"Yes, sir," Dieselhorst said, but then he clucked in mock reproof. "If countries behaved like that, we wouldn't have any wars any more, and then where would the likes of us wind up?"

"Flying for a carnival, I suppose, or else Lufthansa," Rudel answered. "Once I got up into the air, I knew nobody'd be able to keep me on the ground any more. How about you?"

"I worked in a radio studio. That's what I told them when I joined up, which is why I look backwards all the time now." Dieselhorst chuckled as he lit a cigarette. "I didn't tell 'em I just swept up. They probably would have dropped *me* on the Frenchies if I had."

"I won't squeal," Hans-Ulrich promised solemnly.

The sergeant blew out a cloud of smoke. "Doesn't matter any more. I actually know what I'm doing by this time."

They went up again the next morning. Hans-Ulrich wrenched back hard on the stick to yank the Stuka into the air. Lugging those twin 37mm guns under the wings, it really was a lumbering beast. Well, it wasn't supposed to dogfight Spitfires (and a good thing, too!). It was supposed to smash up enemy panzers. It could do that . . . if nobody shot it down on the way.

Rudel peered from the cockpit, looking for concentrations of French or British armor. When he was diving, he had a fine view. In level flight, trying to peer around the long Junkers Jumo engine was a pain in the posterior. Sergeant Dieselhorst could see a lot more than he could.

But Dieselhorst had other things besides enemy panzers to worry about. A yell of alarm came out of the speaking tube: "Fucking fighter on our tail!" The rear-facing machine gun chattered.

Fiery tracers spat past the Stuka. Hans-Ulrich mashed the throttle. He might be flying a spavined old cart horse, but he'd give it all he had anyway. The fighter zoomed past him all the same, and pulled up for another run. It wasn't a particularly modern plane: a French D-500. It was a monoplane, yes, but it had fixed landing gear (like the Stuka) and an open cockpit (which the Stuka didn't). It carried two machine guns and a 20mm cannon firing through the hollow propeller hub.

Without his own heavy armament slowing him down, he could have outrun the Dewoitine. Had he had a choice, he would have. With the panzer-busting guns, he not only didn't have a choice, he didn't have a prayer. He'd have to fight it out up here unless he could scare that Frenchman off. And the fellow wouldn't have become a fighter pilot if he scared easily.

Sure as the devil, here he came, straight down the Stuka's throat. His machine guns winked. A couple of bullets clanged into the Ju-87. The beast could take a beating. It kept flying . . . as well as ever, anyhow. The cannon fired. Its big round missed. Hans-Ulrich thanked heaven—nobody could take many hits from anything heavier than a rifle-caliber gun.

That thought was part of what made him fire both 37mm cannon at the D-500. Scaring the enemy off was the other part. If you saw those big blasts of fire from the underwing guns when you weren't expecting them, if a couple of great honking shells roared past you, you wouldn't need to be *very* cowardly to have sudden second thoughts.

And if one of those great honking shells tore off half your right wing, you'd go into a flat spin and spiral down toward the ground without a prayer of getting out of your plane even if you didn't have to wrestle with a cockpit canopy. Hans-Ulrich didn't see a parachute canopy open. He did see a column of black smoke jet up from where the D-500 went in.

He yelled so loud, Sergeant Dieselhorst asked, "You all right?" If a certain anxiety rode his voice, who could blame him? He had no controls back there, and he couldn't have seen where he was going even if he did. If one of those French bullets had nailed his pilot, his only hope was to hit the silk right now.

"I'm fine," Rudel answered. "Do you know what I just did?"

Dieselhorst was quick on the uptake, but still sounded disbelieving as he said, "Don't tell me you shot that motherfucker down?"

"I did!" Hans-Ulrich sounded surprised, even to himself. Well, why not? He *was* surprised. Not to put too fine a point on it, he was astonished. "Now, where are those panzers?"

"What'll you do if we run into more fighters?" Dieselhorst asked.

"Get away if I can," Hans-Ulrich said, which seemed to satisfy the sergeant, for he asked no more questions.

A column of French machines crawling up the road toward the front sent him stooping on them like a hawk on a column of mice. He blasted the lead panzer first, then climbed again to dive on the others. They went off the road to try to get away, but he still killed two more before the rest got under some trees.

"Now we go back," he told Dieselhorst.

"Sounds good to me, sir," the rear gunner said. "I radioed what you did to the French fighter. By the way the clowns carried on, you might've got yourself a Knight's Cross for that if you didn't already have one."

"Shooting down a fighter's not worth a *Ritterkreuz*!" Hans-Ulrich exclaimed.

"It is if you do it in a Stuka," Dieselhorst replied. These things are made to get shot down, not to do the shooting."

"They're made to hit things on the ground. They're made to get hit and keep flying." Hans-Ulrich knocked the side of his head in lieu of wood. The engine sounded fine. None of the dials showed him losing fuel or oil or water. The ugly bird could take it, all right. He flew back toward the airstrip.

Chapter 18

A newsboy hawked papers on a corner. Sarah Goldman got a look at the big headline as he waved a copy: GERMANY RESCUES POLAND FROM RUS-SIAN HORDES! "Paper! Get your paper!" the kid shrilled. Then he saw the yellow star on her blouse. His lip curled. "Oh. Like *you'd* care."

She wanted to kick the little monster. Only the certainty that it wouldn't do any good and would get her into more trouble than she was likely to be able to get out of made her walk on. And what really infuriated her was that the little prick was wrong, wrong, wrong. For all she knew, her brother was in the middle of the fighting there. If Saul wasn't, he was in France, or maybe Scandinavia.

Wherever he was, Sarah hoped he was all right. The Goldmans had got that one letter from him—actually, the neighbors across the street had got it, and had the sense and kindness to know for whom it was really intended. Then not another word. Saul wasn't a thinker like their father, but he had the sense to realize anything connecting him to his family was dangerous to him and to them.

She wondered how the Poles felt about being "rescued" by Germany.

Better than they would have if the Russians had overrun them, she supposed. Otherwise, Marshal Smigly-Ridz never would have asked the *Führer* to pull his chestnuts out of the fire for him.

And just because troops marched in as rescuers, that didn't necessarily mean they'd march out again so readily. Poland was almost as offensive to the German sense of how the map of Europe ought to look as Czechoslovakia was: or rather, had been. Hitler was doing everything he could to get the map to look the way he wanted it to.

Her mouth twisted. Hitler was doing everything he could to get everything to look the way he wanted it to. Why else would she be wearing the star that said JEW in big, Hebraic-looking letters? Because she wanted to? Not likely! No more than she wanted to go out shopping just before the stores closed, when most of them were sold out—if they'd had anything to begin with.

But the Nazis did as they pleased with and to Germany's Jews. Plenty of Germans were decent, even kind—as individuals. Did they protest the government's laws and policies? Sarah's mouth twisted again. Anyone rash enough to try found out for himself what Dachau was like.

A tram rattled past. Not so long ago, she'd ridden it when she needed to get around Münster. No more. It was *verboten* for Jews. If you had to walk home with a heavy sack weighing you down, that was your hard luck for picking the wrong grandparents. Sarah snorted softly. Even converts, people as Christian as their Aryan neighbors, got it in the neck. As far as the Nazis were concerned, people like that remained Jews even if they went to church. A lot of them had converted to escape such harassment. Well, much good that did them.

She walked on. A car went by. The man driving it wore a black suit and a homburg, so he was probably a doctor. Doctors were about the only civilians who could still get gasoline. The authorities had harvested the tires and batteries from most cars. She didn't know where those batteries and that rubber had gone, but straight into the military was a pretty good guess.

A crew of men in the uniforms of the *Organization Todt* were going through the ruins of a building mashed by a British bomb. One of them pulled out a copper pot and a length of lead pipe. His comrades pounded his back as if he'd just taken a pillbox on the Western front. Scrap metal was precious these days.

How are we supposed to fight a war if we have to scrounge like this? Sarah wondered. Then she wondered why she still thought of Germany and Germans as *we*. They didn't think of her like that. If they had, she would have been worrying about her father at the front along with her brother.

Well, Samuel Goldman had been a genuine German patriot. He'd proved as much with his blood during the last war. And that helped him now . . . maybe a little more than converting to Catholicism had helped the Christians of Jewish ancestry. The discrimination laws didn't come down quite so hard on the families of wounded and decorated veterans as they did on the rest of Jewry. That, Sarah had heard, was one of Hindenburg's last protests after Hitler became Chancellor.

Here was the grocery. She checked her handbag to make sure she had the ration coupons. They'd tightened up on everything since the two-front war got serious. Even potatoes and turnips were on the list these days. When Germany ran short of potatoes . . . she was fighting a two-front war. The stories older people told about what things were like at home from 1914 to 1918 made her glad she hadn't lived through those times herself.

The grocery store had garbage. It didn't have much garbage, either; Aryan shoppers had already picked over whatever was there earlier. Sarah only sighed. It wasn't as if she'd expected anything different. This was what life for Jews was like in the Third *Reich*. She filled her stringbag with what she could, then waited for the grocer to finish with a couple of customers who didn't wear the yellow star. Another German woman came in while she was shopping. This one saw her star and pushed ahead, as the law said Aryans were entitled to do. Sarah said nothing. If she fumed, she tried not to let it show. Some Germans could be personally kind to Jews. Not all, though. There wouldn't have been laws like these if all Germans felt kindly toward Jews.

She parted with Reichsmarks and ration coupons, then went across the street to the baker's. Isidor Bruck stood behind the counter. The bakery, being a Jewish-owned enterprise, had even less than the grocer's shop. But Isidor's smile lit up the bare little room. "Sarah!" he said. "How are you?"

"Still here," she answered. She wanted to tell him that all the Nazis and at least half the German people could go straight to the devil. She wanted to, but she didn't. Even though they'd gone walking together, he might sell her down the river to the *Gestapo* if she left herself open like that.

She didn't care for thinking such thoughts about someone who, she was sure, liked her. Care for it or not, think them she did. That was one of the *Reich*'s worst evils, as far as she was concerned. It made you suspect everyone, because that was the only chance you had to keep yourself safe.

Which only made her feel the more ashamed when he reached under the counter and took out a fine loaf of war bread. It was still black, but it was nice and plump. "I saved this for you," he said. "I was hoping you'd come in today."

"You shouldn't have, Isidor!" she exclaimed, meaning not a word of it.

"I only wish I didn't have to take coupons for it. But—" He spread his hands, as if to say *What can you do?* "You know how things are. They watch us double close because we're Jews. If the flour we use doesn't match up with the ration coupons we take in, well . . ." He spread his hands again, wider this time. "It wouldn't be so good, that's all."

"I bet it wouldn't," Sarah said. "But couldn't you tell them you burned some loaves and couldn't sell them?"

"They'd say we had to unload them anyhow," Isidor answered. "After all, we just sell to Jews. Why should Jews care if their bread tastes like charcoal? They should thank God they have any bread at all."

He trusted her enough to speak his mind. Of course, someone trying to lure her into an indiscretion might do the same thing. If he *was* the *Gestapo*'s creature, he'd have a long leash. He might be hoping she'd say something about Saul and sink her whole family.

Or he might be a baker's son who was sweet on her and trusted her further than she trusted him. If he was, that only made her more ashamed of her caution than she would have been otherwise.

She paid for the fine, fat loaf. She handed over the necessary coupons.

Isidor solemnly wrote her a receipt. Then he asked, "Shall we go walking at the zoo again one day before too long?"

"Sure," Sarah answered. How could she say no when he'd set aside the bread like that? But she would have said yes even without such considerations. He might be a baker's son, but he was nice enough, or more than nice enough. She would have turned up her nose at him in easier times because of what his father did. Well, times weren't easy, and so she was getting to know him after all.

Now . . . If he could be trusted . . . If anyone she hadn't known her whole life could be trusted . . .

She snatched up the bread and fled the bakery. Isidor probably wondered if she was losing her mind. Or maybe he understood all too well. And wouldn't that be the worst thing of all?

"HARCOURT!" That malignant rasp could come from only one smoke-cured throat.

"Yes, Sergeant?" Luc might be a corporal, but in front of Sergeant Demange he suddenly felt like a recruit fresh out of training again—and a recruit who feared he'd face a court-martial in the next few minutes.

Demange paused to stamp out a small butt and light a fresh Gitane, which took the place of the one he'd just extinguished. "How'd you like to do something different?"

"If my girlfriend said that, I might be interested," Luc answered, which won him a snort from the sergeant. But he had to say more than that, no matter how little he wanted to. "What have you got in mind?"

"How'd you like to head up a machine-gun crew?" Demange asked. "Bordagaray came down venereal, the stupid slob. Maybe he knows your girlfriend, too."

"Or your mother," Luc suggested, which got him another snort. Then he paused thoughtfully. It was a better choice than Demange was in the habit of offering him. "You know, that might not be so bad. But who'll take my squad?"

"Any jackass can run a squad. I mean, *you* do, for Christ's sake," Demange said. Luc grinned crookedly; the sergeant loved to praise with faint damn, or sometimes not so faint. Demange took a deep drag, coughed, and went on, "So do you want it? It's yours if you do."

"Sure. I'll take it," Luc said. The army rule was not to volunteer, but this was different. He hoped so, anyhow. You could kill a lot of *Boches* with a machine gun. Of course, they also got especially interested in killing you. If they overran your position, you wouldn't have much chance to surrender. But they hadn't been interested in advancing lately, so that wouldn't come into play . . . he hoped. "Bordagaray's gun, you said?"

"That's right." Sergeant Demange nodded. "Joinville and Villehardouin are waiting for you like you're the Second Coming."

"I'd like a second coming right now. Or even a first one," Luc said. Demange gave him an obscene gesture to speed him on his way. He walked down the trench to the sandbagged revetment that held the machine gun. The other two crewmen eyed him with the apprehensive curiosity veterans gave any newcomer. Joinville was a short, dark Gascon like the disgraced Bordagaray. Villehardouin, by contrast, came from Brittany. He was big and blond, and understood French better than he spoke the national language. Unless he thought about it ahead of time, Breton came out of his mouth more often than not.

Luc hadn't had much to do with machine guns since training, but he remembered how to use one. It wasn't heart surgery. You aimed it, you fired it, you tapped the side of the gun to traverse it, and you tried to use short bursts. His instructor—who would have reminded him of Demange if the fellow hadn't been half again as big—had had some eloquent things to say about that.

It was a Hotchkiss, a serious machine gun, not the lighter Châtellerault. One man could carry a Châtellerault and move forward with an attack. One man could serve it, too, though a two-man crew worked better. The Hotchkiss gun had soldiered all the way through the last war, and looked to be good for this one and maybe the next one as well. The thick doughnut-shaped iron fins on the heavy barrel dissipated heat—sometimes they glowed red when the work got rough—and let you keep laying down death as long as you needed to.

There was a story about a Hotchkiss section at Verdun in 1916—a place far worse than any Dante imagined—that fired 100,000 rounds at the *Boches* with nothing worse than a few minor jams. Somebody must have lived through it to let the story spread. Hundreds of thousands in old French horizon-blue and German field-gray hadn't.

"How are we fixed for ammunition?" Luc asked.

Joinville—his Christian name was Pierre—nudged a couple of wooden crates with his foot. "Both full," he said. He had a funny accent himself, though nowhere near so bad as Villehardouin's. And his voice held a certain measured approval: Luc knew the right question to ask first.

He nodded now. "*C'est bon,*" he agreed. And good it was. You fed an aluminum strip full of cartridges into the gun, chambered the first round, fired till the strip ran dry, then put in another one. No, nothing to it . . . except that you were liable to get killed doing your job, of course. But, once they made you put on the uniform, that could happen to you all kinds of ways.

Luc took the canteen off his belt and tossed it to Joinville. "Have a knock of this," he said. "Then pass it to Tiny."

The Gascon sipped the non-regulation brandy. He whistled respectfully. "That's high-octane, all right," he said, and gave Villehardouin the canteen. The burly blond—tagged, as soldiers often were, on the system of opposites—also drank. He said something that wasn't French but definitely was admiring. When he handed the canteen back to Luc, it felt lighter than it had before he turned it loose.

Cost of doing business, Luc thought, not much put out. You wanted the guys you worked with to like you. You especially wanted them to like you when they could help keep you alive. Pierre might have thought he'd get to command the Hotchkiss gun himself now that Bordagaray was on the shelf. If he tried to undercut Luc, he might be able to pull it off yet.

"Anything I need to know about this particular gun?" Luc asked.

"If you ever get the chance, you ought to boresight it," Joinville said. "Till you can, don't trust the sights too far. If you do, you'll end up missing to the right."

"Got you. Thanks," Luc said. The sights were less important than they were on a rifle, because the Hotchkiss gave you so many more chances.

Still, that was worth knowing. Another relevant question: "German snipers give you much trouble?" The *Boches* knew what was what. They'd knock off machine-gun crews in preference to ordinary rifleman. Who wouldn't?

"We're still here," Joinville answered. He said something incomprehensible to Tiny. The Breton nodded vigorously. Luc scratched his head. Had Pierre picked up some of the big peasant's language? That was interesting. Most Frenchmen, Luc among them, put Breton only a short step above the barking of dogs and the mooing of cows.

Well, he could wonder about it some other time. For now, he peered out through a gap between sandbags at the German lines a few hundred meters. Not much to see. Sure as hell, the Germans did know their business. They weren't dumb enough to show themselves when they didn't have to. He'd been worrying about *Boche* snipers. The boys in *Feldgrau* would worry about men peering through scope-sighted rifles from under the brims of Adrian helmets.

"I wouldn't mind if it stays quiet," Luc remarked.

Joinville eyed him. "You may turn out all right," he said. "I was afraid you'd want to shoot at every sparrow you saw. Some new guys are like that, and it just brings shit down on our heads."

"I may be a new guy on a machine gun, but I've been in since before the fighting started," Luc said. "If I haven't figured out the price of eggs by now, I'm pretty fucked up, eh?"

"You never can tell." Joinville's grin took most of the sting from the words.

And Tiny Villehardouin brightened. He'd heard a French word he understood. "Fuck your mother!" he said cheerfully.

"Yeah, well, same to you, buddy," Luc replied. He didn't *think* Tiny would try to murder him for that. When he turned out to be right, he breathed a small sigh of relief. You didn't want to fight a guy that size without a lot of friends at your back.

Tiny threw back his head and laughed. Luc glanced over at Pierre Joinville. The Gascon gave back a small, discreet nod, as if to say Villehardouin was like that all the time. Luc shrugged with, he hoped, equal discretion.

Then something else occurred to him. He asked Villehardouin, "You know the commands, right?"

"Ah, *oui*," Tiny said. " 'Shoulder tripod!' 'Carry gun!' 'Advance!' 'Lower weapon!' " He looked proud of his linguistic prowess.

Luc glanced at Pierre Joinville again. This time, Joinville looked elaborately innocent. The gun weighed twenty-five kilos. The tripod had to be a couple of kilos heavier yet. Tiny was anything but. Still, to burden one man with both seemed excessive. "That's how Corporal Bordagaray did it," Joinville said. "Me, I lugged cartridges."

Which meant the former gun commander hadn't carried anything heavy. Rank did have its privileges. Did it have so many? "Well, I don't think we're going anywhere any time soon," Luc said. "We'll see how we handle things when we do."

Tiny didn't follow a word of that. Joinville's nod said he figured Luc would do things the way Bordagaray always had. Luc wouldn't have to work hard if he did. *We'll see,* Luc thought again.

MOVIE THEATERS IN SHANGHAI WERE . . . well, *different* was the first word that came to Pete McGill's mind. You could watch a flick in English or French or German or Russian or Chinese or Japanese. Pete had no interest in films in anything except English, but he noticed the other places the way a man happy with his woman (which the Marine sure was at the moment) will notice others: he doesn't intend to do anything about them, but they're there, all right.

The ones that catered to Japanese soldiers in and around Shanghai or on leave in town amused him most. He couldn't read word one of the squiggles the Japs wrote with, but the posters at those joints always seemed more hysterical than any of the others. The colors were brighter, the action more fervid, the actors' and actresses' faces more melodramatically contorted.

From across the street, he nodded towards one of them. He wasn't showy about it: he didn't want the tough little men in yellowish khaki who were buying tickets to notice him. But his buddies got the message. "I'd almost like to see what that one's about. It looks exciting."

"Yeah, well, how come you don't walk over and put down your ten cents Mex?" Herman Szulc said. "You can sit with all the lousy slant-eyed sonsabitches. Boy, I bet you'd see all kinds of stuff you never saw before."

Pooch Puccinelli laughed. "Starting with stars. Then you'd see their boots, when they stomped the living shit out of you."

"Cut me some slack, okay?" Pete said irritably. "I said *almost*, didn't I?"

"You couldn't pay me enough to sit down with a bunch of Japs," Szulc said. "I had my druthers, only way I'd ever look at 'em was over the sights of a Springfield."

"You can sing that in church," Pooch agreed. "Day is coming, too. Soon as those mothers finish off the Reds, they'll jump on our asses next."

"One guy might get away with it," Pete said. "They'd think he was crazy or something, and leave him alone. Or they'd figure their own brass knew he was there, and they'd get in Dutch if they worked out on him."

"My ass," Szulc said succinctly. "I wouldn't go over there for a hundred bucks."

"Me, neither," Puccinelli said.

That put things in a different light. Pete had drunk a couple of beers, but he wasn't remotely bombed. He didn't think so, anyhow. But what came out of his mouth was, "I would—if you clowns got a hundred apiece. I come out in one piece, you pay up."

"Yeah? What happens if you don't?" Szulc said. "What do we tell the officers then?"

"Tell 'em I died for my country." The words sounded grand. Then Pete realized he might have meant them literally. Killed—for a movie? *Nah,* he thought. *For two hundred bucks.*

Maybe he'd get lucky. Maybe Szulc and Puccinelli wouldn't have a hundred apiece, or two hundred between them. They put their heads together. Pooch laughed. It wasn't what you'd call a pleasant sound. He stuck out his hand. So did Herman Szulc. "You're on, Charlie," the big Polack said.

If Pete didn't cross the street now, he'd never be able to hold up his head again. He shook hands with the other two leathernecks. Vera would think he was nuts, too. If this went wrong, he'd never find out what Vera thought about it or anything else. He'd never feel her nipple stiffen under his lips, or her tongue teasing the bottom of his. . . .

He stepped out into the street to keep from thinking about stuff like that. Brakes screeched. A furious horn blared. A taxi driver shook his fist. A car could mash you even better than the Japs. Well, faster. Pete advanced again. He made it to the other side without getting run over. Was that good news or bad? He'd find out pretty damn quick.

The Japanese soldiers gaped at him as he took a place in their queue. He towered over most of them, though they did have a few guys large even by American standards. One of them said something he didn't get. It had to mean *What the hell are you doing here?*, though.

Pete spread his hands and smiled and bowed. They liked it when you bowed. "Take it easy, pal," he said in English. "I just want to watch the movie." He pointed to himself, then to one of the lurid posters.

Something astonished burst from the Jap. If that wasn't *Oh, yeah?*, Pete had never heard anything that was. He nodded and bowed again, doing his best to show he didn't want any trouble. If the foreign soldiers decided they wanted to, they'd mop the floor with him, and that would be that. Boy, would it ever!

They batted it back and forth among themselves, the way he and Herman and Pooch had on the far side of the street. The other Americans stood there watching. If the Japs jumped on him right now, they'd both run over here to try and help, and they'd get creamed, too. If any of them lived, they'd really thank him for that.

But then the Japs started to laugh. One of them thumped him on the back. Another grabbed his hand and shook it. They led him up to the ticket-seller. A chunky guy who looked like a sergeant laid a coin on the counter for him—they wouldn't even let him pay. All he could do was bow his thanks. That got him pounded some more, but in a friendly way.

Once he got inside, somebody bought him a snack—tea without sugar and some salty little crackers that weren't too bad even if they did have a funny aftertaste. They escorted him to the best seat in the movie house. "Good show!" said one who knew a little English. "Good show—you see!"

"Thanks! Hope so!" Pete figured his best chance was to act like a happy moron. They'd think he was squirrely, or at least harmless. He grinned till the top half of his head threatened to fall off.

Down went the lights. The projector whirred. As in American theaters, a newsreel came first. Japanese soldiers escorted Russian prisoners through pine woods. The men around Pete howled cheers. The camera focused on a downed bomber, a big Soviet star on the crumpled tail. More cheers. The narration was just gibberish to Pete, but it had to mean something like *We're knocking the snot out of the Reds.*

The scene shifted. Now Japanese soldiers and little tanks moved across an obviously Chinese landscape. An aerial shot showed bombs dropping from a plane onto a Chinese city. More excited narration—*We're kicking the crap out of the Chinks, too.* The soldiers in the theater ate it up. One of them lit a cigarette and handed it to him.

After the newsreel, the feature. Everybody wore samurai clothes. The haircuts and the armor looked ridiculous to Pete. He understood no more of the dialogue than he had of the newsreel narration. After about fifteen minutes, he realized it didn't matter one goddamn bit. Give them ten-gallon hats and six-shooters instead of helmets and swords and it would have been a Western back home at the Bijou.

There was the villain, a fat, middle-aged guy with a mustache who wanted to run things—a four-flushing ham. He had the hots for the heroine. By now, Pete had seen enough Oriental women to know she was plenty cute. If he'd had any doubts, the Japs' reactions to her would have straightened him out in a hurry. But she had eyes only for the hero, the young sheriff—um, samurai—who rode in to clean up the place. He did, too. The climactic swordfight was more exciting than a gun battle would have been. The villain lost his head at the end, even if you didn't see it bounce from his shoulders. And boy and girl would would live happily ever after. What more could you want from a movie?

Everybody looked at Pete when the lights came up. "Good show!" he said with a big nod—and damned if he didn't mean it, too. "Real good show!" The Jap who knew scraps of English translated for his buddies. They all clapped.

The biggest trouble he had was getting away from them. They wanted to take him drinking. But he pointed to Herman and Pooch when they got outside. The other Marines were still waiting, all right. He would have been astonished if they hadn't been. He made the Japanese soldiers understand he had to get back to his buddies. They reluctantly let him go.

He was more careful crossing the street than he had been when he headed for the theater. For one thing, he'd had a couple of hours to sober up. For another, Szulc and Puccinelli owed him a C-note apiece. Of course you watched yourself better when you knew you had some cash coming in.

RUSSIAN BOMBERS DIDN'T COME OVER the Japanese positions astride the Trans-Siberian Railroad so often any more. Hideki Fujita didn't miss them a bit. But the Reds hadn't quit, even if newsreel cameras made things here look easy. Russian artillery remained a force to reckon with.

Fujita had seen in Mongolia that the Red Army had more guns, bigger guns, and longer-range guns than his own side used. He'd hoped things in Siberia would be different. The difference between what you hoped for and what you got was life . . . or, if you weren't so lucky, death.

Japanese bombers kept going after the Red Army artillery. But the only thing the Russians were better at than building big guns was hiding them. The Russians were masters of every kind of camouflage there was. They were hairy like animals, so of course they were good at hiding like animals. That was what Japanese soldiers said. It sure made sense to Fujita.

Every so often, higher-ups who lived safely distant from the front sent raiding parties through the Russian lines to try to do what the bombers couldn't. The big Russian guns went right on tormenting the Japanese. If any of the raiders made it back to their own lines, Fujita hadn't heard about it. That might not prove anything. On the other hand, it might.

Russian gunners had come up with a deadly new trick, too. They'd started fusing some of their shells with maximum sensitivity. As soon as a shell brushed a tree branch—even a twig—it went off, and rained deadly fragments on the Japanese soldiers huddled below. Fujita wanted to kill the bastard who'd had that bright idea. Too many Japanese were dead or maimed on account of him.

Like a lot of other soldiers, Fujita had dug a recess into the front wall of his foxhole. He balled himself up to huddle in it. That wasn't very heroic, but he'd seen enough fighting to know heroism was overrated. What good was a dead hero? As much as any other sixty kilos of rotting meat, and not a gram more. Staying out and exposing yourself to artillery fragments wasn't heroic, either, not so far as he could see. It was just stupid.

But spending too much time in that recess was stupid, too. The Russians sometimes followed up those tree bursts with infantry attacks of their own. A Red Army man who came upon you when you were all rolled up like a sowbug would probably laugh his ass off while he shot you, but shoot you he would.

Japanese soldiers grumbled about the way things were going. Their bombers couldn't find the Russian guns, and their own cannon didn't have the range to respond to them, let alone knock them out. "We have to be careful not to complain too loudly," Superior Private Hayashi said in the middle of one gripe session.

"What? why?" Corporal Masanori Kawakami was always looking for excuses to put Hayashi down. That was what superiors in the army did with—did to—whenever they could. And Kawakami was also bound to fear Hayashi could fill his place better than he could himself. Not only that, he was liable to be right.

"Please excuse me, Corporal-*san*," Hayashi said, sounding lowly as a worm. He knew what was wrong with Kawakami, all right. "But if the officers hear us saying how much trouble the Russian guns are, what will they do? Send us out to silence them, *neh?*"

Corporal Kawakami grunted. That seemed much too likely. The corporal stabbed out a blunt forefinger. "You afraid to die for your country?"

"No, Corporal-*san*." Hayashi shook his head. Fujita believed him—he'd proved he made a good enough soldier. After a moment, he went on, "I'd rather give my life where it means something, though, not throw it away like a scrap of waste paper. What chance have we got of sneaking ten or fifteen kilometers behind the front, knocking out the guns, and coming back in one piece?"

Kawakami grunted again. If he said they had a good chance, all of his underlings would have known he was a liar. So would Sergeant Fujita, who'd already started having nightmares about that kind of raid. Officers might order it. Some of them might even go along. That didn't mean they—or the enlisted men they led—would see their foxholes again.

The only trouble was, officers could get ideas even without enlisted men giving them away. The officers at the front enjoyed those tree bursts no more than did the soldiers they led. A captain in a battalion a few hundred meters away lost his manhood to a shell fragment. Like anybody else, Fujita knew such disasters could happen. Men spoke of them only in whispers, though. Even thinking about that one made Fujita want to cup his hands in front of his crotch. But how much good would that do if your number was up? Wouldn't you just lose some fingers along with your cock?

A whole platoon—Fujita only thanked heaven it wasn't his—went forth to infiltrate the Soviet positions and do something about those damned guns. None of the Japanese soldiers came back. The Russian guns kept flaying the men in the forward positions. Worst of all, nobody seemed much surprised.

After it became obvious that the platoon was sacrificed on the altar of a god who didn't care, Superior Private Hayashi came up to Fujita and said, "May I please speak with you, Sergeant-*san*?" By the way he kept his voice down and looked around after he spoke, he wanted no one overhearing him.

"*Nan desu-ka?*" Fujita asked, his own voice carefully neutral.

"I'll tell you what it is, Sergeant-*san*." Before telling him, Hayashi took a deep breath and licked his lips. Then he charged ahead: "Why do we have donkeys commanding us, Sergeant-*san*? They must have known a platoon's worth of infantry couldn't get near those guns, much less take them out. But they sent them across the line anyhow, so it would look like they were doing *something*." Another deep breath. Another charge forward: "It's murder, Sergeant-*san*—nothing else but."

No wonder he shivered when he finished. He'd just put his life in the palm of Sergeant Fujita's hand. If Fujita wanted to squeeze it out, all he had to do was report this conversation to any officer. That would be the end of the clever young superior private. Corporal Kawakami would have extinguished him in a heartbeat. Kawakami knew where his rice bowl came from.

Fujita only sighed. "Before you go on about how they're big jackasses, tell me what you'd do if you were in charge."

"Keep bombing them. At least that has a chance of doing some good," Hayashi said at once. He must have been brooding about this for a long time. Well, who could blame him? Taking courage because Fujita wasn't calling him a traitor (or simply beating the devil out of him for saying the wrong thing, as was a sergeant's privilege), Hayashi hurried on: "And we ought to fortify this line the way the French did with the Maginot Line. We don't have to go any farther. All we have to do is keep the Russians from opening the railroad to Vladivostok again. Why do we need to waste men the way we've been doing?"

He waited. Sergeant Fujita opened his mouth, then closed it again. He sighed again. "Bugger me with a pine cone if I know, Hayashi. You want to ask questions like that, you should ask an officer who can give you a proper answer."

"Please excuse me, Sergeant-*san*, but no thank you. I don't think that would be a good idea." Hayashi shuddered to show how very much he didn't think that would be a good idea. "They would give me to the *Kempeitai*, and that would be that. To them, anyone who thinks they're stupid has to be bad."

Thinking about the *Kempeitai* was plenty to make Sergeant Fujita shudder, too. The secret military police were like mean dogs: all bared teeth and growls. And they would also bite down. They'd bite down hard. They existed to chew up and spit out—or swallow—anyone judged to be a danger to Japan and the Emperor. Foreigner? Japanese? They cared not a sen's worth.

And now, because Fujita had listened to Hayashi without immediately bawling for his arrest, he too was complicit. If the *Kempeitai* came for Hayashi, they'd come for him as well. Maybe not right away, but they would. And once they got their hands on him . . . In spite of the disgrace, he would almost rather the Russians caught him.

"Get out of here," he said roughly. "*Shigata ga nai, neh?* You can't do anything at all about it—except make sure your foxhole has as much top cover as you can put on it and still be able to fight. Go on, kid. Scram." Hayashi went away. All the answerless questions he'd asked lingered in Fujita's mind like the snow in a long Siberian winter.

Chapter 19

Another hotshot on this stretch of the line. Willi Dernen saw the need. The son of a bitch with the monster rifle on the other side was still killing people at ranges that stretched to almost two kilometers. He'd sure put paid to the last fellow the *Wehrmacht* sent against him. Willi was one of the men who'd brought in Sergeant Fegelein's body under cover of darkness. The late sergeant had very little head left north of the bridge of the nose. Willi'd seen a lot of dreadful wounds. He was damn glad he hadn't seen this one by daylight.

Oberfeldwebel Marcus Puttkamer was younger than his late, lightly lamented predecessor had been. He took the guy on the other side seriously. Well, Willi took anybody who carried an antipanzer rifle seriously. Using that thing to kill people was like using a U-boat's torpedo to sink a canoe . . . which didn't mean it wouldn't work. Oh, no. It worked fine.

Puttkamer set about slaughtering any officers and men he could reach with his own Mauser. It bore about the same relation to Willi's rifle as a thoroughbred did to a cart horse. Still . . . "How come you don't use one of those big mothers, too?" Willi asked.

A lot of senior noncoms thought they were gods. (So did some junior noncoms—Arno Baatz, for instance.) But Puttkamer seemed like a human being, as Fegelein had before him. He drank beer or wine when he came off duty. He played skat—not too well, either. He laughed at dirty jokes, and told some of his own.

Now he said, "I like the piece I've got. He may have a little more range, but I've got more accuracy. This baby's made to special tolerances. It's tighter than a five-hundred-mark whore's pussy. I've got special ammo, too. If I can see it, I can hit it—you'd best believe I can."

"I'm not arguing," Willi answered. Puttkamer had a sharpshooter's arrogance, all right. Well, if you weren't self-confident, you had no business going into his line of work.

Willi wondered how Wolfgang Storch was doing in a French POW camp. He hoped his buddy'd made it into a camp, that the froggies hadn't just knocked him over the head. Either way, though, he was bound to be better off than if the SS bastards started gnawing at his liver.

"Matter of fact," the *Oberfeldwebel* went on, "I hit the fucker square in the helmet. Only thing wrong was, he didn't have his head in it. He had it on a stick—in the scope, I watched it spin. Oh, he's cute, all right, but not cute enough."

"Does he think you think he's dead?" Willi inquired.

"I hope so, but I don't believe it. He's no dope," Puttkamer replied. Fegelein had said the same thing. The current sniper went on, "I kind of wish I hadn't rung his bell, too. He was wearing a Czech helmet, and there aren't that many of them over there. Now he's bound to have an Adrian, so he'll look like every other froggy who isn't a tadpole any more."

"Would he get another Czech job to fool you?" Willi asked.

"Hmm." The sniper eyed him. Unlike the other sharpshooter, Marcus Puttkamer was dark and not especially big. "You're pretty cute yourself, aren't you?"

"I'm glad you think so, sweetie." Willi batted his own eyes.

Puttkamer laughed and made as if to punch him. "Ah, you got me there. Yeah, he might be that cute. Never can tell. One more thing to worry about. *Danke schön.*"

"Glad to help," Willi said.

"Are you?" Puttkamer's gaze sharpened. All at once, Willi felt as if a goose were walking over his grave. The *Oberfeldwebel* had sniper's eyes after all, even if they were dark. "Feel like being my number two? I could use somebody with his head on straight."

"Your decoy, you mean? How many have you gone through? Are any of them still breathing?" Willi tried to keep his tone light, but he was kidding on the square. He knew some of what a sniper's number two did: drew the enemy sniper's fire, so the fellow with the scope-sighted rifle could find his target. That was an honor Willi could do without. He remembered Fegelein's ruined head, and wished he hadn't. You wouldn't stop a round from an antipanzer rifle. Anything made to punch through a couple of centimeters of hardened steel would punch right on through flesh and blood, too.

"I'm not asking you to stick your head up," Puttkamer said, reading his mind—but not answering his question. "You can hold a *Stahlhelm* up on a stick, same as that Czech mother did with his pot. Where's the risk in that?"

"Oh, I'm sure it's there somewhere," Willi said dryly. A few months of combat were plenty to convince him there was risk in anything that had anything to do with the enemy.

Marcus Puttkamer laughed again, on a different note this time. "You do have to put some chips in the game if you expect to take any out."

"I don't want to cash in my chips," Willi retorted.

"You get up to the front, that can happen any old place," the sniper said. "Come on, man. Do you *want* to keep taking orders from—what do you call the asshole?—from Awful Arno, that's it? And he is, too."

If anything could pump Willi up about the prospect of serving as a sniper's assistant, getting out from under Corporal Baatz's thumb did the trick. "Where do I sign up?" he asked, suddenly champing at the bit.

One more laugh from Puttkamer. "Leave it to me. I'll talk the guy into it." He sounded altogether matter-of-fact. Willi suspected he would have sounded the same way had he said *I'll plug the guy if he gives me any grief.* And if Awful Arno did give him any grief, Puttkamer might threaten to plug him, too. He also might follow through, and Awful Arno would have to be a real jerk not to understand as much. Of course, he *was* Awful Arno. . . .

The corporal came up to Willi the next morning. "The sniper says he wants you for his number two."

"That's right." Willi nodded.

"You want to do it?"

If Willi seemed too eager, Baatz would tell him no on general principles. Long acquaintance made Willi sure of it. So he only shrugged and said, "I don't mind. It's something different, anyhow."

"Good way to get yourself blown up, you mean." Awful Arno had also heard the stories about what happened to a sniper's helper. Puttkamer had seemed sympathetic. Baatz sounded as if he looked forward to Willi's untimely demise. Chances were he did. Why not? If Willi caught one with his face, it wouldn't hurt Arno a bit.

Willi shrugged again. "Can happen to anybody. Those SS guys were just visiting the village. French guns didn't know—or care. They chewed that one fellow up regardless."

Baatz's fleshy face hardened, or maybe congealed was the better word. "I still say you had something to do with Storch going missing when the SS wanted him."

"You can say whatever you want. Talk is cheap."

"Funny man." Awful Arno made as if to spit. "Go on. Hang with Puttkamer—for as long as you last. Won't be long, I bet, but don't come crying to me after you get your balls blown off. I'm glad to be rid of you."

"Well, we're even, then." Willi flipped Baatz an ironic salute and ambled off to find his new master. Looking at it that way made him feel like a hound that had just been sold. Could any hound be as glad to get a new master as he was? He didn't believe it.

"Baatz hopes you'll get killed," Puttkamer remarked. "What did you do to make him love you so much?"

"Oh, this and that. Maybe even some of the other thing, too." Willi didn't trust the sniper far enough to tell him more than that. If Puttkamer wanted chapter and verse, he could get them from Awful Arno.

Or maybe he already had. "If you think I love the blackshirts, Dernen, you'd better think twice."

"Sure," Willi said. What was he going to say? *Bullshit!*? Not likely! "Let's go get that Czech, huh? He's what we've got to worry about now, right?"

"Right," Puttkamer said, and then, "Well, come on. You can see how I do this shit. And you know your stretch of line better than I do. Maybe you'll show me some stuff I didn't already spot."

They went up and down the line. Willi saw it in ways he never had before. He knew there were places where you had to keep your head down if you wanted to keep it on your shoulders. But he hadn't worried about the spots from which you could peer across to the enemy's position and see what the French and the Czechs and the rest of that rabble were up to.

"You don't want to do your observing from the same spot twice in a row," Puttkamer said, like a teacher explaining how to multiply fractions. "Somebody'll be watching for you to be stupid. No patterns. Never any patterns. Flip a coin and follow it if you have to, to keep from giving them a handle on you. If you don't know ahead of time what you'll do next, the other boys can't, either."

"That makes sense," Willi said. "What will you want me to do? Draw the Czech's fire, right? Sounds like a good way for my folks to get a wire they don't want."

"The idea is to get him to shoot at you, not to get him to shoot you. There's a difference, you know," the sniper answered. "You'll do the kind of things the Czech did with me—show your helmet without leaving your head in it. Keep an eye peeled for the sun shining off a telescope or binocular lenses. For God's sake, let me know if you see anything funny. Maybe we'll get you a sniper's rifle, too, instead of the worthless piece of shit you're lugging around now. How's that sound?"

"All right, I guess." Willi's grin was twisted. "Besides, I'm yours for now. Awful Arno's washed his hands of me."

"That's good luck, not bad," Puttkamer said. Willi had to hope he was right.

SERGEANT HALÉVY SET A HAND on Vaclav Jezek's shoulder. "You're not the hunted," the Jew said. "You're the hunter. That's how you've got to look at it."

"I'm the hunter. Uh-huh. Sure." If Vaclav sounded distinctly unenthusiastic, the way he sounded reflected the way he felt. And he had his reasons. He picked up the helmet the German sniper had ventilated. "If I'm the hunter, how come he did this to me and I haven't done a goddamn thing to him?"

"You weren't wearing it." Halévy looked on the bright side of things. He could afford to—the Nazi wasn't trying to spill his brains out on the bottom of a trench.

"No shit!" Vaclav said. After a little while wearing a French model brain bucket, he'd got his hands on another Czech pot. This one didn't fit as well as the older helmet had, but it didn't have those two neat 7.92mm holes in it, either. He did like it better than the Adrian, which protected less of his head. Of course, nothing protected you from a direct hit by a rifle round. You'd need a helmet as thick as the side of a tank to do that. And you'd need a rhino's neck muscles to wear it. He did think the Czech model was better than the Adrian for keeping shell fragments from needling through his skull.

Halévy made a small production out of lighting a cigarette. "Aren't you happy, though?" he said after a couple of puffs. "Now the French officers are glad you carry that antitank rifle. They aren't trying to get you to turn it in any more."

"Terrific!" Jezek said. "That's on account of the Fritz is punching their tickets for them, and they want me to make him quit."

"Even French officers think they're entitled to live." Benjamin Halévy spread his hands, as if to say *What can you do?* "Poor bastards don't know any better."

Vaclav opened his mouth, then closed it again without saying anything. He had to work that through before he answered. After a moment, he tried again: "Only a Jew would come out with something that knotted-up."

"Why, thank you!" Halévy said, without any irony Vaclav could hear. "Maybe I should wave my circumcised cock at the German. Then he'd want to kill me as much as he wants to get you."

"I wish I could work out how he thinks," Jezek said fretfully. "The other Nazi was easier."

"He figured he'd get you because he was a German and you weren't. This guy is better than that, anyway," Halévy said.

"He's a lot better than that, dammit," Vaclav said. "Half the time, I don't even think *he* knows where he'll shoot from next."

"How could he not?"

"Shit, for all I know he rolls dice or something. One he goes here, three he goes there, six he goes somewhere else. Wherever he goes, he nails people."

"You're doing the same thing to his side," Halévy said.

"I know. But I haven't got a glimpse of him." Vaclav hardly heard his own reply. Rolling dice . . . He'd only been running his mouth when he said that. But it sure made sense now that it was out. How could you stalk a man if he had no pattern you could find? You couldn't. Vaclav had a couple of yellowish ivories in his own pocket. He'd made a little money with them—lost a little, too. Maybe they had uses he hadn't thought of before.

He had his favorite places from which to observe the German line, and from which to fire at the Fritzes when he found the chance. Now, knowing the Nazi sniper was on the prowl behind the barbed wire and shell holes separating the two sides, he gave up on those familiar places. He had the feeling that, if he put an eye up to one of his loopholes, a Mauser bullet would greet him an instant later. Maybe he was only being jumpy, but he didn't believe in taking chances.

Of course, he was also taking chances in finding new spots from which to watch the enemy. One of the reasons his favorite places were favorites was that they were good places. He could watch the Germans and shoot at the careless ones with little risk to himself. When he went somewhere else, the Nazis had a better chance to spot him and knock him over.

But—he hoped—the sniper wouldn't be looking for him in these new spots. He had a dirty green cloth he draped over his telescope so the German wouldn't notice it, and to keep the lens from flashing in the sun.

Plenty of *Wehrmacht* men passed through his field of view. He wished he could kill them all, and more besides. He didn't shoot at all of them, though, or even at very many. By the nature of things, a sniper had to pick and choose. He wouldn't last long if he got greedy.

Some of the Germans had taken to twisting their shoulder straps so they covered up the pips and embroidery that marked higher ranks. Sometimes Vaclav noticed that. When he did, he tried to hit the men who'd got cute. How often he didn't notice, of course, he couldn't begin to guess.

Every so often, he saw Germans scrutinizing the lines the Czechs and French held against them. One of them was simply too brazen for belief. The way he stood head and shoulders above the parados, binoculars in hand, infuriated Vaclav. Did the son of a bitch think nobody would punch his ticket for him? He might as well have mailed out engraved invitations with SHOOT ME! on them.

Vaclav took care of that for him. The antitank rifle thundered and slammed hard against his right shoulder. As soon as he fired, he ducked, a habit he'd acquired not long after he started sniping. You could see what you did later, and from somewhere else. After you'd taken your shot, you couldn't change anything anyway.

A split second after he lowered his head, a bullet cracked through the space where it had been. "Hello!" he said, and didn't come up again, the way he might have otherwise.

"Somebody's laying for you," Benjamin Halévy remarked.

"Thanks a bunch. I never would have guessed without you," Vaclav said. The Jew laughed. Vaclav didn't. "God damn it to hell, that bastard was just standing there asking for it. I know I got him. Not even the Nazis would waste a man of their own for the sake of killing me . . . would they?" He heard the doubt in his own voice. Who could guess exactly how ruthless the Germans were?

"I'll have a look." Halévy did, cautiously, from ten meters down the trench. "I don't find him now."

"I wonder who he was. He acted like an officer, and a dumb officer to boot," Vaclav said. "You wouldn't see an enlisted man standing there giving that kind of target. The guys who really fight know better."

"Maybe he was from the General Staff," Sergeant Halévy said. "If half of what you hear about them is true, the Nazis with red stripes on their pants don't know shit about the real world."

"Easy to say that," Jezek answered. "They're here in France. They're in

Poland. They're all over Czechoslovakia, fuck 'em up the ass. I don't see anybody else's soldiers in Germany. Do you?"

"Well, no," Halévy admitted. "But—" Before he could say anything more, German artillery came to thunderous life. He and Vaclav both dove for cover. Were the Fritzes shelling like that to avenge the *Dummkopf* Vaclav had knocked over? They did things like that. If the *Dummkopf* was an important *Dummkopf*, the Czech had accomplished something worth doing. He consoled himself with that—and hoped the Nazis' vengeance wouldn't come down on him now.

WILLI DERNEN EXAMINED what was left of the head from the department-store dummy *Oberfeldwebel* Puttkamer had kitted out in German helmet and tunic. Even less was left of the dummy's noggin than of the other sniper's head. Willi let out a low, respectful whistle. "That piece packs a fuck of a wallop," he said.

"What makes you think so, Sherlock Holmes?" Puttkamer enquired. Willi's ears felt incandescent. The senior noncom went on, "He knows the tricks, damn him. He was down again before I could fire. I'm sure of it."

"Too bad," Willi said.

"You'd better believe it," Marcus Puttkamer said. "He's still out there. He's still learning. He's still got his goddamn peashooter, too. I slip up even a little, he's gonna smash my skull just like the shitass dummy's." He considered Willi the way an entomologist considered a beetle before sticking a pin through it. "Or maybe yours."

"Thanks a lot, *Feld*," Willi said. He'd thought about that possibility before agreeing to become the sniper's number two, but not too much. Getting out from under Awful Arno counted for more. Well, he'd done that. But everything you got in this world came with a price tag attached. Part of the price here was drawing the notice of a sharpshooter who carried a gun that could kill you out to a couple of thousand meters. Next to that, even Awful Arno seemed . . . not quite so awful, anyhow. Willi glanced toward the enemy's lines—but made sure he didn't raise his head above the parapet to do it. "What do we try now?"

Puttkamer lit a Gitane. Like Willi, he liked French tobacco better than the hay-and-horseshit smokes the *Reich* cranked out these days. After a moment's pause, the *Oberfeldwebel* offered Willi the pack. With a nod of thanks, Willi took a smoke from it and leaned toward Puttkamer for a light. The first drag made him want to cough. Yeah, this was the real stuff, all right—no ersatz here.

"I don't know what to try right this minute," Puttkamer answered, snorting smoke out his nostrils like a puzzled dragon. "He's good, sure as hell. Oh, and you're right—screw me if he wasn't wearing a Czech helmet again." His stubbled cheeks hollowed as he inhaled.

"*Wunderbar*," Willi muttered.

"How about that?" the *Oberfeldwebel* said with an acid chuckle. "What I've got to do is, I've got to get him to make a mistake. If I'm there when he does it, he'll never make another one."

"Sounds great, but didn't you just say he was good?" Willi returned. "So how do you think you can make him screw up?"

"Best idea I've had so far is to keep murdering as many French officers as I can, as far back from the trench as my rifle reaches," Puttkamer answered matter-of-factly. "That won't put *his* wind up—too much to hope for. But if all his superiors start screaming at him to get rid of the horrible Nazi gunslinger . . . They might make him move too fast and get careless. Or they might not, *natürlich*. But I think it's worth a try. If you've got a better notion, sing out. Believe me, I'll listen."

Dernen did believe him. Puttkamer wasn't like Awful Arno, always sure he was right no matter what he said or did. Yeah, there were advantages to getting away from Baatz, sure as hell. "What can I do to help?" Willi asked. He felt like an assistant at a chess tournament. But they wouldn't take pieces off the board. No, they'd take at least one body.

"You can help kill them, that's what. Let's go get you a proper rifle, one with a scope on it," Puttkamer said. "That piece of yours . . . Well, the factories turn out worse, but they sure as hell turn out better, too."

Having seen what the sniper could do with his special Mauser, Willi didn't argue. He was used to his own weapon, but he felt no forsaking-all-others attachment to it. And even if he had, he couldn't just mount a telescope on it and start picking off French officers a kilometer and a half away. Snipers' Mausers had a special downturned bolt: the telescope interfered with the travel of an ordinary one.

The quartermaster sergeant was as snotty as quartermaster sergeants usually were. "You want one for *him*?" the fellow exclaimed, as if Willi had a girlfriend prettier than the one a proper quartermaster would have issued him.

"That's right." Marcus Puttkamer left it there. Not only was he an *Oberfeldwebel* himself, he was also a sniper. Who wanted to argue with him? Nobody with any sense, not even a quartermaster sergeant.

And so Willi got his rifle. "Bolt will take some getting used to," he said. "I reach for the wrong place."

"I did, too. You won't take as long to get it as you think," the sniper said. "But do you feel how smooth the action is? Sniper rifles are made the way they're supposed to be. Now you'd better take care of it. You don't keep it clean, you don't keep it greased, I'll mount a bayonet on it and *then* I'll shove it up your ass. Get me?"

"*Jawohl, Feld*," Willi answered. Every sergeant he'd ever served under growled about keeping your weapon clean. Willi was as good about it as anyone, better than most. He could see why it would be especially important for a sniper.

"I want you to spend the rest of the day practicing with the scope," Puttkamer said. "Don't look toward the French lines. They'll see you, and somebody will stop your career before it gets going. Look at our trenches instead. If there's somebody you wouldn't mind seeing dead, find out what he looks like with crosshairs on him. But you're such a sweet guy, you don't have anybody like that, right?"

"Oh, sure," Willi said innocently.

Puttkamer chuckled. "The other thing is, you have to be able to wait. The better you are at holding still, the more targets you'll service. And that's the idea, right?"

"Right," Willi said. The veteran didn't care to talk about killing people. He did it, but he didn't like to talk about it straight on. That was interesting, in its own way.

"Practice," the veteran sniper repeated. "When I think you're ready, we'll go out to a hide at night, and you can start potting froggies. Pick ones well back of the line, if you can. They're more apt to be careless back there, anyhow. And if you do that, they'll think it was me, and they'll go buggier than they would if you showed a different style."

"I understand. But what I do if I spot the Czech asshole with the antipanzer rifle?" Willi asked.

"Dispose of him," Puttkamer said at once. "You think I'll be mad? You think I'll be jealous? Not a chance, kid. I'll get you promoted. I'll get you a medal. I'll get you so fucking drunk, you'll still have a *Katzenjammer* three days later. That's our number one piece of business right now—dealing with that son of a bitch. You hear?"

"I hear." Willi not only heard, he believed. Awful Arno would have tried his hardest to grab the credit if Willi did anything worth noticing. If *Oberfeldwebel* Puttkamer wasn't like that, more power to him.

Baatz watched and sneered and made rude comments as Willi got used to his new weapon. Willi ignored him for a while. Then, as if by accident, he did get the corporal in the crosshairs. He didn't have a round chambered. His finger was nowhere near the trigger. Awful Arno found something else to do in a hurry even so.

After a few days, Puttkamer said, "Well, kid, let's find out how you do." After dark, he led Willi out to a shell hole that had a shattered door splayed half across it. "Get under there. Whatever you do, don't move where they can see you till tomorrow night—and they won't see you then, either. Wait. When you get a target, service it. Need to know anything else?"

"Don't think so," Willi answered. Puttkamer set a hand on his shoulder, then silently crawled away.

Willi slithered under the scarred door and went to sleep. When he woke up, the sun had risen behind him. Hidden by shadows, he ate black bread with liver paste on it. He looked through his binoculars. It was getting on toward noon when he spotted a Frenchman in a kepi striding along importantly half a kilometer behind the enemy line.

Slowly, slowly, he moved the Mauser into position and picked up the Frenchman in the telescopic sight. He made sure nothing was out in the sunlight to give him away. Pierre or Gaston or whoever he was seemed not to have a care in the world. Willi took a deep breath. He let it out. He pulled the trigger—gently, as if with a lover's caress.

The Mauser kicked: not too hard, since it was pressed tight against his shoulder. The magnified Frenchman in the sight took another step. Then he fell over. Willi didn't move. He didn't shout or whoop or even light a cigarette. All the same, he knew he'd just joined the club.

That night, two men brought what was left of Marcus Puttkamer back in a shelter half. From the neck up, he pretty much wasn't there. The bullet that killed him must have caught him right under the chin and blown off most of his head. He looked worse than Sergeant Fegelein had, which wasn't easy. Willi realized his new club had higher dues than he wanted to pay.

A STUKA SCREAMED DOWN out of the hazy, gray-blue sky. Staff Sergeant Alistair Walsh fired a couple of shots at it. He knew that was long odds, but he did it anyhow. What did he have to lose?

Bombs fell from the dive-bomber. It leveled off only a couple of hundred yards above the machine-gun nest it was attacking, then roared away. Sandbags, the gun and tripod, and bodies and pieces of bodies arced through the air.

"Hell," Walsh muttered. "Bloody fucking hell. This is where I came in."

When the German blow fell in the west the winter before, the *Luftwaffe* had had things all its own way for a while. In France, it didn't any more; the RAF and the French were making the Fritzes pay for everything they got there. But that was France. Here in Norway, the deck still seemed stacked in the Nazis' favor.

Before the Germans jumped them, the Norwegians hadn't had much of an air force of their own. They flew Italian Caproni bombers, Dutch Fokker monoplane fighters, and English Gloster Gladiators: biplanes outdated by both Hurricanes and Spitfires. They didn't fly very many of any of them. The *Luftwaffe* could reach this part of Norway from newly occupied Denmark, and from airfields captured farther south in the country: Oslo was firmly in German hands.

More Stukas dove, their sirens wailing like damned souls. More British strongpoints in front of Trondheim went up in smoke and fire. The

Stukas flew away. They'd bomb up again, maybe refuel, and pretty soon they'd come back to blow up more of the defenses around the town.

Somewhere out to sea, there was supposed to be a Royal Navy carrier. The planes that took off from its flight deck might help till England and France could bring in land-based fighters. Then again, they might not. Walsh had seen a Stuka outrun an English Skua. The lumbering German dive bombers couldn't get out of their own way. What did that say about the poor miserable Skua? Nothing good, surely.

Jock pointed south. "Are those bloody fucking German tanks?" the Yorkshireman asked.

Walsh looked, too. Safe enough: no German foot soldiers close yet. How long would that last, though? Not long enough, plainly. "Afraid they are, chum," the NCO said.

"Well, what do we do about them?" Jock pressed.

The ideal answer would have been *Turn our own tanks loose on them.* Walsh saw no English, French, or Norwegian tanks. He wasn't sure there were any Norwegian tanks to see. There were a few Bren-gun carriers: tankettes, some people called them. They carried two men and a machine gun, and were well enough armored to keep out rifle bullets. If the other side had no tanks at all, tankettes were world-beaters. If, on the other hand, they ran up against real armor, they were doomed. And those were real tanks coming. Not first-rate real tanks, maybe: Panzer IIs, or perhaps captured Czech models. Anything that mounted a cannon was plenty to put paid to a Bren-gun carrier.

Thrushes chirped among the tussocks. Fieldfares, wheatears: birds of the far north. One of them plucked a worm from the newly turned dirt in a bomb crater and swallowed it. Walsh laughed in spite of himself. Sure as hell, it was an ill wind that blew no one any good.

An officer had some field glasses. After staring through them, he said, "Those are Czech T-35s."

Wonderful, Walsh thought. *Always good to know what's about to do you in.* Before long, he saw that the young lieutenant was right. The Czech machines were bigger than Panzer IIs. Their road wheels were much bigger. And they carried bigger cannon: 37mm against the German tanks' 20mm guns.

The men in the Bren-gun carriers had guts. They rattled out ahead of the position the Tommies, *poilus,* and squareheads were manning. They would stop the German tanks if they could. Trouble was, Walsh knew too damn well they couldn't. He also knew they knew they couldn't.

Somewhere along the line, there were said to be a couple of antitank cannon. Walsh had no idea where they were. They weren't anywhere close by, so they were unlikely to make any difference in the upcoming fight. His hand shook when he lit a Navy Cut. Nothing was likely to make any difference in the upcoming fight.

Jock's thoughts were running on a similarly gloomy track. "We need the bloody fucking cavalry riding in to chase off the bloody fucking Indians, is what we need," he said.

"Too right we do," Walsh agreed. "This isn't what they call a Hollywood ending. Wrong bloody side is winning."

For some little while, he paid no attention to the rising buzz in the air. If he noticed it at all, he assumed it came from more *Luftwaffe* aircraft. But it didn't. Damned if those weren't Skuas, winging in from off the ocean. They could carry bombs as well as chasing planes faster than they were. Whatever bad things you could say about the Blackburn Skua—and you could say plenty—it was, by God, faster than a tank.

Walsh pointed into the sky. "It's the bloody fucking cavalry!"

Jock stared. A grin as big as all outdoors slowly plastered itself across his face. "Well, up me arse if it ain't, Sarge!"

Doing their best impression of Stukas, the English fighter-bombers dove on the advancing tanks. They dropped their bombs. Then they climbed and dove again; their machine guns chattered as they shot up the Fritzes moving forward with the tanks.

"That'll scramble 'em!" Jock said exultantly.

"It will!" Walsh said. That kind of treatment had scrambled English and French troops often enough—no, too bloody often.

But the Germans, unlike their Allied counterparts, didn't stay scrambled long. With what might have passed for majestic deliberation, the Skuas climbed and dove yet again, and then one more time still. That last pass proved one too many. Majestic deliberation turned out to be only a synonym for too goddamn slow.

Messerschmitts roaring up from the south tore into the Skuas. The English planes streaked back toward the carrier that had launched them. It was, unfortunately, a slow streak, at least by the standards the 109s were used to. Wolves killing sheep could have had no easier time than the German fighters. One Skua after another tumbled out of the sky in smoking, flaming ruin. A couple of parachutes opened, but only a couple. Walsh reminded himself that each English plane carried not one but two highly trained young men.

Quietly, Jock said, "That's murder, is what that is."

Walsh nodded. "Nothing else but. Whoever expected them to be able to fight in those sorry machines ought to come up on charges. They haven't got a chance."

"Like Bren-gun carriers against proper tanks, ain't it?" Jock said.

"It's *just* like that, by God," Walsh answered. "How the bleeding hell are we supposed to fight a war if the equipment they give us is ten years behind what the Nazis have?"

"Isn't that what they call muddling through?"

"That's what they call fucking up," Walsh said savagely. In the last war, the Germans had said their English counterparts were lions commanded by donkeys. Some things didn't change from one generation to the next.

More German planes appeared overhead: broad-winged He-111s and the skinny Do-17s that Englishmen and Germans both called Flying Pencils. The level bombers ignored the troops outside of Trondheim. They started pounding the docks. Thick black clouds of smoke rose. Walsh wondered what was burning. The town? Or the ships that kept the defenders supplied? Which would be worse? The ships, Walsh judged. You couldn't keep fighting without munitions.

Or, for that matter, without food. Maybe you could live off the land in summertime, but summer in this part of Norway was only a hiccup in the cold. The Fritzes could bring things up from the south. The defenders had to do it by sea . . . if they could.

A Heinkel spun toward the ground, flame licking across its left wing. It blew up with a hell of a bang: it hadn't got rid of its bombs. Several Tommies cheered. Walsh wasn't sorry to watch the bugger crash, either—not half!—but how much difference would it make? Any at all?

Chapter 20

hy this is hell, nor am I out of it.

What the devil was that from? For the life of her, Peggy Druce couldn't remember. She'd studied way too much literature in college, but how much good did it do her? She could remember the quote, but not the source. Her professors would have frowned severely.

Well, tough shit, she thought. Even if she couldn't remember who'd written the line, it fit her all too well. The Nazis had even extended their hell to keep her in it. She'd thought getting into Denmark meant escaping. Sadly, just because you thought something didn't make it so.

No more flights from Copenhagen to London. No more ships plying the North Sea from Denmark to England, either. The Nazis were acting as mildly as anybody could after invading and overrunning the country next door. They loudly proclaimed that Denmark was still independent. If you listened to them, they were only protecting the Danes from invasion by England or France.

If.

Had any Danes invited them to protect the country? "Not fucking likely!" Peggy said out loud when she first thought to wonder. She was having lunch in a seaside café at the moment. Her waiter did a double take worthy of Groucho. Peggy's cheeks heated. She'd already seen that a lot of Danes spoke English. Quite a few of them spoke it better than your average American, in fact. She couldn't just let fly without scandalizing somebody. She left the waiter a fat tip and got out of there in a hurry.

Moments later, she wished she hadn't. A couple of dozen Danish Fascists were parading down the street behind a Danish flag—white cross on red—with the words FRIKORPS DANMARK in gold where the stars would be on an American flag. She wasn't the only person staring at the collaborators. Every country had its Fascist fringe, but now the Danish loonies enjoyed Hitler's potent backing.

Slowly and deliberately, a tall blonde woman turned her back on the homegrown Fascists. One by one, the rest of the people on the street followed her example. Peggy was slower than most. She got a good look at the Danish would-be Nazis. By their expressions, they might have bitten into big, juicy lemons.

From behind them, somebody called out something in Danish. Peggy didn't understand it, but the local traitors did. Their faces got even more sour. She hadn't dreamt they could. More and more people took up the call, whatever it was. As the Fascists rounded a corner and disappeared, a helpful Dane who must have noticed Peggy's blank look spoke a few words of English: "It means 'Shame!'—what we shouted."

"Good for you!" she said. If she'd known the word, she would have yelled at the goons herself.

The worst of it was, she had to deal with the Germans again. Her disappointment seemed all the crueler because she'd thought she'd escaped both Nazis and *Wehrmacht* forever. No such luck. No luck at all, as a matter of fact. The Germans might say Denmark was still independent, but the "free" Danes had no control over travel between their country and neighboring Sweden. The occupiers damn well did.

Knowing Nazi arrogance, Peggy would have expected the *Wehrmacht* to take over the royal palace and to run Denmark from it. But General Kaupitsch or his aide had better sense than that. King Christian X went right on reigning. Even his Danish bodyguard remained intact. The Germans administered their new conquest from a drab modern office building three blocks away.

If that was where they were, that was where Peggy had to go. She wished Hitler had issued her a letter instead of calling her on the phone to let her know she could go from Germany to Denmark. (And had he been laughing up his sleeve when he gave her that permission? Sure he had! He must have known his own army would be only a few days behind her.)

No big swastika flag flew over or in front of the German headquarters. The *Wehrmacht* wasn't going out of its way to be hated . . . unless you counted invading Denmark to begin with, of course. Peggy would have bet the Germans didn't. She had no doubt whatsoever that the Danes damn well did, and always would.

She displayed her American passport and told one of the sentries, "I want to see General Kaupitsch. *Sofort, bitte.*" *Sofort* sounded a lot more immediate than *immediately.*

"Why?" one of the Germans asked. Under the beetling brow of his helmet, his features were blank.

"Because the *Führer* said I could come to Denmark so I could go on to the States, and this invasion has screwed things up. That's why," Peggy answered. "Do you understand that?" *Or shall I bounce a rock off your goddamn* Stahlhelm *and wise you up?*

Both sentries' eyes widened. One set was blue, the other brown. *You're a crappy Aryan, kid,* Peggy thought, feeling how far out on the ragged edge she was. "Please wait," the one with the blue eyes said. He disappeared into the office building.

If he didn't come out pretty damn quick, Peggy was going to lay into his buddy with both barrels. But he did. He conferred with Brown Eyes, who spoke up: "I will take you to Major von Rehfeld."

"Oh, yeah? How come not to the general?"

"I am ordered to take you to Major von Rehfeld." For a German, nothing else needed saying. "You will please come with me."

Peggy please came with him. Major von Rehfeld proved to be a tall, handsome man of about thirty-five who was missing the lower half of his left ear. That and a wound badge said he'd seen real fighting somewhere. "So you are the notorious Mrs. Druce," he said in excellent English.

"That's right, buster. Who in blazes are you?" Peggy snapped.

"Among other things, I am the man assigned to get you to Stockholm," the German officer answered. "Believe me: we do respect the *Führer's* order to give you all the help we can. Once you reach Sweden, you are on your own, however. I do not know how soon you will be able to travel from there to England and on to the United States. It is a pity, but Norway remains a war zone."

"And whose fault is that?" Peggy said.

The major shrugged. "I would say it is the fault of France and England, but I am sure you would call me a lying Nazi if I did. So I will not say anything about that. Never mind whose fault it is. It *is* a war zone. Nothing travels through it without grave risk of being attacked by both the two sides. Is this so, or is it not so?"

It was so. Of that Peggy had no doubt whatever. Nobody in her right mind could. "How long do you think I'll have to stay in Stockholm?" she asked.

"This I cannot say." The major spread his hands, doing his best to look and sound as reasonable as he could. "It is not up to the *Reich* alone, you know. The enemy has also something to say about it. I can tell you that we are making much better progress in Norway than we were only a few days ago. We prove that air power is stronger than sea power. The Royal Navy is sorry to learn this, but learn it they do."

Maybe that was so, too. Or maybe he was parroting Goebbels' propaganda line as if it were *Polly wants a cracker!* Peggy couldn't tell. Since she couldn't, she asked, "How do I get to Stockholm?"

"The usual ferry is sailing again. Tickets are easy to come by. You will have no trouble with an exit visa—I promise you that," Major von Rehfeld replied.

"Will you have German soldiers on the ferry, the way you did on the ships in Copenhagen harbor?" Peggy gibed.

To her astonishment, the major blushed scarlet. "We saved needless bloodshed," he said, but he sounded none too proud of it. A moment later, he added, "It was a legitimate ruse of war," but that didn't seem to convince him, either.

If he meant what he said about getting her to Stockholm, Peggy wasn't inclined to be fussy. "How soon can I go?" she asked.

"As soon as you have your ticket, come back. I will provide you with an exit visa. No one will stand in your way," von Rehfeld said.

"You aren't planning to, uh, protect Sweden as soon as I get there, are you?"

"Why would we? With Denmark and Norway safe from English interference, iron ore can travel from Sweden to the *Reich* without risk of interruption."

Had the major claimed that Germany would never do such a wicked thing, Peggy wouldn't have believed him for a minute. When he talked about national self-interest, he was much more persuasive. That didn't mean he was telling the truth. It also didn't mean Peggy would be able to get out of Sweden once she got in. But she was willing to try it. *What can go wrong now?* she asked herself. But the question had a simple, obvious answer. Damn near anything could.

SERGEANT HERMANN WITT MADE a panzer commander very different from Heinz Naumann. Theo Hossbach noted the differences with nothing but relief. Most important, Witt could laugh at himself. He didn't have to feel he was better and tougher than everyone else in the panzer to give orders. He didn't go out of his way to give people a hard time to show he was tougher than they were.

If that came as a relief to Theo, it had to be something close to heaven for Adalbert Stoss. Witt hadn't taken long to realize the driver was missing something most German men had. Imagining three men living closer together than they did in a Panzer II was next to impossible. Theo sure didn't want to think about it, anyhow. Only bedbugs and lice lived closer to him than his crewmates did.

Naumann hadn't been able to quit riding Adi Stoss about his circumcision. No wonder they hadn't got along. Theo wouldn't have wanted anybody razzing him about his dick, either. A couple of days after taking charge of the panzer, Witt looked up from the skinny little chicken he was roasting and said, "Ask you something, Adi?"

"Sure, Sarge. What's up?" Stoss answered—about how Theo would have responded to a casual question.

"When they drafted you—"

"They didn't, Sarge. I volunteered."

"Did you? Well, all right. Good for you. When you did, you filled out about a million forms, right?" Witt said.

Adi nodded and made a face. "Sure. Pain in the ass, but you've got to do it."

"Yeah. You do. You gave all the right answers on the one about your ancestors, didn't you?" the new panzer commander said.

Stoss didn't even try not to understand him. "You bet I did—in spite of the operation, if you know what I mean."

"I expect I do," Sergeant Witt replied. "That's what I needed to know." He turned the chicken's carcass on the branch that did duty for a spit. "And I think this bird's about ready to eat. White meat or dark?"

As Theo gnawed the meat off a drumstick and thigh, he belatedly realized Witt hadn't asked Adi if he was a Jew. He'd only asked if the driver had given the right answers on the military paperwork. Of course Adi had. They wouldn't have let him into the *Wehrmacht* if he hadn't. But the question covered the sergeant's ass. If by some chance Stoss did turn out to be Jewish, Witt could say the driver had denied it.

Theo'd wondered himself. Yes, some gentiles did have a medical need to part with their foreskin. But if you ran into somebody without his, what would you think first? You'd think the guy was a Jew, that was what.

The idea made Theo want to giggle. A Jew in the *Wehrmacht* was like a chameleon on a green rug. You wouldn't look for one on the rug to begin with, so of course you wouldn't notice it if it happened to be there. Theo wouldn't have said anything about his wonderings, even if the *Gestapo* decided to interrogate him. He never said much about anything. And he had his reasons not to. When you didn't love the regime under which you lived, keeping your mouth shut was the smartest thing you could do.

Besides, if Adi really was Jewish, wasn't that about the richest joke anyone could play on the Nazis? Theo might have thought otherwise if Stoss were a bad soldier, or a gutless one. He wasn't. He did fine. As long as he made a good *Kamerad,* who gave a rat's ass about the other crap?

With sizable help from the Polish infantry—which seemed to view retreat as a worse affront than treason—it looked as if they'd be able to hold the Red Army outside of Warsaw. The Poles had managed that after the last war, too. If they hadn't, Germany and Russia might not be quarreling on Polish soil right now. They'd be at each other's throats, the way they had been in 1914.

Quite a few Polish foot soldiers were obviously Jews. What did they think of fighting on the same side as the German National Socialists? Theo was tempted to ask some of them. A German who put some effort into it could make sense of Yiddish. In the end, though, the radioman kept his mouth shut. That was what he usually did, so it wasn't hard for him. And his sense of self-preservation warned him his fellow soldiers would give him funny looks if he all of a sudden started chatting up Jews.

Some of the villages they went through were full of them: men in beards, wide-brimmed hats, and black clothes straight out of the eighteenth century. One of the guys from another panzer in the company said, "Boy, you can sure see why the *Führer* wants to clean out the kikes, can't you? They're like something from Mars. Shame we can't wipe these places up any which way."

"Poles wouldn't like it," another crewman said.

"My ass," the first fellow replied. "They don't like Jews any better'n we do—less, maybe. I bet they'd cheer us on."

"Maybe," the other man said. "But then all the kikes would go over to the Reds. We need that like a hole in the head."

"I guess," the first man said unwillingly. "Their day's coming, though. It's gotta be. I mean, they're like niggers or Chinamen or something, only they don't even live a long piss away from us."

Theo glanced over at Adi. The panzer driver kept his head down and shoveled stew into his face from his mess tin. That meant exactly nothing. Most of the Germans in black coveralls were doing exactly the same thing.

A sergeant with the ribbon for an Iron Cross Second Class and a wound badge said, "The less people who want to shoot me or plant mines or pour sugar in my gas tank, the better I like it."

No one seemed eager to quarrel with that. Theo knew damn well he wasn't. He hadn't liked it when the French shot at him. His own wound badge—and the half a finger he could still feel sometimes even if it wasn't there any more—said he had good reason not to argue. The Czechs could have done the same to him, or even worse. The Russians might yet.

They got another chance the next morning. A Polish cavalryman rode back to warn the crew that enemy panzers lay ahead. The Poles called them *pancers*, pronouncing it the same way German did. To the Russians, they were *tanks*; they'd borrowed the word from English instead.

"Big pancers," the horseman warned. The Poles used cavalry as if they'd never heard of machine guns. Their riders had more balls than they knew what to do with. To an outside observer, that often made them nutty as so many fruitcakes. Germans who'd been in Poland longer than Theo talked about horsemen in the square-topped caps called *czapkas* charging Russian panzers with lances. Maybe that was true, maybe not. That Theo could wonder spoke volumes about what Polish cavalry might be capable of.

"Well, let's see how big they are," Hermann Witt said. "Forward, Adi. Take it slow till we find out what we're up against."

"Will do," Stoss said, and he did. Back in his own armored space, Theo might not find out how big the enemy panzers were till a shell hit the Panzer II and either did or didn't smash the soft-skinned people inside and set the machine on fire. He wondered if getting surprised by death was worse than seeing someone take dead aim at you before you got it. Pretty bad both ways, as a matter of fact.

"Ha!" Sergeant Witt said, and then, "Those damned fast panzers, Theo. Report 'em to division."

Theo did. His gut clenched. No way in hell the Panzer II's armor could hold out a 45mm round. But this machine had teeth, too. Witt fired several short bursts from the 20mm gun. His shouts and whoops and curses said he was doing some good.

Adi's voice came through the speaking tube: "They're running away!"

A couple of other German panzers had come forward with theirs. All the same, Theo wasn't sorry to hear Witt say, "I think I'm just going to let them go. You borrow trouble, half the time you're sorry later on. More than half."

Heinz Naumann would have charged after the Reds. Theo was sure of that. He was also sure Heinz was dead. They still hadn't scrubbed all the former commander's blood off the floor of the fighting compartment; it clung in cracks and crevices. Neither Theo nor Adi had said anything about that to Sergeant Witt. Theo knew he didn't intend to. He didn't know whether Adi Stoss had equal discretion. No, he didn't know, but he thought so.

INSHORE WATERS. Julius Lemp didn't like them for beans. He didn't need his Zeiss glasses to see the corrugated Norwegian coastline. The ocean deepened swiftly as you moved away from the outlets to the fjords, but not fast enough to suit him. If you had to dive in waters like these, you couldn't dive deep enough to have good odds of staying safe—and you were liable to dive straight to the bottom. That wouldn't be good, which was putting it mildly.

But this was where the fighting was, so this was where he had to be. The Royal Navy had nerve. Well, that was nothing he didn't already know. The English were ready to take on the *Kriegsmarine* and the *Luftwaffe* both if that meant they could screw the German troops in Norway to the wall.

And the limeys were knocking the snot out of the *Kriegsmarine*'s surface ships, too. They'd sunk nearly a dozen German destroyers, and a couple of cruisers, too. They had lost a carrier—overwhelmed and sunk by German battlewagons before she could get away. And they'd lost some destroyers of their own, but mostly to air attack. Ship against ship, the damned Englishmen were better.

On the surface. When it came to U-boats, that was a different story. *It had better be*, Lemp thought. Like any U-boat skipper, he felt proprietary about these boats. The Kaiser's *Reich* had come *that* close to bringing England to her knees a generation earlier. This time, the *Führer*'s *Reich* would do what didn't quite come off in the last war.

Lemp scanned the fjord's mouth. Smoke rose from the far end of the inlet. That was Trondheim, catching hell from the air and the ground. The town wouldn't, couldn't, stay in enemy hands much longer. The English, the French, and the Norwegians would have to retreat farther north if they wanted to stay in the fight.

RAF bombers didn't have the range to cross the North Sea and hit back at the Germans in Norway. And so the English were using warships to take up the slack. Even destroyers mounted guns usefully bigger than any a panzer carried. Those shells could mash a submarine. Lemp didn't suppose foot soldiers enjoyed getting hit with them, either.

But if you put a warship where its guns could strike ground targets, you also sent it into danger. British warships these days were painted in crazy stripes, the way zebras would have been were God drunk when He made them. It did a good job of breaking up their outlines, especially when seen from the sea against a background of shore. Nothing broke up the outline of muzzle flashes, though.

Before the sound of the guns reached the U-30, Lemp said, "We'll go below." The ratings on the conning tower tumbled down into the U-boat's fetid bowels. The skipper followed. "Periscope depth!" he called as he dogged the hatch.

With any luck at all, it would be an easy stalk. The destroyer's crew would be paying attention to their targets. They'd be watching out for air attack. The *Luftwaffe* had hit the Royal Navy hard in these waters. How much attention would the limeys pay to submarines? With luck, not much. Yes—with.

Lemp had no intention of leaving things to luck. He swung the periscope in wide arcs to the right and left. He hadn't seen any frigates or corvettes shepherding the destroyer, but that didn't mean they weren't there. Some clever young English officer might be stalking him the way he was stalking the destroyer.

That English officer might be, but the periscope gave no sign of it. Without taking his eyes away from the periscope, Lemp asked, "You there, Gerhart?"

"Yes, I'm here," the *Schnorkel* expert answered. "What do you need, Skipper?"

"Nothing. I'm just glad we've got the snort, that's all." Lemp wouldn't have believed he'd ever say anything like that when the technicians first saddled his boat with the gadget. But ... "We can make our approach a lot faster than we could on batteries. When I write up the action report, I'll log it."

"I've said so all along." Gerhart Beilharz sounded ready to pop his buttons with pride.

"People say all kinds of things," Lemp answered dryly. "Sometimes they're true, and sometimes they're crap. You have to find out. It's a good thing we didn't have to find out the hard way, eh?"

"Er—yes." That took some of the toploftiness out of the tall engineer.

"Torpedoes ready?" Lemp called into the speaking tube that led to the bow. The boat had an electrically powered intercom, but nothing could go wrong with the tube.

"Yes, Skipper. Four eels loaded and ready to swim." The answer came back by the same route. It sounded brassy but perfectly comprehensible.

"All right. Won't be long." Lemp fed speeds and angles to Klaus Hammerstein. The exec turned them into a firing solution. The camouflaged destroyer swelled in the periscope's reticulated field of view. She went right on shelling whatever shore target had raised her ire. No sudden evasive moves, no sign she had the faintest idea death and ruin were slipping up on her. Things were supposed to work that way. They seldom did. Every once in a while, though ...

He got within a kilometer. He could have have fired at her without Hammerstein's calculations, but he was glad he had them. The Englishmen went right on with their shore bombardment. Lemp turned the periscope all about, walking in a circle there under the conning tower. No, no one was sneaking up on him.

"Fire one!" he barked. "Fire two!"

Wham! ... *Wham!* The eels shot out of the tubes. Running time to the destroyer was a little more than a minute. Lemp watched the wakes. Both torpedoes ran straight and true. That didn't happen every time, either. Now ... How long before the Englishmen saw what was coming at them? Would they have time enough for evasive action?

As the seconds ticked off, that became less and less likely. The destroyer showed sudden urgent smoke . . . bare seconds before the first eel slammed into her, just abaft the beam. The second hit a moment later, up near the bow. Over and through the deep rumbles of the explosions, the crew whooped and cheered.

Destroyers weren't armored. They depended on speed to keep them out of harm's way. When speed failed, they were hideously vulnerable. The first hit would have been plenty to sink that ship.

"Back's broken," Lemp reported, watching the enemy's death agonies through the periscope. "She won't stay afloat long."

"She's not far from shore. Some of her crew may make it," Lieutenant Hammerstein said. "Our boys on land can scoop them up when they take Trondheim."

Lemp didn't answer. Even in summer, the North Sea was bloody cold. He wouldn't want to have to swim ashore, with or without a life ring. He didn't think the destroyer would be able to launch her boats. Those might have given the limey sailors a fighting chance to live. If the exec wanted to imagine he hadn't just helped kill a couple of hundred men, he could. Lemp knew better.

He spoke to the helmsman: "Give me course 305, Peter. We don't want to stick around, do we?"

"Folks up top might not be real happy with us if we do," the petty officer agreed. "Course 305 it is." He swung the U-boat around to the north and west, away from the Norwegian coast.

"Break out the beer!" somebody yelled. They kept some on board to celebrate sinkings and other notable events. It wouldn't be cold—the U-boat had no refrigerator—but no one would complain.

Lemp swung the periscope around through 360 degrees again. No hunters. Only ocean and the ever more distant shore. He nodded to himself. "We got away with it," he said, and the sailors cheered some more. "And England and France won't get away with trying to take Norway away from us, or with stopping the Swedes from shipping their iron ore to us through Norwegian ports."

The crew didn't cheer about that. They weren't grand strategists. Neither was Lemp, but he had some notion of how important the iron ore was. The Baltic froze in the winter, the North Sea didn't. If the Swedes were going to keep shipping the stuff when the weather got cold, they'd have to do it through Norwegian ports: through ports the enemy couldn't interfere with. Well, the *Reich* was taking care of that, sure enough.

One more check. No, no other Royal Navy ships in the neighborhood. "Yes," he said. "Break out the beer!" Even inside a cramped, stinking steel tube, life was good.

"OUR MISSION," Colonel Borisov announced, "is to bomb Warsaw."

Most of the pilots and copilots in the squadron just sat there and listened. Some of them nodded, as if in wisdom. Sergei Yaroslavsky sat tight like the rest. The less you showed, the less they could blame you for.

"Any questions before we carry out the mission?" the squadron commander asked.

"Excuse me, Comrade Colonel, but I have one." Of course that was Anastas Mouradian. He'd never fully mastered the fine art of keeping his mouth shut.

"Well? What is it?" Borisov growled. He never wanted questions.

"Warsaw is the capital of Poland. It is a large city. Are we supposed to bomb some special part of it, or do we let the explosives come down all over?" Mouradian asked.

Borisov glared at him. Yaroslavsky wondered why—it was a perfectly good question. Maybe *that* was why. "The orders transmitted to me say 'Warsaw,'" the colonel answered. "They give no more detail. We shall bomb Warsaw—with your gracious permission, of course, Comrade Lieutenant."

"Oh, it's all right with me, sir," Mouradian answered, ignoring Colonel Borisov's heavy-handed sarcasm. "I just wanted to make sure of what was required of us."

"What is required of you is to do as you are told," Borisov said. "Now you have been told. Go do it, all of you." The meeting broke up immediately after that. There didn't seem to be anything left to say.

"Well, well," Mouradian remarked as he and Sergei strode toward their SB-2. The Chimp was already watching the armorers as they bombed up the plane. "Warsaw. How about that?" He sounded bright and cheerful.

Maybe that was *maskirovka:* camouflage. Then again, maybe he'd gone out of his mind.

"As many antiaircraft guns as the Poles can beg, borrow, or steal," Yaroslavsky said. "All the fighter planes they've got that still fly. As many Messerschmitts as the Germans can spare."

"Now, Sergei, how many times have I told you?—if you're going to piss and moan about every little thing, you'll never get anywhere." The Armenian reached over and patted him on his stubbled cheek, as if he were a little boy fretting about hobgoblins under the bed. Sergei spluttered. What else could he do?

Ivan Kuchkov had already got the word, even if he wasn't at Borisov's meeting. "Warsaw, huh?" he said cheerfully. "About fucking time, if you want to know what I think. Time to start hitting those Polish cocksuckers where they live. Then they'll know better than to dick around with us."

What would he do without *mat*? He probably wouldn't be able to talk at all. Sergei waited till the armorers had finished their work, then climbed into the cockpit. He and Anastas ran through the preflight checklists. The engines fired up right away. He eyed the gauges. Things looked better than usual. *They would,* he thought darkly. He waited his turn to take off. The SB-2 seemed eager to fly. Would it be so eager to come back to the Motherland? He could only hope.

"One thing," Mouradian said consolingly as they took their place in the formation. "It's a big target. Borisov can't very well gig us for missing."

"Well," Sergei said, "no. He can gig us for getting killed, though."

"We won't have to listen to him if he does." Anastas seemed to think that was good news. He was welcome to his opinion.

The Poles and Germans were still holding the Red Army east of Warsaw. The line wasn't too different from the one Marshal Pilsudski's forces had held in the fighting after the Revolution. The stakes were higher now, though. The Soviet Union had already punished Poland then. Poland hadn't threatened the peasants' and workers' paradise any more. Smigly-Ridz's Poland and Hitler's Germany now . . . That was a different story. Hitler's Germany threatened everything it could reach, and its arms seemed to stretch like octopus tentacles.

Antiaircraft guns fired at them as they crossed the front. A couple of near misses made the bomber bounce in the air. "Some of those guns are ours!" Sergei said angrily. It happened every time. If it was up in the air, a lot of Russians assumed it had to be hostile. "I'd like to bomb the morons screwing around down there!"

"Do you think their replacements would be any smarter?" Mouradian asked. Sergei considered and reluctantly shook his head. The supply of damn fools was always more than equal to the demand. Then Anastas said, "What do you want to bet the Fritzes shoot at their own flyers, too?"

"Huh," Sergei said in surprise. To Russians, Germans were alarmingly capable: that was what made them so dangerous. It wasn't so easy to imagine them screwing up like ordinary human beings. But if they were so wonderful, why could you drop Germany into Russia and hardly notice where it hit?

They flew on. Poland was a big place in its own right—too big, at any rate, to have antiaircraft guns everywhere. Once they got beyond the front, things grew quiet again. All the same, Sergei wished for eyes that could see above, below, and behind the SB-2 as well as ahead—and all at the same time. It wasn't the first time he'd made that wish. You never knew where trouble would come from next.

"Well, one thing: we'll know when we get to Warsaw," Mouradian said.

"All the buildings and things underneath us, you mean?" Sergei asked.

"Mm, those, too," Anastas said. "But I was thinking, that's when they'll start shooting at us again."

"Oh." After a moment, Sergei nodded. "Yeah, they will, the bastards."

With a wry chuckle, Mouradian said, "We need to get the Chimp up here. He'd call them something that'd set 'em on fire from four thousand meters up."

"He would, wouldn't he?" Sergei agreed. "But don't let him hear you call him that. He'll throw you through a door headfirst, and he won't care that you're an officer or about what they'll do to him afterwards."

"I said it to you, not to him." And, in fact, Mouradian's hand had been over the mouthpiece of his speaking tube. In meditative tones, he went on, "I wonder what Ivan's service jacket looks like. How many times have they busted him down to private for doing things like that? How many times has he made it back to sergeant because he's brave and strong and even kind of clever when he isn't breaking heads? If only he didn't look like a chimp . . ."

"In that case, he'd get another nickname—Foxface or whatever suited the way he did look," Sergei answered. "Some people just naturally draw them, and he's one."

"Yes, I think so, too. Interesting that you should notice." Stas eyed him as if wondering what to make of such unexpected perceptiveness. Sergei didn't know whether to feel proud or nervous under that dark Southern scrutiny.

Then he stopped worrying about it. He had bigger things to worry about: they'd reached Warsaw's outskirts, and, sure as hell, the Poles were shooting at them from the ground. The formation loosened as all the pilots started jinking. They sped up; they slowed down. They swung left; they swung right. They climbed a little; they descended. The more trouble the Poles—the Germans?—had aiming at them, the more likely they'd make it back to base.

Jinking or not, if your number was up, it was up. A direct hit tore off half an SB-2's right wing. The stricken bomber tumbled toward the ground. Sergei flew past it before he could see whether any parachutes blossomed. *That could have been me,* he thought, and shuddered.

There lay the Vistula, shining in the sun. Everything built up on the other side was Warsaw proper. "Ready, Ivan?" Sergei called.

"Bet your stinking pussy," Kuchkov answered.

"Now!" Sergei said. If they had no orders to aim at anything in particular, he wasn't about to make a fancy straight bombing run. Why let the gunners get a good shot at him?

As soon as the bombs fell away, he hauled the SB-2's nose around and gunned it back to the east. A few more shell bursts made the plane buck in the air, but he heard—and felt—no fragments biting. And if enemy fighters were in the air, they were going after other Red Air Force formations.

"One more under our belts," Anastas Mouradian said.

"*Da.*" Sergei nodded. Along with rubber and oil and gasoline, he could smell his own fear—and maybe Mouradian's with it. How could you go on doing this, day after day, month after month? But what they'd do to you if you tried to refuse . . . Yes, not flying missions was even scarier than flying them.

Chapter 21

Fog shrouded the airstrip in northeastern France. Nobody was going anywhere this morning. Chances were, nobody was going anywhere all day. The idled *Luftwaffe* flyers did what idled flyers had been doing since the first biplanes took off with pilots carrying pistols and hand grenades: they sat around and shot the shit and passed flasks of applejack and cognac.

Hans-Ulrich Rudel was happy enough to join the bull session. When one of the flasks came to him, he passed it on without drinking. "*Danke schön,*" said the pilot to his left. "More for the rest of us."

"Nobody got out any milk for him," another flyer said.

Everybody in the battered farmhouse that did duty for an officers' club laughed. But the laughter sounded different from the way it would have not too long before. Then it would have been aimed at him, deadly as the bullets from a Hurricane's machine guns. Now he was an *Oberleutnant* with the *Ritterkreuz* at his throat. His comrades might not love him, but he'd earned their respect.

"Coffee will do," he said mildly, and got another laugh.

"Coffee's harder to come by than booze these days. Coffee worth drinking is, anyhow," said the pilot next to him. "The footwash they issue with our rations . . ." The other flyer made a horrible face.

"Frenchies don't have much of the good stuff left these days, either," another pilot complained. "Or if they do, they're hiding it better than they used to."

"I don't think they've got it," a third flyer said. "We've been in France since last year, and here it is, just about autumn come round again. You can only scrounge so much. After that, there's nothing left to scrounge."

"There'd be plenty if we'd got into Paris the way we thought we would," someone else said. Rudel couldn't see who it was; the farmhouse was twistier than a fighter pilot's mind. He wouldn't have been surprised if the French family who'd lived in it before fleeing in the early days of the war had unrolled balls of thread of different colors to guide them as they navigated from one room to another. What was left of the upstairs seemed even worse.

A long silence followed the flyer's remark. Anything that touched on politics was dangerous these days. Yes, the squadron was a band of brothers. But brothers could turn on one another, too—look what happened to Joseph. Some people feared that the *Gestapo* got word of any even possibly disloyal remarks. Others—Hans-Ulrich among them—hoped the security service did. He didn't want to inform on anyone else himself, but he also didn't want to fly alongside people whose hearts weren't in the fight.

"We'll get there yet," he said.

"Sure we will," said another voice he couldn't easily match with a face. "But when, and what will it cost? Will we get to Moscow first?"

Someone else whistled softly. Hans-Ulrich knew the two-front war wasn't popular with his comrades. Maybe it was even less popular than he'd thought. Again, no one seemed to care to take that particular bull by the horns. At last, the pilot sitting next to Rudel said, "I'd rather have the Poles on our side than against us."

"They aren't on our side." To Hans-Ulrich's dismay, that was Colonel Steinbrenner. The squadron commander went on, "Right this minute,

Stalin scares them worse than the *Führer* does. There's a difference. You'd better believe there is, my friends."

"*Jawohl, Herr Oberst*," Rudel said. "But it makes an army of a million men march against the Bolsheviks side by side with us. We ought to get the French and the English to do the same thing—a crusade to rid the world of something that never should have been born."

A different kind of silence descended on the farmhouse: one rather like the aftermath of a thousand-kilogram bomb. At last, the fellow next to Hans-Ulrich said, "You've always been an optimist, haven't you?"

"When it comes to Germany, of course I have," he answered proudly.

"We're all optimists about the *Vaterland*." Colonel Steinbrenner spoke as if challenging anyone there to argue with him. When nobody did, he continued, "But there is also a difference between optimism and blind optimism."

"Are you saying that's what I show, sir?" Rudel asked.

"No, no. You're a good German patriot," Steinbrenner replied. Rudel would have thought hard about reporting him had he said anything else. After all, he'd been brought in here to replace an officer in whom the fires of zeal didn't burn bright enough—or so the *Gestapo* had concluded, at any rate.

More high-octane liquor made the rounds. Several separate conversations started in place of the general one. That was safer: nobody could hear everything at once. Lickerish laughter said some of the flyers were talking about women—a topic more dangerous than politics, but in different ways. Hans-Ulrich might be a teetotaler, but he didn't stay away from the French girls. His father wouldn't have approved, but he didn't worry about that. When he was with a girl, he didn't worry about anything. *More precious than rubies*, the Bible said, and, as usual, it knew what it was talking about. The Biblical context might be different from the one Hans-Ulrich had in mind, but he didn't worry about that, either.

"If we didn't fuck up this stupid goddamn war—"

Rudel heard the words through all the other chatter, as one might hear a radio station through waves of static and competing signals. His ears pricked up. Treason would do that. You could say some things in some ways, but there were limits. This shot right past them.

He thought so, anyhow. He wondered how Sergeant Dieselhorst would feel about it. Dieselhorst was an older man and a veteran noncom. Both factors generated a broader view of mankind's foibles than a young officer who was also a minister's son was likely to have. Rudel suspected as much, but only in a vague way. He would not have been himself were he mentally equipped to grasp the full difference between how he thought and how Albert Dieselhorst did.

He didn't enjoy being the only sober man in the middle of a drunken bash. Who in his right mind would? But this was nothing he hadn't been through before. They'd think him a wet blanket if he stayed. They'd think him an even worse wet blanket if he got up and walked out. They'd think he thought he was better than they were. He did, too, but he'd learned that showing it only made things worse.

Somebody not far away was going on about the vastness of Russia, and about how a war against a country like that could have no sure ending. Sober or not, Hans-Ulrich got angry. "Once we smash the Reds, we'll run the country for ourselves," he said. "Russia is our *Lebensraum*. England and France have colonies all over the world. We'll get ours the way the Americans did, by grabbing the lands right next door."

"Yes, but the Americans only had to worry about Red Indians. We've got Red Ivans, and they're tougher beasts." The other flyer chuckled in not quite sober amusement at his wordplay.

Ignoring it, Hans-Ulrich said, "We can beat them. We will beat them. Or do you think the *Führer's* wrong?"

The other fellow's mouth twisted. He couldn't say yes to a blunt question like that, and he plainly didn't want to say no. What he did say was, "We all hope the *Führer's* not wrong."

That was probably safe. Rudel would have had to push to make something out of it. He didn't want to push. He wanted his comrades to like him. The easiest way to do that would have been to act like them. He couldn't bring himself to do it. Showing he was brave and skillful in combat was the next best thing. The others didn't despise him any more, anyhow.

Progress. He could throw it away in a flash if he got too strident about politics or about the way he thought the war ought to be going. He said, "Wherever we run into the enemy, we'll whip him, that's all."

"That's what the Kaiser's General Staff told him, too," the other flyer remarked.

"We beat the enemy," Hans-Ulrich said. "It was the traitors inside Germany who made us lose." He'd been two years old when the last war ended. He was parroting *Mein Kampf*, not speaking from experience.

The other flyer was probably younger than he was. "That's not what my old man says," he replied. "He was a lieutenant on the Western Front the last year and a half of the war. They had swarms of panzers by the end of 1918, and most of ours were retreads we captured from the Tommies. He says we got whupped."

"What's he doing now?" Rudel asked.

"He's a lieutenant colonel in Poland. Why?"

"Never mind." If the complainer was fighting, Rudel couldn't call him a defeatist. Not out loud, he couldn't. What he thought . . . he kept to himself. Little by little, he was learning.

CHAIM WEINBERG'S SPANISH was still lousy. It would never be great. But it was a hell of a lot better than it had been, especially when he talked about the class struggle or dialectical materialism.

He hadn't liked the political agitators who indoctrinated the Internationals so they would fight more ferociously. If they needed that kind of indoctrination, they wouldn't have come to Spain to begin with. Or it looked that way to him. The leaders of the International Brigades, and the Soviet officers and apparatchiks who stood beside them, held a different opinion. Theirs was the one that counted.

Indoctrinating prisoners with the ideals of the Republic—and of the USSR—was different. Chaim told himself it was, at any rate. The hapless *campesinos* the Nationalists had dragooned into their army needed to understand that everything they'd believed in before they were taken prisoner was a big, steaming pile of *mierda*.

"They exploited you," he told the tough, skinny, ragged men who came to the edge of the barbed wire to listen to him. He didn't fool himself into thinking he was all that fascinating. Time hung heavy for the POWs. Anything out of the ordinary seemed uncommonly interesting. "They were shameless, the way they exploited you." *Sinverguenza*—he loved the Spanish word for *shameless*.

One of the captured Nationalists raised a hand. Chaim pointed to him. "Excuse me, *Señor*," the fellow said apologetically, "but what does this word 'exploited' mean?"

Chaim blinked. He'd known these peasants were ignorant, but this took the cake. They literally had to learn a whole new language before they could understand what he was talking about. Before he answered the prisoner, he asked a question of his own: "How many others don't know what 'exploited' means?"

Two or three other grimy hands went up. After some hesitation, a couple of more followed them. How many other Nationalists were holding back? Some, unless he missed his guess.

"*Bueno*," he said. "If you don't know, ask. How can you understand if you don't ask? When the priests and the landlords exploit you, they take advantage of you. You do the hard work. They have the money and the fancy houses and the fine clothes and the pretty girls who like those things. They take your crops, and they make most of the money from them. *¿Es verdad, o no?*"

The POWs slowly nodded. That was how things worked in Spain— how they *had* worked before the Republic, and how they still worked where Marshal Sanjurjo and his lackeys governed. Joaquin Delgadillo raised his hand. Chaim nodded to him. He had a proprietary interest in Joaquin.

"What you say is true, *Señor*." Delgadillo had learned to slow down a little to give Chaim a better chance to stay with him. "But how can things be different? How can anyone do anything about it?"

"Land reform," Chaim answered at once. "There are no landlords in the Republic." There were no *live* landlords in the Republic, not any more. "Peasants own their lands. Sometimes they form collectives, but no one makes them do that." Plenty of Republican enthusiasts wanted to impose collective farms, as Stalin had in the USSR. Oddly, Soviet officials discouraged it. They didn't want to scare the middle classes in the cities and towns.

"But what about the holy padres?" another prisoner asked. "Haven't terrible things happened to them?"

"They sided with the reactionaries, or most of them did. They wanted to go on living well without working," Chaim said. "Progressive priests follow the Republic." There were some. There weren't very many. He didn't go into detail. His job here was to persuade, after all.

"The priests say God is on Marshal Sanjurjo's side. They say the Republic is the Devil's spawn," the prisoner said.

"¿Y así?" Chaim asked. *And so?* "What do you think they will say? No one says God fights for his enemies, but Satan is with him. No one would be that stupid. But do you believe everything the padres tell you?"

"They're holy men," the Spaniard said doubtfully. He wasn't used to questioning assumptions. He probably hadn't imagined assumptions *could* be questioned till he started listening to Chaim. Exploited, indoctrinated . . . Was it any wonder that, when the people of Spain found out they could overthrow the system that had been giving it to them in the neck for so long, they often threw out the baby with the bath water?

"How do you know they're so holy?" Chaim asked. "Are they poor? Do they share what they have with people who are even poorer? Or do they suck up to the landlords and piss on the poor?"

"Some of them are good men," the captured Nationalist answered. "Perfection is for the Lord." He crossed himself.

As long as their grandfathers had put up with it before them, a lot of Spaniards would put up with anything. They would be proud of putting up with it, in fact, *because* their grandfathers had before them. Well, Eastern European Jews had put up with pogroms for generation after generation, too. Chaim's grandfather had—and, no doubt, *his* grandfather before him. But Chaim's father had got the hell out of there and hightailed it for the States. And here stood Chaim in a bomb-scarred park in Madrid, not screwing around with the Talmud but preaching the doctrine of Marx and Lenin and Stalin.

"Some are good, eh?" he said.

"*Sí, Señor,*" the prisoner replied with dignity. People here had immense dignity—often more than they knew what to do with.

"Okay," Chaim said, and then, remembering which language he was supposed to be speaking, "*Bueno.*" He tried a different approach: "Isn't it true that most of the priests you call good favor the Republic?"

That made the prisoner stop and think. It made all the prisoners listening to him stop and think, in fact. They argued among themselves in low voices. One man threw his hands in the air and walked away in disgust when the argument didn't seem to be going the way he wanted. The rest patiently went on hashing it out. They had plenty of time, and they weren't going anywhere.

Chaim squatted on his heels and smoked a cigarette. He wasn't going anywhere, either, not right away. He owned more patience than he'd had before coming to Spain, too. If army life, and army life in the land of *mañana* at that, wouldn't help you acquire some, nothing would.

He'd given the little cigarette butt to Joaquin and lit another smoke— and got almost all the way through that one—before the POWs came to some sort of consensus. The fellow who'd called priests holy men came up to the edge of the wire. "It could be, *Señor,* that you have reason," he said gravely. "Many of these men, the ones who did most for the poor, did favor the Republic. Some got into trouble for it. Some ran away to keep from getting into trouble."

"And what does this mean, do you think?" Chaim inquired.

Instead of yielding as he'd hoped, the Nationalist prisoner only shrugged a slow shrug. "*¿Quién sabe, Señor?*" he said. "Who can be sure what anything means? Very often, life is not so simple."

In spite of himself, Chaim started to laugh. Only in Spain would a prisoner answer a political question with philosophy. "*Muy bien,*" the American from the International Brigades said. "What does *this* mean, then? Italy and Germany can't help Marshal Sanjurjo any more. England and France can help the Republic. Who is likely to do better now?"

"*¿Quién sabe?*" the Nationalist repeated. "We were winning before. You are doing better at this moment. But who can say anything about *mañana*?" Several long, strongly carved faces showed somber agreement.

The response only made Chaim laugh harder. The prisoners gave him fishy stares, wondering if he was mocking them. He wasn't, or not for that. "This is Spain, the land of *mañana*. I was just thinking about that. If you can't talk about it here, where can you, *Señor*?"

They had to talk that over, too, before they decided how to feel about it. It was almost as if they had their own little soviet here. Chaim didn't tell them that; it would have scandalized them. Slowly, one at a time, they started to smile. "We did not think men from the Republic could joke," one of them said.

"Who says I was joking?" Chaim answered, deadpan. The POWs thought he was joking again, and their smiles got broader. He knew damn well he wasn't. He grinned back at them all the same.

THE BROWN BEAR in the cage stared out at Sarah Goldman and Isidor Bruck through the bars. He looked plump and happy. People in Germany might have to shell out ration coupons for everything they ate, but the zoo animals remained well fed. Germans were uncommonly kind to animals. Everyone said so.

When Sarah remarked on that, Isidor looked around. No Aryans stood close enough to overhear him if he kept his voice down, so he did: "They think Jews are animals, so why don't they treat *us* better?"

Sarah stared at him in something not far from amazement. She would have expected a crack like that from her father, not from somebody her own age. But she didn't need long to figure out why the baker's son would come out with it. If being a Jew in National Socialist Germany didn't bring out gallows humor in people, what the devil would?

Isidor took a chunk of war bread out of his jacket pocket. He tossed it into the bear's cage. The animal ambled over to it. Sarah wondered if he'd turn up his nose at it—he probably got better himself. Animals were harder to fool than people. But he ate the treat and ran his blood-pink tongue across his nose.

A guard bustled up. He wore an impressive, military-looking uniform. "Do not feed the animals! It is forbidden!" he said importantly. Then he saw the yellow stars on their clothes. He rolled his eyes (Aryan gray, not brown and therefore of questionable breed). "You should be in cages yourselves! Obey, or things will go even worse for you!" Sarah was afraid he would grab the billy club on his belt, but he turned on his heel and stomped off.

"If we were in cages, do you suppose anyone would feed us?" she asked bitterly.

"Some people would—if they came by when nobody could see them do it, and if they were sure the guard was somewhere else," Isidor said.

"Yes, that sounds about right." Sarah remembered the Germans who'd sympathized with her after she had to start wearing the star. She also remembered that no one had told the Nazis they shouldn't make Jews wear stars to begin with. "They wouldn't keep us out of cages, though. Not a chance."

"You bet!" Isidor looked around. "I wish we could do something to the people who're putting the screws to us. All I ever wanted to be was a German, and look what I've got." He brushed his hand across the yellow star.

Samuel Goldman could also have said that. Could? Her father had, many times. Sarah didn't find it surprising: she'd said the same kind of thing herself, too. She almost told Isidor about her brother. But no. What he didn't know, he couldn't blurt out. Saul's life rode on secrecy.

And Saul's fate rode on the tracks of a panzer. He was bound to have Aryan crewmates. He was also bound to be fighting as hard as he could to help the Nazis win their war. How perverse was that? As perverse as anything Sarah had ever imagined.

Perverse enough to let Isidor notice the look on her face. "What is it?" he said. "Are you all right?"

"It's everything," Sarah answered at once. "I'm a Jew in Münster. How can I be all right?"

"Well, it all depends on the company," Isidor said, and then he turned a flaming red, as if he were standing in front of one of his father's back ovens with the door wide open and the heat blasting into his face.

He was sweeter on Sarah than she was on him. He was earnest and nice—no two ways about that. It wasn't even that she felt no spark when he took her hand. But she thought she ought to feel a bigger one if something serious was going to happen.

Or maybe she was crazy. What kind of prospects did a Jewish girl in Münster—or anywhere in the *Reich*—have these days? If somebody not too bad liked you, shouldn't you grab as hard as you could?

Before he went into the *Wehrmacht,* a young professor who'd studied under her father and done what little he could for him had been interested in her. But he hadn't been interested enough to risk courting her. She couldn't even blame him. If she were an Aryan, she wouldn't risk courting a Jew, either. Life gave you plenty of *tsuris* at the best of times; you didn't need to look for more.

She and Isidor walked on. A lion slept in the corner of his cage. His head was twisted to one side, as if he were an enormous tabby cat. He seemed to sleep most of the time. At least, Sarah hadn't seen him awake in several visits to the zoo lately. Well, what else did he have to do, shut away behind bars?

As if picking that thought from her mind, Isidor said, "I know just how the lion feels."

"Me, too," she exclaimed, liking him better for that.

A giraffe stripped leaves from branches set on a bracket high up in its tall enclosure. Its jaws worked from side to side as it chewed. A camel stared at the humans with ugly disdain, then spat in their direction. "See?" Isidor said. "Even the camel knows we're Jews."

"Nah." Sarah shook her head. "It would have got us for sure if it did." They both laughed. Sometimes you couldn't help it.

People walked by carrying steins. A fat man (his saggy skin suggested he once might have been fatter yet) with a big white mustache sold beer from a handcart he pushed along in front of him. "Want one?" Isidor asked.

"I've love one," Sarah said. "But—" She didn't go on . . . or need to.

"He doesn't have 'I don't serve Jews!' plastered all over everything like a lot of the pigdogs," Isidor said. "Let's try it. What's the worst he can do? Tell us no, right?" He hurried over to the beer-seller. Sarah followed briskly. As if Isidor weren't wearing a yellow star, he told the man, "Two, please."

"Sorry, kid," the fellow said. "I'd like to. Honest to God, I would. My mother's father, he was one of your people. Sometimes the clowns at city hall, they give me a hard time about it—but only sometimes, on account of I just got the one grandfather. But if they was to think I wanted to be one myself . . ." He turned a thumb toward the ground, as if he were shouting for blood in a Roman amphitheater. (So Sarah thought about it, but her father taught, or had taught, ancient history. Isidor might have seen things differently, but he also couldn't miss the beer-seller's meaning.)

The baker's son sighed. "They'll come for you anyway, you know. They may come later, but they'll come."

"Oh, sure." The old man whuffled air out through his mustache. "But when you've got as many kilometers on you as I do, I figure it's about even money I crap out on my own before the bastards get around to it." He dipped his head to Sarah. "Sorry for the way I talk, miss."

"It's all right." She set her hand on Isidor's arm. It might have been— she thought it was—the first time she'd reached out to touch him, even innocently like that, instead of the other way around. "See? I said he wouldn't."

"Yeah, you did." Isidor touched the brim of his ratty cap in a mournful salute to the beer-seller. "Good luck."

"You, too." With a grunt, the fellow lifted the handcart's handles. The iron tires rattled on the slates as he shoved it down the path between the cages.

"Did you notice something?" Sarah said after he got out of earshot.

"I noticed he was a jerk," Isidor said, probably in lieu of something stronger. "What else was there to notice?"

"He wouldn't say 'Jew,' " Sarah answered. "His grandfather was 'one of you people.' He had 'just the one grandfather.' He didn't want to be 'one.' He knew what he didn't want to be, but he wouldn't say it."

"Ever since Hitler took over, I bet he's been going, 'Oh, no, not me. I ain't one of them,' " Isidor said. "By now, he may even believe it. Whether he does or not, he sure wants to." He scowled after the man. "And he's right, dammit. He may not last till they decide to land on him with both feet. *We* aren't so lucky."

"They've only landed on us with one foot so far," Sarah said. And maybe that was the worst thing of all: she knew, or imagined she knew, how much worse things could get.

WIND WHISTLED through the pines. It came out of the northwest, and it carried the chill of the ice with it. When winds brought blizzards to Japan in the winter, people said they came straight from Siberia. It wasn't winter yet—it was barely fall—but you could already feel how much worse things were going to get here. Sergeant Hideki Fujita was *in* Siberia. As he had in Mongolia farther west, he discovered that the winds just used this place to take a running start before they roared over the ocean and slammed into the Home Islands. They were already frigid by the time they got here.

"When will the snow start?" he asked another noncom, a fellow who'd served in northeastern Manchukuo for a long time.

"Tomorrow . . . The day after . . . Next week . . . Maybe next month, but that's pushing things," the other sergeant said. "Don't worry about it. When the snow *does* start, you'll know, all right."

"*Hai, hai, hai,*" Fujita said impatiently. He looked north. "Miserable Russians'll cause even more trouble than they did when the weather was good—or as good as it gets around here, I mean."

"They're animals," the other sergeant replied with conviction. "Where they come from, they live with winters like this all the time. It's no wonder they're so hairy. Their beards help keep their faces from freezing off."

"I believe it," Fujita said. "I wanted to let my own whiskers grow when we were in Mongolia to try and keep my chin warm, but the company CO wouldn't let us do it. He said we had to stay neat and clean and represent the real Japan."

"Officers are like that," the other fellow agreed. "*Shigata ga nai, neh?* We grew beards along the Ussuri, I'll tell you. We tried, anyhow. Most of us couldn't raise good ones. It just looked like fungus on our faces. But this one guy—he had a pelt! We called him the Ainu because he was so hairy."

"Did he come from Hokkaido?" Fujita asked with interest. The natives the Japanese had largely supplanted lived on the northern island, though they'd once inhabited northern Honshu as well.

"No. That was the funny thing about it. Sakata came from Kyushu, way down in the south." The other noncom lit a cigarette, then offered Fujita the pack.

"*Arigato.*" Fujita took one and leaned close for a light. Once he had the smoke going, he continued, "Maybe he had a *gaijin* in the woodpile, then. Isn't Nagasaki where the Portuguese and the Dutch used to come to trade?"

"I think so. He didn't look it, though. He wasn't pale like a fish belly, the way white men are, and he didn't have a big nose or anything. He was just hairier than anybody else I've seen—anybody Japanese, I mean."

"I understood you," Fujita said. Foreigners were big-nosed and hairy and pale—or even black!—which marked them off from the finer sort of people who lived in Japan. Oh, there were foreigners who didn't look too funny: Koreans and Chinese, for instance. But their habits set them apart from the Japanese. Koreans slathered garlic on anything that didn't move. Chinese were opium-smoking degenerates who were too stubborn to see that they needed Japanese rulers to bring sense and order to their immense, ramshackle country.

The wind blew harder. A few crows scudded south on its stream. High above them, a raven sported. Crows were businesslike birds, flying from here to there straight as airplanes. Ravens performed, gliding and diving and looping. Fujita liked crows better. But they were leaving, getting out while the getting was good. He wished he could do the same. If some *kami* touched him and gave him wings, he'd fly straight home. Unless a kindly *kami* touched him, he was stuck here.

"When do you think Vladivostok will fall?" the other sergeant asked, not quite out of the blue.

"It should be soon," Fujita answered. "All the news reports say the Russians can't hold out much longer. And we're sitting on their lifeline." If not for the Trans-Siberian Railway, this would have been the most worthless country anywhere.

"The news reports have been saying soon for a long time now. When does soon stop being soon?"

"It'll work out," Fujita said confidently. "The last time we fought the Russians, Port Arthur took a long time to fall, but it finally did."

"Well, that's true," the other noncom admitted. "I'd rather be here than trying to break into Vladivostok, too. They're fighting there like they fought in front of Port Arthur—with charges and trenches and machine guns everywhere."

"How do you know?" Fujita asked. It wasn't that he disbelieved it—it sounded only too probable. But he hadn't heard it before, and nothing like it had been in the news.

"I've got a cousin down there. I hope he's all right. Casualties are pretty high," the other man answered. "And I hope like anything they don't decide to ship us down there."

"*Eee!*" Fujita made an unhappy noise. They were liable to do that if they ran low on men—or if they decided they didn't need so many here to keep the Russians from opening the railroad line again. Russian snipers firing from high in the trees were bad. Fujita thought about Russian machine guns sweeping the ground in front of Vladivostok. He thought about rushing from a Japanese trench to a Russian one and running into a stream of Russian machine-gun bullets halfway across the broken landscape. "Makes my asshole pucker and my balls crawl into my belly."

The other sergeant laughed—unhappily. "I wouldn't have come out with it like that, but it does the same thing to me. You stay in this game for a while, you get a feel for what's bad . . . and what's even worse."

"That's right," Fujita said. "You do if you're a noncom, anyway. I'm not so sure officers can tell." He never would have said that where an officer could hear him, of course, but he was confident a fellow sergeant wouldn't betray him.

And the other man nodded. "You're lucky if your officers know enough to grab it with both hands." Now each had something slanderous on the other. They both grinned.

Not long before, Fujita had been thinking about Russian snipers in the trees. A Mosin-Nagant rifle cracked, a couple of hundred meters off to the left. The report was deeper and louder than the ones that came from Japanese Arisakas. Yells and commotion from the Japanese lines said the sharpshooter had hit somebody.

A moment later, another shot rang out. That raised a bigger uproar. *"Zakennayo!"* Fujita exclaimed. "What do you want to bet they showed themselves getting the wounded man to cover, so the sniper hit somebody else?"

"You're bound to be right," the other sergeant answered. "The Russians like to play those games. You have to be stupid to fall for them, stupid or careless, but sometimes people are."

"We wouldn't be people if we weren't," Fujita said. "Or weren't you sweet on some girl or other before you got sucked into the army?"

"Oh, sure. But when you're talking about girls, at least you get to have fun being stupid."

"There is that," Fujita allowed. Just for a moment, loneliness knifed him in the heart. Fun . . . He'd almost forgotten about fun. The most fun you could have in war was not getting shot. That negative made for cold comfort. Of course, with this wind there was no warm comfort for heaven only knew how many kilometers.

Vladivostok . . . Of their own accord, Fujita's eyes slid south. He didn't want to stay where he was, but he sure didn't want to go down there, either. As far as he was concerned, they could starve the stinking Russians into submission. If it took a while, so what? It wasn't as if Japan needed to use Vladivostok right away. All she needed was to keep the Russians from using it, and she was already doing that.

The people who ran things would see it differently. Fujita had no doubts on that score. He wished he did, but he didn't. They would worry about things like prestige. The sooner Japan took the Russian city, the better she'd look. They wouldn't care about how many soldiers turned into ravens' meat in the doing.

Fujita did. He didn't want to be one of those soldiers. The only trouble was, he could do exactly nothing about it. If they ordered his regiment to storm the works in front of Vladivostok, it would damn well storm them—or die trying. That was what worried him.

Chapter 22

Luc Harcourt looked around. More and more *poilus* kept coming into the line. More and more tanks and other armored contraptions sheltered in groves or under camouflage netting not far behind it. "I think they really mean it this time."

The other members of his machine-gun crew shrugged in a unison that looked staged, all the more so as Pierre Joinville was small and swarthy while fair Tiny Villehardouin was anything but. Tiny said something incomprehensible, presumably in Breton. Joinville said something perfectly comprehensible, in southern-accented French: "The *cons* have meant it before. That doesn't matter for shit. What matters is whether they can do it right for a change."

Tiny nodded, so either that was what he meant or it was something else he might have said. You never could tell with him. But he was strong as an ox and he'd go forward when he got the order, so who cared? You didn't know what he was talking about? Big deal. As often as not, you didn't want to know what a private was saying. That was one of Luc's discoveries since becoming a corporal.

"We've got a chance this time, I think," he said. "Damn *Boches* don't have their peckers up the way they did before they started fighting in Poland, too."

"It could be," Joinville said: as much as a private was likely to give a corporal. Luc remembered that from his days with no rank at all. Oh, yes. The Gascon went on, "Other question is, do we have *our* peckers up now?"

That was the question, all right. Its answer would also go a long way towards answering the other question, the one from the English play. *To be or not to be?* Luc glanced down at his hands. They were battered and scarred and filthy, the nails short and ragged. But they opened and closed at his command. They could yank the cork from a bottle of cognac or cup a girl's soft, warm breast or knock down half a dozen Germans at five hundred meters with the Hotchkiss gun. They were marvelous things, marvelous.

Hanging around in the trenches was pretty safe. Oh, you might be unlucky, but your odds were decent. But if the French advanced . . . There he'd be, out in the open, just waiting for a shell fragment or a machine-gun bullet to do something dreadful. And how much would his clever hands help then?

They could slap on a wound bandage. They could give him a shot of morphine so he didn't hurt so much. It seemed . . . inadequate.

He hunted up Sergeant Demange. If anybody was likely to know what was going on, Demange was the man. He greeted Luc with his customary warmth: "What the fuck do *you* want?"

"Love you, too, Sarge," Luc said. Demange grunted and waited. He wouldn't wait long. He'd start snarling—or worse. Luc hurried ahead: "Are we really going to give the *Feldgrau* one in the teeth?"

"Sure as hell looks that way," Demange answered. "Any other questions? No? Then piss off, why don't you?"

Instead of pissing off, Luc asked, "How bad will it be?"

"All things considered, I'd sooner get a blowjob," the sergeant said, and lit a fresh Gitane.

"*Merci beaucoup.*" Luc left. Behind him, Demange didn't even bother laughing. And yet he'd found out what he needed to know. The attack was coming, and the sergeant wasn't looking forward to it. Demange had done his attacking in 1918. The dose he'd got then cured him of eagerness forever after.

Luc gauged the temper of the new fish instead. When the war first broke out—good God! was it really a year ago now?—he and his buddies had tiptoed into Germany, then tiptoed right back out again. They'd been waiting to get kicked in the teeth. As soon as the *Boches* were ready, they'd got what they were waiting for, too.

The new guys weren't intimidated by the Germans, or by the idea of advancing against them, the way Luc and his buddies had been. Or maybe their officers weren't intimidated the way the fellows with the fancy kepis had been a year earlier. They thought they could go forward and win. That was half the battle right there. If you weren't licked before you even set out, you had a chance.

4 October 1939. 0530. The day. The hour. Luc had his machine-gun team ready. Villehardouin and Joinville were pretty much self-winding. They tolerated Luc not least because he didn't try to pretend they couldn't do it without him. They knew damn well they could. So did he.

It was chilly and drizzly in the wee small hours, but nowhere near enough rain came down to bog the tanks that had rattled forward under cover of darkness. At 0435, right on schedule, the French artillery roared to life. "See how you like that, cocksuckers!" Luc yelled through high-explosive thunder.

German artillery started shooting back inside of five minutes. Some of the *Boches'* shells went after the French batteries. Others pounded the front line. The Germans knew their onions. A big barrage meant the French were going to follow it up. The worse the Germans could hurt them, the better . . . if you were a German.

At 0530, whistles shrilled in the French trenches. "Forward!" officers shouted. Tanks growled toward the German lines, cannon blasting and machine guns braying. Joinville and Villehardouin lugged the machine gun and its tripod ahead. A pair of glum new fish carried crates full of ammunition strips. Luc had his rifle and an infantryman's usual equipment. For the moment, nothing more—rank did have its privileges. But he would turn into a beast of burden in a hurry if one of his crew went down. A machine gun was important in the grand scheme of things, a corporal's dignity much less so.

The French guns increased their range so they didn't land shells on the advancing *poilus*. The German guns shortened range so they did. A round from a 105 came down right on top of a tank. Fire fountained from the stricken machine. A black column of smoke mounted to the sky. Machine-gun ammo cooked off with cheerful little popping noises.

"Poor buggers," Joinville said.

"Wouldn't even be that much left of us if the shell hit here," Luc answered. The Gascon grunted and nodded.

A German MG-34 the bombardment hadn't silenced started spitting death across the field. Luc envied the *Boches* their weapon. It was lighter than a Hotchkiss gun, and it fired faster, too. You could carry it and fire it from the hip if you had to. He tried to imagine firing the twenty-odd kilos of the Hotchkiss from the hip. The picture wouldn't form, and for good reason.

Tracers from the German machine gun sparked closer to the Hotchkiss crew. "Down!" Luc yelled. He followed his own order, diving into a shell hole.

"We set up?" Joinville asked.

Anything that gave Luc an excuse not to stand again sounded good right then. "Yeah, let's," he said. Joinville and Villehardouin got the heavy Hotchkiss onto the even heavier tripod. One of the new guys fed a strip into the weapon. Staying as low as he could, Luc peered over the forward lip of the shell hole. The MG-34's bullets had gone past it; now they cracked by again, maybe a meter and a half above the ground: chest-high on an upright man.

Those shapes in the misty, rainy morning twilight were Germans: Germans trying to get away from oncoming Frenchmen. Having been a Frenchman trying to get away from more oncoming Germans than he cared to remember, Luc relished the sight of field-gray backs. He fired a couple of bursts at them. Maybe he'd knock some of them down. He'd sure as hell make the ones he didn't hit run faster.

A French tank shelled the MG-34 into silence. "Come on," Luc said. "Let's get moving again." His crew hid their enthusiasm very well, but they obeyed. Luc didn't want to hit his own countrymen in front of the gun.

Tanks smashed paths through the German wire. Here and there, Fritzes still stayed and fought in their battered holes. One by one, they died or gave up. A *Landser* with a scared, whipped-dog grin on his face showed himself, hands high. *"Ami!"* he said.

"C'mere, *friend,*" Luc said, and relieved him of his watch and wallet. Some of these Germans carried fat wads of francs—on their side of the line, French money wasn't worth much. Luc gestured with his rifle. "Go on back."

"Danke! Uh—*merci!"* the new prisoner said. Hands still over his head to show he'd surrendered, he stumbled off into captivity. He didn't have to worry about the war any more.

Luc did. "Let's go," he said. They pushed on through the shattered German defenses. It couldn't be this easy, could it? It had never been this easy before—he was goddamn sure of that. He had no idea how long it would stay easy, either. As long as it did, he'd go along with it.

OF COURSE THE REPUBLICANS set up a radio outside the POW camp in the park in Madrid. And of course they always tuned it to their own stations. Joaquin Delgadillo hadn't listened to those when he fought in Marshal Sanjurjo's army. It wasn't that the Nationalists jammed them, though they did. And the Republicans jammed Nationalist radio. Sometimes the whole dial sounded like waterfalls and sizzling lard.

But this was Radio Madrid, and they were right next to the sender. It overpowered the jamming with ease. The Republican announcer might have been standing right there, reading from a script. "And now the news," he said. "French and English armies have gone over to the offensive against the German invaders. Gains of several kilometers are reported. So are rumors that German commanders in France have been sacked because their troops retreated."

"Sacked? I'm surprised they didn't shoot them," someone behind Joaquin said. He found himself nodding. Both sides in Spain had executed officers who went back when their superiors thought they should go forward. As for common soldiers . . . That went without saying. Common soldiers always got it in the neck—or the back of the head, depending.

"In Poland, the forces of the workers and peasants, the glorious soldiers of the Red Army, continue to press forward against the Fascists and their sympathizers," the newsreader went on. "Many Germans and Poles willingly surrender to join the Socialist cause."

Nationalist radio continually reported German and Italian triumphs. Somebody had to be lying. Before Joaquin was captured, he would have been certain it was the Republicans. He wasn't so sure any more. These days, he wasn't sure of anything. Maybe both sides were lying as hard as they could. That wouldn't have surprised him—oh, no, not even a little bit.

"American President Roosevelt has proposed an end to the war on the basis of all sides' returning to their positions before the fighting began," the announcer said. "In rejecting this, Hitler likened it to unscrambling an egg. He said Czechoslovakia would never be independent again, and that Germany would fight on to ultimate victory." The man let out a dry chuckle. "How Germany can gain ultimate victory while retreating in both east and west, Hitler did not explain."

Joaquin didn't know what to make of that. Every time he saw the Germans in action here in Spain, they made things go forward. The Italians who came to help Marshal Sanjurjo didn't care about the fight one way or the other. But Germans . . . Germans made things happen.

He made the mistake of saying that to Chaim Weinberg. The Republic agitator from the United States turned the color of a sunset. "Fuck 'em all," he said. "Fuck their mothers, too, up the ass."

"You hate them so much because they're Fascists?" Delgadillo said.

"Because they're Fascists, *sí*," Weinberg answered. "And because they hate Jews."

A light dawned. Weinberg was a Jew himself. He might have put that reason second, but he meant it first. "Spaniards hate Jews, too," Joaquin said. "Do you hate Spaniards? Why did you come here if you hate Spaniards?"

"It's different here," the American mumbled.

"Really? Different how?" Joaquin asked, honestly puzzled. "Hate is hate, isn't it?"

"With you Spaniards, hating Jews is only a—a tradition, like," Weinberg said. "You don't go out of your way to do it."

"How can we?" Joaquin laughed out loud. "You're the first Jew I ever saw in my life. We threw ours out hundreds of years ago."

"Maybe that's it," Weinberg said. "You people just know you used to hate Jews. There are still plenty in Germany, and the Nazis go to town on them."

That had to be an English idiom translated literally; Joaquin had heard Weinberg do such things before. The American made himself understood, but you never doubted you were listening to a foreigner. After working out what he had to mean, Delgadillo said, "What about the *Estados Unidos*? Is your country a Jews' paradise?"

Weinberg snorted. "Not hardly. But it could be worse. Some people there do hate Jews, yes. But more of them hate Negroes worse. They treat Negroes the way Europeans treat Jews."

"But you would sooner change how Spain does things than how your own country does them, eh?" Joaquin said shrewdly.

The American—the Jew—started to say something. Then he closed his mouth with a snap. When he opened it again, he let out a sheepish chuckle. "Well, you may be right," he said, which surprised Joaquin. He hadn't thought Weinberg would admit any such thing. Weinberg went on, "Other Americans are trying to make things better for Negroes. I thought fighting against the Nazis was more important."

"How many of the Americans working for your Negroes are Jews?" Delgadillo asked.

"Quite a few. Why?"

Now Joaquin found himself surprised again, in a different way. "I would have guessed your Jews would let your Negroes go hang. As long as other Americans have Negroes to hate, most of them leave Jews alone. Isn't that what you said?"

"Yes, I said that, but it doesn't mean what you said it means." On the far side, the free side, of the barbed wire, Weinberg paused to figure out whether that meant what he wanted it to mean. He must have decided it did, because he went on, "Injustice to anyone anywhere is injustice to everyone everywhere. You have to fight it wherever you find it."

"You must enjoy tilting at windmills." Joaquin had never read *Don Quixote*. He'd read very little. But Cervantes' phrases filled the mouths of Spaniards whether they could read or not.

"Fighting against Fascism isn't tilting at windmills," Weinberg said. "Fascism is the real enemy."

"On the other side of the line, they think the same thing about Communism," Joaquin said.

"On the other side of the line, they're wrong." Weinberg sounded as sure of himself as a priest quoting from the Bible. Delgadillo didn't think that would be a good thing to tell him. The Jew went on, "Communism wants to treat every man and every woman the same way."

"Badly—they would say over there." Joaquin still more than half believed it himself. He couldn't insist on it too strongly, though, not when he depended on good will from these people if he wanted to keep breathing.

"How well did they treat *you* over there?" the Jew asked. "You were a peasant, and then you were a private. Do you want your son to live the way you used to live?"

Through most of Spain's history, the only possible answer to that would have been *Well, how else is he going to live?* Things changed only slowly here, when they changed at all. But Joaquin had seen that there were other possibilities. He didn't like all of them—he liked few of them, in fact—but he knew they were there. Stalling for time, he said, "I have no son."

Weinberg snorted impatiently. "You know what I mean."

And Joaquin did. "Well, *Señor*, I mean no disrespect when I say this—please believe me, for it is true—but I am sure I do not want my son to grow up a Red."

"Why?" Weinberg challenged. "What's so bad about equality?"

"Making everyone equal by pushing the bottom up would not be so bad," Joaquin said slowly. "Making everyone equal by pulling the top down . . . That is not so good, or I don't think so. And it seems to me that is what the Republic aims to do."

He waited for the top to fall down on him. He'd probably said more than he should have. But the American had asked, dammit. On the other side of the wire, Weinberg paused thoughtfully. "You really are smarter than you look," he said at last. "The only thing I'll say to that is, sometimes you have to tear down before you can build up."

"Well, *Señor*, it could be," Delgadillo replied, by which he meant he didn't believe it for a minute.

Weinberg wagged a finger at him. "What are we going to do about you?"

"It is your choice. You caught me."

"Maybe I should have shot you when I did."

"Maybe you should have. I thought you would."

"Better to reeducate you," the Jew said. Joaquin wondered if he was right.

PETE MCGILL ENJOYED TALKING with officers no better than any other Marine corporal in his right mind. Officers, to him, were at best necessary evils, at worst unnecessary ones. Sometimes, though, you had no choice. Like St. Peter, officers had the power to bind and to loose.

Captain Ralph Longstreet had never said he was related to the Confederate general of the same last name. Then again, he'd never said he wasn't. He did have a drawl thick enough to slice. A hell of a lot of Marines—and even more Marine officers, it seemed—were Southern men. Looking up from his paperwork, he said, "Well, McGill, what can I do for you today?"

"Sir, you may have heard I've, uh, got friendly with a lady here in Shanghai," McGill answered. His own New York accent was about as far from what Longstreet spoke as it could be while remaining American English.

The captain capped his fountain pen and set it on his battleship of a desk. "A dancer named Vera Kuznetsova," he said. "Vera Smith, that would be in English."

"Uh, yes, sir." Pete hadn't known what Vera's last name meant. He hadn't cared, either, and still didn't. But he knew exactly what Longstreet's tone meant. "It's not like she's Chinese or anything, sir. She's as white as you or me."

"White Russian, to be exact," Longstreet said. "What nationality does she have on her passport?"

He had to know the answer before he asked the question. "Sir, her folks got out of Siberia a length ahead of the Reds. *She* got out of Harbin a length ahead of the Japs. They had papers from the Tsar. I guess she did, too, when she was a baby. Now—" He shook his head.

"Officially, she's stateless, then." Captain Longstreet made it sound like a death sentence. For a lot of people, it had been. The wrong papers or no papers at all could be a disease deadlier than cholera.

"Well, sir—" Pete took a deep breath. "She wouldn't be, sir, not any more, not after she married me."

Longstreet had been about to light up an Old Gold. He paused just before striking the match. "Why don't you shut the door, son, and sit your ass down?" he said. Gulping, Pete obeyed. He didn't think Longstreet sounded friendly all of a sudden—the tone was more like the warden asking a condemned prisoner what he wanted for his last meal. Pete's anxiety only grew when Longstreet offered him a cigarette: it made him think of firing squads. Not knowing what else to do, he took the coffin nail anyhow. Longstreet waited till he'd got halfway down the smoke before continuing, "You've got it bad, don't you?"

"Sir, I'm in love," Pete said. "She loves me, too. Honest to God, she does."

"Well, it's possible. I reckon stranger things have happened," Longstreet said. He *was* a captain; Pete couldn't bust him in the face. Marrying Vera while he was stuck in the brig would be hard, to say the least. Longstreet went on, "But do you figure she hasn't got you tabbed for a meal ticket, too?"

All of Pete's buddies said the same goddamn thing. He was sick of hearing it. "Well, what if she does, sir? She could've picked other guys to play games with, but she didn't. She *does* love me, and I—" He stopped, his tongue clogging up his mouth. Talking about what he felt for Vera— even trying to talk about it—was far and away the hardest thing he'd ever done. Charging a Jap machine-gun nest would have been nothing next to it. The Japs could only kill him.

Had Longstreet yelled at him (or, worse, laughed at him), he would have sat there and taken it, but something inside him would have died. He expected one or the other. Looking for sympathy from an officer was a losing game. But the captain said, "Well, your sentiments do you credit. And you aren't going into this with your eyes shut tight, anyhow. That's something."

"How do you mean, sir?" Pete asked.

"If you reckon you're the first Marine to fall head over heels for a Russian dancing girl or a Chinese singsong girl, I have to tell you you're mistaken," Longstreet said. "A lot of 'em think their sweethearts were virgins till they charmed the girls off their feet and into bed. You seem to know better than that."

"Er—yes, sir." Pete's ears heated. He'd wished he might have been Vera's first, but he hadn't been able to imagine he really was. He mumbled, "She never tried to pretend anything different."

"One for her, then," the captain said. "You've got it bad, but you could have it worse."

"All I want to do is make it legal. She does, too."

"I'm sure she does." Longstreet's voice was dry as dust. "The advantages for her are obvious. I'm sure the advantages for you are obvious, too, but they aren't the kind that's got anything to do with what's legal and what isn't."

Pete's ears caught fire again. "Well, sir, what the . . . dickens am I gonna do?"

"It's not a simple question. First, there's the issue of whether you ought to marry the, mm, the young lady." Captain Longstreet raised a hand. "I know you think so now, but whether you will a year from now may be a different story. Like I said, you aren't the first Marine I've seen in this boat."

"Yes, sir," Pete muttered. As far as he was concerned, whatever Longstreet knew about love he'd got out of books. You could read about bar brawls, too, but reading about them wouldn't tell you what getting into one was like.

"And I hate to have to remind you of it, but you *are* a Marine on active duty," Longstreet added. "You can't just go marrying somebody, the way you could if you were a couple of civilians back in the States."

"I understand that, sir. That's how come I came to see you."

"Okay. Now we get down to the really hard part. It's not easy for a Marine on active duty to get married. He's supposed to be a Marine first, not a husband first. The country does expect that of him." Longstreet sighed. "And if you reckon it's hard for a Marine to get hitched in a regular way, it's at least five times as hard for him to tie the knot with a stateless person. At least." He spoke with a certain somber satisfaction.

"Tell me what I've got to do. Whatever it is, I'll do it," Pete declared.

To his surprise, the captain smiled. It was a wintry smile, but it was a smile even so. "You sound like a Marine, all right," Longstreet said.

"Sir, I am a Marine, sir!" Pete sprang to his feet and came to rigor mortis-like attention.

"At ease, son," Longstreet told him. "At ease. Sit down. Relax. Take an even strain. This may happen. I won't tell you it's impossible. But it won't be easy, and it won't be quick. If you think it will, you'll burn out your bearings and you won't get anything for it but heartache."

"Tell me what to do," Pete repeated.

"You've done the first thing you needed to do: you've brought it to my attention. Now I'm going to have to talk to the judge advocate. He'll tell me where the mines are, and how you can go about sweeping them." Longstreet must have had a lot of sea duty, to think of mines in the water instead of mines buried under the ground. Well, he wasn't old enough to have gone Over There in 1918.

"When will you talk with him, sir? When will he figure out what needs doing?" Pete was all eagerness.

It was his life, of course. It was only Ralph Longstreet's job, and a small, annoying part of his job at that. "I see Herb every day, of course," he answered. "I'll fill him in on what's troubling you, and after that it's in his hands. He may have to talk with some other people, too."

Pete had thought—had hoped—this might be a matter of days. Now he saw all too plainly that it would be weeks or months if not the threatened year. His shoulders lost the iron brace they'd kept even while he sat in the hard wooden chair in front of Longstreet's desk. "Well, thanks for starting things, anyway, sir."

"You did that," the officer said. "And if you're still as ready to go through with it by the time we're all done as you are now, I'd say your chances with this girl will be a lot better than they are today." He picked up the fountain pen. "Anything else on your mind as long as you're here?"

"Uh, no, sir."

"Okay. Dismissed." Longstreet went back to work. Pete stood up, saluted, and left the captain's office. He wondered if he'd done himself and Vera more harm than good.

WILLI DERNEN DIDN'T KNOW where the hell he was. Somewhere in France—somewhere between where he had been and the border with the Low Countries. He couldn't smell Paris, couldn't taste victory, any more. All he smelled was trouble.

He shivered under his summer-weight tunic. It was cold as a witch's tit. If the winter was as bad as it gave signs of being, it'd freeze his balls off. His breath smoked. That was bad. An alert enemy soldier could spot the fog puffs rising into the chilly air and lie in wait to pot the poor bastard who was making them. But he didn't know what he could do about it. Stop breathing? No, thanks!

A gray-haired French peasant watching sheep in a meadow stared at him with no expression at all. Chances were the fellow'd gone through the mill in the last war. Would he sneak off to tell the *poilus* where the Germans were? He might.

The froggies had been polite, even friendly, while the *Wehrmacht* had the bit between its teeth. And why not? They'd figured they would stay German a long time, the way they had after 1914. Now they were wondering. That would mean more trouble down the line, sure as hell it would.

Something else moved. Willi's scope-sighted rifle swung that way as if it had a life of its own. But it wasn't a *poilu*. It was Corporal Baatz coming out of the bushes. Reluctantly, Willi lowered the rifle's muzzle. Tempting as it was, he couldn't go and plug Awful Arno. He didn't suppose he could, anyhow. The unloved corporal was his lord and master again. He'd been reattached to his old unit within hours after *Oberfeldwebel* Putt-kamer got his head blown off. He was still surprised they hadn't made him turn in the fancy Mauser. Somebody'd slipped up there.

Baatz saw him, too, and waved. He didn't raise his hand too high. You never could tell what would draw a sniper's eye. Willi wondered what had happened to the goddamn Czech with the antipanzer rifle. He was prob-ably still busy nailing Germans. Puttkamer wasn't around to quarrel with him any more, that was for sure.

"*Wie geht's?*" Awful Arno asked.

Willi shrugged. "I'm still here. If I get hungry, I'll shoot me a sheep." He paused, considering. *Hell with it,* he thought, and went on, "War's pretty goddamn fucked up, though, isn't it?"

He might have known Baatz wouldn't admit what was as plain as the nose on his piggy face. "You can't talk like that," the noncom insisted.

"Why the hell not?" Willi said. "It's true, isn't it?"

"It's disloyal, that's what it is," Baatz answered. "I knew the *Gestapo* guys knew what they were doing when they started sniffing around you and your asshole buddy Storch."

And they had, too. All the same, Willi said, "Oh, fuck off, man. If you can't tell we screwed the pooch, you're too dumb to go on living."

Awful Arno turned red. "Watch your big mouth, before you open it so wide you fall in and disappear. You keep going on like that, I'll report you—so help me God I will."

"Go ahead," Willi said wearily. "Maybe you'll get me yanked out of the line. If you do, I'll be better off than you are."

That only made Baatz madder. "You don't know what the devil you're talking about. Wait till they chuck you into Dachau. You'll wish you only had machine guns to worry about."

The blackshirts had said the same thing. Willi wasn't about to take it from Awful Arno. "Give me a break. If telling the truth is disloyal, then I guess I am. Jesus Christ, the war *is* screwed up. Even a blind man can see it. Even *you* should be able to."

"You're not just talking about the war," Baatz said. "You're talking about how we're fighting it. And if you say that's gone wrong, you're say-ing the *Führer's* leadership isn't everything it ought to be."

"Yeah? And so? He's the *Führer.* He's not God, for crying out loud. When he takes a crap, angels don't fall out of his asshole," Willi said.

Awful Arno's eyes widened. He looked like an uncommonly sheltered child hearing about the facts of life for the first time. "He's the *Führer*," he said, on a note as different from Willi as could be.

"*Ja, ja,* and the *Grofaz,* too," Willi said: the cynical contraction of the German for *greatest military leader of all time.* "But if he's so goddamn great, how come we're retreating? How come Paris is way the hell over there?" He pointed west.

Before Baatz could answer, a mortar bomb burst a hundred meters behind them. They both threw themselves flat. More bombs came down, some of them closer. Fragments whined and snarled overhead. Willi looked around without raising his head. Sure as hell, that Frenchman had bailed out. And a couple of sheep were down and kicking. Spit filled his mouth. Mutton chops!

Arno Baatz shielded his face with his arm, as if that would do any good. "So Dachau is worse than this, is it?" Willi said.

The corporal nodded without raising his head. "You'd better believe it is. And everybody who doubts the *Führer* will end up in a place like that." Conviction filled his voice.

"*Scheisse,*" Willi said. "If he messed up the war—and he damn well did—somebody needs to doubt him, don't you think? I hope to God I'm not the only one, or Germany's even more screwed up than I figured."

"He's the *Führer.* If we live through this, Dernen, I will report you."

"Go ahead," Willi said, wondering if he would have to make sure Awful Arno damn well didn't live through it. He would if he had to, but he didn't want to. Killing someone on his own side in cold blood wasn't what he'd signed up for. He went on, "I'll call you a motherfucking liar and say you always had it in for me—and that's the truth, too. You think the officers don't know what kind of asshole you are, Baatz? Yeah, report me. It's your word against mine. I bet they believe me, not you, and you end up in the concentration camp."

"You don't get it, do you?" Baatz sounded almost pitying. "This is *security* we're talking about. Of course they'll believe me."

"They'd believe somebody with a working brain, maybe, but not a fuckup like you," Willi retorted. "Like I said, they know better. Go ahead, report me, cuntface. You'll find out." Maybe he was right, maybe he was wrong. Maybe nobody'd take any chances, and they'd both wind up in Dachau. If they did, he was willing to bet he'd last longer than Awful Arno.

And maybe they wouldn't live through this, and it would all be moot. Willi lifted his head a few centimeters. Something that wasn't a sheep moved atop the next little swell of ground to the west. Willi brought his rifle to his shoulder and snapped a shot at it. It disappeared down the back side of the hillock.

"What was that?" Baatz asked.

"Well, it might have been a hippo escaped from the zoo. Or it might have been a Frenchman." Willi chambered a fresh round. "Odds were it was a Frenchy. So if you want to live long enough to rat on me, get your empty ostrich head out of the sand and start acting like a soldier." He'd never had the chance to tell off a noncom like this. It was fun. It might almost be worth getting shot. Almost. If Baatz got shot, too. . . .

Two French soldiers came over that hillock. They were more cautious than the first fellow had been—they knew there were *Landsers* on this side, which he hadn't. Willi fired at one of them. Then he rolled away from Baatz and into the bushes. Once the shooting started, you wanted as much cover as you could find.

Awful Arno fired at the *poilus,* too. He was a decent combat soldier; even Willi, who'd despised him for a year now, would have admitted as much. He headed for something that might be cover, too. Off to the left, a German MG-34 started sawing away. A small smile crossed Willi's face. He loved machine guns—his own side's machine guns, anyhow. They were the best guarantee a poor ordinary ground pounder had that he'd go on pounding ground a while longer.

The MG-34 didn't just knock over enemy soldiers. It made them concentrate on it, so they forgot all about Willi and Baatz. He got a clean shot at a fellow crawling along in a khaki greatcoat. The fancy Mauser thumped his shoulder. The *poilu* doubled up. *Sorry, buddy,* Willi thought, *but you would have done the same thing to me.*

They held the French in place till the late afternoon. By then, Willi had a well-positioned, well-protected foxhole—but no sheep carcass to keep him company, dammit. Even so, he was ready to stay a while, but a runner came up to order the line back half a kilometer. The Germans withdrew under cover of darkness.

Willi and Arno Baatz almost tripped over each other. They exchanged glares. *"Grofaz,"* Willi said again, defiantly. If the *Führer* was so fucking smart, how come they were going backwards? Pretty soon, even Awful Arno would start wondering about things like that. Wouldn't he?

Chapter 23

Sailors threw lines from the U-30 to the men waiting on the pier. The other ratings caught the ropes and made the U-boat fast. "All engines stop," Julius Lemp called through the speaking tube.

"All engines stopped," the reply came back, and the diesels' throb died into silence.

Lemp sighed. Especially since the *Schnorkel* had come to let the diesels run almost all the time, that throb had soaked into his bones. Doing without it felt strange, unnatural, wrong. He sighed again. "Wilhelmshaven," he said to no one in particular. "Home port."

"Sounds good to me," Gerhart Beilharz declared.

"Well, sure it does," Lemp said. "You won't have to wear your iron pot all the time."

"No, and I'll probably clonk myself a couple of times when I don't have it on," the tall engineering officer answered. "Too goddamn many doorways aren't made for people my size, and sometimes I forget to duck."

"That is a bad habit for a U-boat officer," Lemp said with mock severity.

"I'll try to unlearn it." Beilharz stretched. The space right under the conning toward was the only one in the boat where he could do that without clouting somebody. "Be good to get my feet on dry land again, even if it'll feel like it's rolling under me for a little while."

"They'll probably pin an Iron Cross First Class on you for the snort," Lemp told him. "It did us some good, no two ways about it."

"I'm glad you think so, Skipper. I know you had your doubts when the technicians installed it."

That was putting things mildly. Lemp didn't feel like rehashing it, though. All he said was, "We've earned some time ashore."

As the sailors trooped off the U-boat, a commander nodded to Lemp and said, "Admiral Dönitz's compliments, and he would like to speak with you at your convenience. If you would care to come with me . . ."

At your convenience plainly meant *right this minute*. And if Lemp didn't care to go with the commander, he damn well would anyway. Two unsmiling sailors with rifles and helmets behind the officer made that obvious. "I am at the admiral's service, of course," Lemp replied, which meant just what it said.

Dönitz sat behind a broad desk piled high with papers. He had a broad face that tapered to a narrow, pointed chin. But for a thin beak of a nose, his features were rather flat.

"Well, how do you like the *Schnorkel*?" he asked without preamble.

"Sir, it's more useful than I thought it would be," Lemp answered. "It's given less trouble than I expected from an experimental gadget, too. And Beilharz does a fine job of keeping it healthy. He's a good officer."

"He didn't fracture his skull inside the boat?" Dönitz inquired with a smile. Lemp blinked. Did the admiral keep every junior lieutenant in his mental card file? Maybe he did, by God.

"A couple of flesh wounds. Nothing worse," Lemp said after a beat.

"That's good. And it's good you sank a Royal Navy destroyer. We're going to win the Scandinavian campaign, even if England and France haven't quite figured that out yet," the admiral in charge of U-boats said.

"I'm glad to hear it, sir. I know we've hurt the Royal Navy badly."

"Yes, mostly with U-boats and land-based aircraft, though the big ships did get that one carrier," Dönitz said. "They've hurt our surface forces, too, and we have less to spare than they do. But we dominate the waters in the eastern North Sea, and that's the point." His telephone rang. "Excuse me." He picked it up. "Dönitz here."

Someone gabbled excitedly in his ear. Lemp was astonished to see his jaw drop. Dönitz was for the most part an imperturbable man. Not today.

"What?" he barked. "Are you sure? . . . What is the situation in Berlin? . . . Are you sure of *that*? . . . Well, you'd better be. Call me the minute you have more information." He slammed the handset into its cradle.

"What's up, sir?" Lemp asked. "Anything I need to know about?"

Dönitz took a deep breath. *He's going to tell me to get lost,* Lemp thought. What the devil *was* going on? But the admiral didn't do that—not quite. "Maybe you and your men should stick close to barracks for the next couple of days," he said.

"Sir, we just got in after a cruise," Lemp protested. "The boys deserve the chance to blow off some steam. It's not as if—" He broke off.

"As if you'd sunk the *Athenia* again?" Dönitz finished for him. Lemp gave back a miserable nod. That was what had been in his mind, all right. Admiral Dönitz went on, "No, this isn't your fault. But they should do it anyhow, for their own safety. Things may get . . . ugly." He seemed to pick the word with malice aforethought.

"Can you tell me what's going on?" Lemp asked.

"Only that it's political," Dönitz replied. "Listen to the radio. You'll probably piece things together—as well as anyone can right now. Oh, and don't be surprised if you find the barracks under guard."

That raised more questions than it answered. Lemp chose the one that looked most important: "Political, sir? What do you mean, political?"

"What I said." Dönitz seemed to lose patience with him all at once. "You are dismissed." Lemp saluted and got out. He hadn't closed the door before the admiral grabbed for the telephone again.

The commander was waiting in Dönitz's anteroom. "What's up?" he asked when he got a look at Lemp's face.

"Ask your boss . . . sir," Lemp said. The commander looked impatient. As best he could, Lemp recounted what had gone on after the phone rang.

"*Der Herr Jesus!*" the other officer said after he'd finished. "Something's gone into the shitter, all right. You'd better do what the admiral suggested. Things are liable to get nasty in a hurry."

If he didn't know what was going on, he had his suspicions. "What do you mean?" Lemp inquired.

"Just sit tight. I hope I'm wrong," the commander said, which only frustrated Lemp more. Instead of giving him any answers he could actually use, the other officer hurried into Dönitz's sanctum.

"Why don't you do what Commander Tannenwald says, sir?" one of the armed ratings said. Now Lemp had a name to go with the face. The fellow with the *Stahlhelm* and the Mauser should have had no business giving him orders. His muscle, and his friend's, and their weapons, were very persuasive. The two of them escorted Lemp back to his crew.

A few minutes after he got to the barracks, rifle shots and a short burst from a machine gun rang out not nearly far enough away. "What the hell is going on?" Peter demanded. No one answered. No one could—no one else knew, either. The helmsman turned on the radio in the barracks hall. Syrupy music poured out of it. That was no help.

When the tune ended, the announcer said, "Remain obedient to duly constituted authority." Then he played another record.

"What's *that* supposed to mean?" Lemp asked. He got no more answer than Peter had.

More gunfire came from the edge of the naval base. The lights outside the barracks hall suddenly went out. One of the guards stuck in his head and said, "The watchword is '*Heil Hitler!*' Remember it." He shut the door before anybody could ask him any questions. Lemp wasn't sure what to ask anyway. And if people were running around with guns, the wrong question was liable to have a permanent answer.

Lieutenant Beilharz took him aside and spoke in a low voice: "Skipper, I think some kind of coup is going on. What do we do?"

The same unwelcome thought had crossed Lemp's mind. "What *can* we do? Go back to the U-30 and start shooting things up with the deck gun? We don't even know which side is which. Best thing is to sit tight and wait to see what happens. Or have you got a better idea?"

"Well . . ." What wasn't Beilharz saying? What were his politics? What did he think Lemp's were? Terrible for a fighting man to need to worry about things like that. The engineering officer sighed and nodded. "*Ja,* that's probably best. What else is there?"

"Nothing that won't put us in worse hot water," Lemp answered, and they were in plenty. A bullet shattered a window and buried itself in the opposite wall.

"Douse the lights! Get down!" Peter sang out. Somebody hit the switch. The hall plunged into blackness. Thumps and shuffling noises said quite a few men were hitting the deck anyhow. Lemp only wished he knew who was shooting at whom, and why. *Wish for the moon while you're at it,* he thought as he flattened out himself.

WHEREVER PEGGY DRUCE WENT in Stockholm, she kept looking over her shoulder. Would Nazi soldiers suddenly come out of the woodwork like field-gray cockroaches, the way they had in Copenhagen? Germany loudly insisted she had no aggressive designs on Sweden. Of course, she'd said the same thing about Denmark and Norway. If she did end up invading, she would swear on a stack of Bibles that she'd been provoked. An oath like that was worth its weight in gold.

If you listened to the magazines and radio reports coming out of occupied Denmark, all the Danes were happy as could be with their Aryan brothers from *Deutschland.* If you listened to the people who'd got out of Denmark just ahead of the *Gestapo,* you heard a different story.

You could hear both sides in Sweden. You could pick up both Radio Berlin and the BBC. Papers printed reports from the Nazis and from the Western Allies (mostly in Swedish translation, which did Peggy no good, but even so . . .). You could buy the *International Herald-Tribune* and *Signal,* the Germans' slick new propaganda magazine. The Swedes took such liberty for granted. Well, so had the Danes. Sweden didn't know how well off it was, or so it seemed to Peggy.

Still, Stockholm wasn't too bad. London or Paris (or Brest or Bordeaux) would have been even better. Peggy soon discovered, though, that the German major in Copenhagen had been right: she couldn't get there from here. Planes weren't flying. Ships weren't sailing. The Germans were driving English, French, and Norwegian forces up the long, skinny nation to the west, but Scandinavia and the North Sea did indeed remain a war zone.

She was so desperate to get out of Europe, she even visited the Soviet embassy to see if she could reverse Columbus and get to the west by heading east. None of the Russians at the embassy would admit to following English, but several spoke French or German. Peggy preferred French for all kinds of reasons. Once they saw she understood it, so did the Russians.

"Yes, Mrs. Druce, we can arrange an entry visa for you," one of their diplomatic secretaries said. "We can arrange passage to Moscow. There should be no difficulty in that. Once in Moscow, you may travel on the Trans-Siberian Railway as far east as, I believe, Lake Baikal. We would gladly ticket you through to Vladivostok, you understand, but the Japanese have a different view of the situation."

"Aw, shit," Peggy said in English. Just so the Russian official wouldn't feel left out, she added, *"Merde alors!"* Sure as hell, Columbus had got it right: the world was round. And a skirmish on the far side of the immense Eurasian land mass could screw up her travel hopes just as thoroughly as the one right next door. It not only could—it had.

"You have my sympathy, for whatever it may be worth to you," the Russian said.

"Thanks," Peggy answered, and left. His sympathy was worth just as much as the Germans' nonaggression pledge . . . and not a nickel more.

If you had to get stuck somewhere, plenty of places were worse than Stockholm. The weather was getting chilly, but Peggy didn't worry about any winter this side of Moscow's. There was plenty of food, as there had been in Copenhagen till the Nazis marched in. Plenty to drink, too—she needed that. The town was extraordinarily clean, and more than pretty enough. A lot of the buildings were centuries older than any she could have seen in America. For contrast, the town hall was an amazing modern building; the locals couldn't have been prouder of it. The south tower leaped 450 feet into the sky, and was topped by the three crowns the Swedes also used as the emblem on their warplanes.

Plenty of those flew over Stockholm. Maybe the Swedes were sending

Germany a message: if you jump us, we'll fight harder than the Norwegians. Or maybe they were whistling in the dark. They certainly seemed serious. Men in rather old-fashioned uniforms and odd helmets positioned antiaircraft guns on top of buildings and in parks and anywhere else that offered a wide field of fire.

Peggy figured out the placement for herself. She needed no one to explain it to her. And when she realized what was going on, she went out and got drunk. She'd seen too goddamn much of war. She was starting to understand how it worked, the way she could follow a baseball game back in the States.

She woke the next morning with a small drop-forging plant pounding away behind her eyes. Aspirins and coffee—real coffee, not horrible German ersatz!—dulled the ache without killing it. Instead of going out and acting touristy, she went back to her room and holed up with the *Herald-Trib.*

The war news in the paper was often several days old: it had to clear God knew how many censors, get to Paris, get printed, and get to Stockholm before she read it. She turned on the massive radio that sat in a corner of the room. She wanted fresher stories. If things in Norway calmed down—no matter who won—she was six hours by air from London. And if pigs had wings . . .

"BBC first," she said. The English sometimes stretched the truth in their broadcasts. They didn't jump up and down and dance on it the way Berlin did. Or she hadn't caught them at it, anyhow, which might not be the same thing.

It was a few minutes before the top of the hour. She put up with the music till the news came on. The Nazis, who hated jazz, wouldn't broadcast it. The English thought they could play it themselves, and insisted on trying. Most of the results argued against them.

Then the music went away, so she could stop sneering at the poor sap who imagined he could make a sax wail. Without preamble, the announcer said, "Reports of a *coup d'état* against Adolf Hitler continue to trickle out of Germany."

"Jesus H. Christ!" Peggy exploded.

"Military leaders, dissatisfied with the course the war has taken, are said to have attempted to overthrow the *Führer*," the suave, Oxford-inflected voice continued. "Whether the coup has succeeded is unknown outside the *Reich*, as are Hitler's whereabouts and fate. Nor does anyone but the disaffected generals as yet have the faintest notion of how, or whether, they will continue the war in the event they do succeed in overthrowing the German dictator."

"Son of a bitch!" Peggy added, in case her first exclamation hadn't been heartfelt enough.

"In the meanwhile, the fight continues," the BBC man continued. "Anglo-French forces have made new gains against the *Wehrmacht* north of Paris, while French sources indicate that their armies also continue their drive to the northeast that began east of the capital city. In the fighting in Poland, the two sides' claims and counterclaims appear irreconcilable. The situation there, accordingly, remains in doubt."

Peggy knew what that meant. The Russians were lying just as hard as the Germans and the Poles. "And they said it couldn't be done!" she said. She was mad at the Reds for losing their grip on Vladivostok. One more thing that conspired against her going home.

As if reading her thoughts, the newsreader went on, "Fighting in the Far East is similarly confused. The only things that can be stated with certainty are that the Trans-Siberian Railway remains cut in eastern Siberia, and that Vladivostok is still in Soviet hands. His Majesty's government has offered to mediate in this conflict, but the Empire of Japan unfortunately declined."

Of course England wanted to mediate. If the Russians weren't fighting Japan, they could throw their full weight against Germany. But London couldn't insist. How long would Hong Kong and Malaya last if Japan went to war against England? People said Singapore was the greatest fortress in the world, but people said all kinds of things that turned out not to be true.

Then there were the Dutch East Indies, which had to be upside down and inside out now that Germany had occupied Holland. And how much attention could France give to Indochina with a war right in her lap? England had excellent reasons for not wanting to antagonize the Japs. The only question was, would Japan head south regardless of what England did?

If Japan chose to jump that way, what would America do? There were the Philippines, way the hell out in the western Pacific. Could U.S. forces there make life difficult for the little yellow men? Peggy thought so. What was the point of holding on to land like that if you weren't going to use it?

"In British news, Prime Minister Chamberlain has named Winston Churchill the new Minister of War," the broadcaster said. "The P.M. praised Churchill's dedication and steadfastness. Churchill himself said, 'Let the Hun do his worst. We shall do our best, and God defend the right.' "

"Wow!" Peggy said. Chamberlain didn't talk like that—he talked like a greengrocer with too much education. If England had had somebody who talked like that from the minute Hitler started getting cute, maybe the war never would have got off the ground. She hoped it would go better now.

CABBAGE. Potatoes. Turnips. A little sour cheese. A Jewish supper in Münster: no damn good, and not enough, either. Sarah Goldman was ashamed of the way she gobbled up her portion. She knew how bad it was, but that didn't seem to matter. Her body demanded fuel. If poor fuel was all it could get, she'd make the most of that.

Her father got more than she did. He worked harder than she did, too. There wasn't much between his skin and his bones these days, but what there was was all gristle and tough, stringy muscle. He was somewhere between the best shape of his life and starvation.

He inhaled his supper. Afterwards, he rolled a cigarette from the tobacco in his pouch. It was tobacco scavenged from fag ends picked up on the street. Before the war, only poor people would have scrounged like that. Now the ones who did were mostly Jews, because the Nazis had cut off their tobacco rations.

Samuel Goldman didn't seem to mind. After a couple of puffs, he remarked, "My gang was fixing a bomb crater just fifty meters or so down the street from *Wehrkreis* headquarters this afternoon."

"And?" Sarah asked. He wouldn't have used a gambit like that for no reason—he had a story to tell.

"And part of me was wishing the bomb would have come down on the headquarters," he said. The recruiters there wouldn't let him and Saul join the *Wehrmacht*. They'd been embarrassed to refuse, but they'd done it, all right. No wonder he despised the place.

"Only part?" Hanna Goldman said.

Sarah's father nodded to her mother. "Yes, only part. Some of the fellows there, they're not so bad. They have to do what their bosses tell them, or else they get it themselves. The army's not as nasty as the Party—nowhere near."

"Well, all right," Sarah said. "So what happened while you were filling in this crater?" Not long before, she would have been humiliated beyond words at her father's doing such menial work. So would he—he was an academic to the tips of his toes. He took hard labor for granted these days. As with gravedigging in *Hamlet*, familiarity lent it a quality of easiness.

"We'd just about got things fixed when we heard motors coming up the street towards us—and toward *Wehrkreis* headquarters," Samuel answered.

That was enough to make Sarah sit up and take notice. Horses and donkeys—and sweating men—hauled goods through Münster's streets these days. Gasoline and motor oil went straight to the front. Except for ambulances, doctors' cars, and fire engines, the city might have fallen back into the nineteenth century. All of Germany might have.

"What were they?" Mother asked, as she was surely meant to do. "Was it connected to.... to the trouble on the radio?"

There was a safer way to talk about things than Sarah could have come up with. Any time the announcer told you to follow duly constituted authority, you started wondering what duly constituted authority was and why you should follow it. That was the opposite of what the announcer had in mind—but that was his worry, not yours.

Father nodded impressively. "You'd best believe it was. There were four trucks, and shepherding them along fore and aft were brand new half-tracked armored personnel carriers. Very nasty machines to be on the wrong end of." He spoke with a veteran's trained judgment.

"What did they do?" By the way Mother looked at her, Sarah got the question out first by no more than a split second.

"What did they do? I'll tell you what," Father said. "They stopped right in front of the recruiting headquarters, and SS men started jumping out of them and running inside."

"The *Gestapo*?" Mother's voice quavered. You didn't have to be a Jew in Germany to quaver at the thought of the secret police—although it sure didn't hurt.

But this time Samuel Goldman shook his head. "No. These fellows belonged to the *Waffen*-SS—the fighting part. Hitler's personal bodyguards, I guess you could call them. Much as I hate to say it, they were very impressive men." Again, he delivered the verdict with the air of a man who knew what he was talking about.

"There were regular soldiers at the headquarters, right? What did they do? Did they shoot these *Waffen*-SS men?" Sarah hoped the answer would be yes. She thought shooting was too good for the SS, but it would do in a pinch.

Her father shook his head again, though. "No. The SS took them by surprise. The regular soldiers never had a chance to fight. They don't keep many weapons at the headquarters, anyhow. The SS men stormed in with rifles and machine pistols. They came out again a few minutes later. Colonel Ziegler—the head of the *Wehrkreis*—came out with them, with his hands high. They seized a couple of his aides, too. They threw all of them into one of the personnel carriers, and then they drove away."

"What will they do with them? To them?" Mother asked.

"Nothing good." Father had smoked the hand-rolled cigarette down to a tiny butt. He stubbed it out and put the little bit of leftover tobacco back into the leather pouch. It wouldn't go to waste. Once he'd finished, he looked up again. "No, nothing good," he repeated. "You don't grab someone that way to pin the *Ritterkreuz* on him. Ziegler must have been involved in the plot against the *Führer*—or the SS must have thought he was."

"It doesn't seemed to have worked, does it?" Sarah said. Her father pointed to corners of the room. For a second, that meant nothing to her. Then she remembered the house still might have hidden microphones. If she talked about Hitler's overthrow, she shouldn't sound disappointed because it hadn't happened. She fluttered her fingers to show she got it.

When Samuel Goldman said, "I don't think so. We would have heard by now if it had," he sounded glad the *Führer* remained in power. Whether he was might be a different story, but he sounded that way.

Mother found a different question—or rather, the same one she'd asked before, but on a larger scale: "What will the Party do to the officers who violated their oath to strike at the *Führer*?"

"It won't be pretty." Again, Father spoke with what seemed like grim satisfaction. "To do such a thing in wartime . . ." He shook his head like a judge passing sentence. That really might have affronted him. His desire to be German sometimes showed in peculiar ways.

"Would the officers have tried to make peace?" Sarah wondered.

Her father's chuckle was desert-dry. "You might have done better to ask Colonel Ziegler. I have no idea whether those people wanted to end the war or to fight it better than the *Führer* was doing. It isn't likely to matter now."

"What did the other men in your labor gang think of—of what you saw?" Mother asked.

"Most of them were all for it. They're loyal Germans, after all." Yes, Father was speaking for the benefit of the microphones that might not be there. After a small pause, he went on, "But there were a couple who wanted to take their shovels and clout the SS men. They were behind me, so I couldn't see who they were."

That last sentence, surely, was also for the benefit of the hypothetical microphones. Sarah would have bet Father knew just who'd hooted the *Waffen*-SS. She also would have bet more than a couple of laborers wanted to go after the men in black with their shovels. Backing the Nazis was easy when Hitler led the *Reich* from one triumph to another. But when he took the country into a war that wasn't going so well, wouldn't the "*Sieg heil!*"s start to ring hollow?

She also wondered whether Father was smart to mention the carpers at all. If the *Gestapo* was listening, its minions were also liable to decide he knew more than he was letting on. That wouldn't be good—for him or for any of the Goldmans.

Sarah wasn't used to worrying that her father might have missed a trick. He didn't miss many, and she was sure she hadn't noticed most of the ones he had missed. But she'd noticed this one. Realizing your parents could make mistakes—realizing they were as human as anybody else—was part of growing up. All the same, it was a part she could have done without right now.

She didn't get a choice, not on things like that. Any Jew in Germany after the Nazis took over, young or old, could have given chapter and verse on not getting choices. You had to go on, and to hope you could go on going on.

VACLAV JEZEK HAD FORGOTTEN just how heavy his antitank rifle was. On the march, the damn thing was ponderous as hell. It wasn't as if he weren't lugging another tonne and a half of soldierly equipment. In the trenches, where the front wasn't moving and where he could set the piece down whenever he felt like it, it wasn't so bad. With the Allied armies advancing, he couldn't do that.

But he *was* advancing. That made the antitank rifle seem lighter—when he wasn't too tired, anyway. Advancing against the *Wehrmacht*! Ever since the Nazis invaded Czechoslovakia, he'd dreamt of the moment when he could do that. Now it was here.

It was here, and he was scared. The trenches were pretty safe, as far as war went. He was out in the open, vulnerable to bullets and fragments and potato-masher grenades and all the other tools German ingenuity had crafted for maiming other human beings. (And, if his luck went bad, French ingenuity could do him in, too.)

He didn't hurry. Everything he was carrying made sure he couldn't very well hurry, but he wouldn't have even if he could. The Germans might be falling back. They hadn't given up. They rarely did. They skirmished, yielded a few hundred meters, set up their mortars and machine guns, and skirmished some more. Vaclav had no doubt that they dealt out more casualties than they took.

Whenever one of their MG-34s started firing, he hit the dirt. He might have been a dog, salivating at the sound of a bell. But he wasn't the only one who did. The Germans who manned those vicious machine guns might have thought they worked even more slaughter than they did in truth. They didn't even have to point their weapon at a man to get him to fall over. But if they didn't, he was liable to get up again and go on trying to kill them.

"Yes, you just can't trust us, can you?" Sergeant Halévy said when Vaclav remarked on that as they sprawled in a shell hole. "We do keep fighting."

"Every now and then. When we can." Vaclav remembered his dreary weeks in the Polish internment camp. If he'd stayed there, he would have ended up a German prisoner of war after Marshal Smigly-Ridz jumped into bed with Hitler.

"Enough to make the German generals sick of us," Halévy said. "That's how it looks to me, anyhow."

"Too bad they didn't do what they set out to do," Vaclav answered. "Trust a German to do things right most of the time and fuck it up when it really matters."

"True. No Nazis in Paris," the Jew agreed.

"I didn't mean that."

"I know. It's still true, though."

A French tank clattered past them. Several soldiers trotted behind it almost in Indian file, using its steel bulk to shield them from the slings and arrows of outrageous MG-34s. As machine gunners often did, the one in front of them concentrated on the tank. Bullets spanged off the armor one after another. They chipped its camouflage paint but did it no other harm.

"That's a fool," Halévy said. "There—you see? The Germans can screw up the ordinary stuff, too."

"I only wish the cocksuckers would do it more often," Jezek answered.

No sooner were the words out of his mouth than a 37mm armor-piercing round from an antitank gun slammed into the French machine. That made the 13mm slugs Vaclav fired seemed door-knockers by comparison. The tank slewed to a stop, smoke and fire spurting from every hatch. Inside the doomed machine, ammunition started cooking off. Nobody got out.

That left the men who'd followed the tank in a horrible spot. If they pushed on, the machine-gun bullets that had hit armor plate would go after their soft flesh instead. If they stayed where they were, they might as well have been out of the fight. They were no more thrilled about taking chances than Vaclav would have been. They started digging foxholes behind the burning tank carcass.

"Some sergeant will come along in a while and make them get moving, poor saps," Benjamin Halévy said.

"You're a sergeant. What about you?" Vaclav asked.

"Nah." Halévy shook his head. "I saw why they're holing up. And I know that goddamn gun is waiting for them to show themselves. Some other sergeant who comes along in a couple of hours won't care. And by that time the machine gunners will be thinking about something else, so these guys should be able to go forward again."

"Huh," Vaclav said. "You better be careful, or people will start thinking you're a human being or something."

"Don't be dumber than you can help, Jezek. I'm a sergeant, and I'm a Jew. How can I be a human being with all that shit piled on my shoulders?"

"Sergeant's a problem, yeah. I didn't say anything about you being a Jew," Vaclav answered uncomfortably.

"No, but you were thinking it," Halévy said without rancor, putting a finger on why the Czech felt uncomfortable. "If it weren't for the fucking Nazis, you wouldn't want anything to do with me."

"Of course I wouldn't. You *are* a sergeant," Vaclav said, which made Benjamin Halévy laugh. But it wasn't as if the Jew were lying. Back before Vaclav got drafted, he'd had little use for Jews. Czechs didn't despise them as thoroughly as, say, Poles did, but all the same . . . Even after he got drafted, he'd preferred Jews to Slovaks or Ruthenians only because they were more likely to stay loyal to Prague and fight the Germans.

"Well, you're a corporal yourself," Halévy said.

"A Czech corporal in France! That's worth a lot," Jezek returned.

He still couldn't get a rise out of the Jew. "If Czechoslovakia hadn't gone to pieces, you'd be a sergeant for sure. They aren't exactly equipped to promote people here."

"If I hadn't got out, I'd be a dead man by now, or else wounded, or sitting in a POW camp somewhere—I was just thinking about that a minute ago," Vaclav said. "And those all sound better than being a goddamn sergeant. What do you think of that?"

"I felt the same way till they promoted me," Halévy answered easily. "Now I see that sergeants are the salt of the earth. It's the officers who're silly clots."

"Shows what you know." Vaclav dug a grubby pack of cigarettes out of his pocket. Benjamin Halévy looked hopeful. The Czech gave him one. It wasn't as if he hadn't bummed butts from the Jew.

After a while, Vaclav cautiously peered over the lip of the shell hole. There in the distance, between a couple of tree trunks . . . Was that the painted shield on the Germans' antitank gun? Something—no, somebody—moved behind it. Yes, the son of a bitch wore *Feldgrau*. Grunting, Vaclav heaved his heavy piece up onto the dirt lip. He flipped off the safety and stared down the sights. The Nazi had crouched down again. Maybe Vaclav could put a round through the shield; it wasn't made to stop anything more than ordinary ammo. But he might get a better target if he waited.

And he did. The German stood up and looked out through field glasses to try to spot the trouble heading his way. The worst troubles, though, were the ones you didn't see. Vaclav exhaled slowly to steady himself. He pulled the trigger. The antitank rifle slammed his shoulder. The German threw his hands in the air and fell over.

Vaclav worked the bolt as fast as he could, chambering a fresh round. As he'd guessed, another German jumped up to find out what had happened to his buddy. Vaclav fired again. The second Fritz's head exploded into red mist.

"Two?" Halévy asked.

"Two," Vaclav agreed. "One dead for sure. The other I don't know about." Any hit from the antitank rifle might kill. Rubbing, he added, "They ought to requisition me a new shoulder, too."

"Talk to the French quartermasters," the Jew said.

"Fuck 'em," Jezek replied with great sincerity. "Maybe the Germans have a supply dump in Laon. If we can chase 'em out of there, I'll go through it and see."

"If we can chase them out of Laon, we really are doing something," Halévy said. "They took it early on. Maybe we can push on up to the coast and cut them off."

"Maybe we'll get out of this shell hole in a while," Vaclav said. "One goddamn thing at a time." Halévy nodded and scrounged another smoke.

Chapter 24

Theo Hossbach hadn't had much to do with Lieutenant Colonel Koch. A radio operator who was happiest by himself didn't hobnob with a regimental commander. Theo wouldn't have hobnobbed with his crewmates if he could have helped it. But he'd never heard anything bad about Koch. The officer was supposed to be brave. He didn't punish his troops because he enjoyed punishing people. Men who knew about such things said he had a good tactical sense. Theo hadn't seen anything to make him disbelieve it.

None of that did Koch any good now. He stood blindfolded, tied to a post in front of a stone wall in a Polish town. Along with quite a few other panzer crews, Theo and Adi Stoss and Hermann Witt had been summoned to see what happened to officers who dared go against the German government.

A *Waffen*-SS captain—they had their own silly name for the rank, but it amounted to captain—spoke in a loud voice: "This man is guilty of treason against the *Reich* and against our beloved *Führer*, Adolf Hitler.

For treason in wartime, there is only one sentence—the supreme penalty."

He turned to his own men: a dozen more asphalt soldiers. They all carried rifles. When he looked at them, they stiffened to attention.

Maybe they didn't realize it, but the watching panzer crewmen packed a lot more close-range firepower than they did. Lugers, Schmeissers . . . The SS men could wind up dead before they knew it. None of the *Wehrmacht* troops in black coveralls looked happy at what was going on in front of them. What would it take to turn dismay to mutiny?

Not much, not if Theo was any judge. A word from Koch would have done it. And what would have happened after that? War between the army and the SS? Theo would have been ready, even eager, for it. He knew he wasn't the only one, either—nowhere close. But it might also have been war between rebel and loyalist *Wehrmacht* units. He couldn't stomach that. And, while the Germans were bashing one another, what would the Red Army do? Stand around watching? Not likely!

"Raise your weapons!" the SS captain ordered. The firing squad obeyed. "Aim your weapons!" he said, and they did.

Lieutenant Colonel Koch did cry out then. Had he yelled *Save me!* or *Down with Hitler!*, the mutiny might have started then and there. But all he said, in a loud, clear voice, was, "Long live Germany!"

"Fire!" the SS man shouted. A dozen shots rang out as one. Koch slumped against his bonds. Blood darkened the front of his tunic. The sergeant who headed the riflemen went over to him and felt for a pulse. He must have found one, for he grimaced. "Finish him!" the SS captain snapped. The sergeant drew a pistol and shot Koch in the back of the head. That surely ended that. The SS captain looked out at the panzer troops. "You may bury him," he said, as if he were granting some large concession. By his lights, he probably was.

He and his men piled into a half-track and a truck and sped away. What other luckless officer was next on their list?

"Fuck," Adi Stoss said next to Theo. "I hope I never see anything like that again."

"Amen," Hermann Witt said. "He was a good soldier."

The sergeant who commanded another panzer in the platoon said, "You can't plot against the government, not in the middle of a war you can't."

"If he did that," Adi said, which made that sergeant's jaw drop. Theo thought it was a reasonable comment. The SS did things and chose victims for its reasons, which often made no sense to ordinary mortals.

"And even if he was a lousy politician, he was still a good officer," Witt added. "As far as I'm concerned, that counts for more, 'cause chances are it saved my ass—and yours—a few times."

"Huh," the other sergeant said, and walked away.

"Well, that's that. We just went on his list." Adi sounded cheerful about it.

"As long as we're fighting the Ivans, it doesn't matter." By contrast, Witt sounded like a man trying to convince himself.

"Here's hoping," Theo said. His crewmates eyed him in mild surprise, the way they did whenever he opened his mouth.

He never found out how the panzer men decided who would bury the regimental commander. But Koch got a much fancier grave than most German soldiers who met death at the front. And the large cross had *Fallen for the* Vaterland written on the horizontal bar in big black letters.

"If the SS goons see that, they'll pitch another shitfit," Adi predicted.

"Good," Theo said. They exchanged conspiratorial grins. Again, they could ruin each other with a few words whispered in the wrong ears. It wasn't the first time. It wouldn't be the last. They wouldn't have said such things if each didn't already have good reason to trust the other with his life.

Hermann Witt came up and looked at the grave, and at the inscription on the cross. "I got a letter from my father a few days ago," he said, after looking around to make sure no one but his crewmates could hear him. "He says some of the death notices in the paper go 'Fallen for *Führer* and *Vaterland*' and others just say 'Fallen for the *Vaterland*.' It's a way of letting people see how you feel about things, you know?"

"I'm surprised he talked death notices with you," Stoss remarked. "Doesn't he think it's bad luck or something?"

"Nah. He's a freethinker, my old man," the panzer commander said, not without pride. "The way things are these days, he has to keep his mouth shut more than he used to. I'm the one he can let loose with."

"As long as the army censors don't come down on him," Theo said. He liked Witt much better than Heinz Naumann. He didn't want anything bad to happen to him, or to his family.

"He's careful, the way he puts things. I know him, so I can read between the lines," Witt said. "The blockheads the army has reading mail, they don't know crap from cabbage."

"They may seem dumb a lot of the time, but they're smarter than you make them out to be," Stoss said.

"How do you know?" Witt retorted. "Next letter you get will be the first."

Adi shrugged. "My folks died in a train crash when I was little. My grandfather raised me, but he died a few years ago, too. The Stosses never were a big family. Now there's me."

"No girlfriend?" Witt asked slyly.

Another shrug. "I *had* one. She didn't feel like giving me what I wanted before I headed off to training, and I told her what I thought about that. Haven't heard from her since, the lousy bitch."

The panzer commander set a sympathetic hand on his shoulder. "Some of 'em are like that, and damn all you can do about it. If they didn't have pussies, there'd be a bounty on 'em. Ought to be a bounty on some of 'em any which way."

"Well, you can sing that in church," Adi said. Witt asked no more questions. He just looked at Lieutenant Colonel Koch's grave one more time, shook his head, and walked off.

Theo asked no questions, either. Questions of that kind weren't his style. He'd served with Adi a lot longer than the new commander had, and had also noticed that the driver never got any mail. Stoss didn't seem to miss it; it was as if he knew he wouldn't.

If he had no family, if he'd told his girlfriend to piss up a rope . . . Well, hell, didn't he have any friends? He was a good guy. Theo thought so, anyway. Didn't anyone else in the whole wide world? Didn't anyone else like him well enough to send him a note saying *I hope you're still in one piece?*

Evidently not.

But why not?

Several possibilities had occurred to Theo. He'd long since decided which one he thought most likely, and it had nothing to do with singing in church. If the blackshirts ever came to ask him about it, he'd also decided he would deny everything as hard and as long as he could. Of course he would. You didn't tell the blackshirts anything about your buddies, not if you could help it. But Theo would have kept his mouth shut absent that ironclad injunction. He had a keen sense of the absurd, even if he didn't let other people see it very often. A working sense of the absurd often came in handy in the Third *Reich*. And if his conclusion didn't fit in well with the general preposterousness of life, he was damned if he could imagine one that would!

SOMETIMES THE WORST THING you could do was imagine something. Sergeant Hideki Fujita discovered that painful truth for himself, as so many had before him. The idea of getting transferred to attack Vladivostok hadn't so much as crossed his mind till he and that other sergeant sat around chewing the fat and wasting time.

Once it got into his head, though, it wouldn't go away. It stayed there and stayed there, like an eyelash you couldn't rub out of your eye. Other units had been called away from the blocking position. It could happen to his regiment, too. When you were a soldier, anything that could happen could happen to you. It could, and sooner or later it probably would.

You didn't want to have thoughts like that. They meant that, if you kept at this trade long enough, you *would* stop a bullet, you *would* get ripped up by a shell fragment, you *would* get blasted into chunks of raw meat. How could you keep on soldiering if you kept worrying about such things?

How? Your own side would deal with you if you tried *not* to soldier, that was how. And if you found yourself in the middle of the trackless Siberian woods (well, not quite trackless—there was the railroad line that had sent the Japanese army blundering among the firs and spruces to begin with), your best chance—maybe your only chance—was to do your job like everybody else.

This was bad. Nobody in his right mind would have called it anything else. But soldiering had taught Fujita one thing, anyway: the difference between bad and worse was much bigger than the difference between good and better.

"My father fought at Port Arthur," Superior Private Hayashi said one afternoon. The squad huddled around a small, almost smokeless fire in the bottom of their trench. It wasn't snowing now, but it had been, and it looked as if it would start up again pretty soon, too. They had thick great-coats and fur-lined gloves and Russian-style felt boots (although the ones they took from dead Red Army men were even better), but that didn't mean the cold didn't seep into a man's bones. Fire and hot tea or soup were the best weapons against it.

Yet even fire and tea were powerless against the chill that seeped into a man's head. "Two of my uncles did," Fujita said. "They never liked to talk about it afterwards. I didn't understand that till I went into the army myself. You can't tell somebody what combat's like till he's done it himself—and after that he doesn't need to hear it from you."

"*Hai*, Sergeant-*san*." Shinjiro Hayashi nodded. Well, of course a superior private would agree with his sergeant. A sergeant would knock your block off if you were crazy enough to do anything else. But then Hayashi added, "That's very well put."

Fujita smiled before he realized he'd done it. When a smart kid said you'd said something well, of course you were tickled. Yes, he might be flattering you—he knew where his bowl of rice came from, all right. He'd found a good way to go about it, though. Fujita's voice lacked some of the growl he usually put into it speaking to inferiors when he said, "So what did your father tell you about Port Arthur?"

"He never talked about it much, either, not till just before I had to go in for basic training," Hayashi said. "Then he said he hoped I never ended up in a spot like that. He said the Russian artillery was bad—"

"That sure hasn't changed!" somebody else exclaimed. All the soldiers nodded. No matter what other mistakes the Russians made, their artillery was always trouble.

"And he said that our machine guns fired right over the heads of our men when they were attacking the Russian forts," Hayashi went on.

"*Right* over their heads. Sometimes our gunners would shoot our men in the back."

"It happens," Fujita said. "*Shigata ga nai.*" Life was hard to begin with. Soldiering was a hard part of life. If the generals decided killing some of the troops on their own side would help the rest take an objective, they'd do it without thinking twice. It was just part of the cost of doing business. He could understand that. A sergeant sometimes had to make those choices, too, if on a smaller scale.

"*Hai.* It does happen." Hayashi had seen enough to leave him no doubts on that score. "But, please excuse me, Sergeant-*san*—I don't want it to happen to me."

"Well, who does?" Fujita said. "Me, I aim to die at the age of a hundred and three, shot by an outraged husband."

The soldiers all laughed. Fujita couldn't remember where he'd heard that line before. Somewhere. It didn't matter. It was funny. When you heard something funny, of course you used it yourself and passed it along.

"*Eee,* I like that," a private said. "An outraged husband with a pretty young wife, *neh?*"

"Oh, yes," Fujita said. "What's the point to getting shot for screwing some ugly old woman, eh?"

No one saw any. As soldiers will, the men started talking about young women, pretty women, women they'd known, women they claimed they'd known, women they wished they'd known. Fujita told a little truth and more than a few lies. He figured the other soldiers were doing the same thing. Well, so what? Talk like that made the time go by. In their foxholes and trenches farther north, the Russians were probably telling the same stories.

As if to remind the Japanese that they hadn't gone away, Red Army gunners greeted the next day's dawn with an artillery barrage. Bombers flying above the ugly gray clouds dropped tonnes of explosives through them. They were bombing blind, and none of their presents fell anywhere close to the front. For all kinds of reasons, that didn't break Fujita's heart. He was in no danger himself. And the soft-living men who called themselves soldiers but never saw the trenches—the clerks and the cooks and the staff officers—got a taste of what war was like. He hoped they enjoyed it.

A couple of days after that, the regiment got pulled out of the line. The first place they went was to a delousing station. Like any Japanese, Fujita was glad to soak in almost unbearably hot water. He was even gladder the Russian bombers had missed the bathhouse. If the soap smelled powerfully of medicine, so what? Getting his clothes baked to kill lice and nits was less delightful, but he could put up with it.

Some of the soldiers thought they were going home. Some people could smell pig shit and think of pork cutlets. Fujita was willing—even eager—to be surprised, which didn't mean he expected it.

The men marched off to the west, toward the Ussuri River and the border with Manchukuo. The officers said nothing about where they were headed, or why. Maybe they didn't know, either. More likely, they didn't want the troops to find out till they couldn't do anything about it but complain.

A small flotilla of river steamers waited by the riverbank. They'd all seen better decades. Some of them looked as if they'd seen a better century. Sergeant Fujita's company and another filed aboard one of the riverboats. They filled it to overflowing. It waddled out into the stream and headed south. Fujita feared he knew what that meant . . . which, in the grand scheme of things, mattered not at all.

Spatters of snow chased the steamers. The clouds overhead remained thick and dark. For that, the sergeant thanked whatever weather *kami* ruled in these parts. Clear skies would have let Russian airplanes spot the steamers and shoot them up at their leisure. Each boat mounted a machine gun at the bow and another at the stern. From everything Fujita had seen, they wouldn't do a sen's worth of good in case of a real attack.

He said as much to Hayashi. The conscripted student looked back at him. "What difference does it make? If the Russians don't shoot us from the air now, they'll shoot us on the ground pretty soon."

"Maybe they won't," Fujita answered. You had to look on the bright side of things. That was about as far on the bright side as he could make himself look, though.

"*Hai. Honto.* Maybe they won't. Maybe our own machine gunners will do it for them, the way they did in my father's day." Hayashi had his share of cynicism, or maybe more than his share.

"Your father made it. So did my uncles," Fujita said. Again, just surviving seemed like optimism. The steamers lumbered south through the snow flurries.

PERONNE WAS A NORTHERN TOWN that had kept some of its brick-and-stone walls. German bombs and French artillery—or maybe it was the other way around—had done horrible things to them. Big chunks were bitten out of the church of St. Jean. Despite the chill of crisp fall days, the stench of death fouled the air.

In the French drive to the east, Luc Harcourt had seen—and smelled—a lot of towns and villages like this one. He smelled bad himself. He couldn't remember the last time he'd bathed. Joinville and Villehardouin were just as grimy and unshaven and odorous as he was. So were all the other *poilus* pushing the Fritzes back.

Joinville pointed to a parade of sorts going through the streets of Peronne. "By Jesus, there's something you don't see every day!"

"Too bad," Tiny Villehardouin added in his bad Breton-flavored French.

Luc Harcourt thought it was too bad, too. The locals were forcing a dozen or so young women to march along bare to the waist, their breasts bouncing at every step. Some had had their heads shaved. Others, more humiliatingly still, wore scalps half bare. One was very visibly pregnant.

People yelled at them as they went: "Whores!" "Cunts!" "Scumbags of the *Boches*!" Rotten vegetables flew through the air. No one seemed ready to cast the first stone, though.

"I bet this happened after we chased the Germans out the last time, too," Joinville said. The Gascon had his eye on one of the girls in particular. His chances were probably pretty good, too. If she'd sleep with a German, or a bunch of Germans, why wouldn't she sleep with a Frenchman?

"Not with the same broads, I bet," Luc said. Joinville laughed so hard, the Hotchkiss gun on his back almost fell off. Villehardouin, who was burdened with the tripod, fixed his crewmate's straps.

The rumble of aircraft engines swelling out of the east made Luc's head rise like that of a dog scenting danger. If those were Stukas, he wanted to find somewhere else to be, and in a hurry. Another country, by choice.

But this flight wasn't full of vulture-winged dive bombers. In fact, the flying machines looked like something left over from his father's war. They were biplanes with open cockpits. Antiaircraft guns opened up on them. Black puffs of smoke marked shell bursts. Some came quite close to the planes, but the old-fashioned, ungainly machines buzzed on.

Luc had trouble taking them seriously even when they swooped down on Peronne. But then, all of a sudden, it sounded as if God were firing giant machine guns up in the sky. The townsfolk suddenly lost interest in tormenting their wayward women. They ran, screaming. Luc wanted to do the same thing. Only the fear of losing his men's respect forever held him in place. "Hit the dirt!" he yelled, and suited action to word.

Both machine gun and tripod clanked as Joinville and Villehardouin followed suit. That fearsome *ratatat-tat* grew louder yet as the German biplanes neared. *They're doing it with their engines,* Luc realized. It was the same kind of trick as the sirens in a Stuka's landing gear. It was designed to make people afraid. And, as with most things German, it did what it was designed for. Did it ever!

The biplanes carried real machine guns: Luc saw them spitting fire. And bombs fell from under their wings: not the monsters Stukas could haul, the ones that pierced reinforced concrete and wrecked fortresses, but even so. . . . Luc rolled himself into a ball like a hedgehog. He only wished he had real spines.

Bullets sparked off brickwork and cobblestones. Bombs bounced him as if he were a basketball. A round clanged off metal somewhere much too close. And then the biplanes were gone—he hoped.

He needed a moment to take stock of himself. Both arms work? Check. Both legs? Check again. No holes? No blood? No pain? No and no and no. "Fuck me," he said. "I'm all right."

Then he looked around to see how his buddies were doing. Villehardouin seemed to be going through a checklist like the one he'd just used himself. The big Breton nodded and gave a thumbs-up. Joinville had taken off the Hotchkiss gun and was looking it over. "Look!" he said, pointing to a dent and a lead splash on one of the iron cooling fins at the base of the barrel. "It hit here and ricocheted. If it hadn't ricocheted, it would have gone into my back."

"Sometimes you'd rather be lucky than good." Luc took his water bottle off his belt. "Here. Have some of this."

"*Pinard?*" Joinville asked, taking the flask.

"Better—applejack," Luc said.

"Ah. *Merci, mon ami.*" The Gascon's throat worked. After a couple of swallows, he handed Villehardouin the bottle. The big man also took a knock. Then he gave the water bottle back to Luc. Luc drank, too, before he stowed it on his belt. He needed a little distilled courage, or at least an anesthetic.

Luc looked around again, this time for the soldiers who'd been hauling the Hotchkiss gun's ammunition. None of the bullets from the biplanes had hit the aluminum strips of cartridges, which was also lucky. They might have started going off like ammo inside a burning tank, which wouldn't have been healthy for anyone within a few hundred meters.

But one of the troopers was methodically bandaging his calf. Red soaked through the white cotton gauze. "How bad is it, Émile?" Luc asked.

"Hurts like a motherfucker, but I don't think it'll kill me," Émile answered. "Hell, if you get me a stick I bet I can walk on it."

"Chances are they'll send you home, then," Luc said.

"Not fucking likely—I grew up in Verdun," Émile said. The eastern town had held in the last war, but fallen in this one.

"Oh." Luc had forgotten that, if he ever knew it. "Well, they'll take you out of the line for a while, anyway."

"It'll do," Émile said. "I only wish to Christ they'd done it sooner."

Loud shouts came from around the corner. That was Sergeant Demange's voice. Of course he'd live through a strafing and a dive bombing. Luc didn't think anything could kill him. He'd probably never been born, but manufactured in some armaments plant during the last war. Maybe he had a serial number tattooed on his ass—or stamped into it.

Now he was trying to pull order out of chaos. He bawled for medics, for stretcher-bearers, for Peronne's firemen, for water, for anything else blasted houses and wounded people were likely to need. He might have restored something resembling calm, too, if the church of St. Jean hadn't chosen that moment to fall in on itself with a crash.

Shrieks from inside announced that people had sheltered there against the German biplanes. Sergeant Demange effortlessly shifted gears. "Come on!" he yelled to whoever might be listening. "Let get the sorry sons of bitches out!"

"Let's go," Luc told his men—or all of them except Joinville, who'd somehow disappeared after his slug of apple brandy. "We'll do what we can."

They followed him. He was proud of that. Till he'd got a corporal's stripes, no one had ever wanted to follow him. Maybe the rank helped make the man. He didn't feel like complaining any which way.

The church wasn't burning: a small thing on the scale of miracles, but Luc would take it. He flung aside stones and chunks of brickwork and tugged at beams. His hands were hard, but he tore them up anyhow. And the first woman he uncovered didn't need help: falling masonry had made sure she never would. He turned her over so he wouldn't have to look at what was left of her face.

He and the other soldiers—and some townsfolk—did pull several people out alive. That made him feel a little better. Joinville showed up about twenty minutes after he started heaving wreckage. "Where the hell were you?" Luc growled.

"I found that broad," the Gascon said with a lazy smile. "Never did it with nobody with no hair up top before. Didn't matter—she had plenty down below." He set to work as if he'd been there all along.

"*Merde!* I ought to kick your sorry ass!" Luc didn't know whether to laugh or to pound the soldiers's thick head with a brick.

He ended up laughing. *Life is too short for anything else.* Joinville's presence probably wouldn't have meant life for anyone who'd died. That being so, why resent him for tearing off a piece when he saw the chance? *Because I didn't get to, goddammit.* Yes, that one answered itself, didn't it? Luc bent to the task once more.

*　　*　　*

HANS-ULRICH RUDEL WATCHED the Hs-123s land one after another. The biplanes were as near obsolete as made no difference. But they could still carry the fight to the enemy, even if Stukas could do more and do it better.

Those Henschels could take it, too. One of them had a hole in the aluminum skin of the fuselage big enough to throw a cat through. It flew, and landed, as if it had just come off the assembly line. Rudel didn't like to think what that kind of hit would have done to his Ju-87. Nothing good—he was sure of that.

Groundcrew men pushed the biplanes toward revetments after they shut down their engines. Before long, the Henschels would fill all of them. Hans-Ulrich's squadron, and the Stukas the pilots flew, were heading east to teach the Red Russians a thing or two.

Sergeant Dieselhorst ambled up. "I was talking to one of the guys in the radio shack," he said. "Sounds like they gave that Peronne place a good pounding."

"All right by me," Rudel said. "But they can't carry cannon under their wings, you know—not a chance in the world."

"*Ja, ja.*" Dieselhorst nodded. "But the scuttlebutt is, the Ivans have more panzers than England and France put together."

"Well, if they do, we'll just have to make sure it doesn't last." Hans-Ulrich spoke with the confidence—with the arrogance—of youth. Dieselhorst, an older man, smiled and nodded and said not another word.

The Stukas flew off to the east two days later. The sun was rising in Hans-Ulrich's face when he rose from the airstrip in France and setting behind him when he put down on the smooth, grassy runway at Tempelhof, just outside of Berlin. He and Dieselhorst both eagerly hopped out of their Stuka; long flights were tough on the bladder.

Rudel was happier once he'd eased himself, but only for a little while. Then he noticed the armored cars crewed by *Waffen*-SS men near the edge of the airport. Their turrets were aimed at the just-arrived bombers. "What's that all about?" he asked.

"What do you think?" Sergeant Dieselhorst answered. "They don't want us to bomb up and go after the Chancellery."

"That's crazy!" Hans-Ulrich exclaimed. "We wouldn't do anything like that."

"They're kind of jumpy right now," Dieselhorst said dryly.

"You can't blame them, after . . . whatever happened here," Hans-Ulrich said. He didn't know the details of the plot against Hitler: only that it had failed. He was glad it had. Treason had brought down the *Reich* at the end of the last war, and now it was raising its ugly head again? If it was, it needed to be slapped down, and slapped down hard.

"We aren't going to do anything like that. They've already been through us once to make sure we don't." Dieselhorst looked around and lowered his voice before going on, "And they didn't need to do that."

"They thought they did. You can see why. If the *Führer* couldn't trust the generals right under his eye, how can the *Reich* trust anybody without checking him out real well?" Rudel said.

"Sir . . ." Dieselhorst hesitated again, much longer this time. He finally shook his head and started to turn away. "Oh, never mind."

"Spit it out," Hans-Ulrich told him.

"You'll spit in my eye if I do."

"By God, I won't." Rudel raised his right hand with index and middle fingers extended and slightly crooked, as if taking an oath in court. "We watch each other's backs. Always."

"Always? Well, I hope so." Sergeant Dieselhorst's jaw worked, as if he were chewing on that. After another hesitation, he picked his words with obvious care: "You know, sir, there's a difference between not fancying the *Führer* and being a traitor to the *Reich*."

"No there isn't!" Hans-Ulrich exclaimed.

Dieselhorst's chuckle held no mirth whatever. "I knew you'd say that. But a devil of a lot of people think there is. That's the biggest part of what this ruckus was all about."

"If you try to overthrow the *Führer* of the German *Reich* in wartime, what are you but a backstabber?" Rudel demanded, as stern and certain as his father was about the tenets of their faith. If he hadn't promised Dieselhorst . . . But he had, and his word was good.

"Some people would say, a German patriot," the sergeant replied. "I don't know that that's true. But I don't know that it isn't, either. What I do know is, there's usually more than one way to look at things."

"Not this time," Hans-Ulrich said.

"I knew you'd say that, too." Dieselhorst stepped well away from the Stuka to light a cigarette. "Well, we'll go on and hit the Reds a good lick. If you think I'm going to sing songs about how wonderful Stalin is, you're even crazier than I give you credit for . . . sir." He blew out a stream of smoke.

They slept in tents guarded by *Waffen*-SS men. When they got mush and doughy sausages and ersatz coffee the next morning, the fellow who served them wore the SS runes on his fatigue uniform. No one said much at breakfast. Even Hans-Ulrich was sure the mess-hall attendants who carried off the dirty dishes were listening.

Going back to the airplanes was a relief. Flying off toward the front in the east was a bigger one. At the front, things were simple. You knew who was a friend and who was a foe. Politics didn't get in the way—not so much, anyhow.

Before long, the communication from the ground came from men who spoke German with an odd accent, stressing the next-to-last syllable of every word whether they should have or not. "I'd say we're over Poland," Dieselhorst remarked through the speaking tube.

"I'd say you're right," Hans-Ulrich answered. A flight of gull-winged monoplane fighters badged with the Polish red and white four-square checkerboard paced the Stukas, escorting them through an ally's airspace. That Poland was an ally most Germans disliked almost as much as the Soviet enemy didn't matter . . . for the moment.

Hans-Ulrich eyed the fighters with wary attention. He didn't think they were anywhere near so good as German Bf-109s. Of course, they wouldn't have to be anywhere near that good to make mincemeat of a Stuka squadron. But they just flew along, friendly as could be. One of the Polish pilots caught Rudel's eye and waved. Hans-Ulrich waved back. What else was he going to do?

He also kept a wary eye out for Russian fighters. The Reds had monoplanes and biplanes, both models with noticeably flat noses. German pilots who'd faced them in Spain said they weren't so good as Messer-schmitts, either. Again, though, they didn't need to be to shoot him down. How did they stack up against these Polish planes? He didn't know, and hoped he wouldn't have to find out.

A couple of antiaircraft guns fired on the Stukas when they flew over Warsaw. Colonel Steinbrenner screamed at the Poles over the radio. The firing abruptly cut off. It hadn't hit anybody. What that said about Polish air defenses . . . It sure didn't say anything good.

They landed at an airstrip about forty kilometers east of the capital. When Hans-Ulrich got out of his Ju-87, artillery was grumbling in the middle distance. Well, it wasn't as if he hadn't heard the same thing plenty of times in the Low Countries and France. He wasn't used to hearing it come out of the east, though.

And he wasn't used to the scenery, either. The land looked almost as flat as if it had been ironed. A cold wind that had a long start did its best to blow right through him. He was glad for his fur-and-leather flying suit. Off in the distance, a shabby village looked like something out of the seventeenth century, at least to his jaundiced eye.

To Sergeant Dieselhorst's, too. "Jesus, what a dump!" the noncom said.

"Now that you mention it, yes," Hans-Ulrich said.

"Don't let the Poles hear you talk like that, or they'll smash your face for you," a groundcrew man advised. "They think we're on their side, not the other way around."

That made Hans-Ulrich laugh out loud. "And the flea thinks the dog is his horse, too," he said scornfully. "We've got our soldiers and our planes here, and we aren't going to leave until *we're* good and ready." If the Poles didn't like that, it was their hard luck. They were only Poles, after all.

Chapter 25

No one had ever claimed Wales was a place where you went to enjoy the weather. There were good and cogent reasons why no one had ever said such a damnfool thing. Alistair Walsh had seen plenty of bad weather there, and even more in his army service. All the same, he'd never imagined anything like winter in central Norway.

The wind howled like a wolf. Snow blew as near horizontal as made no difference. He had a wool balaclava under his tin hat and a sheepskin coat a herder had pressed on him that was far warmer than his British-issue greatcoat. He wore greatcoat and sheepskin one on top of the other, and two pairs of mittens on his hands. He was cold anyway.

A British captain who was stumbling north with him said something. Whatever it was, that vicious wind blew it away. "Sorry, sir?" Walsh shouted back.

"I said"—the captain put his mouth as close to Walsh's ear as a lover might—"I *said*, without the bloody Gulf Stream, this country wouldn't be habitable at all."

Walsh considered that. "Who says it is, sir?"

"Ha!" The officer nodded. "Makes you understand why the Vikings went pirating so often, what?"

"Damned if it doesn't," Walsh agreed. "Even Scotland looks good next to this, and by God I never thought I'd say that in this life." The country up in the north there was bleak as could be, but this outdid it.

After nodding again, the captain said, "No fucking Germans in Scotland, either."

"Right." Walsh wished there were no Germans in Norway, either. Unfortunately, wishing didn't make them go away. They weren't nearly far enough behind the retreating Allies. German mountain troops had snowshoes and skis, and moved much faster than poor ordinary buggers stumbling up these indifferent roads.

Oh, the Norwegians had ski troops, too, and a few French *chasseurs alpins* were also equipped for winter warfare. But most of the allied expeditionary force was plain old infantry. And the plain old infantry was in trouble.

"One good thing," the captain bawled into Walsh's none too shell-like ear.

"What's that, sir?" Walsh answered. "It's one more than I've come up with."

"With the weather so beastly, the *Luftwaffe* can't get off the ground."

"Mm. There is that," Walsh said. "We can get shot and shelled, but the blighters won't bomb us for a while."

"Of course, our own planes are also grounded."

"Yes, sir," Walsh replied, and said not another word. The *Luftwaffe* ruled the skies in Norway and above the seas west of it. The RAF, along with a few French planes and what little was left of the Norwegian air force, did what it could against the Germans, but it wasn't enough. Stukas swooped, sirens screaming. Messerschmitts strafed almost as they pleased. The Fritzes' artillery spotting planes, the ones that could take off and land in next to nothing and hover in a headwind like a kestrel, flew here, there, and everywhere, showing the Nazis what to strike next. Clear weather favored the enemy. Well, there hadn't been much of it lately.

He trudged on. For all he could tell, the Germans were shelling them right now. The wind and snow cocooned him tightly. If the bastards didn't score a direct hit, he'd never know it. And if they did, he figured he'd end up in a warmer place than this. At the moment, eternal flame didn't seem half bad.

"Do you think they'll be able to pull us out, sir?" he asked.

"Maybe. If the bad weather holds and lets our ships into Namsos," the captain answered. He studied Walsh. The veteran noncom wondered why; neither of them showed more than his eyes. "What about you, Sergeant? I daresay you have more experience in these matters than I do."

Walsh only shrugged. "I may be older than you are, sir, but I've never been in anything like this."

"Last bugger who was in anything like this was Scott, and look what happened to him." The captain laughed harshly. "No, there was bloody Amundsen, too, and he was a Norwegian himself. He must have felt right at home at the South Pole, eh?"

"Wouldn't surprise me one bit." Walsh turned away from the wailing wind, cupped his hands, and lit a cigarette. Some people could strike a match in any weather, no matter how dreadful. The harsh smoke—he'd taken a packet of Gitanes off a dead Frenchman—gave him something to think about besides the blizzard.

"If only the German generals had given Hitler the boot," the captain said.

"If ifs and buts were candied nuts, we'd all have a bloody good Christmas," Walsh answered. "D'you really suppose they would have stopped the war? They're Fritzes, too, remember. I've never known those sons of bitches to pack it in while they can still fight."

"Something to that, I shouldn't wonder," the captain said. He brought up a mittened hand to the brim of his helmet. "Some sort of checkpoint up ahead."

"Maybe they'll tell us which way Namsos is." Walsh wasn't a hundred percent sure he'd been going north. He'd been steering more by the wind than by anything else: that and flocking with his friends. If they were wrong, so was he. Sheep liked to flock together.

"Maybe they will," the captain said as he and Walsh neared the crossroads. A squad's worth of men stood there—vague shapes through the flying snow. The officer let out a formidable bellow: "I say! Which way to Namsos?"

They didn't answer (or if they did, Walsh couldn't hear them, which was at least as likely). The staff sergeant clumped on. He and the captain were almost close enough to spit on the waiting soldiers when the other man shouted his question once more.

They heard him this time. One of them answered, "For you it does not matter."

"What do you mean, it doesn't matter?" the captain said indignantly.

"Sir—" Walsh grabbed his arm. "Sir, he's got a Schmeisser!" One German submachine gun wouldn't have meant much—he carried a Schmeisser himself. But . . . "They've *all* got Schmeissers!"

"You are our prisoners, gentlemen," the German said in excellent English. "Drop your weapons and raise your hands. Try nothing foolish. It would be the last mistake you ever made—you may be sure of that."

Some of the men with them started laying their rifles on the snowy ground. Walsh didn't know what made him take off and run. Stupidity, odds were. But there were a few soldiers between him and the *Boches*, and the sheepskin coat was a dirty white that might camouflage him in the swirling snow. Maybe they wouldn't even notice he was missing.

The captain ran with him. Misery loving company? Whatever it was, it queered the deal. The Fritzes shouted. Shouting was bad enough. Then they started shooting, and that was a lot worse. But sure as hell, they couldn't exactly see what they were shooting at. Some of the flying bullets came pretty close to Walsh, but he'd had plenty of nearer misses. And Schmeissers, wonderful as they were in close-in combat, weren't the least bit accurate out past a couple of hundred yards.

They could run after him. He risked a look back over his shoulder. They were running after him, as a matter of fact. It wasn't as if he didn't leave a big, juicy trail in the snow. But if he could get to the pine woods a bit more than a quarter of a mile away before he got shot or tackled, they'd have a lot more trouble catching up to him.

That captain—Walsh wasn't even sure of his name—was running on a different line. If the Germans wanted to grab both of them, they'd have to split up. They might not like that. Maybe the Allied soldiers were leading them into an ambush.

Maybe there weren't any more Allied soldiers for miles and miles. That was what Walsh feared most. In that case, he was running for nothing. He might end up freezing to death for nothing, too. Was England worth it? His feet must have thought so, or they never would have taken off.

As he panted toward the pines, he damned all his years and damned all his cigarettes—except he wanted another Gitane. Well, that would have to wait. Couldn't those young, fit Nazi privates outrun an old reprobate like him? Evidently not, because he got into the woods ahead of them.

It was like being in among all the Christmas trees in the world—little ones, big ones, enormous ones. Even the smell was right. He yanked his Schmeisser off his shoulder and put a couple of Mills bombs in the sheepskin coat's right-hand pocket. Now he could fight if he had to. He wasn't just a target the Germans hadn't been able to knock down.

Which way was north? He hadn't been sure before, and now he'd got all turned around. It would be a hell of a note if he blundered straight back to the Fritzes, wouldn't it? They didn't seem eager to come into the woods after him. Nor could he blame them. A man might get hurt trying something like that. Capturing troops who didn't even realize you were on the other side was a hell of a lot easier.

"Fuck 'em all," he muttered, and his breath smoked around him even though he hadn't pulled that next Gitane out of its packet. He thought north was *that* way. If he turned out to be wrong, well, he'd given it his best shot. The Germans might be taking Norway, but they hadn't taken him. Yet.

CHAIM WEINBERG HAD A NEW SACRED TEXT from which to preach. "Thieves fall out," he told the Nationalist prisoners in the park in Madrid. "The Germans are fighting among themselves. Some of them can see that Hitler is only leading them into disaster. And if that is true for Germany, isn't it even more true for Spain?"

He got somber looks from the POWs. German efficiency was a watchword in Spain, especially among the Nationalists. If the gangsters who lined up behind Hitler could go for each other's throats, what about the goons who said they were for Sanjurjo? What would they do if they saw a better deal in going out on their own? It was something for everybody to think about, not just a bunch of hapless prisoners. It seemed that way to Chaim, anyhow.

Because it seemed that way to him, he said so to anyone who would listen. He had discovered his inner missionary while haranguing the POWs. What he hadn't discovered was how to make his inner missionary shut up.

He got into arguments in line for meals. He got into arguments in *cantinas,* and on street corners. He got into fights, too. He won more often than he lost. Few people who hadn't been to the front wasted less time fighting clean than he did. After he left a couple of loudmouthed Spaniards groaning on *cantina* floors—and after he discouraged their friends with a foot-long bayonet held in an underhand grip that warned he knew just what to do with it (which he did)—the arguments stayed verbal. He got a name for himself: *eso narigón loco*—that crazy kike. He wore it with pride.

Of course, by running his mouth he also set himself up for Party discipline. He'd faced Party discipline in the States. They told you to quit doing whatever you were doing that they didn't like. Either you did or you dropped out of the Party.

Party discipline in Spain was a different business. They told you to quit doing whatever you were doing that they didn't like. Either you did or they threw your sorry ass into a Spanish jail or a punishment company or they said to hell with it and shot you.

Chaim wasn't altogether surprised when a scared-looking runner summoned him to appear before a Party organizer and explain himself. He wasn't altogether thrilled, either, which was putting it mildly. But what choice did he have? He could try going over to the Nationalists, assuming they or the Republicans didn't shoot him while he was trying to desert. But that would have gagged a vulture. He certainly couldn't stomach it himself.

And so he reported to the organizer. She had her office in a beat-up building (the most common kind in embattled Madrid) that had housed government bureaucrats before the Spanish civil war got going. That she was a she he'd inferred from the *nom de guerre* the runner gave him: *La Martellita,* the Little Hammer (with feminine article and ending). That was a good name—Molotov meant *son of a hammer,* too.

Sure as the devil, she wasn't very big. He'd expected that. He hadn't expected her to be drop-dead gorgeous, but she was: blue-black hair, flashing dark eyes, cheekbones, a Spanish blade of a nose, and the most kissable mouth he'd ever seen. That she looked at him as if he were a donkey turd in the gutter somehow only made her more beautiful. He had no idea how come, but it did.

"Well, Comrade, why are you throwing around such bad ideology?" she snapped, her voice cold as the North Pole.

"I did it so I could meet you," Chaim answered. Not for the first time in his life, his mouth ran several lengths ahead of his brain. "People said you were very pretty, and they were right."

"If you think you can flatter me, you had better think again," La Martellita said, in tones not a tenth of a degree warmer than they were before. "You will only end up digging a deeper hole for yourself—maybe one deep enough to bury you in." She sounded as if she looked forward to shoveling dirt over him. Odds were she did.

"I have a question for you," Chaim said.

"Yes?" she asked ominously.

"What's your real name?"

"None of your business."

"That's a funny name," he said. Her nostrils flared, and not with pleasure. He sighed. "Okay. Um, *bueno.* I have another question for you."

"If you keep wasting my time, you'll regret it."

"I believe you," he said . . . regretfully. "Why is it such a sin to say the Fascists have contradictions of their own, and that we ought to do everything we can to take advantage of them?"

"Because you are only a soldier," she answered. "Higher-level policy is none of your business—none, do you hear me? For all you know, for all I know, for all anyone knows, we *are* trying to exploit those contradictions. But soldiers have no business proposing policy."

"I'm not just a soldier," he said. "I'm a propagandist, too, trying to bring Nationalist soldiers over to the Republic. If I can't talk politics with them, I can't do my job."

"Did you get your views approved before you presented them?" La Martellita asked.

"Uh—no," Chaim admitted. He was a Communist, a loyal Communist. But he was also an American. He was used to doing things on his own hook and worrying about consequences later. Well, here it was, later, and here were the consequences. If this stunner in shapeless denim coveralls— a crime, that!—wanted him shot, shot he damn well would be.

She looked through him. "And why not?"

"It didn't seem necessary," he answered feebly.

"That was very stupid," La Martellita said.

"I thought every man was free to be anything he wanted, even stupid, under the Republic." Chaim threw out the line like a chess player offering a poisoned pawn.

And she took it: "Every man may be stupid under the Republic, Comrade, but you abuse the privilege."

"Didn't Trotsky say something like that?" Chaim knew perfectly well Trotsky had. His voice was pure innocence all the same. If you accused somebody of quoting the Red Antichrist, you needed to sound innocent.

La Martellita's eyes flashed again, terribly. She looked as if she hated him. No doubt she did. But now he had a hold on her. Even if they were dragging him off to the nearest wall, he had a chance of getting her stood up against it right after him. She took out a pack of cigarettes, lit one, and smoked in quick, furious puffs. She didn't offer it to him.

She stubbed hers out while it was only half done—a rare thing in Spain these days. When she spoke again, she came straight to the point: "What do you want from me?" She knew what she'd done. Oh, yes.

"A little understanding would be nice," Chaim said.

"What do you mean, 'understanding'? If you think I'll be your mattress or suck your stupid cock, I'd sooner cut my throat." She sure as hell did come straight to the point.

"No, no, no," Chaim said, thinking *Yes, yes, yes!* He went on, "I was talking about politics. I didn't mean any harm when I said what I said, any more than you did just now. I don't think I should get in trouble for it."

"Oh. Politics." The way La Martellita said the word, it sounded more obscene than cocksucking. She drummed her fingers on the rickety little table she used for a desk. "Can you try not to talk about your own so loudly when you're not reeducating the Nationalists?"

It was like getting sent out of the confessional with a penance of three Our Fathers and five Hail Marys. "I'll try," Chaim said. He didn't even have to promise to do it.

"All right. Get the fuck out of here." La Martellita wanted to pretend she'd never had anything to do with him.

"Tell me your name first."

He would sooner have faced Nationalist artillery than her glare. "Magdalena," she spat. "*Now* get the fuck out of here."

"See you again, I hope," Chaim said.

"That makes one of us," she said, and for once he quit while he was ahead and got out.

PETE MCGILL STOOD SENTRY OUTSIDE the American consulate in Shanghai. Because he wore two stripes on his left sleeve, he commanded the two-man detachment out there. He could have done without the honor. Shanghai was a good bit south of Peking. You couldn't have proved it by him, not this freezing early December morning.

"Fuck, it's cold," he muttered.

"Bet your ass," Max Weinstein agreed. They both spoke with barely moving lips. No one more than a few feet away would have had any idea they were talking. They were there to look impressive, and they did that. Like convicts, they managed to go back and forth without letting the outside world notice.

There wasn't much outside world *to* notice. Shanghai wasn't used to this kind of godawful weather. Hardly anybody was on the streets. The people who had to go out bundled up in all the clothes they owned. A lot of them seemed to be wearing two or three people's worth, and to be freezing even so. Inside his thick wool coat and tunic and trousers, Pete felt himself slowly turning into a block of ice.

"Liable to be fires in the Chinese part of town," he said. That was something over ninety percent of Shanghai, but he didn't think of it that way. "They'll throw anything that burns onto the brazier."

"Sure they will. And they live in those crappy little houses that go up like billy-be-damned, too," Max answered. "They're the exploited ones."

Sighing out fog, Pete said, "Don't get all Red on me, man. I was just saying it was something we need to be on the lookout for."

"Yeah, yeah. I was saying why we needed to be on the lookout for it. Don't you think why counts?" Weinstein said.

"What I think is, a Commie Marine's as crazy as a fish with fur or a general with sense," Pete said. "You take orders from guys like me, not from Stalin."

"Yeah, yeah," Max said again. "Don't remind me."

"Somebody better." Talking out of the side of his mouth, Pete felt like a movie gangster. But if a sergeant or an officer came out to check on the sentries, he wouldn't be seen moving his lips. "Why'd you join the Corps if you're a fuckin' Red?"

"On account of I like banging heads, an' they'd jug me if I did it back in the States," Max answered. "I thought about going to Spain instead. Sometimes it still looks like I shoulda done that. Wonder how many Fascists I woulda shot by now."

"They shoot back," Pete said dryly. "Besides, you're liable to get your chance against the Japs."

"Ain't like they don't deserve it, too. But I'd rather shoot Nazis any day," Max said.

"Gee, how come?" Pete asked.

Weinstein gave him a sidelong dirty look. "Two guesses, asshole, and the first one don't count."

"That's Corporal Asshole to you." Pete had given Max grief first. If the other Marine came back with something snappy, he couldn't very well resent it. Oh, he could, but then he'd really be an asshole.

"Funny guy. Funny like a truss," Max said.

Before McGill could answer, something blew up a couple of blocks away. Pete was on the ground before he knew how he'd got there: not knocked over by the blast but automatically hitting the deck. He'd brought his Springfield to his shoulder and had a round in the chamber and his finger on the trigger, ready for . . . well, for anything. Marine training and drill were wondrous things.

Weinstein sprawled a few feet away, as ready as Pete was. "The fuck?" he said.

"Yeah, I—" Pete got interrupted again. Another blast went off, and then another and another. "Son of a bitch!" he said. "I think they're trying to blow Shanghai up."

"Who's 'they'?" Max asked through several more booms, some almost as close as the first, others much farther off.

It was a good question. As far as Pete could see, it had only one possible answer: "Gotta be the Chinks. If this doesn't drive the Japs squirrely, what's going to?" More bombs went off as he spoke. No airplanes buzzed overhead; guerrillas inside the city must have planted the explosives. They'd get better results from bombs aimed right at the occupiers than they would have if the ordnance fell thousands of feet from a speeding plane.

They got the results they wanted, all right. Pete and Max had hardly climbed to their feet before Shanghai started bubbling like a pot with the lid on too tight. Chinese and Westerners came running out to see what the hell was going on. The American consul, a pink, double-chinned Rotarian named Bradley Worthington III, a worthy whom Pete had seen only two or three times before, came out for a look around. "Wow! That was something, wasn't it?" he said in Midwestern accents.

"Yes, sir," Pete said. He noticed Max's trousers were out at the knee from his dive to the pavement. If the consul said anything about it, Pete would have to gig the other sentry. Then Max would find ways to make him sorry, even if the Red Jew was only a private.

But Worthington wasn't going to get excited about pants with holes. He had bigger things to worry about. "The Japanese will turn this place inside out and upside down to catch the terrorists who just did that," he predicted.

"Yes, sir," McGill repeated, in a different tone of voice. He'd always assumed anyone plump, prosperous, and Midwestern was unlikely to have two brain cells to rub together. But Bradley Worthington III had just come up with the same conclusion he had himself. If that didn't make the consul a clever fellow, what would?

Shooting broke out a couple of minutes later. Max cocked his head to one side, listening. He was supposed to hold his stiff brace, but the times were irregular. "Arisakas—most of 'em, anyway," he said.

"Yeah. They are," Pete agreed.

"Not wasting any time, are they?" the consul said.

"No, sir," Pete answered. Suddenly, painfully, he hoped Vera was okay. The Chinese shouldn't have had much reason to target the joint where she danced and slept, but he knew he was going to worry any which way till he heard from her. How long till his relief came? He figured he'd go check on her as soon as he could.

Then a fire engine tore past, red lights blinking and bells clanging. More noise said ambulances were hauling casualties to hospitals. *Please, God,* went through Pete's mind. *Don't let anything bad happen to her. Please.*

A platoon of Japanese soldiers went by at a quick march. The lieutenant in charge of them shot the American consulate a look full of vitriol. Because it hadn't been bombed? That was how it seemed to Pete. One of the ordinary Japs started to aim his rifle at Worthington. A noncom yelled at him, and he didn't follow through. The platoon rounded the corner and disappeared.

Pete decided going to check on Vera might not be such a hot idea after all. If the Japs could think about firing at the consul on the steps of his own building, what would they do to a Marine they caught running around by his lonesome? Nothing good—Pete was sure of that.

Rifle fire crackled, almost close enough to make him dive for cover. Bradley Worthington III started to do the same thing, and checked himself at about the same time. That was interesting. Had the consul gone Over There in 1918? Pete wouldn't have been surprised.

"This could get very bad," Worthington said. As if to underscore the words, a machine gun went off in the distance: a long, somber stutter of death. McGill wondered whom the Japs were shooting at. He wondered if they knew—or if they cared.

"Bad? This could be another Nanking," Max said.

"Christ! I hope not!" Pete said, and the U.S. consul nodded. When the Japs took Nanking, they went blue-goose loony. Most of the stories that came back from there were too outrageous to seem possible. Which proved exactly nothing, because some of the worst stories had photos to back them up. You wouldn't think people could do such things to other people, let alone have fun while they were doing it, but that was what the photos seemed to show.

Another machine gun started up, this one closer. The gunner was an old pro, squeezing out one murderous burp after another. Pete could hear screams, too. Again, who were the targets? Some of the Chinese who'd planted bombs, or poor luckless devils who happened to have wound up in front of the gun?

A pause. Another short burst, and then one more. Pete didn't *know* who the gunner's targets were, but he knew too well what he guessed.

THEY GAVE JOAQUIN DELGADILLO his very own set of denim coveralls. His old uniform was so torn and tattered, it was almost falling off of him. Several Nationalist prisoners were already wearing the unofficial uniform of the Republic. He was glad of that; he wouldn't have wanted to be the first one.

He got razzed even so. "Gone over to the other side, have you?" said a middle-aged POW still in the Nationalists' yellowish khaki.

"I'm the same as I was yesterday," Joaquin answered. "Only the clothes are different."

"The same as you were yesterday?" the older man returned. "Well, how were you then, by God?"

"Why, the same as I am today, *claro*," Delgadillo said. The other POW laughed and let him alone.

He was glad of that. He didn't know himself how he'd been yesterday, not in the way the older man meant. Everything spun round and round inside his head, making him wonder which way was up—or if any way was. He had all the things he'd believed since he was a kid. And he had Chaim Weinberg; the Jew threw grenades at those old certainties every time he opened his mouth.

If what Weinberg said was true, the Republic had been right all along. If what he said was true, the future lay in its hands. Things would be richer, freer, better than anything Marshal Sanjurjo could deliver.

If. But it was a big if. Joaquin had been fighting the Republic for a long time before he got captured. He'd been in the Republican trenches. He'd taken prisoners before he became one. The bastards on the other side— on this side—were at least as skinny, at least as sorry, as the fellows he'd fought alongside. They could claim to be the wave of the future, but their present looked pretty sorry.

Of course, so did what he'd been fighting for. What did landlords do? Why, they took. Factory owners? The same thing, no doubt about it. Priests? Them, too. Them more than any of the others, because what did they give back? Nothing you could eat, nothing you could wear, nothing you could *use*.

They give you heaven, or a chance for it. Everything that got pounded into him while he was growing up was still there. It hadn't gone away, even if the Jew—the Jew!—had done his best to exorcise it. But now it had company inside his head. New ideas and old warred in there like Republicans and Nationalists.

Yes, just like that, he thought unhappily.

Plainly, the Republic wasn't the tool of Satan he'd thought it was before the trench raid that went south. As plainly, more things were wrong with the Nationalist regime than he'd imagined. But did that make the Republic the new earthly paradise? If it did, how come he was still lousy?

"Free love!" called another Nationalist still in decrepit khaki, pointing to his overalls.

"Oh, piss off," Joaquin said, and his fellow prisoner chuckled. It was an article of faith among the Nationalists that all the women who favored the Republic would lie down for you if you snapped your fingers. Joaquin didn't know of anybody who'd had the chance to find out whether that was true, but he did know everybody on his old side believed it.

Which meant . . . what? Weinberg went on and on about how stupid it was to take anything on faith. Unless you had a reason to think this, that, or the other thing, why do it? He would ask that over and over, and nobody had a good answer for him.

Joaquin had had a question that gave the Jew pause, though: "Why do you think Stalin is so wonderful? Have you met him? Have you gone to Russia?"

"No," Weinberg said slowly. "But I have seen the bad things Hitler and Mussolini are doing. There's a saying in English. It goes, *The enemy of my enemy is my friend.* Hitler and Mussolini are the enemies of the workers and peasants. Stalin has to be their friend, then."

"We think Stalin is Spain's enemy," Joaquin said. "Where is Spain's gold? In Moscow, that's where. Stalin stole it."

"No, he didn't." Weinberg shook his head. "The Republic bought weapons from Russia. Nobody else would sell to us, but Stalin did."

Maybe that was true, maybe it wasn't. Joaquin realized he shouldn't argue. He believed some of what the guy who'd captured him came out with. If he tried to convince Weinberg and the other Reds on the far side of the barbed wire that he believed all of it, maybe they'd turn him loose. Once he was on the far side of the wire himself . . .

Well, what then? Would they hand him a rifle and send him to a trench somewhere to fight against the men for whom he'd formerly fought? If they did that, he might be better off staying right where he was. Some people *did* switch sides. About half of them fought harder for the side they chose themselves than for the one where they'd started. The rest were spies or worthless for some other reason. Sorting out who was who got . . . interesting.

Then again, it was also possible that a distant trench was a better place than a POW camp in the middle of Madrid. Nationalist bombers still visited the capital. Joaquin had cheered them on when they flew over the lines. He'd wanted the Republicans to get what was coming to them. Now there was a chance that some of what was coming to them would land on him instead.

Before, they'd unloaded on Madrid in broad daylight. They mostly came at night these days. The more modern fighters the Republic had got from France and England made day bombing too costly to try very often any more. Even coming by day, the bombers weren't very accurate; the craters pocking the park proved as much. Flying by night did nothing to improve their aim.

Pounding guns and wailing sirens woke Joaquin from a fitful sleep. It was cold. It had been bitterly cold lately—this was going to be a winter to remember, and in no fond way. The drone of engines overhead penetrated the rest of the din.

"Fuck 'em all," somebody in the big tent said, and promptly started snoring again.

Joaquin envied him without being able to imitate him. Too much racket, and too much in the way of nerves, too. Swearing under his breath, Joaquin went outside to watch the show.

The sky was black as a sergeant's heart. The stars seemed even farther off than usual—grudging little flecks of light. The blue ones might have been cut from ice; the red ones didn't feel warm, either.

Searchlights darted and probed. Antiaircraft tracers and bursts were beautiful, but they didn't make Joaquin think of celebrations, the way they usually did. He knew too well that this was war, and all the bright lights intended nothing but death.

A searchlight speared a three-engined bomber—an Italian plane—in its glare. Antiaircraft fire from half a dozen guns converged on the machine the gunners could see. The bomber twisted and jinked, writhing like a stepped-on bug. The searchlight hung on to it. Others also found the bomber. Fire licked along its right wing. It tumbled toward the ground.

Bombs whistled down. Not all the sirens that screamed belonged to the warning system. Some came from ambulances and fire engines. Joaquin wondered if he should jump into a trench. The POWs had dug them to try to stay alive through air raids. But the show in the sky held a horrid fascination. He didn't want to miss any of it.

He could have been smarter. He could have done a better job of gauging the screams of falling bombs. One went off close enough to knock him ass over teakettle. Fragments shouted and screamed past him. Once bitten, twice shy—he stayed flat as a run-over toad.

He did, anyhow, till he saw prisoners joyously running out through a big hole blasted in the wire. Then he scrambled to his feet and ran with them. No guards shouted warnings or opened fire. Had they been blown to hell? Or were they just cowering in their own foxholes, the way any men with a gram of sense would? Joaquin didn't care. As soon as he got out into Madrid in these overalls, he'd look like anybody else. And, thanks to Chaim Weinberg, he knew how to sound like a Republican, too. They'd never catch him once he got loose. Then he could . . .

What? he wondered. What could he do? Something. Anything! As long as he was doing it for himself, who cared? If somebody needed him to haul sacks of shit, he'd do that. He'd like it, too. He'd never been afraid of work. Nobody who grew up on a Spanish farm could possibly be afraid of work.

Another bomb whistled down. Joaquin flattened out again. This one was going to be even closer. Maybe he should have waited before he

Chapter 26

Snow. Wind. Cold. Gloom. Sergei Yaroslavsky took them for granted in wintertime. He could think of very few Russians who didn't—the lucky handful who lived on the Crimean coast, perhaps. The bad weather was settling in earlier than usual, but even ordinary winters were long and hard.

By contrast, Anastas Mouradian gave forth with a melodramatic shiver. "*Bozhemoi,* this weather's beastly," he said in his accented Russian. He swigged from a bottle of vodka and passed it to Sergei. Nobody would fly today: not the Red Air Force, not the Poles, not the *Luftwaffe.* Nobody. By all the signs, nobody would get off the ground any time soon, either.

"It's winter, Stas," Sergei answered. "You got out of Armenia a while ago now. You know what winters are like once you come north."

"Like hell. Like Dante's hell in the *Inferno,*" Mouradian said. "He put Satan in ice, not in fire."

"Either one would work, if I believed in God or Satan or hell." Mouradian tacked on the coda to keep the other officers sitting around there getting drunk because there was nothing more interesting to do from thinking him a believer. He wasn't, or not much of one. Believing in God and worshiping weren't illegal, but they wouldn't do your career any good.

Another bottle came by. Sergei swigged, then passed it on to Mouradian. The Armenian said, "What do you suppose the other ranks are doing now?"

Overhearing that, Colonel Borisov laughed raucously. Everybody'd put away a good deal by then. "Those motherfuckers? They're already under the table—you can bet your balls on it. When they settle in with the popskull, they don't dick around," the squadron commander said.

Maybe he'd poured down enough vodka to leave his tongue loose at both ends. Or maybe he was just using *mat* to tell the truth as he saw it. Either way, Yaroslavsky thought he was bound to be right. "I hope Sergeant Kuchkov doesn't get into a brawl," Sergei said. The liquor was making him fussily precise instead of careless and sloppy.

Even Mouradian smiled at the way he spoke. "The Chimp will do whatever he does," he said. "He proves Darwin was right—if we still have ape-men among us, we must have come from them a long time ago."

Kuchkov's reputation had spread through the whole squadron. "Better not let him hear you talk like that," a pilot warned. "He'd tear your head off and piss in the hole. He'd be sorry afterwards, but—"

"So would I," Mouradian broke in, and got a laugh.

"You bet you would be," the other officer said. "Wouldn't do you a kopek's worth of good, though."

One more drunken truth. "He's still a good man to have in the bomb bay," Sergei said.

"Sure he is," the other fellow agreed. "He's got more muscles in his cock than most guys have in their leg." That was an exaggeration. Sergei thought so, anyhow.

Colonel Borisov looked at his wristwatch. That made several other people, Sergei among them, do the same thing. It was three or four minutes before the top of the hour. Borisov stood up. A moment later, he involuntarily sat down again. Swearing, he tried again. He swayed this time, but stayed on his feet. Proud as a sozzled peacock, he shuffled over to the radio set and turned it on.

The tubes needed half a minute or so to warm up. When sound started coming out of the set, a children's chorus was singing of the glories of Marx, Lenin, and Stalin. Listening, Sergei suddenly understood how a fly had to feel while it was drowning in a saucer of sugar syrup. His face showed none of that. Even drunk, he had no trouble hiding what he thought. Few Soviet citizens had that kind of trouble; most of the surviving ones who did were in a gulag these days.

Mercifully, the chorus ended. An announcer spent a minute urging his listeners to buy war bonds. "Work like Stakhanovites, save like Stakhanovites!" he boomed. Then he too shut up and went away. Sergei wondered how many exhortations like that he'd heard. Thousands. It had to be thousands. And the radio was a new invention, too. He remembered the first time he'd ever listened to one. He'd been sure it was magic. What else could it be?

"Moscow speaking," a familiar voice said. You could set your watch by the hourly news bulletins. Sergei had, plenty of times. If he tried it now, he'd make a hash of it. Enough antifreeze coursed through his veins to make that a certainty.

"Moscow speaking," the newsreader repeated. "Fierce fighting continues east of Warsaw. Fascist claims to have driven the heroes of the Red Army back in headlong retreat are, of course, nothing but the usual lies that spew like vomit from the Hitlerite and Smigly-Ridz regimes. Advances by the forces of progress, however, have proved less rapid than our beloved General Secretary, Comrade Stalin, would have preferred. Changes in the command structure of Red Army units fighting in Poland are expected to improve matters in short order."

Someone whistled softly. Sergei didn't see who it was, but he shared the sentiment. How many generals who hadn't advanced fast enough to suit Stalin were advancing on Siberia right this minute? How many had died of 9mm heart failure? When you shot a man in the back of the head, his heart *did* stop beating. "Heart failure" made for a nice, neat death certificate.

"English, French, and Norwegian forces continue to retreat in Norway," the newsreader continued. "We must resign ourselves to the fact that the capitalist and imperialist forces cannot be relied upon to check the Nazis, and that another country is vanishing down the Hitlerite maw. If Norway falls, it will bring the German cannibals dangerously close to the Soviet Union's northwestern border—only a thin slice of Finnish territory separates Norway from the USSR. And Finland, under the reactionary rule of Marshal Mannerheim, cannot be relied upon the remain neutral."

What did that mean? Was Stalin thinking about taking Finland himself before the Nazis could? If he was, would he get away with it? The Soviet Union had had a tougher time in Poland than anyone expected. How tough were the Finns? Sergei had no idea, and wasn't eager to gain a first-hand education on the subject.

"In the Far East, fighting continues against the Japanese imperialists," the newsman said, and not another word on that score. The bald announcement could mean only one thing: the fighting wasn't going well for the Soviet Union.

Sergei had wondered if the squadron would be detached from the fighting in Poland and sent across the USSR to bomb the Japanese invaders. Since it hadn't happened yet, he doubted it would for a while: not till spring, at the earliest. Days of decent flying weather were so scarce in this season, it might be faster to disassemble the SB-2s and ship them and their crews by train, then put the machines back together again.

The trouble with that was, the planes couldn't go far enough by rail. Barring a miracle, Vladivostok would fall. And Marxist-Leninist doctrine had no room for miracles. *Too bad,* Sergei thought. The Motherland could really use one over there.

"On another front, Japan's intolerable aggression and oppression have reaped what the historical dialectic would predict," the newsreader continued. "Chinese guerrilla strikes against the brutal enemy continue in Shanghai, Peking, and other centers occupied by the invaders. Anything that damages Japan on one front cannot help but damage her on all fronts."

He was right . . . Sergei supposed. He also sounded like someone whistling in the dark to try to show he wasn't afraid. If Japan were fighting the United States in the Pacific, that might draw off enough energy to weaken her against the USSR. Chinese guerrillas weren't a big enough cause to create the same effect.

But the United States remained neutral. If Japan beat the USSR, that would be all right with the Americans. And if the Soviet Union finally beat Japan, that would be all right, too. Why not? Either way, each country would hurt the other badly, and the USA would end up facing a weakened foe.

The newsreader started bragging about aluminum production, hydroelectric plants, and kilometers of copper wire. Sergei stopped listening. Industrial output was important, but he couldn't do anything about it. The vodka bottle came round once more. He damn well could do something about that. He could, and he did. The bottle felt noticeably lighter when he passed it again. Outside, the wind raved on.

CHRISTMAS WAS COMING AGAIN. Peggy Druce hadn't expected to spend one holiday season away from Herb, let alone two. She couldn't do anything about that. Before this latest trip to Europe, she'd always thought she was too important, or at least too clever, for anything bad to happen to her.

She knew better now. When the world went to hell around you, you discovered you weren't fireproof after all, no matter what you'd thought before. *Well, I'm doing asbestos I can,* she thought, and smiled and flinched at the same time. Herb would make that kind of horrible pun at any excuse or none.

Making it here wouldn't do her any good. A lot of Swedes, maybe even most of them, knew some English. But they wouldn't get the wordplay—which might be just as well.

Still, this was better than the joyless Christmas and New Year's she'd spent in Berlin the year before. The lights were on—no blackouts in Sweden. Food wasn't rationed. People here wore better clothes, and they went around looking happier than the Germans had. Why not? Sweden wasn't in the war. She wouldn't be, either, unless the Nazis dragged her in.

The Swedes were ready to fight if Germany tried it. You saw plenty of men in uniform in Stockholm. Sweden had stronger industries than either Denmark or Norway. She bought planes and tanks from other countries, but also built her own. She made her own artillery, too. Peggy didn't suppose Sweden could actually lick Germany, but she'd let Hitler know he'd been in a fight.

Didn't he already have enough on his plate? He seemed likely to win in Norway, and Germany and Poland were doing all right against Russia. Peggy was sure Hitler would happily fight Stalin to the last drop of Polish blood.

But things weren't going so well for the Nazi supermen in the west. And that was the key front . . . wasn't it? When the war first broke out, she would have been certain it was (with the exception that the German attack on Marianske Lazne almost killed her, and what could be more important than that?). She wasn't so sure any more. One way or another, the Russians would have their say. Peggy was no Red—Herb would have bopped her over the head with something had she leaned that way—but she could look at a map and make sense of what she saw. There was an awful lot of Russia, and there were an awful lot of Russians. Sooner or later, that had to count . . . unless, of course, it didn't.

Only one way to tell: wait and see. Peggy had just reached that brilliant conclusion when a knock on the door to her hotel room chased it out of her head. She opened the door without the least hesitation: certainly with less than she would have shown in a hotel back in the States. Stockholm wasn't the kind of place where a burglar was likely to cosh you and make off with whatever he could carry.

"Yes?" she said, and then, *"Ja?"* The word was the same in Swedish as in German, but she tried to make it sound different. Jut because she could speak some German didn't mean she wanted to.

"Hello. My name is Gunnar Landquist," the man standing in the hallway said in almost perfect English. "I am a reporter from the *Handelstidningen,* in Göteborg." That was Sweden's second-largest city, right across the Kattegat from Denmark. Landquist was about her own age, tall, with brown hair going gray, very fair skin, and blue eyes.

"Isn't that the newspaper the Germans don't like?" she said.

"One of them," Landquist answered with a small-boy grin that made him look much younger. No, the Nazis weren't happy about freedom of the press, and the freer the press was to call them the SOBs they were, the less happy they got. The Swede went on, "You have seen of the war more than most civilians, or so my friends tell me. Our readers, I am sure, would be interested in the views of an intelligent American traveler."

"That's nice," Peggy said. "Where do you think you'll find one?"

The Swede blinked, then threw back his head and laughed. "Oh, it will be a pleasure to interview you!" he exclaimed. He was armed with a pencil and a spiral-bound notebook nearly identical to the ones reporters in the USA carried.

"I doubt it, but come on in anyway." Peggy stood aside so Landquist could. He laughed again. When he perched on a chair, Peggy sat on the edge of the bed. "Okay. What do you want to know?" she asked.

"How do you feel about the Germans and their war?" He poised pencil above paper, waiting.

Peggy was about to rip Hitler for all she was worth. Then she wondered what would happen if she did and German troops suddenly appeared in Stockholm, the way they had in Copenhagen. Nothing good, not to her—and not to Sweden, either. The Nazis had long memories when it came to slights: at least, to slights aimed at them.

And so she was more prudent than she might have been: "What I want to do most is get back to the United States. The German diplomats have done everything they could to give me a hand. Even Hitler himself cleared up some red tape for me once. But"—she gave Gunnar Landquist one of her crooked smiles—"they won't stop the shooting just to let me go back, darn it."

He scribbled. "You have been under attack by the Germans and by England and France, is it not so? Which is worse?"

Her smile grew more crooked yet. "The one that's going on right this minute is the worst attack ever. The one you lived through yesterday, you don't need to worry about any more."

"I see. Yes. That makes good sense." Landquist wrote some more.

"Sorry. I'll try not to let it happen again," Peggy said.

He blinked again. Peggy got the feeling he had to put it into Swedish inside his own head before he could realize it was meant for a joke. Once he figured it out, he didn't hold back. He had a big, booming guffaw that made you want to like him. "You are wicked!" he said, plainly meaning it for a compliment.

"Thank you," Peggy answered, deadpan, which produced another explosion of merriment from him.

"My, my," he said. "How am I to write a story when I am laughing so hard? Let me ask you a more serious question: with all the rationing she uses, how long can Germany go on fighting?"

That was serious, all right. Peggy gave it the best answer she could: "A long time, at least by what I saw. The food isn't so great, but there's enough of it. Nobody's going hungry. People can't get many new clothes, but they can manage with their old stuff. Most of what's new goes straight to the *Wehrmacht.* But I've heard there's rationing in England and France, too. You'd know better than I would, and more about how tight it is."

"I know it is there. Past that . . ." Landquist shrugged. "No one on either side seems happy to admit he has not got plenty of everything."

"You're bound to be right."

Landquist lit a cigarette: an American Chesterfield. Seeing Peggy's wistful stare, he offered her the pack. They hadn't been her brand back in the USA, but they came closer than any of the European blends she'd been smoking. She sighed with pleasure after he gave her a light. Then he said, "With the fighting to our west, not many more of these will come through."

"The war to the west is why I'm still here," Peggy answered, floating on clouds of tobacco-flavored nostalgia. "I mean, Sweden is a nice country and everything, but I'd still rather go home. I want to, but I can't."

"I am sorry." Unlike a lot of people who said that, Gunnar Landquist actually sounded as if he meant it. "If there were something I could do—"

That subjunctive was correct. Even so, most Americans would have said *If there was.* Sometimes you could tell foreigners because they spoke your language more accurately than you did.

"Since you cannot go, what will you do?" Landquist asked.

"Stay," Peggy said, which made him laugh yet again. She went on, "If I have to stay somewhere that isn't America, this is a nice place to be."

"I am glad to hear it. I shall write it down and quote you." Write it down he did. He tipped her a wink. "So you like us better than Germany, do you?"

"Oh, Lord, yes!" Peggy blurted. Gunnar Landquist wrote that down, too. Peggy wondered if she ought to ask him not to. If—no, when—the Germans read it, it would only piss them off. She'd been trying to avoid that, even in this interview. *Well, too goddamn bad this time,* she thought. It was nothing but the truth.

THEO HOSSBACH HADN'T MUCH ENJOYED spending a winter in the field in the Low Countries and France. By the way things were going, spending a winter in the field in Poland would be even less fun. He came from Breslau, not that far west of where he was now. Winters got pretty beastly there, too. Not so beastly as this, though. He didn't think so, anyhow.

Adi Stoss came from some lousy little town near Münster, way the hell over on the other side of Germany. He pissed and moaned about the cold and wind like you wouldn't believe. "This weather ought to be against the Geneva Convention," he said with an exaggerated shiver, huddling close to the fire the panzer crew had made of boards taken from a wrecked farmhouse. The peasant whose house it had been was in no position to complain; they'd found his body, and his wife's, and a little boy's, in the ruins.

"Screw the weather," Hermann Witt said. The panzer commander didn't get far from the fire, either, no matter what he said. He *wasn't* one of the people who could light a cigarette in any weather. Finally giving it up as a bad job, he went on, "What ought to be against the fucking Geneva Convention are the Russians."

A puff of fog escaped from Adi's mouth as he grunted. Theo made some kind of small noise, too, but the wind grabbed it and blew it away. Neither of his crewmates paid any attention. Chances were they wouldn't have even if they'd heard him. He didn't worry about that. It wasn't as if he *wanted* people paying attention to him, for God's sake.

Adi looked east. He pounded his mittened hands together to try to get some blood flowing in them. "You suppose it's true? What the damn foot soldiers were going on about, I mean?"

"That the Ivans cut the cocks off our guys in that patrol they caught? That they stuffed 'em in their mouths afterwards?" Gloomily, Witt nodded. "Yeah, I believe it. I went through basic with one of the guys who found 'em. I'm not saying Benno wouldn't tell a lie, but he wouldn't tell that kind of lie—know what I mean?"

"I only wish I didn't," the driver answered. He pounded his hands some more, staring down at the ground between his feet. When he looked up again, his face seemed ravaged and old. "Here's hoping our guys were dead before the Russkis went to work on 'em."

"Yeah. Here's hoping." Witt scowled. "If I thought they were going to do that to me, I'd shoot myself first."

"Christ, who wouldn't?" Stoss cupped his hands in front of his crotch. "Fun old war, ain't it?"

"Fun . . . *Aber natürlich.*" The corners of the sergeant's mouth turned down even farther. "How the hell are you supposed to fight against people who do that kind of shit? They *aren't* people, not really. Nothing but savages."

"How do you fight 'em? You kill 'em, that's how. And you make goddamn sure they don't take you alive." Adi slapped his hip. "I never let loose of my pistol these days."

"Makes sense to me." Witt turned to—turned on—Theo. "How about you, Hossbach?"

"Huh?" Theo said in surprise. A blush heated his face. He couldn't leave it there. A few more words came out: "Adi usually makes sense."

"Fat lot of good it does him, too," Witt said. "Sorry son of a bitch is stuck in Poland just like the rest of us."

"Oh, there are worse places," Adi said lightly.

"Yeah?" Witt challenged. "Name two."

"Dachau. Belsen." All at once, Stoss' tone wasn't light any more. The names came off his tongue flat and hard as paving stones.

He didn't just kill the conversation; he shot it right behind the ear. Witt got very busy—almost theatrically busy—heating meat-and-barley stew in his mess tin. The cooks coyly declined to tell their customers what kind of meat it was. That made Theo suspect it would whinny if you poked it with a fork. He'd eaten horsemeat in the field before. This had the same strong flavor and gluey texture. He didn't worry about it. A full belly beat an empty one any day of the week.

Like Adalbert Stoss, he preferred Poland to a concentration camp inside the *Reich.* That didn't mean bad things couldn't happen to you here. The Russians announced that they weren't shutting down for the Christmas season by shelling the hell out of the position the *Wehrmacht* and the Poles were holding. Shouts of *"Urra!"* and the rumble of enemy panzers coming forward said they weren't kidding around, either.

As soon as the first shells burst, all the German panzer crewmen raced for their machine. Theo slammed his hatch shut behind him. A moment later, fragments clanged off the Panzer II's hull. Theo gave the interior wall a happy pat. He pitied ground-pounders.

"Why aren't you starting this lousy cocksucker?" Witt shouted at Adi.

"What the fuck do you think I'm trying to do?" the driver shouted back. Behind Theo, the starter motor clicked and whined. The main engine didn't want to catch. "It's cold outside," Stoss added.

"Well, the Ivans sure as shit have theirs going," Witt said. That wasn't good news, which was putting it mildly. Sitting in a panzer that didn't want to move made Theo stop envying the infantry.

"Fine, Sarge," Adi said with what sounded like patience stretched very thin. "You can go jump in a Russian panzer, if that makes you happy." He didn't say *You can go jump in a lake,* but if Theo could hear the words hanging in the air the panzer commander was bound to be able to hear them, too.

"If you don't get us started, we'd better bail out, because one of those assholes is heading our way." Witt's patience was also pretty frayed. "We don't want to be here when he starts shooting."

"Right," Adi said tightly, and then, to the Panzer II, "Come on, you—!" He hadn't been in the army very long, but he cussed like a twenty-year veteran. The starter motor ground once more—and then, with a coughing roar, the main engine caught.

"There you go!" Witt yelled. "Get us moving! Make for those bushes. And for God's sake step on it!"

Adi must have stepped on it, because the Panzer II jumped forward. Theo couldn't see what was going on outside. How far away was the Russian panzer the commander'd been having a fit about? How soon before it opened up? The Ivans weren't great gunners, but a hit from anything bigger than a machine-gun round would hole this thin armor.

The Panzer II's little turret traversed. The 20mm gun fired three rounds in quick succession. These Russian panzers weren't so tough, either. Unlike this one, their cannon could fire useful high-explosive shells and give foot soldiers something new to worry about, but the 20mm could get through their armor as easily as they could penetrate a German machine's.

"Ha!" Witt said. "Nailed *that* fucker, anyhow. Now go forward. We'll see what kind of friends were keeping him company."

"Forward," Adi agreed.

Forward they went. Theo's inner ears and the seat of his coveralls would have told him so much, even absent the order. So would the radio traffic dinning in his earphones. Through the voice tube, he told Witt, "Scads of Ivans. This looks like a big push."

"Happy day," the panzer commander said, and then, "Thanks, Theo." He sounded grateful that Theo was talking at all, even to relay the tactical situation. That he did announced that he was getting to know his radioman pretty well. A moment later, he told Adi, "Put us behind that stone fence. We can give them plenty of grief from there."

"Will do," Stoss said. The panzer stopped a few seconds later, so he'd presumably done it. The turret traversed. The main armament fired several rounds. Witt's exultant whoop said one or two of them had done what he wanted. Then the coaxial machine gun chattered. Witt knew how to handle the MG-34: he squeezed off one short burst after another, giving the barrel time to cool between them.

More urgent shouts in Theo's earphones. He said, "Sergeant, we're ordered to pull back. They're breaking through."

"My ass they are!" Witt said indignantly. "I've wrecked two of their panzers and scared off the foot soldiers. And we've got enough infantry of our own—well, Poles, too—to keep them from flanking us out."

"We're ordered," Theo repeated. "They've already torn a hole in our position south of here. We've got to retreat so we can organize the counterattack."

"All right. I'll do it. I'm only a fucking sergeant—I have to follow orders." Witt couldn't have sounded more disgusted. He added, "I sure wouldn't want to be the dipshit officer who gave those orders, though. When the *Führer* finds out about it, that sorry sucker'll be lucky if he's still a corporal. Put it in reverse, Adi—somebody with embroidered shoulder straps has the vapors."

"I'm doing it," the panzer driver replied, and matched action to word. Theo knew what *he* thought of the *Führer*'s military judgment (among other things). He would have been very surprised if Adi Stoss didn't share his views: Adi probably had stronger reasons for such opinions than he did himself.

None of which would matter if the Ivans set this perambulating coffin on fire. As it did so often, the local got in the way of the general. Once they freed themselves from this mess, Theo could worry about other things. Once they did . . . If they did . . . He wished the damned panzer would go faster.

SARAH GOLDMAN HAD GOT USED to the *Gestapo* and the rest of the SS in Münster. Even when the blackshirts weren't harassing her or her family, she had a feel for how often she'd see them. They'd become a familiar if unwelcome part of the local fauna, like rats or cockroaches. The comparison wasn't hers: it came from her father in a low voice when they were both out on the street and away from any likely microphones. Once she heard it, she couldn't get it out of her mind; it fit too well.

When she started noticing far more SS uniforms than usual, alarm filled her. One possible—even probable—reason for a swarm of SS men was a pogrom.

To her surprise, Father didn't seem especially worried. "You may be right, of course," Samuel Goldman said, "but they already had more people than they needed if that's what they've got in mind. Importing more would be like running over a kitten with a panzer."

Checkpoints sprang up on every other street corner. "Your papers!" a blackshirt barked at Sarah, holding out his hand.

Gulping, she gave them to him. "Here—here you are."

He looked them over, then returned them. His lip curled; that seemed a job requirement when Sarah dealt with blackshirts. But she'd heard plenty of his colleagues who sounded nastier than he did when he asked, "You are a native of Münster? You have lived here your whole life?"

"Yes, that's right," she answered.

"All right, then. We don't expect trouble tonight from your kind. Pass on," the SS man said. He glowered at the gray-haired man behind her. "Your papers!"

Pass on Sarah did. She wanted to scratch her head. Only the fear that the SS men at the checkpoint would find the gesture suspicious made her hold back. She hurried home to help her mother peel potatoes and turnips . . . and to pass on the curious news.

"They could have given you a worse time, but they didn't?" Hanna Goldman sounded as if she had trouble believing her ears. Sarah understood that. If her mother had told her the same thing, she too would have had trouble believing it. After a long pause for thought, Mother went on, "I wonder what they're up to."

"Beats me," Sarah said. Noise from the usually quiet street in front of the house made them both stop peeling and hurry out to the living room to see what was going on. Teams of horses drew two enormous antiaircraft guns down the street. The men who served the guns followed in a horse-drawn wagon (but one with modern rubber tires, or it would have been much noisier). Like the fellows in charge of the gun teams, they wore SS black.

"Well, I don't know what's going on, either," Hanna Goldman said. "I wonder whether anyone does these days." That made more sense to Sarah than anything she'd heard outside the house lately.

When Father got home, he had no doubts. He seldom did. He wasn't always right, but he was almost always sure. "Somebody important must be making a speech tonight," he declared. "Göring? Goebbels? Hess? Any one of them is possible, but my money's on Hitler."

"Ah," Sarah said. She didn't *know* if he had things straight, but her money was that he did. His explanation cleared up why Münster was full of blackshirts: they were here to protect Somebody Important from the *Wehrmacht* . . . and, perhaps incidentally, from the British and French. She told her father about the antiaircraft guns and their SS crews.

He nodded. "Yes, that makes sense. If Somebody Important starts talking in Berlin or Dresden or Breslau, the Western democracies can't do anything about it—even if the Russians might. But here? Once they know a big *Bonz* is talking, they can put planes in the air and drop their bombs before he's finished." He gave her a lopsided grin. "That's what you get for letting your speeches run long. An abrupt way to edit, but no doubt sincere."

Sarah kissed him on his stubbly cheek. "You're quite mad," she said affectionately.

"Well, I do try." Father looked pleased with himself.

He turned on the radio. The music that poured out of it would have needed to be more interesting to sound boring. Sarah thought the orchestra must have been dripped in treacle. When the tune ended, an announcer spoke in awed tones: "Tonight, the *Führer* addresses the German *Volk* and the German *Reich* from Münster!"

Father looked even more pleased with himself, almost indecently so. He'd not only figured out what was going on, he'd had the timing down to a T. Even a clever man, which Samuel Goldman was, didn't get to seem so clever very often. Sarah imagined airmen in flight suits jumping into airplanes with roundels of blue-white-red or red-white-blue and roaring off into the night toward her home town.

Stormy applause greeted the *Führer*. She wondered where exactly he was. Did Nazi bigwigs fill the concert hall? Or was he speaking at the stadium? Sudden tears stung her eyes. Saul had played there. He'd won cheers for his skill, if not cheers like these. What good did it do him? She only hoped he was still alive.

"People of Germany!" That hot, familiar, hatefully exciting voice roared out of the radio. "People of Germany, I came here to tell you that the *Reich* can never be defeated!" More applause: waves of sound climbing up and falling back. Hitler went on, "Foreign foes cannot beat us! And neither can our own traitors! They tried their best to stab us in the back again, the way the Jews stabbed us at the end of the last war, but their best was not good enough."

Samuel Goldman made a rude noise. If the *Gestapo* did have a microphone hidden in the house, their technicians might take it for a burst of static. What they'd make of Sarah's giggle right afterwards . . .

Hitler, of course, wasn't finished. "We will hang the traitors!" he thundered. "We will hang them all, small and great together. For we have no right to hang the small ones while leaving the great ones fat and safe at home!" Oh, the listening Nazis cheered! Sarah wondered how they, or anyone, could take him seriously. Those savage sentiments mixed with that sticky-sweet Austrian accent!

"Year ago, the Socialists told me, 'Turn back, Adolf Hitler!' I was only a newly discharged veteran, a nobody, but I never turned back once," the *Führer* declared. "I never have. I never will. The *Reich* goes forward— forward to victory!"

"*Sieg heil!*" the Party faithful cried.

"*Sieg heil!*" Hitler echoed. "And we must go on to victory, for one year of Bolshevism would ruin Germany. The richest, most beautiful civilization in the history of the world would fall into madness and destruction. The Reds would spare nothing, not even our morals and our faith. And I tell you this, *Volk* of the *Reich:* I shall not spare their backers inside Germany, and I shall not spare the godless Jewish masters in Moscow!"

"*Sieg heil!*" the audience shouted again. "*Heil* Hitler!"

"There will be no peace in our country until we smash Bolshevism and treason of every kind," Hitler said. "I put my whole life into this struggle every day, and so must everyone who has joined me in it. I have attacked the traitors and murderers here. With my own hand I have shot them dead. And now the *Wehrmacht,* at last purified from the stupid struggles of internal politics, will show its thanks through devotion and loyalty and victory. For Germany is pledged to victory: to victory over our foolish Western foes, and to a final solution for the Bolshevik-Jewish Russian monster! We shall not falter. We shall not fail. Like St. George, we will slay the dragon, and he will never rise again!"

"*Sieg heil! Heil* Hitler!" the listening Nazis roared. Hitler thumped a fist down on the lectern to show he'd finished. They cheered and cheered.

Two and a half hours later, Münster's air-raid sirens wailed a warning. Flak guns bellowed. Bombs whistled down out of the heartless sky. Banned from any proper shelter, Sarah and her parents huddled under the dining-room table and hoped the house wouldn't come down on top of it.

"I knew they'd show up late." Her father might have been talking about a student who hadn't turned his paper in on time. "They might have nailed him if only they'd hustled, but he's bound to be gone by now."

"He's bound to be gone," Sarah agreed, "and the war's bound to go on." Right that minute, she could think of nothing worse to say.

About the Author

HARRY TURTLEDOVE is the award-winning author of the alternate-history works *Hitler's War, The Man with the Iron Heart, The Guns of the South,* and *How Few Remain* (winner of the Sidewise Award for Best Novel); the Worldwar saga: *In the Balance, Tilting the Balance, Upsetting the Balance,* and *Striking the Balance;* the Colonization books: *Second Contact, Down to Earth,* and *Aftershocks;* the Great War epics: *American Front, Walk in Hell,* and *Breakthroughs;* the American Empire novels: *Blood & Iron, The Center Cannot Hold,* and *Victorious Opposition;* and the Settling Accounts series: *Return Engagement, Drive to the East, The Grapple,* and *In at the Death.* Turtledove is married to fellow novelist Laura Frankos. They have three daughters: Alison, Rachel, and Rebecca.

About the Type

This book was set in Minion, a 1990 Adobe Originals typeface by Robert Slimbach. Minion is inspired by classical, old style typefaces of the late Renaissance, a period of elegant, beautiful, and highly readable type designs. Created primarily for text setting, Minion combines the aesthetic and functional qualities that make text type highly readable with the versatility of digital technology.